Emma Blair was born in Glasgow and now lives in Devon. She is the author of twenty-nine bestselling novels including *Scarlet Ribbons* and *Flower of Scotland*, both of which were shortlisted for the Romantic Novel of the Year Award.

For more information about the author, visit www.emma-blair.co.uk

Also by Emma Blair:

Where No Man Cries
Nellie Wildchild
Hester Dark
Jessie Gray
The Princess of Poor Street
Street Song
When Dreams Come True
A Most Determined Woman
The Blackbird's Tale
Scarlet Ribbons
The Water Meadows
The Sweetest Thing
The Daffodil Sea
Passionate Times
Half Hidden
Flower of Scotland
An Apple from Eden
Goodnight, Sweet Prince
Wild Strawberries
Forget-me-not
Moonlit Eyes
Finding Happiness
Twilight Time
Little White Lies
Three Bites of the Cherry
Sweethearts
Arrows of Desire

This Side of Heaven

Emma Blair

piatkus

PIATKUS

First published in Great Britain in 1985 by Arrow Books Limited
Published by Time Warner Paperbacks in 1997
This paperback edition published by Piatkus in 2009
Reprinted by Piatkus in 2011, 2014

A CIP catalogue record for this book
is available from the British Library.

ISBN 978-0-7499-4282-3

Printed and bound in Great Britain by
Clays Ltd, St Ives plc

Papers used by Piatkus are from well-managed forests
and other responsible sources.

MIX
Paper from
responsible sources
FSC   FSC® C104740
www.fsc.org

Piatkus
An imprint of
Little, Brown Book Group
100 Victoria Embankment
London EC4Y 0DY

An Hachette UK Company
www.hachette.co.uk

www.piatkus.co.uk

This Side of Heaven

1

Sheila hummed to herself as she trudged along the tow path that would shortly join up with the narrow dirt road leading down to Dragonholme. She was on her way back from Bogside Farm, where she'd been buying eggs, a journey she made once a fortnight.

It was early July, and so far the summer of 1911 had been a glorious one. A glance at the fat sun hanging heavily overhead told her it was getting on for teatime. She started walking faster, as some of the eggs she was carrying were wanted for the evening meal.

A few minutes later she came in sight of the sea. What she saw on the horizon caused her to come up short and catch her breath. Could it be? Was it them?

Twenty-eight dots: twenty-eight boats. The number couldn't be coincidental; it had to be the fleet coming home! Excitement gripped her, her da and brothers were coming home, and Eric – beautiful, adorable Eric whom she loved to distraction, he was coming home as well.

There was a strong northerly blowing which meant that the fleet would be tying up before long. She calculated that if the wind didn't change they'd be entering harbour in less than an hour.

From her clifftop vantage, she must be the first of the village to spy the fleet. She must hurry down to Dragonholme and cry the news so that all would be ready in time for when the catch was landed, the first catch to come into Dragonholme that season.

The sound of a horse snorting behind her made Sheila jump. Whirling round, she found herself looking at a middle-aged man on a hunter.

'Who are you?' he asked, in a voice that expected answers. His eyes never left her face.

7

A toff – one of the gentry, Sheila thought, instinctively straightening her shoulders and raising her chin.

'Sheila Beattie,' she replied politely.

'From Dragonholme?'

She nodded.

'You'll be Davey Beattie's daughter then?'

That surprised her. How would her da know a toff like this?

'I am,' she nodded, almost making it sound like a challenge.

'A fine skipper, one of the best along this coast; and that's saying something,' the gentleman replied with a thin smile.

Sheila turned and pointed out to sea. 'That's the fleet coming home. I just spotted them a minute ago.'

The black hunter, a vicious-looking beast, pawed the ground while the man shaded his eye to gaze in the direction she was pointing.

'Aye, so it is. And no doubt that'll be the *Bluebell* leading the way.'

Bluebell was the name of her father's boat. It was a new drifter, a Zulu, launched only the previous year. Davey had invested every penny the family possessed on its purchase.

'As admiral of our fleet it's his place to be out front,' Sheila informed him proudly.

The man's eyes twinkled, amused by her immediate and fierce show of pride. 'How old are you, lass?' he asked suddenly, his eyes no longer on the fleet.

That's none of your business, Sheila thought. 'Sixteen, sir,' she answered grudgingly. Her mother would die if she thought she'd been rude to a gentleman.

Suddenly Sheila knew who this stranger was, who he had to be. He must be the new laird who'd bought Dragonholme Hall after the death of the old laird, Mr Magnussen. Dragonholme Hall was in the valley about half a mile away. The original Hall had been built a thousand years ago by Einar Hairybreeks, the leader of the vikings who'd founded the village. Vikings who'd

8

come, and stayed, and after a while had intermarried with the local Scots.

'You must be Mr Campbell,' she dared, really looking at him for the first time.

'Aye, that's me,' James Campbell smiled.

Sheila immediately curtsied as she'd been taught, as she'd always done when coming into the presence of the old laird, a right kindly man if ever there was one. She looked up at James Campbell, but there was no kindness in those eyes.

'Excuse me, sir, but I'll have to be going,' she said, suddenly anxious to be gone. 'I must away down to the village and cry the news about the fleet.'

James Campbell pursed his lips, his hand thin and white against the neck of his monstrous horse. He was disappointed she was leaving him so soon. He'd taken to the tawny-haired girl. She was pleasant company.

'Till the next time then,' he answered slowly, patting Satan's gleaming skin.

'Good-bye,' Sheila mumbled, and without waiting for a reply started running along the road, her basket of eggs clutched securely to her side.

At the point where the road fell away in its descent to the village she turned to gaze behind her, and he was still there, exactly as she'd left him; facing out to sea, his eyes fixed on the home-bound fleet. For no reason she could think of and despite the heat of the day, an ice-cold shiver ran through her. Then, shaking herself, she hurried on her way.

Mrs Johnstone, whose husband crewed the *Fear Not*, was the first person Sheila saw to shout the news to. Within minutes all of Dragonholme knew that the men had returned from the northern fishing grounds, and that the same number of boats were coming back as had left at the beginning of May when the fleet had set sail for Lerwick in the Shetlands.

Peg Beattie, Sheila's mother, was already looking out the gutting knives when Sheila burst into the house, flushed and breathless. In her mid-forties, Peg was stout but still handsome, her face marked as much by kindness as by hard work and care. Sheila was the youngest of her children, and the only girl. Her sons were all aboard the *Bluebell* with Davey.

Peg paused in what she was doing, her brows drawn, her eyes clouded.

'Ten days earlier than last year. The fishing must have been poor for them to be so far down the coast this early in the month,' she said.

'I hadn't thought of that.' In her excitement Sheila had completely forgotten that the fleet weren't expected till the end of next week.

At that moment Rhona and Maggie came flying in through the door. Rhona was married to Jack, Peg's oldest son, and Maggie to Dougal. Both of them lived close by. Peg's youngest son, Bob, still lived at home and shared the back room of the two-roomed house with Sheila.

Sheila got on great guns with Rhona, but not with Maggie, who was considered a pain in the bumbeleerie. The trouble with Maggie was that she was domineering and overbearing, and though it didn't bother Rhona or Peg, who knew how to handle her, Sheila was too young and fiery herself to bother about diplomacy.

'You and Rhona get the table and I'll help Ma with the packing boxes,' Maggie said to Sheila.

Sheila put her hands on her hips. 'Since when did you start giving orders in our house?' she demanded.

Maggie made a gesture of impatience. 'I'm not giving orders. I'm merely getting things organized.'

'It sounded very much like orders to me.' Sheila glared at her sister-in-law defiantly.

'This isn't the time for bickering. Sheila, do as Maggie has suggested,' Peg said firmly.

'Come on then,' Sheila said to Rhona, and led the way out of the house round to the partially covered lean-to at the rear where the gutting table was kept out of season, wrapped in an old tarpaulin.

'Where are the weans?' Sheila asked as they walked to the back.

'They're already away down to the harbour,' Rhona smiled. 'They were too excited about seeing their father to wait for me.'

They uncovered the heavy table with its hinged legs.

'You shouldn't let Maggie rile you,' Rhona advised.

'It's that manner of hers. It aye puts my back up.' Sheila grunted as she and Rhona lifted the table up into a carrying position.

But even Maggie's faults went from Sheila's mind as she and Rhona staggered down to the harbour where they set the table up in what was traditionally the Beattie spot. Minutes later Peg and Maggie joined them, their arms filled with packing boxes.

'There are more boxes still to come,' Peg said, laying the gutting knives out on the table.

Maggie was already shrugging into one of the heavy leather aprons that had been inside the topmost box she had been carrying. When she saw Sheila glowering at her she said, 'I'll get them if you like.'

'You can both get them,' said Peg, nipping that in the bud. Even though Maggie had volunteered herself for the task there could still have been a fight.

Sheila and Maggie returned to the house leaving Rhona to sort out the boxes that had already been brought down, and Peg to hone the knives to razor sharpness on a whetstone that had been in the Beattie family time out of mind.

Just outside the harbour entrance Davey gave the signal for the lug rig to be dropped. Creaking and flapping, the sails, tanned black from successive dippings in cutch, sank on to the deck where Uncle Matt was waiting ready to square them away.

Sheila watched in admiration as the *Bluebell*'s black painted hull, her name picked out in gold leaf, swung towards that part of the quayside where she was to be tied up. Oh, but she was bonny right enough; with her white wheelhouse and mastheads, blue gunwhales, and dark azure blue coamings and hatches. Sheila thought she had never seen a finer boat.

With a resounding bump the *Bluebell* kissed the quayside, causing its sixty-foot masts to quiver high overhead. It was Bob who sprang on to the quayside to secure her fore and aft. A second later, he was in his mother's arms, hugging Peg tightly and saying how grand it was to be back again in Dragonholme.

One after the other the fleet entered the harbour: the *Muirneag*, the *Star of Hope*, the *Foamcrest*, and the *Gypsy Queen*.

And there was Eric, her darling man, bobbing up and down as he tried to wave to her and attend to his duties at the same time. Like a young tree he was, strong and straight and just a bit wild. His eyes were the palest blue, his blond cropped hair so bleached from the sea as to be almost white. Sheila's heart hammered within her at the sight of him, and she gave up a silent prayer of gratitude to the Good Lord for having seen fit to bring him home safe and sound.

Dougal had his son, wee Dougal, cradled in one arm, and his daughter, Violet, in the other, Maggie beside him, staring up into her husband's face with unconcealed joy.

Rhona and Jack were embracing, while Ian stood by his da's side, one finger in his mouth, the other hand clutching hold of Jack's sweater as though to ensure that Jack wasn't going to suddenly disappear again. A queer, quiet lad was Ian, fairy-touched, said some, but lucky with it, somehow.

There was no wife there to greet Uncle Matt. No wife and no daughters or sons. Auntie Lily had died six years ago, and they'd been a childless couple. Uncle Matt was Davey's older brother, but had never owned a boat of his own or even been the skipper of one. Uncle Matt was a man who liked to take orders, not give them. It was a wise man who knew his own level, Davey had once said, and although the conversation hadn't been about his brother, it was Uncle Matt that Davey had had in mind.

The *Gypsy Queen*, Eric's father's boat, was tied off now, and Eric himself was hurrying towards her. He stopped just short of her, his body trembling, embarrassed to hug her in public.

'You look well,' she said, clasping her hands behind her. What an awful trite thing to come out with, she silently scolded herself. But, like him, she felt constrained by being surrounded by so many folk.

He couldn't seem to hold still.

'Aye, and so do you.'

Eye into eye they stared at one another. All she wanted to know passed between them that way. He still loved her, she was his special lass, his one and only.

'Later then?' he finally whispered, his eyes darting nervously around.

'When?'

'As soon as you can get away. After you've eaten. I'll be waiting.'

'The usual place?'

Eric nodded. 'And I'll bring a wee something to keep out the cold.'

'You daft haddie, it isn't cold at night at this time of year,' she laughed.

The corners of his sparkling eyes crinkled with his laugh. 'I'll bring it anyway, just to be on the safe side.'

She reached out and touched his hard, calloused hand, so filled with emotion that she thought her heart must surely explode.

'All right you lot, can we get back to work now!' Davey called from the deck of the *Bluebell*. As always he was puffing on his old clay pipe which, like nearly all the fishermen he knew, he smoked turned upside down.

The Beattie brothers jumped back aboard the *Bluebell* to begin the business of hand winching the catch on to the quayside. From there it would go to where the women had set up. Eric gave her one last smile and returned to the *Gypsy Queen* to help his da and brothers do the same.

Soon their knives were flashing. Sheila, Peg, Rhona and Maggie expertly gutted cran after cran of herrings, taking it in turn to break from this chore to pack the gutted fish into boxes, covering them with salt to keep them fresh.

The herring scales got everywhere – over their faces, up their arms, even under their clothing and headscarves – but none of the women minded. There was no point in complaining, even if they did. Fish were money. In fact, fish were their whole survival. What was a little physical inconvenience weighed against that?

At long last their boxes were full, but still the gutting continued, for part of the catch was to be taken home and smoked.

McPherson, the carter, put in an appearance, he and his son stacking the Beattie boxes alongside the others he'd already collected. He kept careful tally in his fish book. McPherson would be taking the Dragonholme catch through to Portnessie where the buyers and railhead were. Portnessie was a small fishing port ten miles further up the coast, and the buying and selling centre for all the villages thereabouts. From Portnessie some of the fish would go to the markets in Edinburgh and Glasgow, while another portion would eventually find its way to Poland, Latvia, Germany and other European countries.

Finally, with the sun just about to go down, the gutting was finished for the day. Sheila, Rhona and Maggie started humping the fish to be smoked to the smoke-house behind the Beattie home. While the younger women were doing this, Peg washed down and tidied up the area where they'd been working.

As was the custom on the first day back in the home port, once the catch was unloaded the men had all gone to the pub. Seeing that the gutting was finished and the packed fish on its way to Portnessie, the men would now begin to make their way home for the evening meal.

After that, many of them would return to the pub again to carry on where they'd left off.

When the fish to be smoked were all put away Rhona and Maggie returned to their own homes, and Sheila to hers, making straight for the hand pump in the kitchen where she gave her hands, face and hair a thorough wash.

A pot of lentil soup that Peg had begun that morning was now bubbling invitingly on the cast-iron range, alongside which a dozen herrings were being cooked on the brander.

Peg cut the best part of a loaf into thick slices, then started buttering each slice. Back from the pub, Davey sat in his usual chair by the side of the range gazing deep into the glowing coals. Bob was in another chair, having a quick snooze before the meal was dished up.

'You're home gey early this time round?' Peg prompted quietly, her eyes darting from her buttering to Davey. He had never been a talkative man, but she knew him so well that words weren't needed.

Davey roused himself from his reverie. 'The fishing wasn't so good further north, but picked up a wee bit once we got down to Peterhead. Apart from that, the shoals are coming south more quickly this year.' He paused for a moment, staring past her. 'But don't ask me why, it's just one of those things.'

'We'll do all right out the season though, won't we?' Peg asked softly, a hint of worry tinging her voice.

Davey sniffed and knocked some dottle from his pipe. 'What we brought in today was far and away our best catch to date. Let's just say that from here on in we'd better do an awful lot better than we have up to now.'

Peg bit her lip. Despite her own suspicions, this wasn't what she'd been hoping to hear. Fear clutched at her insides. The fishing had been marvellous for the past thirty-odd years, but that didn't mean it would continue to be so. She remembered only too well the hungry times of her youth when the fishing had been diabolical and poverty had covered the east coast like a shroud.

Sensing Peg's worry, Davey gave her a reassuring smile. 'Wait till we get to the Silver Pits, they've never let us down yet,' he said. The Silver Pits were particularly rich grounds that the Dragonholme fleet fished working out of either Hull or Grimsby.

'Aye, the Silver Pits,' echoed Peg, cheering considerably. Davey had always been lucky there.

A few minutes later Peg told Sheila to rouse Bob, and started to serve out the soup. The eggs that had originally been planned were now forgotten; fish and the sort of soup that sticks to your ribs were what were needed for men who'd been on the sea.

'Ah,' said Davey, as she passed out the dishes. 'Now that's a fair treat for an old sailor.' He quickly finished his soup, holding out his bowl for seconds. As Peg laid the second bowlful before him, she saw that a frown had darkened his face. 'Is something bothering you?' she asked.

Davey broke a slice of bread in half, then into quarters. 'I was just thinking about steam trawlers. There are more than ever fishing this year, including six new ones out of Portnessie.'

'Owned by James Campbell, him that's bought Dragonholme Hall,' chimed in Bob, suddenly remembering that he could use his mouth to talk as well as eat.

'Aye, that's a fact. Campbell's added them to the fleet of sail trawlers he owns. It must have cost him a pretty penny to buy six of them at one go.' Davey was visibly impressed by this show of affluence and success. As a drifterman, Davey disliked sail trawlers and loathed the new steam variety. He believed that the steam trawlers ripped up the beds below the fishing grounds, destroying the feed.

'He's a self-made man, you know,' Davey went on, unusually talkative. 'He's not one of those who comes into this world with a silver spoon in his mouth.'

'I met him the day,' Sheila joined in. 'He said you were one of the best skippers along this coast.'

Davey blinked. 'Met who, girl?'

She had everyone's attention now. 'The new laird. I was coming home from the farm when he came up behind me on a great black horse. I had just spied the fleet at the time.'

'And he talked to you?' Peg prompted, always curious about lives so different from her own.

Davey interpreted Peg's question in his own way. 'And why shouldn't he speak to her?' he wanted to know. 'Sheila's just as good as him who was born in a house in Portnessie exactly the same as this one.' As far as Davey was concerned, being free and Scots were all the qualifications a body needed in life.

'He might have been born in a house like ours, but he speaks right posh now. A proper gentleman and no mistake,' Sheila went on enthusiastically.

Davey tugged at his beard, his sudden indignation already on the wane.

'Aye, well Campbell spends a lot of time in Glasgow and Edinburgh. London even, I'm told. He'll have picked up his new speech and manners there no doubt. But don't be misled by his outward appearance or the way he sounds now. Underneath it all James Campbell is *still* fisher folk, and a damn fine skipper in his own right.' Davey paused, then went on in a tone that was almost coy. 'And he said I was one of the best skippers along the coast, eh?'

Sheila nodded.

A smile teased at the corners of Davey's mouth. He was well pleased by the compliment.

'So what's his wife like?' Peg asked eagerly.

Davey helped himself to another slice of bread. 'I've never seen her, but I've heard she's genuine Edinburgh Morningside.'

'What does that mean?' asked Bob, his face screwed up in puzzlement and his spoon in mid-air.

'Ach, don't you know anything?' scoffed Sheila. 'Morningside is where the Edinburgh toffs live; them that never do a stroke of work and ride around in fancy carriages all day long.'

'And the women wear beautiful gowns and have hands that are like velvet to touch,' Peg added, her eyes taking on a faraway look as she tried to imagine herself with such luxuries. She'd never owned a gown in her life; her hands were as hard and workworn as any man's.

'All I know,' said Davey, 'is that there's a family; two boys. Both of whom go away to school in the English fashion. You know, a school where they actually live.'

Peg shook her head in maternal condemnation. 'I've always thought that a gey uncivilized way of doing things, sending wee mites off on their own like that. But there you are, the English are an uncivilized race if ever there was one.' There was a general murmur of agreement.

'The Campbells can only have moved into the Hall during the past day or two,' mused Peg. 'I know for certain that the decorators were still there at the end of last week.' How long would it be, she wondered, before she clapped eyes on Mrs Campbell? Almost every woman in the village was dying to get a look at her. Wait till they heard that the laird's wife was Edinburgh Morningside!

Sheila cleared away the soup bowls and placed the herrings on the table. After slicing the first one open Davey asked for the white stuff to be passed. The word salt was never uttered by him – every fisherman knew it was unlucky.

'What I don't understand,' said Sheila, 'is why Mr Campbell would want to buy Dragonholme Hall. Why come here where he's a stranger? If he wanted a bigger or grander house why not buy one in Portnessie? Or Glasgow, or Edinburgh?'

Davey chuckled. 'It might well be he fancies being called the laird, as is his entitlement now that he owns the Hall. It's been said before now that there's a streak of vanity in the man.'

Having finished all that he wanted to eat, and not one for sitting around chatting, Bob excused himself. 'I'm away back to The Haven,' he said, giving Peg a peck on the cheek. 'Good food always makes me thirsty.'

'Collecting Thomasina McLean on the way no doubt?' Sheila teased.

'Listen to the pot calling the kettle black,' Bob jibed back. 'As if you won't be seeing Eric Gifford later.'

'I might just go for a walk with him,' Sheila replied airily.

'We all know about your walks,' Bob said, giving his mother and father a meaningful wink.

Sheila blushed and looked away. Bob grinned with his success in embarrassing his sister. It was a rare day when he got the better of her.

Davey cleared his throat and stared into his cup of strong tea. He knew damn well what the young ones got up to, hadn't he and Peg been young themselves once? But it was wrong of Bob to hint at such goings-on in front of his parents, particularly his mother: it showed a certain lack of respect. 'I think you'd better run along before you say any more,' Davey advised quietly.

Realizing that he'd overstepped the mark, Bob muttered his good-byes and strode off into the night.

'I'll clear up,' Sheila said, starting to collect the dirty plates together.

Peg stared at Sheila, remembering what she herself had been like at that age. She and Davey had been courting then, just as Sheila and Eric were now. Davey had been working on a Skaffie called *Buttercup*. Peg brought her gaze on to Davey and a mellow warmth filled her. He was a man in a million, her Davey. She wouldn't trade him for all the tea in China. 'Never mind the dishes. Go off and see your lad,' Peg said to Sheila, shooing her away.

'Are you sure, Ma?'

'Aye, of course I am. Away and enjoy yourself. Just don't come in at all hours. Remember tomorrow's a working day.'

Davey lit his pipe, thinking it was going to be strange when their last two were gone from the house. He was going to miss Sheila in particular. As his only girl he'd always had a special soft spot for her. 'Well,' he said, reaching his hand out to Peg. 'It's good to be home.'

Once outside, Sheila paused to stare over Dragonholme. There was a vibrancy in the very air that had been missing these past few months. It was the men being back; they added something when they were there, and took it away with them when they went.

She turned left at the harbour to head for the Gifford hut which was high above the tide line a little ways along the beach. There were a number of huts on this stretch of beach, used by the families who owned them for storage purposes.

The Gifford hut, as they all were, was an old undecked boat that had been cut in half breadthwise, one half, keel uppermost, embedded firmly into the sand, and planking added to make a wall of the open end into which a door had been set.

The door swung open to her touch and she peered into the darkness, knowing instantly that Eric was already inside, as he'd promised he'd be. She could feel his presence.

An arm encircled her shoulders and he drew her gently to him. She gave a soft moan as his lips found hers.

A few seconds later, he let her go while he knelt at the bottom of the door, stuffing a strip of old sacking into the chink so that the lamp he was about to light wouldn't be seen by passers-by. A Lucifer match flared, and the hut suddenly shone with a soft yellow glow.

He would have taken her in his arms again immediately, but she held him back, wanting to look at him, at every inch of him, leaner and darker than she had remembered. 'It seemed like an eternity,' she whispered, her hands holding his.

'I know,' he breathed. 'I felt the same.'

'I thought about you every day, and dreamt about you

every night,' she said, turning her eyes away from his in shyness.

He touched the top of her head with his lips. 'I forced myself not to think about you during the days. That would have been just asking for an accident. But I did dream about you during the nights,' he whispered, his mouth against her skin.

Suddenly she felt weak. All the months of loneliness and missing him rushing in on her. All the hours spent in dreams. She closed her eyes for a few moments, opening them again to find that she was back in his arms, her breasts hard against his chest, her happy tears trickling down her cheeks.

Gently, almost delicately, he undid her blouse, his roughened hands more pleasing than silk against her skin.

She helped him remove her clothes until at last she stood before him. She watched him as he removed his clothing. If they had been in the best hotel in Edinburgh, she couldn't have been happier. There wasn't a gentleman in the world worth half of Eric. There was no other man whose touch could so excite her, to whom she would offer herself and her love.

There was no finesse about his lovemaking: he was a rough-hewn man making rough-hewn love, but he brought her to heights of ecstasy, made her heart and body soar. Caught in a whirlpool of sensation, every nerve in her body tingling from his touch, she called out his name again and again. At last the world returned to what it had been, and there was Eric. Eric, her lover, her darling man, grinning down at her, his face damp with sweat, his eyes filled with love.

Later, he moved away from her to reach for the bottle of whisky he'd laid on the floor before she'd arrived. Eric swallowed a mouthful of whisky then extended the bottle to her.

'To keep out the cold?' she teased.

'Aye, that's right,' he nodded, giving her a fly,

conspiratorial wink which made her laugh. He often made her laugh. Laughter and love, what more could she want?

She took a sip of spirit, then another. 'That's grand,' she said. She was used to taking a dram, now and then, but enjoyed it more when he was with her. 'Marika will be telling Duncy round about now,' Sheila said, passing back the bottle. Marika Sigurdson was her great friend. The pair of them had been close pals since they were wee. Duncy Laidlaw was Marika's boyfriend.

Eric frowned. 'Telling Duncy what?'

'That he's bairned her. She found out just after he sailed.'

'So it's a wedding then,' Eric smiled, one arm around her.

'And soon. She'll have him at the altar before the fleet moves on.'

It never occurred to either of them that Duncy might not agree to the marriage. Duncy had made Marika pregnant, and when that happened the man married the woman concerned, that was one of the many unwritten rules by which the community lived.

'I'm to be best maid,' said Sheila, thinking of the new dress she'd made for the occasion, and in which, Peg had assured her, she looked a right treat. It was on the tip of her tongue to say that she thought it was high time they were wed also, or was it his intention to wait until she, too, was bairned?

She could just picture her and Eric in *their* own wee house, *their* curtains hanging on the windows, *their* braw wooden press, the status symbol every wife in the village set such store by, in the corner of the kitchen. Coming to the hut was all right at first, but now they'd outgrown it. She was sixteen and he eighteen; how much longer did he plan to wait for goodness sake? They were both more than ready for marriage and settling down.

She decided not to chisel him about it, though, not on his first night back. Soon, however, soon it would have to be settled. Certainly before the fleet sailed south. She'd wait until the perfect opportunity presented itself.

'The fishing's been dreadful,' Eric said, taking another swallow of whisky.

'So my da told us.'

'I've never known a year like it,' he muttered, back at sea in his mind, thinking how few decent catches they'd had so far, and how many bad ones. Hopefully the home grounds would be luckier for them, hopefully. . . .

She ran one hand over his body, down the hardness of his chest and the smoothness of his belly. The male body held no mysteries or embarrassment for Sheila, not when she'd been brought up sharing a bedroom with three brothers, her only privacy a sheet hung up so that it screened her bed from theirs.

'What does your da say?' she asked quietly, her hand stroking his long muscular leg. She wanted a really stunning press, varnished inside as well as out, with elaborate fancy work on the corners; thistles say, or acorns, and intricate scrollwork along the beading.

'He doesn't know what to think,' answered Eric, his voice coming from far away.

January, she decided, that would be the best month for them to be kirked, for the boats would be laid up then, undergoing their yearly overhaul, and he'd be ashore.

True, the season had been a bad one so far, but all that would change when her da took the fleet to the Silver Pits, she was sure of it. Eric would finish the season with a good share, enough for them, on top of everything else, to afford a few days' honeymoon in Edinburgh where the fabled Princes Street was.

There were many fine shops in Princes Street, the best in all Scotland it was said, one of which was bound to have the press of her dreams, a press to outshine all others in Dragonholme.

'Oh, Sheila,' Eric groaned, 'I have missed you so.'

2

Dawn was a distant glimmer on the horizon as the Dragonholme fleet began slipping from the harbour on the high tide.

Sheila stood on the quayside along with the rest of the womenfolk. It was their custom to come down to see their men off. There was a stiff breeze, she noted. The fleet would make good time to the home grounds.

She felt marvellous this morning, overjoyed to be young and alive and so in love. She'd seen Eric and briefly held hands with him before he'd gone aboard the *Gypsy Queen*.

Finally the *Bluebell* pulled away from the quayside. First in, she was last out, but once beyond the harbour she would quickly take her place at the head of the fleet.

There was a clack of clogs behind Sheila, and then Marika was beside her. Marika's eyes shone brightly in the dark. 'A week this Saturday,' Marika said excitedly, the words coming out in a rush.

Sheila swept her friend into her arms and hugged her. 'Who's to be the best man?' she asked when they pulled apart.

'Tarry Dunbar,' Marika replied, pulling a face. Tarry's Christian name was John, but everyone called him by his Tee name, or nickname.

Sheila didn't like Tarry. He was a loud-mouth, a braggart and a bully, who had far too big a tip for himself. She'd never understood how Duncy, one of the nicest lads you could ever hope to meet, could be so pally with him.

'He was Duncy's firm choice,' apologized Marika. Not only did she know of Sheila's aversion to Tarry, she wasn't madly keen on him herself.

'That's all right,' laughed Sheila. 'I can put up with him for the day. I half expected it to be him, anyway, so it's no real shock.'

'We'll get him drunk after the meal and maybe he'll pass out early on,' suggested Marika with a giggle.

'Good idea. Once he's said his speech and done his business I'll make sure his glass is aye brimming,' laughed Sheila enthusiastically. A flat-on-his-back-for-most-of-the-evening Tarry Dunbar would suit her just fine.

Marika hiccuped. 'Indigestion,' she explained. 'It's been terrible these past few days.'

The women had started to move back to the village now, having their own work to be getting on with. Sheila and Marika, who was talking non-stop about her wedding plans, fell in behind Peg, Rhona and Maggie.

As Marika chattered on Sheila couldn't help but feel a wee bit jealous. January wasn't all that far away, she consoled herself. The time would soon fly by, and then it would be Sheila Beattie walking down the aisle to have a gold band put on her finger.

At her front door, Sheila said good-bye to Marika, then hurried round to the smokehouse where she found Rhona and Maggie already hard at it, filling up barrels with brine water into which the fish would be put to soak. Leaving them to get on with that she started getting down the tenters, the long poles on which the fish would be threaded so that they could then be hung on the hooks high overhead.

Peg wasn't there, she was round the back of the smokehouse loading up a wheelbarrow with fuel for the fire. This fuel was oak chips and sawdust, which gave the finished kipper its distinctive and nutty flavour.

Maggie and Rhona had been talking, but now Maggie addressed herself to Sheila. 'You've got a glow to your cheeks that I haven't seen there for some time,' she said lightly, her lips curled into what Sheila interpreted as a smirk.

25

Sheila paused to tuck a stray wisp of hair back under her headscarf. 'What's that supposed to mean?' she snapped back, knowing only too well what Maggie was insinuating.

Maggie's smile got even broader. 'You must have had a good night, I'm thinking, that's all.'

'And what's that to you?'

'There's no need to get so het up Sheila, I'm only passing the time of day,' Maggie replied, assuming an innocent expression.

Oh, how her sister-in-law annoyed her! If Rhona had said that to her they would have had a good laugh together, but not so with Maggie. Maggie was always trying to take the rise out of her, and largely succeeding.

'If I've got a glow on my cheeks this morning then that's more than I can say for you. You look bloody haggard.'

'Don't be cheeky!' Maggie screeched.

'I'll stop being cheeky if you'll stop trying to stick your knife into me!' Sheila snapped back.

'I was doing no such thing!'

'Liar!'

'What in the name of the Wee Man is going on here?' Peg exclaimed, standing in the doorway, hands on hips.

Sheila jerked a thumb at Maggie. 'She started it.'

'And you're too over-sensitive by far,' hissed Maggie.

'So what sparked this off then?' Peg asked.

A sudden silence fell inside the smokehouse. Sheila had no intention of telling her mother what Maggie had said to her, nor had Maggie.

'Am I going to have to do this all by myself?' Rhona grumbled, up-ending a box out of which a cascade of herrings tumbled into one of the barrels of brine.

Maggie grabbed the opportunity. 'I'm right with you, Rhona,' she said, and hurried over to lend a hand.

Sheila took a deep breath. 'The tenters are all laid out ready. What shall I do now, Ma?'

Well, whatever had happened, it seemed the incident

was now closed, Peg thought. Still, best to separate these two for a while, she told herself, and knew the chore she'd send Sheila on. 'Your da's told me he wants the spare net brought down from the loft as there's a lot of repair work needing doing on the one he's using. The change-over will be made the night after they've docked, and we'll start the repairs tomorrow afternoon. We're going to need some new mending needles, so I want you to run up to Taggart's and get them for me.'

At the door of the smokehouse Sheila noticed that Maggie, behind Peg's back, was giving her a filthy look. In reply she stuck out her tongue at Maggie, then put a thumb to her nose and waggled her fingers. Feeling much the better for that she set off on her errand, whistling as she went.

Tom Taggart was a man her da's age who stumped around on a wooden pin. He'd lost the lower part of his left leg in an onboard accident over twenty years before.

Having purchased the needles and had a bit of a crack with Tom, Sheila was about to make her way back to the smokehouse when her gaze fell on a cottage a wee bit up the road. The idea came to her like a bolt from the blue. Why hadn't she thought of it before! The cottage had been lying empty since the previous winter when its former occupant, old Granny Mutch, had passed on at the grand age of eighty-six.

Leaving Tom Taggart with a hasty 'good-bye', she abruptly left the shop.

Going to the cottage, Sheila opened the door and went inside. All Granny's possessions had long since been taken away by McPherson the carter who'd transported them to Lufften, where Granny's only surviving relative lived. The place was manky, but then what could you expect? The walls and floor were filthy, and the range was caked with grease, but aside from that, there was nothing wrong with the kitchen or the second room ben that a good dose of elbow grease wouldn't put right. Nothing wrong with the cottage that some curtains and sunshine wouldn't fix. It would be perfect for Eric and her.

As far as Sheila was concerned, the biggest attraction about the cottage was that it was rented accommodation, and as such ideal for a couple just getting started who'd be needing to watch their silver for quite some time to come. She knew the cottage to be part of the Dragonholme estate, as were about a quarter of the houses in the village. The rest, like her da's, were privately owned. The Dragonholme estate, of which the Hall itself was the centre, comprised much land, several woods, a small trout loch, some houses in Dragonholme, and the entire clachan of Knockhammie, situated roughly mid-way between Bogside Farm and the Hall.

For several minutes, she wandered from one room to the other, seeing it as it would be. Then she realized how time was getting on. She'd better get right back or Peg would be giving her what for. Slamming the door behind her she ran down the hill, the lee wind blowing in off the sea making her cheeks burn and her hair, freed of her headscarf, stream out behind her.

'Now there goes a bonny sight,' said Tom Taggart to Handy Dandy McKechnie, a retired fisherman and former crewmate of Tom's.

Handy Dandy was just quick enough to glimpse Sheila's flying figure as it flashed by the window. 'Oh, aye, oh aye indeed,' he replied, and he and Tom exchanged smiles, each remembering other bonny young lassies long ago, and the good times he'd had with them.

Sheila couldn't sleep. She was hot and sticky, and the bedclothes seemed a ton weight on top of her. Bob had gone off ages back and was now snoring fitfully beyond the curtain.

Throwing the bedclothes aside, she rose and shrugged into a dressing gown, then lit the lamp on her bedside table. Crossing to the far side of the room she laid the lamp on a wooden chair that stood beside a large metal-banded kist, or chest, in which, during the past few years, she'd been accumulating many of the things a bride was expected to provide for her new home.

Kneeling in front of the kist she opened it, staring down at its contents, the items of which she could have reeled off in a list without missing a one.

At the very bottom of the kist were four pillows and two bolsters, each filled with feathers and down which she had gathered herself. On top of these were four fluffy blankets and two baby-blue ones, then came a half a dozen sheets made of Egyptian cotton, one dozen Turkish towels of various sizes and colours, a hard-wearing tablecloth for weekdays, a damask one for Sundays, a complete set of crockery, and finally, a number of kitchen utensils.

It was a well-filled kist; everything the best money could buy. Eric would have no cause for complaint there she assured herself. In her mind she could see the contents of her kist in use in Granny Mutch's cottage, her dream press presiding in the corner, Eric relaxing by one side of the range, she at the other getting on with some knitting or a wee bit of mending, the pair of them talking over the day's events just like her ma and da did when Davey was at home.

That range was gey past it mind, the brander was broken and she'd noticed several cracks along. . . . .

'Will you put that light out and let a body get his sleep?' Bob grouched, pulling himself up on one elbow and glaring biliously at her.

'Sorry,' she mumbled contritely, silently closing the kist. Swiftly, she re-crossed the room, turned out the lamp and got back into bed.

Semple, the factor, would be in Dragonholme this coming Friday, as he was every Friday to collect the estate rents. She'd seek him out during her dinnertime and chisel him about the cottage.

Her last conscious thought was that it had turned awful humid and close, quite unlike the weather they normally had at this time of year.

On the Friday she waylaid Semple who listened sympathetically to her request. 'As there's no one else after the place I don't see why it shouldn't be yours,' he said with a smile.

Filled with elation Sheila thrashed the terms out there and then. When that was concluded she asked the factor not to mention this to any of the other villagers for the moment. 'We've not quite made the announcement yet,' she confided sweetly. 'You know what people are like.'

As she'd expected, Semple had told her that in order to guarantee tenancy she'd have to start paying rent straight away, which she agreed to. Oh well, she thought philosophically, that would give her plenty of time to get the cottage ready for when she and Eric eventually moved in.

That night Eric took her to The Halibut's Tail for a drink. She was bursting to tell him about the cottage. In fact, she had been intending to tell him, using it as a catalyst to get him to propose to her that very night, but had decided against it when she'd seen the mood he was in, which was morose to say the least.

All the way to the pub he'd gone on non-stop about how bad the fishing in the home grounds was turning out to be. 'Disastrous,' he kept saying. 'Bloody disastrous.' What the *Gypsy Queen* had taken so far hardly added up to one full hold. Where were the great shoals? It was the question everyone was asking, but not even Davey had come up with an answer.

No, she decided, watching him leaning against the bar waiting for their refills, it was definitely not the time to winkle a proposal out of him. Although he smiled when he caught her eye, his expression was still grim.

While Eric was at the bar, Tarry Dunbar and several

members of his crew entered the pub. Although only in his early twenties, Tarry owned and skippered the *Locarno*, a small Skaffie that had passed on to him when his da bought a bigger boat. Tarry stopped briefly to chat boisterously with a group of drinkers he was friendly with, then swaggered over to stand beside Eric, where he demanded loudly to be served some pints of heavy, and could Charlie Renton, who was serving, be quick about it.

Eric came back to Sheila. 'He's well guttered,' Eric said, nodding in Tarry's direction.

'They all are. Pissed as newts,' Sheila agreed.

'Ach well, it's a Friday night. If you can't let off a bit of steam then, when can you?' grinned Eric.

'I don't mind folk letting off steam. It's when they get obnoxious with it that I object.'

They sipped their drinks in silence for a few minutes.

'Your da's thinking of moving the fleet on to the Silver Pits the week after next if the fishing doesn't improve,' Eric said at last.

Sheila blinked. That was news to her. Davey hadn't mentioned a word at home about taking the fleet south so soon, at least not in front of her. She said nothing, but the look in her eyes was a question.

'Aye, it really is that bad,' Eric said, shaking his head.

'Now, don't you worry, you'll make up the season's pay when you get to the Silver Pits, I'd stake my life on that,' Sheila smiled, convinced she was right. As Davey had said, the Silver Pits had never let him down yet. No, the fleet would make up its money all right, but if they went south so early it meant she wouldn't have her darling Eric with her for as long as she'd thought. She would have to move quickly. And then a new idea struck her: he was bound to be in a mellow mood the night of Marika and Duncy's wedding. That was when she should get him to commit himself. The night of the wedding it would be, she decided.

They finished their drinks and decided to go for a stroll

31

along the beach. Once outside Sheila commented on the queer weather, saying she found it unusually oppressive.

'Even out at sea it's muggy.' Nor would this strange weather make it any easier for them to locate the missing big shoals. It was a known fact that weather conditions affected upper level fish and the way they ran.

Sheila clutched Eric's arm when there was a sudden commotion round the side of the pub, then the night air was punctuated by a shrill cry of pain.

'What the hell's that all about?' Eric exclaimed, moving swiftly to the corner of the pub to see what was going on.

I might have known, Sheila thought, when she saw that Tarry and his friends were there. But the figure struggling in their midst, who was that?

The figure cried out again, a pathetic sound that tore at her heartstrings.

'It's wee George Jorgesson, I recognize him now,' said Eric grimly. Removing Sheila's hand from his arm he told her to stay where she was, but she was having none of that and hurried after him.

George's face was tear streaked, his eyes starting with terror. His trousers and pants had been pulled down to his ankles, the lower part of his body smeared in hot sticky tar.

Tarry looked up at Eric and Sheila's approach, the tar dripping from the brush in his hand. 'It's my new deck boy's brothering. I'm taking him to sea for the first time on Monday,' Tarry explained.

Wee George averted his head, mortally ashamed that a lassie should see him like this.

Tarry waved the dripping tar brush in front of him. 'It's how I got my Tee name, it was done to me at my brothering.'

Brothering was a tradition on the east coast, a rite of passage performed by a lad's future crew mates before his first expedition. When the brothering was over and done, the boy was acknowledged to be grown-up, a man among men.

Eric had nothing against brothering, ruefully remembering his own, but it was plainly obvious that George had had more than enough.

'And where did you get that tar?' asked Sheila. 'Did that just happen to be on hand?'

Tarry grinned. 'You could say that it was around.'

These were a right bunch of animals, Sheila thought, shooting Eric a look of disgust.

'Not done yet though, eh wee George?' crooned Tarry, and dipped the brush back into the can.

Wee George moaned and started to cry again. In a sudden explosion of energy he tried to struggle free, but the two men holding him fast merely tightened their grip.

'I think it should stop now,' Eric said quietly.

Tarry paused in what he was doing to glance over his shoulder at Eric. 'Why don't you and that bird of yours just fuck off,' he replied with a smile.

The *Locarno* crew members all grinned. Obviously they thought this was great sport.

Eric knotted his fists, knowing that if it came to a fight he was on a hiding to nothing against so many. But he couldn't walk away and leave George to this lot.

Sheila was well aware of how things were developing and knew it was up to her to get George off the hook. For no matter what the provocation, Tarry daren't strike a woman who wasn't his wife.

Going to Tarry she put her hand on the brush handle next to his.

'I think you've proved what a big brave man you are,' she said sweetly.

Tarry coloured, but didn't let go when she tried to pull the brush from his grasp.

'Give it to me, Tarry, or so help me the way I'll tell this story round the village will make you a laughing stock for months to come,' she promised.

Tarry wasn't scared of any man in Dragonholme, or the Lothians come to that, but public ridicule did scare

33

him as Sheila had known only too well it would. Slowly, reluctantly, he relinquished his grasp on the brush handle.

'Why don't you chaps go back to the pub and get yourselves another drink?' Sheila suggested.

There was a hiatus lasting a few seconds while Tarry fought back his anger and frustration. 'Aw to hell with it, I was done anyway! Let's get to The Haven where the next round's on me,' he declared loudly.

Tarry stamped off past Eric, shooting Eric a filthy look as he went by, his crew members hurrying along after him.

Sheila heaved a sigh of relief when they vanished round the corner then turned to George who was sobbing silently now that his ordeal was over.

Wisely she held back and let Eric be the one to help George.

'Come on, stop greeting, you'll live,' Eric said gruffly.

Sheila, Peg, Rhona and Maggie were out front mending the nets that had been used in the northern grounds when a horse and carriage drew up before them, and a short stocky man with a pug face and a blue bonnet got down from the driving seat.

This was Wally Simpson, the laird's ghillie.

'Good-day to you, Mrs Beattie,' said Simpson to Peg, who acknowledged the ghillie with a nod of her head, thinking to herself, now what does he want?

Simpson cleared his throat. 'It's your daughter I'm after having a word with,' he stated simply.

'Which of them did you have in mind?' asked Peg, her mending needle slipping through the net quick as a darting minnow.

Simpson screwed up his right eye, then cocked his head to one side. 'I thought you only had the one daughter and that the others were daughters-in-law?'

Peg had never liked Wally Simpson. He was a sly,

34

sleekit man. 'Are you being impertinent, Mr Simpson?' she snapped in reply, putting her hands on her hips.

Simpson stared at her. Peg standing like that reminded him of a picture he'd seen recently in the newspaper portraying a newly launched Dreadnought.

'Not in the least, only getting my facts straight,' he lied, in the slow, lazy drawl that he knew irritated people. He enjoyed irritating people – probably his only natural talent – and walking all over them given half the chance.

'Well, there's Sheila at the end. State your business to her,' Peg said coldly.

Simpson walked down the line of nets till he was facing Sheila, and insolently eyed her up and down.

'I suppose looking is about all you can manage at your age,' Sheila said, causing Rhona and Maggie to giggle.

'I've never heard the like!' spluttered Simpson.

'Ach, you hear all sorts round here, just as you meet all sorts,' Sheila smiled.

Simpson drew himself up to his full height, which wasn't considerable, and puffing out his chest, said in what he considered to be a crushing tone. 'I'll have you know you're addressing an Elder of the Knockhammie kirk.'

What a pompous wee pipsqueak, Sheila thought. 'Is that a fact?' she retorted, still smiling. 'Dearie me, they must've been right hard up!'

Rhona put a hand over her mouth to smother her laughter.

'So what can I do for you, Mr Sampson?' Sheila asked sweetly.

'Simpson,' he corrected crossly.

'Are you here as an Elder or as the laird's *servant*?'

Simpson went puce, at an uncustomary loss for words. Then, swallowing hard and wishing he'd never started this, he went on, 'Mr Campbell has sent me to fetch you to the Hall. He wants to speak to you.' An expression on his face clearly said that the eccentricities of James Campbell were no concern of his.

Peg's eyes opened wide, while Rhona and Maggie turned to stare both quizzically and speculatively at Sheila.

'What does he want to see her about?' Peg asked.

'I've really no idea,' Simpson answered truthfully.

It had to be about Granny Mutch's cottage, Sheila was thinking, and her heart sank within her. Something had gone wrong with the arrangement she had made with the factor, she just knew it! Hell and damnation, she swore inwardly, that cottage had been perfect.

'Sheila?' Peg prompted.

Sheila was about to explain to her ma about the surprise she'd been planning to spring on Eric, but changed her mind when she saw Simpson gazing quietly into the distance, listening intently to every word.

'I'll tell you the story when I return,' she said, and ran into the house where she put on her best shawl, the Chinese one that Eric had bought for her in Lowestoft the previous year.

Simpson, brandishing a whip and making noises that were supposed to convey his impatience, was back in the driving seat when she returned outside. 'I shouldn't be too long, ma,' Sheila assured Peg, giving her mother a quick peck on the cheek. Rhona held the carriage door open for her as she climbed inside.

'I'll be dying to hear what the inside of the Hall is like now they've had it completely done out,' Rhona whispered through the open window.

Sheila's reply was a conspiratorial wink. Then, in a loud voice, she cried out, 'You can drive on now, Simpson!'

Simpson snorted, his mouth pinched into an expression of distaste. Just who did she think she was, giving *him* orders? Wisely, though, he didn't climb down to dispute the matter with her; he had no wish to be at the receiving end of any more of her jibes. He cracked his whip and muttered darkly to himself.

It was the first time Sheila had ever been in a carriage,

and the experience was certainly a pleasant one. I feel just like Lady Muck, she thought. On spying Mrs Johnstone, she stuck her head out of the window and waved, laughing delightedly at Mrs Johnstone's look of stunned incredulity. She settled back into the plush seat, knowing that word of her being in the laird's carriage would be round Dragonholme like wildfire. Mrs Johnstone would see to that.

On arriving at the Hall they didn't draw up at the main entrance, but round to the side where the staff came and went and general deliveries were made. Simpson jumped down and strode through the door, leaving Sheila to make her own way after him.

Once through the door, she went along a hallway to another door that was ajar, following the sound of Simpson's voice, in conversation beyond. Passing through this door she found herself in a large kitchen where Simpson was talking to a woman who was obviously the cook.

Simpson turned to Sheila. 'Wait here,' he said, more rude than officious, and went marching off, his bandy legs making him sway from side to side as he walked.

'I'm Mrs Tripp,' the cook said, coming to Sheila and smiling.

'And I'm Sheila Beattie. I'm here to see the laird.'

Mrs Tripp's smile was kindly. 'So Simpson was saying. He's gone to tell the laird that you've arrived. While you're waiting, would you like a cup of tea? There's one freshly mashed.'

An Englishwoman, Sheila thought, automatically on the defensive. Tea was masked north of the border, not mashed. 'That's very kind of you. I'd love some tea,' she answered politely, suddenly feeling uneasy and out of her depth.

The girl's reply had been stilted, her manner distant, and Annie Tripp knew why. It was nearly always the same when she opened her mouth to a stranger since coming to Scotland to take up this post. 'Are you surprised that I haven't got horns? I'm told that many of you Scots think we English do,' she asked, but not unkindly.

Sheila had met a number of English men before, but never an English woman. Of course she knew the English didn't *actually* have horns, that was just an old wives' tale. Just as she knew that their woman didn't eat new-born Scots babies, as some inland people still believed, in the more remote areas where they never had any truck with the Sassenach.

Sheila gratefully accepted the cup that was offered her. The woman was doing her best to be friendly. It would be rude of her not to be the same. 'I've never believed the English are as bad as they're painted. Nobody could be *that* bad,' she replied gravely.

Annie Tripp stared at Sheila, then, realizing it had been a joke, burst out laughing. Sheila joined in. When Simpson returned to say that the laird would see Sheila now, he found the pair of them having a good crack together, as though life-long friends.

Sheila thanked Annie for the tea, and followed Simpson out of the kitchen into another hallway which eventually led them into a large reception area. Avidly she glanced about her, taking everything in, the furniture and decorations, the very smell of the place, for she'd be expected to describe what she'd seen down to the last detail when she got home.

They ascended a sweeping staircase that brought them on to the Hall's second level. Here the walls were wood panelled and there was a thick, burgundy-coloured carpet underfoot.

They passed several suits of armour, then plunged into a small tunnel-like hall at the end of which was an oak door. Simpson rapped loudly.

'Come in!' called out a deep, masculine voice.

Simpson opened the door, gestured to Sheila to enter, and closed it behind her once she was inside. James Campbell was seated at a huge desk, a mass of papers spread out before him, his back to the window and the world outside.

This room, clearly the laird's private study, was plain in comparison to what she'd seen of the rest of the Hall. The floorboards were bare but highly polished, the walls and ceiling a clotted-cream colour. Apart from the desk, there were only two items of furniture in the room; one a bookcase crammed to overflowing, the other a small table by the window on which stood a replica of a steam trawler of the latest design.

'I'll be with you in a moment,' Campbell muttered without looking up, as though barely aware that she was there.

An instrument on a corner of his desk caught her attention. She recognized it to be a sextant from the description Davey had once given her. Davey didn't own one himself, scorning such aids to navigation. Davey and his like navigated by the stars and an intimate knowledge of the sea and sea-bed, being able to locate with pin-point accuracy and shoot their nets on any spot they wished.

'Paperwork, the bane of my life,' said James Campbell, and with a sigh threw down the pen with which he'd been writing. And then he raised his eyes to look at her. My God, he thought, she's prettier than I remembered. Pretty and oddly disarming. This was going to be harder than he had thought.

'I usually take a glass of sherry about this time. Would you care to join me?' he asked.

But Sheila was too anxious to perform the rituals of politeness. 'It's about Granny Mutch's cottage, isn't it, sir?' she blurted out.

He dropped his gaze, going on as though he hadn't heard her, opened a drawer in his desk and took out decanter and two glasses.

'Not for me, sir, I've just had some tea,' Sheila said and bit her lip.

James Campbell slowly poured himself some sherry, staring at the rich colour of the liquid as it filled the glass, realizing that she'd brought the smell of fish in with her. It was a smell he could remember as far back as he had memory, and one he had never tired of. The smell of fish was the smell of the sea, and as far as he was concerned the smell of the sea was the very breath of life itself.

He coughed, acutely aware of her presence, of the roughness of her clothes and the wildness in her bearing. How real she was compared to his wife Fiona, that lady of light and air, whose delicateness always seemed so brittle, as though she might break if handled too much, like a Dresden figurine would if grasped too tightly. Who was so much a lady that she didn't seem a woman.

'I'm afraid it is about the cottage. The fault's entirely mine. I neglected to tell the factor I had plans for it,' he explained, in a tone that wasn't at all like the firm but sympathetic one he'd intended using.

Instantly the image she'd had of the cottage, of her and Eric's home, vanished, bursting like a bubble. She'd known that's what it was, what it had to be! Disappointment welled within her at this verification of her worst fears.

'I wanted to tell you face to face that the fault was mine, and that no blame can be attached to Semple for what's occurred,' he went on. He tried to look her straight in the eye, but what he saw there caused him to glance away. It's not at all like you to be so bloody soft, he berated himself.

Despite the depth of her disappointment and hurt, Sheila knew there was no use arguing. The cottage was the laird's property, his to dispose with as he pleased.

'Thank you sir,' she whispered, and turned to go, determined not to let him see her cry.

'Wait!' he called out, not wanting her to leave, not like this. 'Semple said something about you getting married?' He held his glass in his right hand, nervously moving it between his fingers.

She'd asked Semple not to mention that round the village, but the laird was hardly the village. 'It's not settled yet,' she replied quietly, wishing he would let her flee.

He sipped his sherry, studying her over the rim of his glass. A silence as loud as an explosion stood between them. What a magnificent young woman, he thought. There was a wildness and a warmth about her, an air of straightforward determination that he hadn't encountered in years. She was precisely the sort of lassie he would have wanted to marry if he hadn't been so intent on success and status. 'But you are *planning* to get wed?' he prompted at last.

'Oh yes, sir. January, probably. It's just – well, we haven't got round to telling our families yet,' she lied. It was too personal a matter to explain to the likes of him.

He wondered at the pang of jealousy that stabbed through him. After all Sheila Beattie was nothing to James Campbell. 'May I inquire who the lucky man is?'

'Eric Gifford, sir. His da owns the *Gypsy Queen*, of the Dragonholme fleet.'

'Well, I'm sure your Eric is a fine upstanding lad,' he replied with a smile.

'He is,' Sheila whispered in reply, and then suddenly, without warning, tears were rolling down her cheeks. Turning away she hastily dabbed at them with the corner of her shawl.

For the first time in years, James Campbell found himself in a situation he couldn't control. This was awful. There was no place for sentiment in business, he reminded himself, but there was no conviction in his heart. Rising, he crossed to her and handed her his hanky. 'Use that,' he commanded.

She wiped her face, and blew her nose. 'I'm ever so sorry,' she muttered, furious with herself for having broken down.

'I think you should have that sherry,' he said and filled a second glass, which she accepted without protest.

When she was once more in control of herself, although still a little shaky inside, she said, because she could think of nothing else to say, 'My da told us that you're a self-made man, and that you were born in a Portnessie house that's just like ours.'

Campbell nodded, memories of the old times, the hard grafting times, flooding back. 'I started with a Coble that I got for next to nothing because they're not popular on this part of the coast, and went from there.'

'You must be extremely clever.'

Flattery, he asked himself? But no, she was not a girl like that. She would say only what she meant. 'The business side of the fishing industry has always fascinated me as much as the fishing itself. I've worked very hard at each, and been lucky with both.'

'How many boats have you got now?' she asked, feeling better now that they were talking about things she understood.

'Seventy-two.'

She pursed her lips and whistled, forgetting the embarrassment such a gesture would cause her ma. She'd known he owned a lot, but seventy-two! Why he owned nearly three times as many boats as there were in the entire Dragonholme fleet! 'You must be rich as Croesus.'

Campbell laughed. 'Let's just say it's been a long time since I've had to worry where my next crust of bread is coming from. And of course I have interests other than the boats, they're only part of my empire.'

Empire! The word jarred with her, and she remembered her da saying there was a streak of vanity in James Campbell. A rather large streak, she'd say, to use a word like that. Vanity and ego.

'Do you still own the Coble?' She asked impulsively. The answer she got was an insight into James Campbell that she hadn't expected. A strange look came into his eyes so they almost seemed to gleam metallically. 'I do,' he replied softly. 'Once something's mine it stays mine forever.'

Sheila found his words chilling, so that, involuntarily she pulled her shawl close. Here was a man capable of great ruthlessness, even cruelty. A man who thought differently from anyone else she'd ever known. 'I really must be getting along,' she said, and finishing what was left in her glass she laid it beside the sextant.

But still he didn't want her to leave, and wracked his brains for a topic that would prolong the conversation. 'How have the Dragonholme fleet been doing?' he asked, though he was far from ignorant of the bad luck they'd been having.

Sheila shook her head. 'It's bringing back hardly anything at all.'

'It's the same with my fleet. At the moment I'm not even covering costs, let alone making a profit.'

'Have you any idea why the shoals came south early this year?' she asked, as intrigued as all the villagers of Dragonholme were by that mystery. It was the question none of the fishermen could answer.

Campbell barked out a harsh laugh. 'Shoals! It's a bit of an exaggeration to call what's come south shoals. Small schools, I would term them.' Crossing to his desk he shoved various papers aside to reveal an Admiralty map. 'Ever heard of the Royal Society?' he demanded, smoothing the map out flat.

'No,' said Sheila, wondering what he was up to now.

'Well, they're a very august body of gentlemen who have a great thirst for knowledge, and it was several of their members who reported that there have been severe underwater upheavals in the Norwegian Sea just south of the Arctic Circle.'

Sheila stared down at the spot on the map where he was pointing, and there was the Arctic Circle clearly marked. To the north was Jan Mayen Island, with Svalbad, Spitsbergen and a large chunk of the Greenland mainland further north still.

Campbell's finger moved over to come to rest again in Western Russia, just below the Kara Sea. 'And around here, in what was very likely part of the same disturbance, there have been a number of earthquakes and eruptions.'

'Are you saying all this has something to do with the herring?'

'As this all took place in late April, it could very well be so,' he said slowly. 'Thinking about that, after reading the Royal Society's report, I wondered if the great shoals had come south even earlier than we'd imagined.'

Sheila's eyes widened. 'You mean the great shoals might be continually ahead of our fishermen this season and that all they're catching are the stragglers?'

Her own personal scent, mingled with the heady aroma of the sea that she'd brought in with her were making his senses reel, throwing him back to days he'd forgotten he remembered. And that tawny hair, thick and lustrous, the thought of it spread out against his hand, the thought of himself enveloped by the smell of her. . . .

'To discover if that was the case, I sent a couple of trawlers ahead of my fleet, having them fish well in advance of where we would normally be at this time of year.'

'And?' Sheila demanded expectantly.

Campbell shook his head. 'I was wrong. My boats never made contact. Wherever the herring are, it isn't further south.'

Sheila frowned in thought, trying to piece together all the terrible clues. 'You said the underwater upheavals were severe. What if they were so severe they killed the great shoals?'

James Campbell stared at her as though she'd slapped him. 'My God,' he whispered. Could it be true?

'Is it possible?' Sheila asked in a cracked voice.

It was several seconds before Campbell could reply, and when he did it was reluctantly, as though afraid of his own imaginings. 'I suppose it is. Mother Nature has wiped out entire races of people before now, so why not the great shoals of herring?'

Both knew that if she was right not only that season would be affected, but many more to come. It could take a score of years for the herring to breed themselves back to anything like the numbers they'd been. What Sheila was suggesting was the virtual annihilation of the herring industry as it now existed. Whole villages in Scotland and England would go bankrupt at the end of either this season or the next.

The thoughtful silence that had fallen between them was broken by Sheila. 'This mugginess is becoming unbearable,' she complained, suddenly awares that her entire body was sticky with sweat.

Campbell smiled, dabbing at the sweat on his own brow with a hanky.

'It's a direct result of those volcanic eruptions in Western Russia. The ash the eruptions have spewed into the atmosphere has created a sort of hot blanket. Up until now, it's been felt mostly at sea. This section of the east coast and a belt round Stavanger in Norway are the first land areas to be hit.'

Despite his vanity and arrogance, his knowledge and intelligence impressed her. He wasn't bad looking, either, for such an old man.

It was a rare occurrence for James Campbell to change his mind after he'd committed himself, but he did so now. He'd become so taken with Sheila during the past few minutes he didn't want her to think ill of him. On the contrary, he wanted quite the reverse. 'I've decided to let you have the cottage after all,' he said abruptly. 'I had intended building on to the property, but we'll forget about that for the time being. As for the rent as it stands, I won't expect you to start paying that until you actually move in. You can consider that my wedding present to you and your young man.' He set his glass on the desk with finality.

Sheila was completely taken aback. The last thing she'd expected was a total turn around on his part. 'Thank you, sir, thank you,' she stammered, her face glowing with renewed excitement.

'The pleasure is entirely mine, Sheila Beattie,' James Campbell smiled.

*　　*　　*

She was halfway home when it started to rain. At first there were only a few light drops, but these quickly intensified until it was pouring down. The light paled to murky grey, and then grew darker still. In the driving seat, Simpson fought to control the horse which was snorting and rolling its eyes in fright.

When Sheila alighted in front of her house the rain was actually bouncing a foot back off the ground. I hope the fleet's all right, she worried, as she hurried inside.

She awoke as the sound of the crash reverberated round the room. 'What the. . . !'

'Don't fash yourself, it's only thunder,' Bob said from beyond the curtain.

'Are you up?'

'Aye, I'm over at the window watching the gale. It's quite a spectacle.'

As she got out of bed there was another crack of thunder. It might have been her imagination, but it seemed to her that the walls shook from it.

'The thunder started about half an hour ago,' Bob said when she joined him at the window. 'I'm surprised it hasn't wakened you before now.'

A jagged streak of lightning split the sky, followed by another and another. Off in the distance Sheila could hear the roar of surf pounding the beach.

'God help all fishermen who're on the sea this night,' Bob said with feeling, thankful he wasn't one of them.

'Look!' said Sheila, pointing to where a blue glow had suddenly appeared in the north-west.

Bob was well acquainted with the Northern Lights, but he'd never seen anything like this before, nor heard of anything like it.

'Probably something else caused by the ash spewed into the atmosphere by the Russian volcanoes that erupted a few months back,' Sheila said, airing her newly acquired information.

Bob looked down at her, both amused and amazed. There were times when his sister came out with the damnedest things.

'The laird told me about the volcanoes when I was at the Hall,' she explained, and went on to tell him about the Royal Society and the underwater upheavals in the Norwegian Sea.

'My God!' breathed Bob, echoing James Campbell, when she told him it could be a possibility that the great shoals had all been destroyed.

The loudest crack of thunder yet exploded above the house. This time she was certain: the walls *did* shake.

Davey stood on the quayside and stared out to sea, a sea that was a seething green and white cauldron. The thunder and lightning had stopped, but that eerie blue glow was still to be seen in the north-west.

The wind tore fiercely at his oilskins; a warm wind with enormous power and fury behind it. In the harbour the boats bobbed and dipped, yawed and juddered; the heaving water alternately sucking at, then crashing against their hulls.

'Well, Davey, what's the verdict?' Rab Gifford asked.

The men of the Dragonholme fleet had formed themselves into a semi-circle behind Davey, awaiting his pronouncement.

Davey removed the battered clay from his mouth. 'I say we stay in harbour. My feeling is that, bad as this blow is, it's going to get an awful lot worse as the day goes on,' he said slowly.

Several of the men swore in their disappointment at losing a day's fishing. Tarry Dunbar was one of them.

Eric glanced across to where Sheila and the other women were waiting. He gave her the thumb's down sign, then gestured that he wanted a word with her.

As the men started to disperse Eric hurried over to Sheila, pulling her to one side so that their conversation wouldn't be overheard. 'I'll arrange to be doing some work on our gash floats and corks in the hut this afternoon,' he whispered. 'Can you make it?'

'I could well be busy,' she replied vaguely.

His face dropped. 'I don't often get a weekday free this time of year.'

'Ach, don't panic,' she interjected with a playful smile. 'I'll be there.'

'Right then. I'll be expecting you.' She often teased him, and he often misunderstood.

Walking back to the house, Sheila was joined by Davey. Everyone else in the family had gone ahead.

'Now what's this you've been telling Bob about underwater upheavals in the Norwegian Sea?' he demanded.

By that afternoon, as Davey had predicted, the gale had worsened considerably. By the time Sheila arrived down on the beach, mountainous rollers were crashing ashore, filling the air with the hiss and howl of the angry sea.

As she opened the door of the hut a gust of wind caught it, wrenching it from her hand to send it banging inwards. Eric looked up from where he was sitting on top of a coil of new warp line and grinned, thinking how magnificent she looked with her hair whipping to one side and her cheeks burning fiercely from the driving spume that had been lashing her since nearing the beach.

Sheila made no effort to reshut the door, wanting it to remain open so that the dramatic exit she had planned would be unhindered. Planting her hands on her hips, exactly the way she'd seen Peg do countless times, she glanced around her in dismay.

Eric's grin changed to a frown. 'What's wrong?' he asked, rising and tossing aside the knife he'd been using.

'This place. It's been so long since I've seen it in the daylight that I'd forgotten how filthy it is.' An expression of disgust clouded her pretty face.

Eric looked about him in bewilderment. 'All the huts are like this. Our's is no worse.'

'Glue, paint, manky tackle of all sorts,' she sniffed. 'Some love nest!'

'Oh, now Sheila –' he began in alarm, going to her and trying to take her in his arms, only to be pushed away.

'Not here, not any more. I do have some pride!' she snapped, eyes blazing with anger.

Eric was at a complete loss. What had suddenly got into the girl? 'You don't mean that,' he said, trying again to take her into his arms, only to be repulsed a second time.

'Oh yes I do!'

'But you've never complained about the hut before.'

'Well, I'm complaining now. A man expecting a woman to make love in conditions and surroundings like these has no respect for her, no respect at all.' And with that she wheeled around and strode back the way she'd come, leaving a shattered Eric gawping after her.

But as soon as her back was turned on him, her fierce expression instantly changed into a broad smile. Not a bad performance of outraged indignation, even if she did say so herself! That had knocked some of the complacency out of him. It was high time he learned she wasn't to be taken for granted.

She was just rounding a small dune when she saw something that made her come up short. Sitting on its rear, about a dozen feet away, staring at her, was a large hare. Sheila went cold all over. It was an omen of the worst sort to meet a hare. In the old days it had been said that witches turned themselves into hares and in that disguise wrought great evil.

I shall go intill a hare,
With sorrow and sych and meikle care;
And I shall go in the Devil's name,
Ay while I come home again.

Sheila clearly recalled the lines that Peg had told her one dark winter's night when the men had been out and

49

they'd sat huddled round the fire. Peg had got the lines from a travelling spaewife who'd sworn it was the incantation that Isobel Gowdie, the most infamous of Scottish witches, had used when she'd wanted to transform herself into a hare.

The hare's liquid brown eyes gazed into Sheila's, then slowly it lifted its front right paw and jerked it in her direction.

'Oh!' She exclaimed, taking a step backwards.

'Sheila! Sheila, wait up will you!' Eric shouted behind her. She turned as he came puffing to a halt by her side. 'You don't half move quickly when you've got your dander up,' he gasped.

She grabbed hold of his arm, squeezing it so hard in her anxiety that it caused him to wince.

'What is it?'

She swung round to point out the hare, only to find that it had gone, vanished without trace.

Eric's approach must have sent it scuttling away, she told herself. It was well known that hares were naturally shy and timid creatures, although that particular hare had seemed neither shy nor timid. On the contrary, it had been bold in the extreme. The way it had jerked its paw at her! She shuddered at the memory.

As she didn't go on to explain about the hare, Eric mistook her upset, thinking it had to do with him. 'Don't fall out with me, Sheila. It never occurred to me that the hut might be offensive to you. It's just always been such a safe meeting place,' he pleaded.

She took a deep breath, then smiled inwardly. He was netted, but she wouldn't land him yet. That was planned for Saturday night during the wedding reception. 'I haven't fallen out with you, it's just . . . well, I suppose I expected more of you,' she replied, disappointment and sadness in her voice. She resumed walking and he strode beside her.

'In what way did you expect more of me?' he demanded.

She answered obliquely, then a little further on switched the conversation to children, saying what a delight her nephews and nieces were, and how it must be grand to have children of your own, particularly boys to carry on the family name and tradition.

By the time they reached her house she had Eric visualizing himself as a grizzled skipper whose stalwart sons not only idolized him but crewed for him as well. And she had completely forgotten about the hare.

Tarry just wouldn't pass out. Sheila had managed to see he was fed drink after drink – all extremely large ones – but still he kept on his feet, yelling and wheeching like a demented Kelpie.

Sheila and Eric had thought they might have trouble with Tarry after the incident with wee George, but although they'd both been aware of him occasionally glowering darkly at them nothing had actually been said.

'Take your partners for the Gay Gordons please!' cried Murdo Sigurdson, Marika's da, from the raised dais on which the two accordion players were seated.

The reception was being held in the Community Hall, and including the children who were continually running up and down and getting under everyone's feet, there were just under fifty people present.

Sheila and Eric got up for the dance, finding themselves behind the sparkling Marika and the flushed Duncy. The ceremony earlier had gone off without a hitch. Marika had looked so absolutely radiant as she'd walked down the aisle on her da's arm that Sheila hadn't been able to stop herself from crying when Marika said, 'I do'. Despite Eric whispering to her several times to stop 'greeting like some big bairn', she had continued from that point right through to the end of the ceremony.

Sheila brought her attention back to the immediate present as the dance got under way, laughing to see fat Mrs Arbuthnot shaking her enormous backside at the man behind, not unlike the way the Clydesdales on Bog-side Farm shook their bottoms when the summer flies and midges were bothering them.

Out of the corner of her eye she saw McPherson, the carter, arrive to take Marika and Duncy on their honeymoon which was to be spent in Pittlody, a picturesque clachan some seven and a bit miles inland.

She couldn't help thinking of the honeymoon she planned for Eric and herself. Going to Pittlody was all right, but to Edinburgh and Princes Street where she'd find that braw dream press she was after, now that's what she called a honeymoon – one to remember for the rest of her life! She gave Eric such an exuberant smile that he nearly tripped.

It had been a smashing week for her with Eric ashore, a week when all her dreams seemed so within her reach that the world was filled with only happiness and song. Even Eric's restlessness over the fleet's forced inactivity couldn't mar her mood for long.

Sheila glanced across to where Tarry and a few of Duncy's pals were sneaking out of a side door. They'd be off to 'fix' the cart on which Marika and Duncy would be travelling through to Pittlody, she guessed.

At the end of the dance Marika signalled to Sheila and the two of them took themselves off to the cludgie, or ladies' toilet.

'I feel so nervous,' Marika giggled. 'You'd think we'd never done it before.'

'Ach, don't be daft, there's nothing to be nervous about,' laughed Sheila. 'Anyway, Duncy's put away so much of the cratur I'll be surprised if you get more than a peck on the cheek out of him later.'

Marika giggled again. Sheila didn't know her Duncy: drink never affected him in that department.

There was a tap on the door which Sheila answered. Murdo Sigurdson handed in Marika's going away clothes and announced that the newlyweds' cases had been loaded aboard the cart.

When Marika was ready she turned to Sheila. 'How do I look then?'

'Pretty as a picture, *Mrs Laidlaw*,' Sheila smiled.

'You're the first to call me that,' Marika whispered, having been waiting all night for the thrill of being addressed by her new name.

Sheila took her plump friend into her arms and hugged her tightly. 'I'm so pleased for you,' she choked. 'I can't tell you how much.'

On leaving the cludgie they found all the guests lined up waiting for them, a sheepish Duncy standing at their head with his arm crooked for Marika to take.

While the accordionist played 'I Love a Lassie', everyone followed the happy couple outside to cheer them on their way. Old boots, several ancient corsets, and the largest pair of drawers Sheila had ever seen (donated by Mrs Arbuthnot) hung and dangled from the rear of the cart. The *pièce de resistance*, however, was in the centre of the cart where a giant mock carrot with a round white pudding impaled upon it had been stuck.

A cascade of rice fell over Marika and Duncy as they climbed on to the cart. Duncy raised a roar of ribald laughter, catcalls and jeers when, pretending to notice the carrot for the first time, he remarked in a loud aside to Marika that he couldn't for the life of him think what it was supposed to mean.

'Right then, all set for the off?' McPherson asked from the front of the cart, flicking his whip over the horse when Duncy gave him the nod.

Marika's bouquet flew through the air, straight into Sheila's waiting hands.

'You next then, lass,' said Mrs McDuff, who was standing beside Sheila and Eric.

Sheila gave Eric a sideways look to ensure he'd heard that, then turned back to watch the cart roll off into the darkness with Tarry and some other rice throwers pursuing it.

Sheila nudged Eric and whispered that she wanted to

53

show him something. Then, with him following, she forced her way to the rear of the throng and took his arm.

'It's a lovely bouquet, don't you think?' she asked coyly, and held it up for him to smell.

'Oh, aye, real nice.'

'I've never caught one before, did you know that?'

He shook his head, a little confused by all the celebrating he'd been doing. 'Well, it's a fact,' she said softly, and leaned her head against his shoulder.

Arm-in-arm, they started up the street, Eric, roused by the night air, noticing that the wind had fallen again. The clouds were still low, though, and swirling frenetically as if being stirred by some unseen, heavenly spoon. 'Where are we going?' he asked.

'I told you, I want to show you something.'

'But what?'

'Wait and see,' she teased.

He let out a sigh. Women! How exasperating they could be at times. Still, he had to admit that he couldn't do without them, especially Sheila. He couldn't imagine life without Sheila.

She stopped in front of Granny Mutch's cottage. 'What do you think?' she asked.

He stared about, not sure what he was supposed to be looking at. 'Think of what?'

'Follow me,' she said mysteriously, and led him inside.

Just to the right of the door were two candles and a box of Lucifer matches that she'd put there that morning. A match flared, then a candle spluttered alight. 'Hold that,' she instructed, handing him the candle.

Eric was bewildered. What in the name of the Wee Man was she playing at? Why bring him here?

She faced him squarely, a look in her eye of which he might have been more wary were he more sober.

'I've decided there's to be no more lovemaking between us,' she said baldly.

'What!' The candle in his hand shook, throwing crazy shadows on the wall.

'No more lovemaking,' she repeated, her expression one of immoveable resolution.

He stared at her aghast. 'I thought it was only the hut you objected to?'

'So you then went on to think maybe the woods or the dunes or somewhere like that would be all right?'

'Well, where else is there?'

'You're my own darling man, Eric, but you have one tiny fault. You have no imagination.'

That was a relief. He was still her darling man. He couldn't be getting the elbow. 'If the hut, the woods, the dunes, in other words all the usual places that courting couples use are out, then where do you suggest?' he asked slowly.

'I'm sick to death of old tarpaulin and such, and the worry that someone might walk in on us. I want privacy, Eric. Assured privacy.'

'But the only way to get that in a small village like ours is to – ' He trailed off as the penny dropped. So that was it – that was what all this was about! Now he knew why her behaviour had been so odd and erratic since he'd come back to Dragonholme. Marika being bairned must've sparked this off. Aye, that would be it. 'I suppose this cottage is for rent?' he asked quietly.

'I believe it is,' she answered casually, as though he'd been the instigator all along and not she.

'Perhaps someone else has already spoken up for it?' he speculated, unable to repress a smile.

'I happened to have a conversation with the factor just the other day, and if I remember correctly he mentioned in passing that it was still available,' she said with a shrug, and proceeded to light the second candle.

Happened to have a conversation. Mentioned in passing. Eric laughed inwardly. His Sheila was something, that was certain.

Sheila went over to the box cavity bed and peered into the recess. 'With sheets and blankets it must be right comfy, and *private* in there,' she said appraisingly.

He'd been thinking to give it another year before getting wed; at the end of next season, when there might be a bit more money to hand. But maybe Sheila was right and it was foolish to delay what would happen anyway. He certainly had no intention of losing her. 'It would make a fine family home, there's no denying that,' he conceded.

'Needs a few things doing to it. The range, for example, should be replaced, but apart from that there isn't much that some elbow grease wouldn't put right,' Sheila enthused.

He had enough money saved; not quite as much as he would have liked, but enough. The trouble was that some of that was going to be eroded if this damned awful season didn't pick up. 'I suppose a grand wee but and ben like this won't stand empty long,' he mused.

'I shouldn't think it will.'

He tapped at the floor with the toe of his shoe. 'No doubt the fleet will be moving on to the Silver Pits directly this gale is over,' he said.

'Aye, but you'll be back again at the end of December, then it's straight into January. January's always been one of my favourite months.'

So it was a January wedding she planned.

'No lovemaking unless privacy is assured?' he repeated, raising an eyebrow.

'Not a bit.'

He crossed to the window and stared out. She wasn't the only one who could play games, he decided. He'd indulge in a little teasing of his own. 'That Rosie McCullough has fairly grown up I was thinking the night. How old is she now?'

'Fourteen,' Sheila replied, her lips pursing.

'As a wee lassie she was always keen on me, did I ever tell you that?'

'Often,' Sheila answered through gritted teeth.

'I could be mistaken but I thought she was giving me the come hither when we were up doing The Grand Old Duke of York,' Eric said.

'Was she indeed?'

'Some figure, eh? Who would have thought such a skinny runt of a child would grow up to be such a *big* girl.'

Sheila began to seethe. If he thought he was going to give her over for that Rosie McCullough, then he had another thing coming! If he so much as laid a hand on Rosie she'd scratch the eyes out of his head.

Suddenly, Eric laughed, loudly and uncontrollably, unable to keep it up any longer. He was delighted with himself for getting his own back. From now on, Sheila wasn't going to get things quite so much her own way as she had. 'I'll make a bargain with you,' he said, when he'd finally stopped laughing enough to speak.

'What's that?'

'You compromise on the lovemaking and I'll compromise on the wedding.'

She stared at him for a second. Then she, too, started to laugh. He'd had her going that time. This was a new side to Eric, and one she liked.

'It's a bargain.'

He came to her and took her into his arms, his mouth eagerly seeking hers. As they kissed his hand began to caress her breast.

She broke off kissing, her hand on his wrist. 'Haven't you got something to say first?' she whispered.

'You mean *the* actual question?'

'*The* actual question.'

He took a deep breath to steady himself. After all, it wasn't every day a man proposed. He opened his mouth, but before he could utter a word the church bell started to clang loudly and stridently.

'Oh, hell!' Sheila swore, then was instantly filled with remorse. When the church bell rang outwith a Sunday something calamitous had happened.

Eric had gone rigid with the first clang, but now he galvanized into action. 'Come on!' he exclaimed, and blew out the two candles. Grabbing her wrist he pulled her towards the door.

Out in the street they joined a stream of people heading for the church, where a large crowd had already assembled.

Sheila spied her da, with her three brothers at his back, pushing his way to the front. 'What's happened?' Davey shouted, but no one had an answer; nor did anyone know who was ringing the bell.

The minister appeared from the manse. He had no idea either why the bell was being rung.

And then, quite abruptly, the clanging ceased. A few minutes later a red-faced Tarry appeared, breathless from having run down the stairs from the bell tower. With Tarry was Ian McPherson, the carter's son.

'What is it, Tarry?' Davey demanded. 'Why are you ringing the bell?'

Tarry thrust Ian in front of Davey. 'You repeat to the admiral what you told me at the reception,' Tarry commanded.

'My da sent me through to Portnessie with a load this morning and I'm only back ten minutes since,' Ian explained nervously.

'Get on with it!' urged Tarry.

Ian took a deep breath, unused to being the centre of so much attention. 'The Portnessie fleet went out last night and has found a big shoal at the Broken Crags. When their cutter came back at midday it was fair brimming over with fish,' he said. The Broken Crags was located in the most northerly section of the home grounds.

The Portnessie fleet was made of trawlers. Trawlers operated in a different way to drifters, staying at sea for some time and sending their catches back by cutter. Drifters, on the other hand, came in and out of port, usually on a twenty-four-hour basis.

'We must set sail right away to catch the ebb tide,' Tarry commanded.

'Aye, the morning could be too late,' piped up Mr Johnstone. 'The Portnessie men might have scooped the entire shoal by then.'

58

'Now wait – just wait a minute!' ordered Davey. Rubbing a hand over a stubbled chin, he glanced up at the sky as Eric had earlier, to note that the wind had fallen away.

'What do you say, Davey?' Tarry urged with pleading in his voice. 'Do we put to sea?'

'Let's away down to quayside and have a look first,' Davey replied, and instantly the crowd surged in the direction of the harbour.

On the quayside, Davey consulted a barometer, and found it ominously low. The sea itself was choppy, but nothing like the broil it had been.

'We're wasting time,' Tarry said in exasperation, the crew of the *Locarno* ringed about him.

'A big shoal. We need those fish,' Dougal whispered to Davey, and Jack, hard by Dougal's side, nodded his agreement.

Conditions had improved, Davey could hardly deny that. They were certainly far better than the previous night when the Portnessie fleet had gone out. And yet . . . and yet. . . . It wasn't the low barometer that was holding him back, but something intangible, an instinct honed by years of experience, that warned him to stay ashore.

'What's the verdict?' asked Robin McDuff who crewed *The Willie*.

'I say we stay tied up,' replied Davey sternly, his eyes serious with responsibility.

Tarry gave an exclamation of anger, smashing his fist against his thigh.

He's drunk, Sheila thought, then remembered that he should be, considering the amount of whisky he'd consumed that day.

'You can say what you like, Davey, but the *Locarno*'s going after those fish,' Tarry growled defiantly, thrusting out his lower jaw.

'If Tarry's going, then I'm going,' spoke up Olaf Johnstone, skipper of the *Fear Not*.

'You should do as the admiral recommends, that's the way it's always been with us,' Eric said to Olaf.

'There speaks a right coward, a man who hides behind his lassie's skirts,' taunted Tarry.

Eric flushed bright red. 'I'm no coward,' he replied in a low voice.

'Are you not?' leered Tarry. Turning to his crew, he winked lewdly, causing them to laugh and snigger.

'Mind yourself, Tarry Dunbar!' warned Rab Gifford. No one called a son of his a coward.

'So how about you, then, Mr Gifford? Will you put out with me?' Tarry jibed.

Rab looked to Davey, then back to Tarry. 'I do as the admiral says,' he replied reluctantly. 'I'm staying in harbour.'

Tarry hooted. 'I can see where Eric gets it from now,' he howled. 'A real chip off the old block.'

In unison the Gifford lads stepped forward. This sort of insult wasn't to be borne. Just who in hell did Tarry Dunbar think he was!

Pinchie Murray, skipper of the *Happy Return*, decided he could turn this to his own advantage. 'I've done really badly this season, so I'm going with Tarry,' he said to Eric. 'If you'll entertain the idea, then you're welcome to take Duncy's place. I'm a crewman short with him off on his honeymoon.'

'If my da says not to go out, then you shouldn't,' Sheila warned, tugging at Eric's arm.

'Your lassie's speaking,' smiled Tarry. 'Time for you to jump.'

Eric was churning inside. Tarry had put him in such a position that he had to go, there was nothing else for it. If he didn't he'd never live it down. Not to himself at any rate.

Sheila was furious. Tarry's accusation was complete nonsense. No fisherman who went on the boats was a coward. If anything they were all, including Tarry, the complete opposite, the bravest of the brave. Tarry was mixing up cowardice with caution, bravery with foolhardiness.

'I'll sail with you, Pinchie,' replied Eric, the colour having drained from his face.

'No!' bellowed Rab. 'When my boys go to sea it's in the *Gypsy Queen*. We'll sail for the Broken Crags as well,' he declared.

The *Locarno*, the *Fear Not*, the *Happy Return* and the *Gypsy Queen*: four boats out of twenty-eight were now committed against their admiral's advice. Every eye present came to rest on Davey.

If they went on their own, Davey's days as admiral would be over. But that was not what bothered him. It was a fine thing being admiral, but it wasn't the be all and end all. What worried him was making the right decision for everyone. Although his instincts told him to stay ashore, there were times when instincts had to be over-ridden, when a gamble had to be made against the odds. Was this one of those times? If Sheila was right and the great shoals had been destroyed in the Norwegian Sea then this might be the last substantial amount of herring they would take this season. Was his caution foolhardy?

The circumstances were extraordinary, and extra-ordinary circumstances called for extraordinary deci-sions. Not only might this be the last decent catch of the season, it was also clear that the men wanted to go. Four boats were already committed, and many other skippers and crews were straining at the leash: he could read it in their faces.

Davey took a deep breath. 'If you are determined to go, then we'll all go,' he announced. 'We'll take a chance on the weather.'

A collective sigh ran through the crowd. Some of the men smiled, others laughed and jostled each other hap-pily; but there were only tight, drawn faces among the womenfolk. They'd do their smiling and laughing when the trip was over and their men were safely home again.

Tarry looked straight at Sheila and gave her a mocking

61

wink. He'd got his own way, and that never failed to make him happy.

Sheila glared back. She would never forgive Tarry Dunbar for challenging her father's authority and insulting Eric the way he had.

All around Sheila men were hurrying off to get changed into their sea gear. By her reckoning, they had less than half an hour to get the fleet away.

She told Eric she'd wait for him beside the *Gypsy Queen*, then stared after his broad back as he ran to catch up with his father and brothers. It was an image she would never forget: Eric hurrying away, his fair hair flying, his movements urgent with excitement, her darling man, her blond viking.

Jack was the first back to the *Bluebell* to give Rhona a squeeze and a cuddle, and Ian a kiss on the forehead. The so-called fairy-touched lad stared at his father with huge worried eyes, and his lower lip trembled.

'There, there, my wee man, I'll be back before you know it,' Jack smiled, and tousled the boy's hair before setting him down again.

Then came Dougal to say good-bye to his family, Davey and Bob shortly behind him.

'Now don't fash yourself woman, it'll be all right,' Davey said to Peg, abruptly turning away from her to shout out an order to Uncle Matt, who'd just jumped aboard.

At the *Gypsy Queen*, Sheila rejoined Eric. 'Old Granny Mutch's place is a grand cottage, you did well to think of it,' he said, taking one of her hands in his. She looked at his large, strong fingers encircling hers.

'I'll be standing right here when you get back,' she said solemnly. 'You can ask me that question then.'

'What question's that?' he asked innocently.

'You know fine well which question I mean,' she retorted, and stuck a finger into his ribs.

They both laughed. 'Ach, to hell with it, I don't care who sees!' he said, and taking her into his arms, kissed her right there in front of everyone.

On the deck of the *Gypsy Queen*, Alastair Gifford wolf-whistled.

'Would you take a look at that!' he exclaimed, nudging his brother Don.

'Come on Eric, there'll be plenty of time later for the winching!' Rab cried, having just cast off the aft line.

At the harbour entrance the *Muirneag* was already passing out to sea, while behind her came the *True Vine*, *Nonsuch* and *Locarno*.

'See you tomorrow,' Eric whispered to Sheila. Roughly breaking their embrace, he leapt from the quayside on to the bow of the *Gypsy Queen* and loosed the for'ard line.

The last boat to leave the harbour was the *Foamcrest*, and as she did the wind freshened, immediately causing the fleet to pick up speed.

'Good luck to all the bonny men!' cried Mrs Henderson as the *Foamcrest* cleared the harbour entrance, as she did every time the last boat cleared the harbour entrance when the fleet put to sea.

Sheila suddenly felt completely limp, drained of all energy and vitality. It had been a very long day. She wondered how the men, most of them a wee bit drunk from the celebrations, could find the strength to face the sea.

'Let's all go back and have a nice cup of tea,' Peg suggested, forcing her eyes away from the departing fleet. 'I think that's what we all need. A nice cup of tea.'

Halfway home, it began to rain.

Despite the rain, the heat returned and all during the night the temperature mounted steadily. Sheila woke out of a fitful sleep just before three to find she was wet with sweat. In the thick, oppressive darkness, she lay listening to the night sounds, the hammer of rain on the roof, the whistle of wind that was making the chimney pots rattle, the rustle of leaves and the creak of trees.

She could hear Peg snoring in the front room, and thought about the *Bluebell*, the *Gypsy Queen* and the rest, wondering how they were getting on at the Broken Crags.

In her dream, Eric had been making love to her in the bed at Granny Mutch's. So vivid had the dream been that she could still feel his body on hers. But thinking of the fleet reminded her of other things. What if she was right? What if the great shoals had been destroyed in the Norwegian Sea? That would mean terrible hard years lay ahead for them, years with the sort of constant, hopeless hardship that Peg had known in her youth.

If that was to be, had she and Eric a right to get married? Alone in her small bed, she could feel the warmth of his kiss on her lips. If hard times did lie ahead, she'd rather face them as Eric's wife. Anyway, and she gave a rueful grin, two could starve just as easily together as they could apart. It would be a January wedding, then, no matter how the season turned out.

Still feeling restless, Sheila rose and crossed to the window where she frowned. The rest of the village slept peacefully, but there in the north-west that strange blue glow had reappeared. Sheila stared at it with troubled eyes, only certain there would be no more sleep for her that night.

Some with shawls covering their heads and shoulders, others with their hair blowing free, the women of Dragonholme lined the quayside, waiting for the dawn to come up. Off in the north-west the blue glow had grown to twice the size it had been earlier that morning when Sheila had first noticed it.

The sea itself was fierce. Wave after angry wave crashed against the quayside throwing spume high into the air. The rain had stopped. But the wind had worsened, howling and moaning like a demented spirit.

The dawn came weakly over the horizon, frail shafts of pale light struggling to illuminate the thick grey sky.

'Do you see anything yet, Sheila?' Peg asked anxiously.

Sheila strained her eyes, willing the black sails to suddenly appear; but there was nothing to see but the sea and the sky and the dawn coming up. 'No sign yet,' she answered, trying to keep her own voice cheery.

Behind the women, the gutting tables were all laid out ready, the gutting knives upon them. Off to one side stood McPherson, the carter, with his son, and beside them were Handy Dandy, Tom Taggart, and the other old and disabled men of the village.

Handy Dandy started to sing 'Rock of Ages', his strong baritone disturbing some gulls close by, sending them wheeling high into the air, cawing and crying their protests.

Tom was the first to take up his friend's song. But soon everyone there in the strange dawn light joined in, taking comfort and solace from the hymn. 'Rock of Ages' was followed by 'There is a Green Hill Far Away' and that by 'Jerusalem'.

An hour passed, then another and another. The tide began to turn and still there was no sign of the fleet.

Of course, they all agreed, they hadn't expected the fleet home with the morning tide, they'd only been there just in case.

The wag-at-the-wa' clock ticked away the seconds as Sheila busied herself with the day's housework, or pretended to busy herself. For some reason she wasn't really accomplishing very much. Nor was Peg, despite the fact that she was bustling frantically around the house, doing this, that and a dozen other things at once.

'This heat!' complained Sheila pausing to wipe a sheen of sweat from her brow.

'Aye, it's more like I imagine Africa to be than the east coast of Scotland,' Peg replied, dusting an ornament she'd dusted not half an hour since.

Both women looked up as the clock struck the hour and the cuckoo popped out. Another ten or fifteen minutes and the tide would be turning again.

'Shall we get down there then?' Peg asked, abandoning her dusting to reach for her shawl, unable to conceal the concern in her eyes.

They called by for Rhona and Maggie, and with the children trailing along beside them, made their way down to the quayside where a small knot of women had already gathered.

Jack and Rhona's son, Ian, had the saddest expression Sheila had ever seen on a child. He stared disconsolately out to sea, as though he saw things the other watchers didn't.

The strange blue glow in the north-west was larger than ever, spreading across the sky like ink slowly spreading over blotting paper.

She glanced again to the north-west, to find that the colour of the glow had deepened to violet, and in its centre streaks of lightning were flashing one after the other.

She had thought it would be cooler down here by the quayside, but in fact the flying spume and spray which spattered her face might have come from a kettle halfway to being boiled.

'It must be a good catch, don't you think?' asked Peg suddenly. 'They'd be back by now if there was nothing there.'

'I'm sure you're right, ma,' agreed Sheila. And thought to herself of course she's right, the catch must have been even better than they hoped it would be.

It was well over an hour later when Lena Murray gave a sudden cry of joy and threw up her arms. 'There they are!' she shouted. 'Look! There they are! I'm sure it's them.'

Sheila cupped her hands around her eyes. Were those sails or low flying clouds? At this distance it was almost. . . . And then she too let out a shout. Yes, they *were* sails, the fleet was coming in.

Soon afterwards, Sheila was able to count the dots; twenty-eight of them, just as there should be. Peg put her arms around Sheila's shoulders and hugged her close, her smile broad, her eyes shining with relief.

Nearer came the fleet, every boat sitting low in the water, heavy with fish.

It began to rain, lightly, almost gently, but the wind blew harder than ever. Even as they stood there they had to hold on to one another to stop themselves from being blown over, or away.

Thunder shook the heavens. Jagged, powerful bolts of lightning lit up the almost purple sky.

Aboard the *Bluebell* Davey was crouched over the wheel. It worried him that the boat was so sluggish, and he considered lightening his load to regain some buoyancy. Eventually he decided against it; every fish was precious when this might be the last decent catch of the season.

Below deck in the *Gypsy Queen* Eric paused to sniff the air which had suddenly become charged and tainted with a metallic smell which stung his nostrils and made him want to cough.

Tarry Dunbar was grinning broadly as he steered the *Locarno* in the wake of the *Bluebell*. He'd known he was right to go to the Broken Crags, and what a haul it had been! The Portnessie fleet was still there, but wouldn't be able to do much fishing in weather as foul as this. He'd land his catch, and then turn right round again as soon as the weather cleared and get himself another capacity haul out of what remained of the big shoal.

Sheila was eyeing with trepidation the black clouds that were quickly piling up in the south-west, looking like nothing so much as thick, black smoke from a furnace. The clouds stood out eerily against the violet glow surrounding them.

And then, without any warning, the wind dropped completely away, leaving the boats bobbing on a churning sea.

Davey glanced at his aneroid to discover that it was rising at an alarming rate.

Even Tarry's smile had vanished. God damn it! he raged silently. There would be no second haul for him if this lack of wind went on for any length of time.

But the wind stayed down and the sea rose even higher, rushing and leaping in mad fury, tossing the boats about as though they were mere toys.

'Water!' yelled Uncle Matt, and seconds later a huge mountain of water broke over the *Bluebell*. Uncle Matt's legs became entangled in a line and he was smashed against the deck.

Jack and Dougal fought their way for'ard to help him but just as they reached him a second mountain of water, even larger than the first, descended on them from nowhere. Jack and Dougal were swept off their feet and carried overboard. Instantly they vanished beneath the surface of the angry sea.

Davey stared at the spot where his two sons had gone over, his face so immobile it might have been carved from stone. Despair and the most profound grief he'd ever experienced welled through him. His hands gripped the wheel as though not even the ferocity of the wind could dislodge him. Beyond feeling, beyond despair, he stared into the broiling water as though what had happened might be undone. Then something in him snapped.

'Take the wheel,' he ordered an ashen Bob.

From no wind at all to a raging hurricane took less than a minute, and during that brief space the *Fear Not*, and the *Martha Somerville* were both swamped. Chaos ruled the waters. There was not a man aboard the boats who was not stunned by what was taking place.

'Merciful Jesus!' gasped Peg, while a few feet away Mrs Johnstone, whose man crewed the *Fear Not*, gave a great animal cry, and, sinking to her knees, buried her head in her hands.

It was hell on earth. Sheila, battered by the furious

winds, clung to her mother, her eyes fixed on the nightmare before them, while overhead the sky itself seemed about to be torn apart. It was impossible to believe that what was happening was real.

She watched in fascinated horror as the *Muirneag* turned over, then sank almost immediately. Beside her, she could feel Peg shaking.

A giant wave towered over the *Locarno*, drawing the vessel broadside-on and right underneath it, heeling over towards it. And then the wave fell.

The *Orion*, the *Star of Hope* and the *True Vine* all broke apart, while the *Happy Return*, Pinchie Murray's boat, dipped into a trough and just didn't reappear.

On the *Bluebell*, Bob's voice rose against the sounds of death, 'Our Father, which art in Heaven. . . .'

On the quayside Sheila too began to pray. Softly, automatically, 'Dear God in Heaven, please help us. Dear God, please. . . .'

'Sheila!' Eric screamed, the last word he ever spoke, and then the broil closed over him.

Sheila heard that scream, though not through the raging elements, or the roar of death, but in her mind where it rang out clear as a note from a cleanly struck bell. 'Eric!' she wailed, clutching on to her mother's hand. 'Eric!'

Peg had begun to weep. Beside her Rhona and Maggie were frozen with shock. As the *Gypsy Queen* had gone down, so too had the *Bluebell*.

3

Early on the day of the funeral fishermen from up and down that part of the coast started to arrive in Dragonholme to honour and pay their last respects to the dead.

The men of Eyemouth came, followed by those of

Burnmouth, Cove, Coldingham, Portnessie and the Forth ports of Musselburgh and Newhaven.

Grim-faced men in blue serge, they gathered by the kirk where they spoke in soft voices and occasionally, unobtrusively, handed the bottle round.

When it was time to call the congregation the kirk bell tolled, a sad mournful sound that tugged at the heart and caused more than one grim face to turn away and shed a quiet tear.

Sheila knew it to be only her imagination, but it seemed to her that with each toll of the bell the name of a boat that had gone down rang out.

The *Bluebell*, the *Gypsy Queen*, the *Pilgrim*, the *True Vine*, the *Harmony*, the *Muirneag*, the *Locarno* – God damn Tarry Dunbar and may he roast in Hell for evermore! – the *Star of Hope*, and on and on, the names of nineteen boats out of the twenty-eight that had put out to sea. A hundred and five men drowned, and only seven bodies recovered, washed up on the beach during the few days following the disaster.

A few minutes, that's all it had taken for her whole world to be turned inside out. Her da, her brothers, the man she loved, all taken, all gone. At first there had been hysteria; then a still coldness. Now she felt only a numbing emptiness; a week ago she wouldn't have believed that the human body could be so cold and vastly empty.

Peg appeared strong and controlled as they made their way to the kirk, but Sheila knew it to be no more than a brave act. Inside, she knew, her mother was completely destroyed.

The sun shone brightly high overhead in a duck-egg-blue sky, through which a few wisps of cloud floated. It had been like this since the morning after the boats had gone down, that last terrible maelstrom marking the passing of the freak weather.

Women in black were converging on the church from all sides. So many widows, thought Sheila, so many widows, and fatherless children holding their mother's hands or clutching on to their skirts, their eyes wide with fear. There were three fatherless bairns in their own family now: wee Dougal, Violet and Ian. It was some comfort, at least, to know that they'd be financially secure for some time to come. The *Bluebell*, like all the other boats, had been insured. Peg would divide the money equally between herself, Maggie and Rhona, the way Davey would have wanted, and considered just.

A man stepped out of the Cove contingent and raised his cap to Peg. His name was Ramsay McLaren. He was a trawlerman through and through and he and Davey had been old adversaries. All that antipathy was forgotten now, though, for he'd greatly admired Davey as a person, and as a fisherman.

'Thank you for coming here this day, Mr McLaren,' Peg said.

McLaren nodded. He'd come, he was there. He didn't have to tell Peg what that meant. She knew.

Music was playing as they entered the kirk: 'Abide with Me'. The minister's wife was doing her best at the organ which was usually played by Alex Coburn who'd gone down on the *Harmony*.

The Gifford women were already there, as were the Johnstones, Sigurdsons and many others. Marika and Duncy were with her ma, Marika clinging on to Duncy, both only too aware, and profoundly grateful, that he owed his life to their honeymoon. Otherwise he would have been aboard the *Happy Return*, Pinchie Murray's boat, and one of those lost.

When all the mourning relatives were gathered inside, the other members of the village filed in, led by James Campbell and his wife Fiona. When they had been accommodated, the visiting fishermen took those seats remaining.

A throng of fishermen was left crowding at the back, with even more beyond them. The minister ordered all exterior doors to be opened so that the service could be heard outside as well as in. These fishermen then arranged themselves into several large groups round the open doors.

The minister held up his hand. 'Dearly beloved, let us pray,' he said.

Sheila bowed her head, but instead of concentrating on the minister's words, her mind was filled with pictures of Eric during their last short time together. Remorse stabbed at her as she remembered how she'd denied him her body and her love. Days that they could have spent making love had instead been spent holding him at arm's length, playing silly games just to make him propose.

But how was she to know what was going to happen, her heart cried out? How could she possibly have foreseen the dreadful fate in store for him, and so many other fine men?

Oh, Eric! she wailed to herself. Never to see him again or to hold him close, or hear his laugh, or see him smile. It was a sin, she knew that, but she wished she was dead too, her body alongside her darling man's down there in sight of Dragonholme where the *Gypsy Queen* lay.

James Campbell's gaze was fixed on the back of Sheila's head. She'd been in his thoughts night and day since the day in his study when he'd said she could have Granny Mutch's cottage after all.

She haunted him: that tawny hair, those sparkling eyes, that fierce determination, the look of gratitude she'd given him when he'd told her she could have the cottage that had made him go weak at the knees.

When he tried to study his accounts he saw her image staring back at him; when he gazed out to the sea her face appeared before him, calling him on. He was being stupid. He was behaving like a fool. He'd told himself that a hundred times over, but it had done no good. He'd told himself a hundred times that she was young enough to be his daughter, and in love with another man, but even that didn't stop his obsession.

Then the disaster had occurred, and the Gifford lad had gone down with the others. There would be no marriage

72

now; the young man she loved was dead and gone. Did that mean he stood a chance?

James Campbell ground his knuckles into his thighs. A butterfly drawn irresistibly to nectar, that was how he felt every time he saw her now. A moth winging frantically towards the flame. Oh, he told himself, he was being ridiculous; succumbing to middle-age fantasies, searching for his youth in the arms of a girl. But nothing could deter his heart.

With a snort, he raised his eyes determinedly to the pulpit, and tried to concentrate on what was being said. Within seconds, however, his willpower was completely overridden and his gaze was once more on the back of Sheila's head.

James Campbell awoke with a start. He was trembling all over, and filled with a terrible fear. He'd been thinking in his sleep about Sheila Beattie.

With nearly all the young eligible Dragonholme men dead, her own family's source of livelihood gone, and no work in the village, what was to keep her there?

There was the mother of course, but was that enough? He doubted it. Not for a beautiful spirited girl like Sheila.

The mother would have the insurance money from the *Bluebell* to fall back on, of course, so there was no immediate hardship for her or her family. But that in itself worked against keeping Sheila in Dragonholme, for it freed her to go elsewhere to find work – to eventually find herself a new man.

The thought of never seeing Sheila again filled him with panic and a dull sense of loss. In the dark, quiet, lonely room James Campbell made a vow to himself. He vowed that Sheila Beattie would stay in Dragonholme, no matter what.

He knew he wanted her for himself. And what he wanted, he always got. One way or the other.

*　　*　　*

73

Some days later, Sheila and Peg were sitting on either side of the range, each preoccupied with her own thoughts. The house hadn't been cleaned or even tidied since the disaster. Neither of them had the will or the energy to do anything more than get from one day to the next.

Sheila looked up when there was a rap on the door. 'I'll get it,' she muttered, thinking it was one of the neighbours. But it wasn't a neighbour. It was a tall, thin man wearing grey pin-striped trousers, a black jacket and a homburg. In his right hand he carried an attaché case.

'Miss Beattie?' the man asked, doffing his hat.

'Sheila Beattie, that's right.'

'I'm Mr Dunwoodie from Eyemouth. I handled your father's marine insurance.'

'You mean the *Bluebell*?'

'Exactly,' replied Dunwoodie, smiling evenly and politely to hide his nervousness. This was going to be absolutely awful, but it had to be done.

Peg rose and smoothed down the front of her crumpled dress. It was indicative of her state of mind that it didn't bother her that the house was in a mess. She'd been sleeping badly, and it showed in the tightness and pallor of her face.

'Come away in, Mr Dunwoodie. Davey mentioned you to me,' she called out.

Dunwoodie went to Peg, and shook hands with her, then spoke in sombre tones the little speech of condolence he'd prepared.

Sheila offered to make a cup of tea, which he refused. Peg gestured him to a seat, and having sat, he busied himself removing various sheets of paper from his case.

'I've been expecting you, Mr Dunwoodie,' Peg said, giving him a wan smile.

Dunwoodie shuffled his papers, paused, coughed, then shuffled his papers again. This was turning out to be even more difficult than he'd anticipated. For a brief second he considered reneging on the deal he'd made

74

with James Campbell, then told himself not to be a bloody fool. Sentiment had no place in business. It was the chance of a lifetime, and if he didn't grasp it firmly with both hands he would regret it for as long as he lived.

Only five years old, Dunwoodie's was a tiny agency compared with the two giants in this field – Grant and Lisle of Aberdeen and John Kerrigan of Peterhead – who between them handled about seventy-five per cent of the Scottish boats. But that would change when he landed the entire Portnessie fleet, as Campbell had promised. With them on his books his agency would have a chance at the really big time. Besides, he reassured himself, Campbell had assured him that everything would be all right; no one would be hurt by their little deception. All he had to do was adjust the company's records and tell one small lie to Mrs Beattie. What could be simpler?

'I'm afraid I've got some bad news for you,' Dunwoodie said, finally turning his attention to Peg.

Peg glanced in surprise to Sheila, then back again to Dunwoodie. 'What does that mean?'

Dunwoodie, his expression one of sympathy and concern, glibly spoke his lie. 'Mr Beattie's monthly renewal payment fell due the week before the tragedy. The money never arrived in at my office. Consequently, and it pains me to say so, the *Bluebell* wasn't covered when she went down.'

'Oh my God!' whispered Sheila.

Peg shook her head. This just wasn't like Davey, he'd always been so meticulous about such matters.

Dunwoodie brought out the reasons he'd known would make sense. 'I believe your husband invested all his capital in the *Bluebell*.'

Peg stared at him, numb with disbelief, able only to give the smallest of nods.

'As it's been such an appalling season to date, I can only think that he became acutely short of cash and neglected to make his payment on time. It is regrettable and unfortunate that this non-payment coincided with the loss of the boat.' Dunwoodie gave a little cough.

'Had he ever faulted on a payment before?' asked Sheila.

'That was the first time since I started handling his business, and I believe the first time ever.' His eyes showed nothing but concern.

'Then surely the insurance company can make an allowance for one lapse?' Sheila's voice was shrill with desperation.

Peg said nothing.

'I'm sorry,' Dunwoodie said softly.

'You mean you won't even speak to them about it?'

'I mean I already have, and the answer was no.' Dunwoodie turned to Peg for support, but she seemed barely aware that he was still there.

Sheila felt as if the world was crumbling around her. They'd been counting on the insurance money. Without it, things would be bad enough for her and Peg, but what was it going to be like for Rhona and Maggie? They had bairns to clothe and feed.

Peg passed a weary hand across her brow. She felt she'd aged a dozen years since watching the *Bluebell* sink; she felt she'd just aged that again.

Dunwoodie didn't even bother to ask if Davey and his sons carried life assurance, knowing the answer would almost certainly be no. He'd never met a fisherman who didn't believe that it was unlucky and tempting fate.

Dunwoodie slipped his papers, props in this charade, into his attaché case, then rose. Having done what he'd come to do, he couldn't wait to get out of the house. 'And now I'll have to go, I have many other calls to make today,' he said apologetically.

'Yes, of course,' whispered Peg.

'Were any of the other boats behind in their payments?' Sheila asked.

The daughter was certainly a beauty, Dunwoodie

thought as he shook his head sadly, unaware that Sheila was the cause of Campbell's scheme.

Peg and Sheila saw him to the door, and he told them again how sorry he was to be the bearer of such bad tidings. When he was gone, Peg, in a tremulous voice, instructed Sheila to wait a minute to let him get clear, then to run and tell Rhona and Maggie to come over. There was no point in putting off bad news.

Peg poured out some drams, whisky of Davey's that had been lying in the press. When Rhona, Maggie and the weans were assembled, Peg broke the news as gently as she could, in a voice that was barely more than a whisper, then passed around the drams.

Rhona looked down at Ian and started to cry, the tears running down her cheeks, her sobs soaking her otherwise motionless body. Maggie, however, went completely still. She might have been poleaxed.

'What about my house?' Rhona choked through her tears. 'You know it's only partly paid for, Ma. I was counting on my share of the insurance money to pay off the rest.'

'So was I,' Maggie whispered, drinking off her dram in a single gulp.

Rhona rested her head in her hands. 'I have fifteen pounds to my name,' she said softly. 'Fifteen pounds.'

'And I've got seven pounds twelve and six,' said Maggie.

Neither amount was going to get them very far.

Peg alone was calm, as though beyond her own hurt and fear. They'd have to talk this through, she said. It was no time for self-pity. Rhona wiped away her tears, and, clutching Ian to her bosom, brought herself under control. Violet and wee Dougal took themselves off in a corner where they began playing with an old tin tray that Davey had brought back years before as a souvenir of Cromer.

The women talked for hours, their voices strained but unemotional. They might have been discussing anything

– a special occasion, or a daily event – might have been any four women just passing the time of day. In the end, Rhona decided that she couldn't keep her house. She would go to work if she could, but there was no work in Dragonholme not connected with the fishing. No – as far as she could see there was only one path left open to her and that was to try and sell the house and move back in with her parents. She and Ian would be all right there. They'd manage somehow.

But Maggie had no parents to return to. They had died within months of one another after she and Dougal were married. She had a sister in Coldingham, but Lizzie would hardly welcome her with open arms. Lizzie lived in a two room but and and ben with eight bairns and had enough problems of her own.

'Then you must move in here,' Peg said to Maggie after they had been through all the possibilities.

Sheila's heart sank. As sorry and sympathetic as she felt for Maggie, the last thing she wanted was to live under the same roof as her sister-in-law. The pair of them would just never get on together, no matter how great the tragedy that united them.

'There's nothing else for it. She was my son's wife and they are Dougal's children,' Peg said to Sheila later when they were alone again.

'Nothing else we could do,' Sheila agreed. 'Nothing else at all.'

On the same day that Maggie, wee Dougal and Violet came to live with Peg and Sheila, word arrived in Dragonholme that the great shoals had reappeared in the southern North Sea. In Upper Scruff, Clay Deep, Tea Kettle Hole and the Silver Pits they were to be found teeming in unbelievable numbers.

In a world that seemed to have lost all its hope, all reason of existence, the reappearance of the great shoals gave the entire village a new surge of life and the promise of normality. The sense of gloom that had descended on all of Dragonholme with the tragedy shifted. Once again there was activity and an undercurrent of excitement. Once again the village began to bustle and smile.

What remained of the Dragonholme fleet – nine boats out of the original twenty-eight – elected a new admiral and put to sea for the first time since the disaster, heading south. The entire village turned out to wish them luck. Not a soul left the quayside until the last sail had been waved out of sight.

Living together it didn't take long before Sheila and Maggie were squabbling night and day. As Peg said, the only time there was any peace was when both of them were asleep. For her mother's sake, Sheila tried to hold her temper, but on several occasions it got so bad between her and Maggie that she had to run out of the house, not wanting Maggie to see her greet, and had ended up in Old Granny Mutch's place where she cried until she could cry no more, thinking of how things would have been if Eric had lived; if she still had dreams.

One afternoon when they were all sitting outside the house doing various tasks, the weans playing tumble-your-wilkies, there was the clip clop of horse's hooves and the laird, mounted on his black hunter, appeared at the top of the rise.

Peg was preparing to give James Campbell a cordial nod as he passed by, but he surprised all three women by reining in and dismounting. The children, eyes wide, left off their game, following his every movement as he tied off Satan and strolled over to Peg. Only after he had formally introduced himself and engaged her in several minutes' polite conversation did he get around to the real purpose of his visit. 'I've heard about the trouble you had over the *Bluebell*,' he said sympathetically. 'It's a sad business indeed.'

Peg nodded, even more awed by him than the children

were. 'Aye, it was that,' she said softly, embarrassed by his knowledge.

James looked away towards the treacherous sea. 'Aye, a sad business.' Then, turning back to her suddenly, he said, 'I think there's a way I can help you.'

Peg drew herself up to her full height, her shyness gone. It was kind of him to offer and she appreciated his kindness, but things hadn't come to such a pass with them yet that they had to accept charity. They had always got by and they would still.

'You misconstrue my meaning, Mrs Beattie,' Campbell said gently, making it clear that he was one of them, after all. He wouldn't insult the wife of Davey Beattie by making such a gesture. No, what he had in mind was the position of maid that had suddenly fallen vacant at the Hall. 'I thought that perhaps your daughter Sheila would be interested in the post,' he concluded.

The wage he proposed was so handsome that even Peg's natural reservations were weakened. Her eyes moved from Campbell to Sheila and back again. It would certainly solve some problems.

'Would I be living in?' asked Sheila.

'Yes indeed, with all found.'

'It does sound like a good opportunity,' ventured Peg.

'I had to sack the girl we had,' Campbell continued. 'She was lazy and I won't tolerate that at any price. I thought of your Sheila because she struck me as a concientious and industrious worker. I'll warrant I'm not wrong?'

'I'd recommend her to anybody, even the King himself,' Peg replied proudly.

The poor lassie James Campbell had given the sack had indeed had a lazy streak in her, but not nearly enough for her to merit being discharged. She'd gone because it suited James Campbell's purposes. And James Campbell's purposes had become the only important thing in the world. Although he was now standing quite calmly and normally in the bright light of the sun, for all the world like a man who needs a servant, his obsession with Sheila had become the strongest passion in his life.

'Well, Sheila, what's your answer then?' Campbell asked with a smile.

'I think, sir,' said Peg, 'that we'd better have some time to think about it.'

'I accept,' interrupted Sheila. 'There's nothing to think about. When would you like me to start?'

'Shall we say you come up to the Hall on Sunday evening, and begin Monday morning?'

'I'll be there, sir.'

'Excellent, that's settled then!' Campbell beamed, and giving Peg a small salute by touching his riding crop to his hat he walked smartly over to Satan, untied his horse, and swung himself into the saddle.

Satan snorted and pawed the ground, then he and Campbell were clattering away up the street, Satan's hooves striking sparks from the cobbles.

'Now there's a stroke of luck!' cried a still-shocked Peg as they watched man and horse thunder away.

'What a nice man,' said Maggie.

Yes, Peg and Sheila agreed. Imagine him going out of his way to help them because the *Bluebell* hadn't been insured. Yes, he was a nice man, she said, a really nice man.

On Sunday evening after tea, Sheila duly presented herself at the Hall as had been arranged, going to the same side entrance that the ghillie Simpson had taken her to the day he'd brought her to see the laird.

Annie Tripp, the cook she'd made friends with on that visit, was there to greet her, pumping her by the hand and saying how marvellous it was they were going to be working together, and would Sheila like a cup of tea and a slice of cake?

Sheila was halfway through her second slice of cream sponge when a maid called Agnes Robertson joined them, back from her day off. A middle-aged woman, originally from Glasgow, Agnes had been in service all her life. Sheila took a shine to Agnes, who obviously reciprocated the feeling, and soon the three of them, Sheila, Annie and Agnes, were chattering away like old friends.

There was another maid, Agnes said, called Pat Dyer, but her job was to attend to Herself, as Mrs Campbell was known below stairs by the staff. Her ladyship was very grand, Agnes explained with relish. Right out of the top drawer and hoity toity with it as well. Not like his lordship at all.

'Do they get on, then?' asked Sheila, overwhelmed with curiosity.

Agnes shrugged, rolling her eyes at Annie. 'After a fashion,' she said.

There was a warm, friendly atmosphere in the kitchen. Sheila couldn't believe that it didn't extend throughout the house. Laughing at Agnes's impersonation of Herself, she still thought life here was going to be pleasurable, even fun.

Annie was clearing away their dishes when Hay, the butler, appeared. Sheila could tell instantly that what Agnes had said about Hay was right. He was a lovely old man. How could she be anything but happy here?

Hay added his welcome to Annie and Agnes's, then informed Sheila that after she'd settled into her room Mrs Campbell would like a word in the library. The working day started at six, he went on, and she was expected to start promptly. Breakfast for the staff was laid out at five-thirty, and removed again at five minutes to six.

All the introductions out of the way, Agnes then took Sheila along to her room.

'Toilet, my room, Pat's, and this one along at the very end is your,' said Agnes, and on arriving at the last door on the landing, she opened it with a flourish and ushered Sheila inside.

The fragile evening light still filled the tiny room.

'Hardly the Ritz, but it beats some I've had to put up with in my time,' Agnes sniffed. 'I'll let you freshen up and then I'll come back to show you to the library. Herself doesn't like to be kept waiting.'

After Agnes had left, Sheila stared round her new quarters. The room was small but fairly well furnished. There was an iron sprung bed, and a mattress with clean sheets and blankets folded neatly at one end, a washstand with a bowl and jug, a free-standing, ornately decorated wardrobe, and a solitary wooden chair. Inside the wardrobe were two clean uniforms hanging on the rail.

She unpacked her few belongings, hanging her clothes alongside the uniforms and then put the few treasured knick-knacks round the room. Perhaps it was just homesickness, but suddenly she felt the tears come to her eyes. Suddenly, more than anything, she wished she had a photograph of Eric to put out. A photograph of him so handsome and happy – her Eric – but he had never had one taken.

The room wasn't exactly cosy as it was now, she thought, but with a wee bit of effort she'd soon have it a proper home from home. Fussing in her pocket, she pulled out a handkerchief to dry her eyes. Yes, soon she'd have it a proper wee home.

'Come in!' called out an extremely well-spoken female voice when Agnes knocked on the library door. Sheila's heart gave a little leap. Agnes, with Sheila behind her, entered and curtsied.

'Sheila Beattie, the new maid, ma'am,' announced Agnes, giving Sheila a little nudge so that she would curtsey too.

Fiona and James were playing backgammon, he with a glass of claret and half empty decanter on his side of the table, she with a look of determined concentration.

Fiona beckoned Sheila over, and Agnes didn't so much

leave as vanish. Suddenly Sheila felt shy and awkward, a lump of a girl compared to the stunningly graceful and elegant woman before her. Perhaps this was all a mistake and the day-dreams she'd been having since the afternoon of the laird's visit – the fantasies of a new, exciting world free from sadness – were only the foolish dreams of a child.

James Campbell looked up suddenly from the board and smiled at her – almost as though he'd read her mind.

'I'm pleased to meet you Sheila,' pronounced Fiona Campbell, with all the warmth of a December morning. 'I believe you're the girl who lost her father and three brothers in that terrible disaster,' she said, throwing her dice.

Fiona had been deeply moved by the funeral service. As she told everyone who would listen, there had been so great a sense of suffering and loss inside the church that just being a part of the assembly had left her drained and weakened for days afterwards. 'A terrible happening – a terrible happening indeed,' she fretted, knocking her husband's counter from the board.

'It's the price of fish, ma'am,' Sheila replied in a whisper.

Fiona stared at her blankly. 'The price of fish? Whatever do you mean?'

Sheila gave a thin smile. 'Men's lives, ma'am. That's the real price of fish.'

Once more James Campbell raised his gaze to Sheila, a look of open admiration in his smile.

'I think, my dear,' he said, 'that it's your move.'

Sheila was the first to join Annie Tripp in the kitchen next morning. She had had some trouble getting off to sleep the night before, lying nervously awake long after the rest of the house was asleep, dozing fitfully now and then, only to be awoken by her mother's voice or a dream of Eric's face. This morning, though, she was feeling quite cheerful. As the staff gathered around the enormous kitchen table, talking and laughing as they ate the plentiful breakfast, even Sheila's feelings of loneliness began to fade. Last night she had felt frightened and alone, but this morning she felt among friends.

They were all laughing at Agnes's story of Herself taking to her bed for three days when they ran out of her favourite imported mustard, when a shadow fell across the table.

There stood Simpson, the ghillie.

'What's this the cat dragged in?' he demanded, glowering at Sheila.

'This is Sheila Beattie,' Agnes explained. 'She's taken over from Min.'

'Mr Simpson and I have already met,' said Sheila, meeting his eyes.

'The new maid?' Simpson mused, and gave a dry humourless chuckle.

Sheila stared at him boldly, but the others averted their eyes, beginning to talk again, though softly, among themselves.

Simpson sat at the other end of the table, facing Hay. 'I'll be having the porage, then,' he announced.

'None on the day I'm afraid,' replied Annie.

'Why the hell not?'

Sheila glanced at Hay, who was steadfastly addressing his attention to the plate in front of him. For some reason, Hay was scared of Simpson, Sheila guessed. Why else did Hay allow him such liberties in the butler's domain?

'Because we've run out. I can't give you what I haven't got, Mr Simpson, now can I?'

'Bloody bad management if you ask me,' Simpson grumbled. 'Let me have some of the scrambled egg then. I hope it's better than the last lot you made.'

Annie banged a plate on to the table in front of him. Looking across at Sheila, she raised her eyes to heaven.

Agnes excused herself and fled the kitchen.

They're all scared of him, Sheila thought. Did he

85

behave like that all the time, or was it laid on especially for her?

'I'll have a cup of tea then,' Simpson called to Annie, spraying crumbs of egg and bread all round him.

'I thought it was Dragonholme Hall I'd come to, not the piggery on Bogside Farm,' Sheila said suddenly to no one in particular. Simpson's head rose immediately, his eyes dark with fury.

'I'll have no lip out of you, girl. Mind your place.'

Without another word Sheila rose from her place, took her dirty dishes to the sink, then headed for the door. Just before it closed behind her, she popped her head back in.

'Oink!' she said. 'Oink! Oink!'

It was just after midnight as James Campbell reached for the whisky and poured himself yet another dram, well on the way to being drunker than he had been in many a month.

He was sitting at the desk in his study, a pile of important-looking papers spread before him. He'd come here directly after dinner, ostensibly to get on with some pressing paperwork, but had, in fact, been unable to concentrate on clauses and data, unable to drag his thoughts away from waking dreams of a young girl with tawny hair and an impish grin. Sheila had been with them for ten days now, and he could no longer remember what it had been like without her – without the sound of her laughter bubbling in the hallways, without her smile lighting the dour and gloomy, the lonely rooms of Dragonholme Hall. Every day his fascination with her intensified, his need to hear her voice or catch a glimpse of her bustling through her chores became more obsessive. Had it been so long since anything other than work – than his own determination to succeed, to prove himself – had given him any pleasure? So long since he had been able to smile, to feel joy touch his heart like a warming sun?

Now, however, he had to be away from Dragonholme for some time. He had to go down to Grimsby to sort out a problem with the fleet, and from there he had to go to Germany for at least a week. No matter how well things went, it would mean his being away for at least three or four weeks. Three or four weeks away from Sheila.

Getting up from his desk he crossed to the window, staring out over the sea. All his energy, all his passion and all his dreams had been spent on the accumulation of power and of money. And that, he realized, his mind constructing images from the darkness of the night, was all he had. Power and money – not happiness; not love.

Confused by the whisky and by the turmoil in his own heart, James Campbell leaned his head against the glass. There had been several women in his life – many before Fiona, and one or two after – but not one of them had ever touched his soul or roused in him these feelings of longing and hope.

'I love her,' he whispered into the night. 'I love her.' And he was filled with amazement and wonder.

Outside the walls of his mansion, the wind whispered back his words. I love her. I love her.

But would she ever be his? He might hope to have her body – he was not, after all, either an unimportant or an unattractive man – but it was not her body alone which he craved. He wanted her: her friendship and her lips against his own; her sympathy and trust; her passion and her concern. As much as he wanted to make love to her, he wanted her affection even more.

Swaying slightly, he returned to his desk and helped himself to another drink. Perhaps, when he came back from Germany, he would be able to make some changes in his life. If he could convince Fiona to stay in Edinburgh (and surely that would be no difficult task; there was nothing she hated more than being stuck in the middle of nowhere, as she put it), he might be able to approach Sheila as himself, get to know her – let her get to know him.

Perhaps, he thought, losing himself once more in alcoholic fantasies, perhaps there was hope for him yet.

But James Campbell wasn't the only one who was obsessed with Sheila that night. Wally Simpson, lying abed in his cottage a quarter of a mile from the Hall, was thinking about her as well. It was not love, however, that kept him awake.

That Beattie bitch, he thought to himself. She was undermining his authority, making him look a fool in front of the others. More than that, she was turning them against him. It wouldn't be long before they were all laughing at him, right to his face. She needed taking down a peg or two, and he was just the man to do it. To do it and enjoy doing it. Oh, aye, he'd enjoy doing it, all right, he'd certainly do that.

If only he could think of how.

'So tell me about the family,' Sheila said to Agnes. 'I know they have two boys at fancy schools in England, but that's all.'

The pair of them were sitting at the kitchen table, polishing the silver while Hay had a sleep on one of the chairs by the fireplace. Pat Dyer had gone off to Edinburgh with the Campbells when they'd left an hour previously, and Annie was down in the cellar stock-taking her supplies.

'There are just the two boys, Drew and Robert. Drew is the oldest, but he's left school now, although I couldn't say where he is or what he's doing. He's a bit of a strange fish is Drew.'

'And why wasn't Robert home for the school holidays? Don't either of them come to visit their parents?'

'He went to France with friends or something like that,' said Agnes. 'Pat says he'll be back at Christmas.'

'And will Drew be visiting the Hall then do you think?'

'Your guess is as good as mine. He could come. Then again, he might not. You'll meet him eventually, though. Neither of the boys is a patch on their father,' concluded Agnes with a wink.

Their chatter ceased immediately as Simpson came into the kitchen from outside, smirking as though enjoying a private joke.

'Are they away then?' Simpson asked, knowing full well that they were. He'd been standing on a nearby hillside, watching the carriage drive off.

'Aye, they're away,' Agnes answered, without looking at him and vigorously rubbing a soup spoon.

Still smirking, Simpson looked directly at Sheila, who was doing her best to ignore him, and then sauntered over to the sleeping butler.

'Been at the sherry again, Hay?' he bellowed suddenly.

A startled and frightened Hay came instantly awake. 'Eh! Eh!' he exclaimed. 'What?'

Simpson's smirk widened into a leer. 'I said, have you been at the sherry again, old man?'

Hay sat up, straightened his clothes, then smoothed back his hair, playing for time until he'd pulled himself together.

'What are you saying?' he asked at last in a mild voice.

Simpson squatted so that he was on eye level with Hay. 'I know you've got a taste for the laird's sherry, old man, and that not content with helping yourself during the day you pinch bottles of the stuff when you think no-one's looking.'

Hay went white as a sheet. His gaze darted first to Agnes, then to Sheila. Both of them pretended to be so thoroughly engrossed in what they were doing that they seemed unaware that there was anyone else in the room. In reality, though, they were all ears.

Now what's all this in aid of, wondered Sheila as she buffed a gravy boat.

Simpson shook his head and tut tutted. 'Here's the

laird hardly gone, and already you're drunk on duty. Drunk to the extent of passing out,' he accused.

'I am not drunk, and I have never passed out!' replied Hay indignantly. 'I was only enjoying a wee nap, that's all.'

'There's only one type of person the laird hates more than an idler, and that's a thief,' Simpson said evenly.

Hay stared at him in horror. What a totally odious man. If it weren't for Simpson, this would be the most perfect post. And how on earth had Simpson found out about the sherry anyway? He'd thought he'd been so careful, but obviously he hadn't been careful enough.

'The sack with no second chances and no reference, that's what the laird would give you if he found out,' continued Simpson. 'And at your age it wouldn't be so easy for you to get more work.'

Hay stared into Simpson's mean and greedy eyes. 'Why are you telling me all this?' he asked at last in almost a whisper.

Simpson rose and stretched, teasing out the time before replying. He'd blackmailed Hay once before, but what he was holding over Hay now was far more serious. The first time had been only a test. A test that Hay had passed.

At last he spoke. 'With the laird and Herself away for some weeks, you won't be needing the same amount of work done indoors I'm thinking,' he said. 'As I have more than I can cope with, I thought it would be a friendly act on your part to lend me one of the maids as a help.'

Sheila paused in mid buff. So that was it. It wasn't Hay he was after at all. It was her.

Simpson squatted down so that he was face to face with Hay. 'Well?'

Hay licked lips that were dry. What could he do other than comply? He was trapped, snared by Simpson, who only had to pull the snare tight to do for him. Being a ghillie Simpson was a dab hand with snares. Hay couldn't help feeling a certain kinship and sympathy with the many rabbits Simpson had brought back for the pot.

'I'm sure that'll be all right,' he mumbled feebly.

Simpson gave a triumphant smile which he directed straight at Sheila. 'I think I'll have little miss smart mouth there,' he said.

Sheila wanted nothing more than to tell him to take a running jump. How could she though? If she refused to co-operate Simpson would report Hay, and Hay would almost surely be fired. She couldn't let that happen to the old man. He'd been kindness itself to her since her arrival at the Hall. And Simpson, of course, had said all this in front of her so that she would know what a refusal on her part would mean. 'I'll be delighted to help you,' she said pleasantly.

Hay breathed a sigh of relief, and threw Sheila a grateful look. My God, he thought, I've never needed a sherry more than I do right now.

Simpson nodded curtly. Oh, this was going to be rare! 'Tomorrow then. Be ready,' he said, and strode from the kitchen.

'You were right,' Agnes said vehemently after Simpson had gone. 'He is a pig.'

With as much dignity as he could muster Hay thanked Sheila, then hurried off to his room.

There was an autumn nip in the air, Sheila thought, as she followed Simpson along the track through a small wood of firs. They'd come about three miles so far, she judged.

On leaving the wood they skirted a loch, coming eventually to some bogland from which several long strips of peat had already been taken. 'Have you ever dug peat before?' asked Simpson.

Sheila shook her head, understanding now what the unusual-shaped spade he'd brought along was for.

'I'll show you how it's done then,' he said. 'Pay attention.'

He cut the brick of peat expertly, having done it countless times before; then he cut another and placed it beside the first.

Sheila caught the spade when he threw it at her. 'Let's see you do that,' he ordered.

It wasn't nearly as easy as it appeared, but then she hadn't expected it to be. Her initial efforts were disastrous, but gradually she began to get the hang of it.

'Hard graft, wouldn't you say?' Simpson smiled.

'I'm used to grafting,' she answered in an unconcerned tone. 'I was brought up to it.'

For a second anger flashed in his eyes. She had an answer for everything, this one. 'I'll be back when it's time for you to knock off. And no slacking, mind, or I'll be having that word with the laird about Hay after all.' And with that he strode away.

Sheila started to hum, as if she were enjoying what she was doing, sure that that would annoy him. 'Oink!' she said to his retreating back. 'Oink! Oink!'

She woke next morning feeling as though she'd been through the heavy mangle Peg used at home for wringing out the washing. She'd never been so stiff, every muscle in her body aching excruciatingly.

It took her three times longer than usual to get dressed, and when she came to walk she found that she was hobbling.

Outside the kitchen she took a deep breath, willing her body to function and behave as it did normally. 'Morning!' she called out cheerily as she breezed in through the door.

Agnes paled on seeing Sheila's hands. Her palms were covered in blisters and were red raw in patches. 'That's terrible,' she muttered, pointing at them. 'Whatever have you been up to?'

Simpson slurped his tea. Hay seemed to be having trouble with his breathing.

Annie dished out a pair of kippers for Sheila, watching in concern as Sheila had difficulty in holding her knife and fork.

'I'll put something on those hands after you've had your breakfast,' she said.

'There won't be time for that,' Simpson snapped, gesturing at the clock on the wall. There was only a minute left before the staff were expected to start work.

It was Sheila's own fault that her hands hadn't been attended to the night before, but she'd been so totally exhausted when she'd arrived back at the Hall that she'd bypassed the kitchen, and gone straight up to her bed where she'd fallen instantly asleep. Her intention had been to come down later and get a bite of supper and have her hands attended to then, but she'd slept right through till morning.

'Time to get going,' shouted Simpson, getting to his feet. 'It's peat cutting again today. We wouldn't want to get a late start, would we?'

'Oh good! I enjoy the fresh air and exercise,' smiled Sheila forcing herself on to her feet. At least she had the satisfaction of seeing a scowl come to his face.

The sea gently lapped the beach, a playful puppy dog compared to the terrible monster it had been the day it had swallowed her future and her past.

She could see Eric everywhere: here was a large tuft of marram grass on which they'd once sat; there the black rock he'd chased her round on her fourteenth birthday. But most poignant of all was the Gifford hut where they'd spent so many hours making love, and which she was now staring at, dreading entering, yet being drawn there as iron to a magnet.

It was her day off and she'd just been to see Peg. She hadn't intended visiting the beach, or the hut, but somehow, as though they had a separate will of their own, her feet had brought her here.

A lump came into her throat as she entered. Of all places, this was the one she most identified with Eric. It was here she'd given him her virginity and her love.

She remembered the last time – *the last time!* she thought, and moaned softly, still not able to truly believe she'd never see him again, that he was gone forever.

Hot tears burst from her eyes and slowly she sank to her knees. 'Oh Eric! Eric!' she wailed. But only the sound of the sea answered her call of grief.

'You look dreadful,' said Annie Tripp, handing Sheila a cup of tea.

Sheila knew she looked dreadful. She couldn't have expected to look otherwise after the amount of crying she'd done in the Gifford hut. Inside her, though, there was a new feeling of peace.

'It's my ma,' said Sheila slowly, telling at least part of the truth. 'I'm worried about her. She's having a hard time of it right now.'

'Is the money you're giving her not enough?' There was genuine concern in Annie's voice.

'No, it's not that. My sister-in-law is living with her now . . . and – '

'And they're not getting along?'

'No,' sighed Sheila. 'It's just awful. They're not getting along at all.'

'Aye, two grown women sharing a kitchen is always a problem,' agreed Annie.

'I'm really worried about my ma, though,' Sheila went on. 'She used to be so outgoing. She always kept everything going. Now she just wanders around like a ghost. It's as though she died with Da and the boys.'

'And how's her health?'

'She's lost weight. But she doesn't seem to have any energy any more. She acts as if everything is an effort.'

'Ah well,' said Annie gently. 'She's bound to be feeling bad, isn't she. I'm sure she'll get over it in time. It's you I'm worried about right now. You're half dead on your feet.'

For the first time all day, Sheila smiled. 'You are kind to me,' she said. 'I'll be all right. I'm just a bit tired.'

'That's right,' said Annie, nearly helping Sheila to her feet. 'You go upstairs and get some sleep. You'll feel better in the morning. You'll see.'

'Yes,' said Sheila. 'I'll feel better in the morning.'

Simpson stood watching Sheila cut and stack the peat bricks. That's a strong bitch, that one, he thought to himself, his eyes moving along her firm young body, along the muscles of her arms and the swell of her breasts. A strong bitch, that one. Strong and spirited.

His plan that the task would break her wasn't working. By now he had expected her to be begging for his kindness. Please, Mr Simpson, I'll do anything you ask. Please, Mr Simpson, I'll never laugh at you again. Please, sir, isn't there something I can get you that you want?

And suddenly, standing there watching her body strain against her clothing as she worked, Simpson realized what he wanted. And an expression of unholy joy suffused his face.

James Campbell swung himself up on to Satan in such a way that anyone watching him would have thought, now there's a happy man! My, but it was grand being back at Dragonholme. James Campbell exalted to himself. And a full fortnight before he'd thought possible. How thoughtful of Max Abelman to die and make the trip to Germany impossible for several months! How kind of Fiona to insist on staying in Edinburgh! 'I'm not going back to that mausoleum till I'm ready,' she'd screamed at him. 'It may be your idea of living, cooped up in that monstrosity, but it's not mine. I want to be

with people who don't smell of fish. I want to be surrounded by beauty, not by a bunch of fishermen and their
ugly wives.' Thinking of Fiona, he smiled. With a bit of
luck she'd stay in Edinburgh till Christmas.

He couldn't wait to see Sheila. Why she should be out
helping Simpson and not working in the house baffled
him. And what on earth was wrong with Hay? He'd
thought the man was going to faint when he'd shown up
unexpectedly.

Satan trembled beneath him, eager for a good run.
Once clear of the stables, James touched the black horse
on the flanks and Satan immediately broke into a trot and
seconds later into a full gallop.

The directions Hay had given him to locate Simpson
and Sheila hadn't been at all clear; but he'd find them. Even
if it took him the rest of the afternoon he'd find them.

She had been working alone for what seemed like hours,
cutting the bricks and then stacking them, cutting
them and stacking them for what seemed like days, waiting for Simpson to come along with the cart. Every
muscle, every bone in her body ached and her throat was
parched – Simpson had forgotten to give her any ration
of water. She had just stopped for a moment, squinting
up at the sky to try to judge the time, when Simpson and
the cart appeared over a hill. She had been so happy to see
another person, even Simpson, and so eager for a drink,
that she hadn't noticed the peculiar way he watched her as
she hurried towards the cart.

'Did you bring me some water?' she panted as she
reached him.

'It's in the cart,' he said, nodding his head, his eyes not
moving from her. And even when, kneeling on the floor
of the cart, she had turned back to say that she couldn't
find the water, it must be up front with him – and had
seen him there, suddenly standing right behind her with
his belt in his hands – even then she hadn't understood.

'I'm going to give you something that's even better than water,' cooed Simpson, squatting down beside her, one hand already clasped around her wrist, the other reaching out to touch her breast through the thin cloth of her blouse. 'Much much better than water.'

And then she screamed. She screamed, summing all the strength her broken body could muster, and shoved him off balance, scrabbling over the side of the cart and on to the ground. He caught her easily, wrestling her back to the ground, his hands tearing at her clothes, his weight pinning her down, the belt slapping her across the face.

'You little bitch,' he screamed over and over. 'I'll show you who's boss around here. I'll show you – '

Simpson felt the new presence first. Sheila was still fighting and screaming, when he suddenly looked up – up and straight into the eyes of James Campbell. The next thing Simpson knew, he was being jerked into the air.

'It's not my fault,' pleaded the ghillie. 'She was asking for it. I had to teach her a lesson.'

'And now I'm going to teach you one.'

Only when she heard James Campbell's voice did Sheila stop screaming. Streaked with dirt and blood, her clothes in tatters, her body still shaking with sobs, she watched as the riding crop was raised for the first time.

After that, she must have fainted. When she came around, she was back at the hall, in a strange bed, and sitting beside her, lightly dozing, was Annie Tripp. Sheila closed her eyes and tried to remember what had happened. Slowly, it all came back to her: the cart and Simpson, the animal fury of his attack, the terror that had shaken her very soul – and something else. The riding crop, Simpson's gibbering screams – and then a quiet, gentle voice saying 'It's all right, Sheila, it's all over now. You're safe again. It's all right, Sheila', and the strong arms around her, lifting her against his chest and the beating of his heart.

*   *   *

By the time Sheila was feeling well enough to leave the guest room James Campbell had insisted she be put in when he brought her home on that dreadful afternoon, Simpson had been sent packing. The incident in the field had become common knowledge in Dragonholme, although the laird had forbidden its discussion, and Simpson had slunk off in disgrace.

It was also common knowledge, of course, that the laird had Mrs Beattie brought to the Hall on the following day to see her daughter. Peg told everyone not only about the wonders of the Hall itself and the hospitality and kindness of James Campbell, but of his almost fatherly concern for Sheila; how he apologized over and over for letting any harm come to her while she was under his roof.

'Her own da wouldn't have been more upset,' she later commented to Maggie. 'It makes me feel much easier, knowing she's in such good hands.'

While she was confined to her bed, the laird came to visit her several times a day, bringing her presents (a book or two he thought she might enjoy reading, a bunch of flowers, a new dress to replace her damaged clothes) and sitting for hours, teaching her to play backgammon and cards, telling her stories about the world outside Dragonholme. Although he had wanted to immediately dismiss Hay when he first heard the details of her ordeal with Simpson, Campbell eventually gave in to Sheila's pleas for leniency towards the old man.

'I can't keep him around, not after all that's gone on,' he reasoned with her, 'but I can give him a good reference to be going on with. I don't think I can be fairer than that.'

No, thought Sheila, he probably couldn't, not a man like James Campbell with all his private rules and principles, his strict standards of right and wrong. She knew him well enough now to know that though he was, at heart, a kind and giving man, he was so afraid of seeming weak or malleable that he rarely showed any sign of softness or common compassion. His business associates knew him as a hard and remorseless man, and so, too, did his employees, his family and the few people who might consider themselves his friends. Fair, most people would have said of him, James Campbell's a fair man, but no more than fair.

A week after James Campbell rescued her from Simpson, Sheila was ready to start work again, but the laird refused to hear of it. 'You'll take another week off,' he ordered. 'I'll have no arguments.'

On the Tuesday she was summoned to the kitchen, where Annie handed her a picnic basket. 'He gave me instructions last night to make it up and have you carry it down to Kettil's Cut for mid-day,' she explained, shaking her head in perplexity. 'I don't know what's got into him lately. He's not been himself for weeks.'

It was a fine, clear morning, and Sheila enjoyed the walk to Kettil's Cut which was reached through Kettil's Cave. Kettil had been one of the Vikings who'd come over with Einar Hairybreeks, but just why the inlet and the cave were named after him was open to speculation and some wild imagining by some.

Sheila carefully made her way through the hollow-sounding cave, coming out where it opened on to the Cut. To her surprise James Campbell was alone, and near him, tied up at the water's edge, was a boat she'd never seen before, only heard about: a Coble.

He had been sitting on a rock, waiting for her, and rose quickly at her approach. 'Well,' he said, grinning like a boy. 'What do you think of my first boat?'

Sheila put down the picnic basket, then walked up and down the Coble's length. It was well maintained, painted not long since by the looks of her. But she seemed very small compared to the Zulus, Fifies and Skaffies Sheila was used to. The name on the battle-axe bow was *Enterprise*. 'They don't do well running before the wind,' she remarked.

Campbell laughed. She was right. That was the craft's weakest point. 'They're inclined to go too fast then, and when they do that they can easily lose steerage and broach,' he agreed.

'But she's a bonny craft all the same,' said Sheila, fascinated by the way the deep forefoot flattened out and the keel disappeared. She knew from what Davey had told her about Cobles that underneath the flat-bottomed rear section of the boat were fixed twin keels, the aft ends curved like the runners of a sledge. It was rare to see this particular type of English boat, for none were built in Scotland.

'I keep her in the Portnessie repair yard usually,' he explained, 'but suddenly I had the desire to see her in the water again.'

Herring gulls screamed raucously overhead, and Sheila shielded her eyes against the sun to watch them wheel and dive. She'd been taught as a child that gulls were the incarnations of dead fishermen. Listening to their calls, it was not impossible to believe.

'Have you ever been on the sea?' Campbell asked, interrupting her reverie.

'Don't you know it's unlucky to have a woman aboard a fishing vessel?' she laughed. 'My da would've skinned me if I'd so much as stepped on to the *Bluebell*!'

'Fishermen worry too much about luck,' he said sharply. 'A man makes his own luck, and that's an end of it.'

Sheila stared at him in unmasked shock. No other man she'd ever known – not her da, nor her brothers, nor her Eric would ever have said such a thing.

'A man should rule his destiny, not be ruled by it. That's what I believe,' said James Campbell, as though challenging the universe.

Sheila took a deep breath, studying him closely. She could see now how James Campbell was different to other men; and why he'd succeeded where others would never have tried. A man who believed as he did was either a fool or a force to be reckoned with. She watched him as he stared towards the horizon. He was not a fool.

'How about having a trip out with me?' he asked suddenly.

'You mean now?'

'Of course! That's why I had you bring the picnic basket. I thought we could sail out a bit and have lunch together.'

But she was a servant! Servants didn't lunch with the employers; it was unheard of. 'I don't think that would be right, sir,' she stammered.

'I say what's right and wrong. And I want to take you out on the *Enterprise*. But not against your will, mind. I won't do that.'

She glanced out to sea. How often she'd wanted to go out there – knowing that, like the rest of the women in Dragonholme, she never would. Well, here was her chance. Perhaps it was not only men who could rule their own destinies.

She took a deep breath. 'Could you take me out to where the fleet went down?'

Campbell frowned. 'Are you certain you want to go there?' he asked gently.

She nodded, surprised to see the concern in his eyes.

They made the short trip in silence. When they reached the area where the fleet had gone down, he dipped the sail and dropped anchor. Sheila stared into the grey-green depths, in her mind's eye seeing the *Bluebell*, *Gypsy Queen* and all the other boats, for ever imprisoned beneath the surface of the sea. 'Oh Eric,' she whispered, her heart filled with pain and longing; her head with memories. Minutes went by like seconds as she gazed, transfixed, into the secret depths. Hypnotized by her own unspoken grief, by the hurt she'd been denying for so long, Sheila rose slowly to her feet, her eyes fixed on a vision at the bottom of the sea. 'Oh, Eric,' she cried. 'Oh, Eric – '

James moved quickly, grabbing her just as she was about to fling herself overboard. She screamed and tried to fight him off. With an oath, he pulled her back and forced her down on to the floor of the boat.

When finally she was still, the face that looked up into his was terrible in its agony. Wordlessly, he clutched her to his bosom while she sobbed and sobbed.

Later, after her tears had ceased and a tranquil silence had grown around them, he suggested that they have lunch.

'If we don't eat after Annie's gone to all this trouble, she'll get back at me by overcooking dinner,' he joked, pulling the cork out of the wine bottle with a pop.

Sheila smiled. It was obvious that he would not speak about the incident unless she wanted – not even to her.

'Thank you,' she whispered as he handed her a glass.

'Have a sandwich. They're delicious.'

She accepted the sandwich, a hard-boiled egg, a piece of chicken – each new bit of food being pushed on her with the admonition that Annie would be upset if the lunch came back barely tasted.

'No, really,' she began again. 'I must thank you. I don't know what came over me.'

He tilted his head back and drained off the wine in his glass. 'Don't thank me now,' he grinned. 'I haven't done anything yet.'

Out there, in the old boat, far from the wealth and power of his life, he seemed like a different man. She guessed that he talked to entertain her, to divert her, but she soon found herself caught up in his jokes and stories, his anecdotes about the awful gaffes he had made on his first expedition into society.

In a quiet tone he then spoke about Edinburgh and Morningside, and how he'd once been dazzled and impressed by the grand folk who lived there: folk with lineage, sophistication and fine fine manners. Not for him his own kind. He'd make money out of them all right, he'd decided, but he would no longer be part of the common herd. He would be somebody. He would get to the top – and he would stay there.

Fiona had been beautiful, and well connected. Her family was not only descended from the Royal House of Stewart, but they were also wealthy. She had birth and breeding and charm. And he had thought that he could want nothing more.

But as time had passed he'd come to realize that what had so attracted him was without substance and, ultimately, boring.

'Are you saying you don't love your wife?' Sheila asked in a whisper, afraid to look at him.

The sun blazed above them, the sea flowed beneath them. They were all alone in the world.

'I loved the idea of her,' he replied at last. 'I still do, in a way.'

'And does she love you?'

He gave a wry smile. 'I was different. A rough diamond. I brought a sense of danger into her life, something she'd never had before. Her parents were against the marriage, of course, which only made me more desirable. She knew they would never forbid the marriage. Fiona can twist them round her little finger – so she enjoyed becoming my wife. I was scandalous.'

'It's a long chalk from the sort of world I'm used to.'

His smile became broader. 'Yes,' he said, toasting her with his glass. It is that.'

'Why did you invite me out in your boat today?' she asked eventually.

'I was wondering if you'd be interested in a new job,' he smiled.

'A what?' she asked, taken completely by surprise. 'What sort of job? Aren't you satisfied with my work?' she queried cautiously.

'Oh, I'm satisfied with you, right enough.'

'Then what's wrong?'

'Nothing's wrong. I just thought that a girl of your obvious intelligence might like to do more than dusting and cleaning. How would you like to be my clerk at the Hall?'

'A clerk!' she exclaimed in astonishment.

'More my personal assistant, really. I would train you to deal with correspondence and many of the minor details that take up so much of my time.'

'But I've never had any training. What if I make mistakes?'

'Of course you'll make mistakes. That's what life's all about. Besides, there would be another pound a week.'

'It sounds absolutely marvellous!' she breathed, barely able to believe this was really happening. Wait till she told Peg!

'Is it agreed then?' he asked, extending his hand.

'Agreed,' she replied enthusiastically, and took his hand in hers and shook it.

Efficiency, she decided, that was a major key to James Campbell's success. His businesses ran like well-oiled machines.

He'd once described his businesses to her as his empire, and that's exactly what they were. The profits they made were quite staggering. Besides the estate and Portnessie fleet there was the Portnessie repair yard, thirty-six houses in the town, ten shops that supplied most of the domestic needs of his fishermen and their families, another repair yard in Dunbar, a canning factory in Dunbar, extensive property in Glasgow, Edinburgh and Dumfries, and a part share of the Yellow Funnel Shipping Line worth two-and-a-half-million pounds.

Of all his businesses the one that fascinated Sheila most was the Portnessie fleet, and even in the three weeks she'd been James Campbell's clerk she'd picked up an enormous knowledge about it and how it was run so successfully. At the end of this current season, now doing well after the initial terrible start, he intended placing orders for three new steam trawlers, bringing the total owned by him to nine trawlers, and seventy-five boats.

One of the new trawlers was to be called the *Sheila B*. She'd blushed when he'd told her, not knowing where to put herself when he'd laughed at her embarrassment. The *Sheila B*! Every time she thought about it a thrill ran through her.

Her desk was in the study, facing his – not to keep an eye on her he'd explained, but so they could pass letters, invoices and the like to one another without the trouble of having to get up. A typical example of his efficiency that, she thought.

She glanced round when the door banged open and Campbell came striding in. Immediately she knew from his expression that something was wrong. 'What is it?' she asked.

'Ian McPherson, the carter's son, is downstairs. Your sister-in-law has sent him to fetch you. It seems your mother has had some sort of attack.'

Instantly Sheila was on her feet, her face ashen, her mind electric with fear.

Less than ten minutes later, she and Ian were careering towards Dragonholme, the horse pulling the carriage going flat out.

'A lot of fuss and bother about nothing,' Peg said when she saw Sheila framed in the doorway.

Sheila kept quiet till the doctor had finished his examination. 'How is she?' she asked at last.

'Tough as an old guttie boot,' Dr Eckemyr replied.

'Thanks for the compliment,' joked Peg. 'I'm an old boot now, am I?'

Eckemyr ran his fingers through the little hair he had left, then stared down at Peg. 'There really isn't all that much wrong with you – not physically, anyway. My guess is you've been brooding too much,' he said kindly.

Peg's eyes clouded over, and the despair and desolation she'd come to know so well swept through her like a cold, heartless wind. 'My man and three sons. Wouldn't you brood?'

Eckemyr had no answer to that. 'All I can suggest is that you keep yourself as active as possible. There's no medicine I can prescribe to cure what's wrong with you.'

Sheila took her mother's thin and suddenly aged hand. 'You must try and take better care of yourself. What would I do if anything happened to you?' she said gently. 'You must eat more, for a start.'

'I can't eat when I've no appetite, and I haven't had that since . . . since – ' A choke came into her voice and she turned her head away.

'I know. I know,' whispered Sheila, squeezing Peg's hand, a hand that seemed frail and lifeless in hers. And she did know. But she had reached her nadir that day aboard the *Enterprise* with James Campbell, and now was on the road back. But what could help Peg find her way back from all that pain and grief?

Sheila stayed the night and left again for the Hall after breakfast. Peg seemed a great deal chirpier, and even attempted to have a little toast.

As Sheila made her way to the Hall she thought about Ian McPherson and Maggie, and the looks the pair of them had been exchanging when they'd thought no-one was watching. Those looks had told her why Ian had been at the house when Peg had had the attack, and she presumed Ian was now a regular visitor there.

Yes, James Campbell was right in what he'd said to her as they turned the *Enterprise* back towards Dragon-holme that afternoon that seemed so long ago: life did go on.

The Portnessie fleet had returned home from the south the previous day and, as was Campbell's custom, he was giving a dinner for the skippers and their wives, followed by a party for all crew members. He'd asked Sheila to accompany him through to Portnessie as his business associate, saying it would be a good thing for her to meet his people and they her.

They were staying at the Buccleugh Hotel, the larger of the two hotels that Portnessie boasted.

Sheila stood before the full-length mirror smoothing down the front of the new dress the laird had insisted on buying for her that afternoon. It was a braw dress right enough, by far and away the brawest she'd ever owned. It was not the one she'd gone into the shop to buy – which had been far simpler and cheaper – but it was the one James Campbell had chosen for her.

She wasn't at all nervous about the dinner due to start in half an hour, she told herself. After all, she'd been brought up among fishing skippers and their wives: wasn't she herself the daughter of an admiral? But if she was being truthful, she was a wee bit uneasy about going as James Campbell's partner. Working alongside him was one thing, socializing with him quite another.

She thought suddenly of Fiona Campbell, so effortlessly elegant and confident, and felt common. She prayed she wouldn't do anything that would make James Campbell think she'd let him down.

You're being bloody daft, she told herself. How could she do anything among her own kind that would let him down? They'd all be fish out of the same barrel – even James Campbell, despite the fact that he was boss and owner and now spoke with the accent of the gentry. She knew she would have been petrified if she'd been asked to accompany him into a social group other than her own, but there was, of course, no danger of him ever doing that.

For a few moments she gave way to day-dreaming, imagining herself at some posh do, all dolled up in silks and satins, gliding about gracefully the way Fiona Campbell did and speaking with the same Morningside plum in her mouth.

The image conjured up in her mind was too much. Her face creased into a smile and she began to giggle; but there was part of her that had been thrilled by what she'd visualized, no matter how ludicrous it might seem, and yearned for it.

Some minutes later there was a knock on the door and James Campbell entered, carrying a chilled bottle of champagne and two glasses.

He'd prepared a funny little speech, but that was now forgotten as he stared at Sheila. Had she asked him he could have told her she didn't need silks, satins or a posh accent; she was simply quite stunning as she was.

'You're beautiful,' he said, the words out of his mouth before he knew it.

Sheila blushed and turned away. 'It's kind of you to be gallant.'

'No, no. I mean it. You are.'

She glanced at him out of the corner of her eye, very much aware of the strange fluttering inside her that his words had caused. 'Thank you,' she murmured.

'I thought we'd have a glass together before going down. Just to get the evening started on the right note,' he said.

When he popped the cork he made a hash of it, spilling champagne over the carpet and nearby wall. He'd made a hash of opening the bottle because he hadn't been watching what he'd been doing. He'd been watching Sheila Beattie instead.

Wheeches and cries rent the air; the party was well under way – and a rather grand and exciting party it was, too.

Sheila was thoroughly enjoying herself. Her cheeks were flushed from a combination of alcohol, excitement and the noisy heat of so many people having a good time.

At dinner, Sheila had noted the curious looks from the women present, and had known too well the question in their minds. She should have expected it, of course. A powerful and charismatic man such as James Campbell escorting a young and attractive woman, whether or not she was his assistant, was bound to cause comment, if not gossip. Besides, she thought, rather chuffed, if those looks had been curious they had also been envious.

She glanced over to where James was deep in conversation with a skipper called Innes whom she'd been introduced to over dinner. There was a tap on her shoulder and she turned to find Tod McAlpine smiling at her. Tod was a handsome young man her own age whom she'd already been up on the floor with a number of times, and who was obviously much taken with her.

'Would you care for another birl? It's a reel,' Tod said.

'Aye, I'd like that tine,' she replied. Taking his hand, she walked out on to the floor with him to join the other dancing couples.

'You're the belle of the ball here tonight,' he whispered, and gave her a cheeky wink.

Then the music started up and away they went, Sheila wheeching with the best of them. As she whirled round she caught sight of James Campbell looking darkly in her direction, but then he glanced away, pretending he hadn't been staring her. Jealousy, she thought. That look had been one of unabashed jealousy. She liked the idea that that was how he felt about her.

When the dance was over she thanked Tod and joined the energetic group of onlookers around the edge of the room. Could it be true that James Campbell was jealous? Could it be true that a man who might have any woman he chose would choose her?

'It's getting like a bakehouse in here,' said James Campbell's voice beside her. She'd been scanning the room for him, but somehow he'd managed to sneak up on her.

'You gave me a start,' she laughed.

'How about a breath of fresh air?'

'Is it all right for you to slip away?'

'You mean because I'm mein host? If I'm paying for this ceilidh, I'm entitled to do as I like,' he said, more sternly than he'd intended.

109

Did he ever relax his authority? She stiffened. 'Does that mean it's an order?'

He grinned at her like a boy. 'It would give me great pleasure, Sheila, if you'd step outside with me,' he said with mock solemnity, then winked. 'Besides, there's something I'd like to show you.'

'Show me what?' she asked, not sure of whether he was teasing or not.

'Come and see,' he said, already leading her towards the doors.

Outside an icy wind blew off the sea and against their faces. Away from the frenzy and uproar of the party, the night was entirely theirs. Not a soul seemed to be stirring. As they walked, he talked about these Portnessie streets in which he'd grown up, pointing out the places of his childhood almost as though he were a child again.

Even though Dragonholme was only ten miles away, Sheila had only visited Portnessie twice before for an hour or two.

Just as she was wondering where they were headed, they turned into a narrow cul-de-sac, at the end of which was the wreck of what had once been a stone but and ben house. The roof had long since gone, and what remained was falling apart.

James Campbell gestured to the ruined house. 'Where I was born,' he announced.

There was a sad, forlorn atmosphere surrounding the house that tore at Sheila's heartstrings. 'Do you still own it?'

He went to the house and laid his hand against it. He might have been delicately touching another person. 'Aye, I never sold,' he replied softly.

'Then why have you let it get to this state? It's a criminal waste, so it is,' Sheila flared. It angered her to see what could be a respectable dwelling allowed to rot away.

James smiled at her anger, understanding it. 'I don't want to live here, nor do I want anyone else to. Then again, I also don't want to pull it down. This house is very important to me: it's where my ambition was lit. I want to be able to return here from time to time and remember how it was. See and hear the past, if you like,' he explained, his voice thin and strained.

He looked lost standing there, she thought. Lost and lonely – not at all the confident and iron-willed James Campbell she was used to. She was pleased she'd seen him like this. It made him more human. 'Did you have it hard as a wee boy, then?'

He was a while in answering, his mind in the past, recalling, remembering. Finally he spoke. 'My da was a drunk, and a mean bastard with it. Just after my third birthday he came home at the end of the season to announce he'd never go fishing again, which, a man of his word, he never did. Nor did he ever work again, not a hand's turn. So it was left to my ma to provide for the family which she somehow did by bait gathering, net mending, and anything else that would turn a copper coin.

'There were two older than me: a sister and brother. Maggs died when she was six, Kenny when he was ten; both of consumption. Money my ma earned that should have gone on food for them went down da's throat instead. I can remember Kenny's funeral as if it were yesterday. Mum cried her eyes out, but I never shed a tear. "You're a hard wee bugger, son," Da said to me after we'd buried Kenny. And I replied, "When you finally go to Hell I hope the Devil puts you in the fieriest furnace he's got."

'I expected a good clout round the lug for that, but he didn't hit me, or even reply. Instead he took himself off to the pub and drank himself into a blind stupor on rum bought him by sympathetic fishermen who knew he'd just come from burying his eldest boy.'

Campbell paused to pull out a packet of cigarettes and light one for himself. Then he went on. 'I ran around for years with no shoes and my bare arse hanging out of my breeks; a figure of fun to some, a figure of pity to others.'

He blew a perfect smoke ring which the wind caught and whipped away. Leaning against the front of his house he said, 'As soon as I was old enough I signed on as crew for a chap called McLaren. I started as galley boy, saved every farthing I could, and worked like three slaves.

'I had the incentive to work that hard, you see, for I'd sworn a great oath that I was going to be a somebody one day. That I would rise above the poverty and squalor by hard graft and using the brain the good Lord had given me. I'd show everybody.'

He paused to draw on his cigarette, face hidden in shadows and smoke. 'From a tiny spark, that ambition grew inside me till it became like some huge, hungry beast needing to be forever fed, never satisfied no matter how much it was given.' He paused, as though undecided about continuing, then took an audible breath. 'To achieve the ends I'd set myself I became ruthless in the extreme. I did a few things I'm still ashamed of, but I couldn't stop. I had to win.

'The *Enterprise* was the first rung on my ladder to success. Two years after buying her, I bought my first decked trawler: and, the year following that, one became two, and then two became four, and four eight, until, finally, I was the man you now know, the success I'd always dreamed.'

He was no longer lost and lonely as he'd been a few minutes before. He was now potent; yes, that was the word: potent – and in this mood reminded her of his black hunter, Satan.

'What happened to your ma and da?' she asked quietly.

'I hadn't long joined McLaren when Ma passed away, worn clean out. Without her to take care of him, Da died less than six months later.'

'Why did your da refuse to work any more?'

James gave a bitter smile. 'Ma used to make excuses for him, talking about bad arthritis, bronchitis – itis this and itis that – but the real truth was that he was just plain lazy.'

'Your ma would have been proud to know what you'd achieved.'

His bitter smile became a sneer. 'She might have been proud of me, but I never had anything but contempt for her.'

Sheila looked at him in shock. 'Why? You admit your ma worked her fingers to the bone for you!'

'Maybe so, but this house aye belonged to her, so there was never any need for her to keep my da on like she did. When he stopped working she should have thrown the sod out on his ear. Maggs and Kenny might still be alive if she'd done that. I blame her as much for their deaths as I do the old man.'

'Perhaps she wasn't as strong as you are. Perhaps, for all his faults, she always loved your da?' Sheila suggested softly.

But his expression became grim and thunderous. 'What about Maggs and Kenny? Didn't she love them, too?'

'You make it sound so black and white. Even I know things in life are just never like that.' She searched his face in puzzlement, looking for some kindness. 'You're a very unforgiving man,' she said at last.

'I am that,' he fairly shouted. 'I always have been and and I always will be.' He threw what was left of his cigarette down on to the ground and ground it beneath his heel.

'This wind is starting to cut through me,' she said, shivering. 'I think we should go back.'

But he just stood there, looking past her, his face locked by some powerful emotion. 'James,' she said gently. 'James, I think we should go.'

It was done before he'd realized it. He caught her to him and pressed his lips on hers. She stiffened, her mouth unyielding, but then the sheer force of him overcame her and her lips parted.

Had she forgotten what it was like to be lost in a kiss, to forget everything within the power of an embrace? Or

113

had she never known before such a hungry passion, such an overwhelming longing? When at last they pulled apart, he held her at arm's length, his expression both serious and concerned. 'As we've been talking about love,' he said thickly, 'I think you should know that I've fallen in love with you.'

Love! But he couldn't love her! It had rather excited her to think that he fancied her – just as it had always pleased her to flirt a little with an attractive man. But love? A man like him, and she little more than a girl – a fisherman's daughter who knew little of the world beyond their harbour – was he lying to her to seduce her? 'I think we'd better get back now,' she said quickly, turning away. 'They'll be missing you.'

He caught her chin and pulled her head to face him. 'I know exactly what I'm saying, Sheila. I've thought about nothing else for months and months now. I love you, Sheila. I need you.'

She jerked her head and turned her back on him – but did not shrug herself free when his arms encircled her from behind. 'Did you bring me here just to tell me this?'

'No. I just wanted you to see where I was born. And then . . . and then I couldn't bottle up my feelings any longer.' He moved his hands to her shoulders and turned her around. 'Have I made a complete fool of myself then?'

'No,' she answered quickly, reaching out to touch his cheek. 'No, never a fool.'

They stood staring at one another in silence, for minutes that might have been hours; for hours that might have been minutes. 'I think we *had* better return,' he said eventually, and, tentatively taking her arm, led her back up the cul-de-sac.

Sheila lay in bed, knowing he was going to come to her. Ever since bidding him good-night and coming upstairs, leaving him behind to have a dram with a skipper who wanted a private word, she'd been waiting nervously for his rap on the door, unsure of what she should do – listen to her heart or her head.

She knew what Peg would say. How would she feel about being the mistress of a married man? But he was not just a married man: he was James Campbell, and his kiss had awakened in her yearnings she'd never known before and a feeling of joy that made her want to run shouting through the village, he loves me! *He* loves *me*! Peg would say she was a silly girl. Silly and wrong. Wrong to take up with a man who already had a wife. But Sheila had learned something in the past months. She had learned that happiness is fleeting. She had learned to take the moments as they came – to use them and enjoy them, for they might never come again.

But Eric had been dead such a short time. Would it be a betrayal to his memory, to what they'd had together, to give herself to someone else?

There was no rap. The door opened, and he was standing before her.

'I knew you'd come.'

He closed the door behind him. 'I knew you knew. I want you Sheila,' he said simply. 'I need you.'

The time for bereavement was over. Yesterday was gone, but not forgotten. This moment signalled a new beginning. 'And I need you,' she whispered back, her eyes warm with tears.

The days flew past. Winter gave way to spring, and spring to summer, the world all new and dancing with colour. James Campbell was like a man reborn. If it had been love for Sheila that he had felt before, all those long and lonely nights of his wanting her, of imagining what it would be like to lose himself in her arms, then there were no words to describe what he was feeling now. For years his only thought had been of winning, of getting everything he wanted no matter what the price. Mad with his obsession, he had forgotten the things that now seemed all that mattered: he had forgotten how to love, how to give, how to laugh.

If anyone noticed the change in him – if Fiona, for instance, wondered what had lifted the severity and gloom from his manner, or wondered where he was going when he passed her door in the late hours of the night – they were wise enough not to let him know.

Sheila had, in fact, had a complex conversation with Fiona – a conversation about flowers that, beneath its surface talk of blooms, and seasons and the art of arrangement, had held a clear message: I don't mind about the *affaire* as long as you are both discreet. But she had kept it from James because she was unsure of what the message might mean. That Fiona had enough to occupy her time and was glad to be relieved of some of her more distasteful wifely duties? Or that Fiona was used to his flirtations and was not going to bother herself over her husband's going to bed with a servant? When he was with her, she was sure that he loved her, and felt her own love growing day by day as Eric's memory began to fade away. The guilt and confusion she had felt at first had been replaced with affection and trust. But on those nights when she lay by herself, wondering if he might still come that night, no matter how late the hour, she found herself questioning not only Fiona's passive complicity, but James's motives as well; and she was a girl once more, wishing she were home with Peg where things were safe and she knew what was what. In the morning, however, she would forget her fears with his first smile or his brusque 'Good morning'.

The pleasure she took in being with him was matched by the joy she took in working with him. He often said that it was a stroke of genius that he had thought of making her his assistant. She had a natural head for figures and a natural aptitude for business. Not only was she able to instantly grasp the most complex problems, but she had an intellect that he knew rivalled his own.

116

'You are the perfect partner for my life,' he repeatedly told her. 'Without you I am halved.'

Sheila ran out of the house around the corner to where the smokehouse stood. With a hand against one of its walls to steady herself, she threw up, again and again, until finally she was retching on an empty stomach.

Peg, her ma, was gone. 'Don't worry about me, lass,' Peg had whispered. 'I'm going to join your da and brothers. I'll be a lot happier there than I am here. But it grieves me sore to leave you behind.'

'Don't die, Ma!' she'd wailed, but Peg's mind had been made up long since, and no tears could change the course she chosen.

Peg had smiled softly, and the lines and years had seemed to drop away with the cares of her life. The breath had whistled from her and her chest had stilled.

'Is she . . . ?' Maggie had asked in a quavering voice.

Sheila had nodded and Maggie had stumbled backwards, collapsing into a chair and bursting into tears.

At least the end had come quickly. There hadn't been more than a few minutes between Peg collapsing and her dying; not even long enough for the doctor to get there, though Ian McPherson had gone running for Doctor Eckemyr moments after the collapse.

Sheila was grateful she'd been there when it had happened. That had been some consolation. It was Sheila's day off and they'd had the entire day together. She couldn't help but wonder if Peg had somehow controlled events to fall out as they had, dying on a day of her own choosing when her last remaining child was by her side.

Sheila straightened, then went to a free-standing water tap by the side of the smokehouse where she rinsed out her foul-tasting mouth.

Feeling better, she returned to the house to find that Dr Eckemyr had arrived and was in the process, assisted by Ian, of lifting the body into the cavity bed. When the body was laid out, Eckemyr covered it with a sheet. 'I am sorry,' he said to Sheila.

'There didn't seem to be any pain.'

'Heart failure, I think,' Eckemyr said, and Sheila gave him a grateful smile. So he also thought that Peg had died of a broken heart.

Being the weekend Ian had brought over a bottle of whisky with him so he poured out drams for them all. Shortly afterwards Eckemyr took his leave, saying he'd be back in the morning to make out the death certificate.

After the doctor left, Sheila went to sit beside the cavity bed, where, lost in a dream, she recalled many scenes from her childhood. Aye, it had been a rare house to be born and brought up in. What fine people her ma and da had been. So many memories, so many happy times: a vibrant family, full of life, which was now, with the exception of herself, all gone.

As the hour was getting late, she decided to return to the hall for some things and to explain that she would be returning home that night to sit with Maggie.

On arriving at the Hall she let herself in by the front door, not wanting to face anyone else just yet, and made her way upstairs to seek out James. She desperately wanted James's arms about her, to lay her head against his chest, to cry and have him comfort her.

'And neither the girl nor the rest of the family ever suspected?' a male voice was saying.

Sheila stopped and frowned. James was with someone, and it was a voice she knew; but whose?

'Everything's fine, Dunwoodie,' James said shortly.

Dunwoodie! Of course, the insurance agent.

'It nearly broke my heart to lie to them like that,' whined Dunwoodie.

'But you forced yourself, eh?' said James with a humourless laugh.

118

'Aye, I did that, Mr Campbell. We all have our price in this none too savoury world we inhabit, and you certainly knew mine.'

Both men had been hard at the bottle, she could tell that from their slurred speech. But what did Dunwoodie mean by saying that he had lied? And what was fine?

'At the time I didn't realize it was the lassie you were after. It wasn't till I heard she'd come to work for you that I put two and two together. I can't say I blame you for wanting to get her in your power,' Dunwoodie chuckled. 'I remember thinking at the time what a handsome piece she was. A real cracker!'

'Aye, you have as fine an eye for the lassies, Mr Dunwoodie, as for an extra few bob.'

Dunwoodie chortled. 'It was all so easy. I didn't even have to change my books. The *Bluebell* payment hadn't been put through yet.'

Sheila went cold all over. Had that man just said that the *Bluebell* had been covered after all? She was suddenly overcome with nausea. When she was once more sufficiently in control of herself to listen to what they were saying it was only to discover that they'd changed the subject and were now talking about London where, it seemed, Dunwoodie had recently had occasion to visit for the first time.

Quietly as a mouse Sheila stole away to her bedroom where she sat in the darkness, lost in thought.

. . . *The lassie you were after . . . wanting to get her in your power . . . didn't even have to change my books . . .*

These words reverberated round and round inside Sheila's head as she tried to make sense of what she'd overheard.

To begin with, she knew James had switched agencies handling the insurance of his fleet from John Kerrigan of Peterhead to Dunwoodie, but when exactly had that been? Then she recalled the date: *after* the disaster.

So what was James's part of this arrangement? And Dunwoodie's part?

. . . It broke my heart to lie to them . . . I didn't even have to change my books . . . the Bluebell payment hadn't been put through . . .

Dunwoodie's involvement, on James's instructions, was clearly to make it appear that Davey hadn't paid that last premium. But why should James Campbell not want what remained of the Beattie family to get their due?

. . . The lassie you were after . . . it wasn't till I heard she was working for you that I put two and two together . . . .

Oh, my God. All this was because of her. Because James Campbell always got what he wanted, no matter what the price.

'You bastard. You devious, callous, conniving bastard!' she whispered into the empty room.

She'd known from the beginning that he was ruthless, but to capitalize on the Dragonholme disaster and upset so many lives for a whim – that was beyond forgiveness.

She began to weep; soft, warm tears which trickled down her cheeks. 'Oh, Eric!' she whispered, and the trickle became a torrent. 'Oh, Eric! What have I done? Oh, Ma!'

She was still weeping when she decided she'd have to leave the place. She couldn't continue on at the Hall after what she'd learned.

She could go home, except Maggie was ensconced there, and she couldn't bear the idea of living with her sister-in-law. Anyway, if she went home James would soon seek her out and she never wanted to see or speak to him ever again.

Let Maggie and Ian McPherson have the house. It would be her wedding present to them, for they'd soon be getting married, no doubt about that.

As for the funeral arrangements, Maggie would have to take care of those. Peg would understand why she didn't attend the service and burying after, why she had to away that very night.

She had some money; not a great deal but certainly

enough to pay a train fare and keep her going for a few days. Then there were several items of jewellery James had given her: nothing excessively valuable, but what they would realize from a pop shop should keep her going till she found another job.

With the room still in darkness she packed a small case, keeping what she would be taking to a minimum, as she was going to have to walk to Portnessie, all ten long miles of it. And from there to where? That was a question for which as yet she had no answer.

When she was ready she sat down again. She would wait until James and all the servants were fast asleep before leaving the Hall.

Midnight was chiming when she heard him stagger up the stairs, the last to go to bed. She waited a further hour to be completely on the safe side before slipping from her room.

On the clifftops overlooking Dragonholme, she paused to stare down at the village where she'd been born.

'Wish me luck Ma,' she whispered, and, turning abruptly she strode off towards Portnessie, heel and toe, never looking back.

PART TWO

The Harvest Red Christmas 1913–17

'You have sown for the Day, you have grown for the
  Day;
Yours is the Harvest red.
Can you hear the groans and the awful cries?
Can you see the heap of slain that lies,
And sightless turned to the flame-lit skies
The glassy eyes of the dead?'

From 'The Day', author unknown
Daily Express, 1914

4

John Kelly, one of the fly men, had a reputation for being obnoxious when drunk, which he was certainly being right then. 'Come on, give us a kiss,' he said to Sheila, having trapped her against some flats stacked in the passageway waiting to be taken to the paintdock and turned into a part of the house William Wallace once owned in Elderslie.

Sheila liked John well enough – he could be a good laugh at times – but she had no intention of kissing him, even in Christmas fun.

'Let me pass, John,' she pleaded.

'Not until I get a big smacker,' he persisted, grabbing her round the waist and attempting to pull her closer. She did her best to resist.

'Think about your wife!' Sheila hissed.

'Bugger her, what she doesn't see she'll no' be worried about.'

She pushed and strained. He might be small, but by God he was strong. Of course, heaving the flying scenery up and down night after night was bound to develop his arms.

'Are you all right, Miss Beattie?' a cultured voice inquired.

John Kelly whirled, pressing Sheila into the flats with his back, to glare at the speaker. It was Mr Lack, the actor playing the pirate king in the pantomime. 'Piss off, Englishman!' John ordered angrily.

Mr Lack looked from John back to Sheila who pulled a pleading face. 'Perhaps you'd like to accompany me downstairs, Miss Beattie?' Lack suggested, taking a step forward.

The knife appeared in John's hand as though by magic,

125

its blade viciously hooked and encrusted with rust. 'On your way,' he spat.

It was the first time anyone had ever pulled a knife on Lack and he was quite stunned by it. He managed to keep cool, however, appearing as unconcerned as though John were threatening him with no more than a strand of wet spaghetti.

Sheila knew John: he was a hard wee nut and that knife was no empty threat. Having pulled it he'd use it. Better a kiss than a stabbing. 'I'll manage Mr Lack, thank you very much,' she said in a tight voice.

'You heard the bint, now fuck off!' snarled John, his knife hand weaving a figure of eight pattern in front of him.

Lack was blond and slim, almost boyish in looks and build, but he wasn't as soft or the pushover that he looked – as opponents on many a rugger field had found out. When circumstances called for it, as he deemed these did, he could be quick-witted and articulate as well as packing a punch.

Lack stared at the knife, then up again at John. 'Just a nick from that rusty thing would be enough I think. A couple of days and I'd be a mortuary case as a result of septicaemia,' he said.

John blinked. 'Septi what?'

'Septicaemia. Blood poisoning. In other words what I'm saying is that the chances are exceptionally high that even a nick from that knife would kill me.'

'It would serve you fucking right for sticking your neb in where it's no' wanted,' retorted John.

Lack gave a lazy smile. 'It would be first-degree murder, and the penalty for that is the hangman's noose,' he said evenly, and clenching his fist made a pulling gesture at the side of his neck.

John recoiled a fraction, and blinked again. The actor's mime had been extremely explicit; he could almost feel the hemp round his throat.

'Now I'm escorting Miss Beattie downstairs, so will you please stand aside,' Lack said in an inoffensive tone, but still with command and authority in his voice, and coming forward laid his hand on Sheila's arm.

For several moments John hesitated. Then his nerve broke and he lurched away, thereby releasing Sheila. It was only a kiss he'd wanted, he told himself. How in the Hell had they got on to the hangman's bloody nooses!

Sheila would have hurried off down the passageway, but Lack held her back, forcing her to walk at a normal pace. Neither spoke until they were downstairs and backstage when Sheila said, 'Would that really be first-degree murder?'

Lack smiled, his eyes twinkling. 'I've absolutely no idea; but our friend from the flys believed it would be,' he laughed, 'and that's all that matters.'

Sheila laughed as well. He had some nerve to him, this Mr Lack, with his youthful good looks and his polished good manners.

'Well, I'd like to thank you for putting the fear of God into him.'

'I am at your service,' he said with a mock bow. 'Obnoxious drunks my speciality.'

They began to chat about the success of the show, and the success of the party, when suddenly a high voice interrupted them.

'Oh, there you are. I've been looking everywhere for you. Are you ready then?' Trisha Alexander asked Lack, breathlessly appearing from nowhere. Trisha was the female juvenile lead playing Princess Ismela in the season's production of *Sinbad*.

So that's how the land lies, Shiela thought, with an unexpected twinge of disappointment.

'You know Miss Beattie, of course,' said Lack.

'I should think so. She fitted me for some of my costumes,' Trisha replied, and gave a tinkling laugh.

'I didn't have that pleasure. It was the other wardrobe lady who fitted me for my solitary costume,' smiled Lack. The Queen's Theatre boasted two wardrobe mistresses: Pat McLuskey was one, Sheila the other.

They chatted for a few minutes, then Lack and Trisha said good-night and left Sheila to make her way on to the stage where, despite the lateness of the hour, the theatre's 1913 Christmas party was still in full swing. She was searching for Pat, with whom she shared digs, finally finding her in the auditorium getting well acquainted with a bottle of malt whisky. 'Pished as a newt,' said Pat, and hiccuped.

'You're not the only one,' grinned Sheila.

He wasn't a bad actor at all. She'd certainly seen a lot worse, Sheila decided from her vantage point in the wings where she'd been watching Lack in his biggest scene, his dual with Sinbad, at the conclusion of which he and the other dastardly pirates were thoroughly routed.

It was the day after the party and the first house. Hangovers and their cures were the main topics of conversation around the theatre.

Thrust, cut, parry by Sinbad, then a whack with the flat of the sword on Lack's bottom, the sound of the whack coming from a pair of clapper sticks operated off stage. Clutching his bottom dramatically Lack leapt up and down, the audience roaring, shouting, 'ooh! ooh! ooh!' then ran from the stage followed by his band of cut-throats.

'So may all pirates be vanquished!' Sinbad boomed to the audience, flourishing his scimitar above his head, and was rewarded with an enthusiastic round of applause.

Sheila hadn't realized she was standing where Lack made his exit. She was right in his way when he came off, which flustered her as she hadn't wanted him to know she'd been watching him. Once he was masked from the audience by the return, he stopped to smile at her. 'How are you today?' he whispered.

'Not too bad, considering,' she replied, pretending to be engrossed by Sinbad.

'It was a good party, I enjoyed it.'

'I did too,' she replied, flashing him a brief smile.

He was about to ask her if she'd like to come to the green room with him for some tea when she excused herself, saying she had to get on, and walked away. He stared after her thoughtfully.

'Miss Beattie?'

Sheila turned to find Lack hurrying along the corridor to catch up with her. 'Hello again,' she smiled. It was four days since he'd caught her watching him from the wings and they hadn't spoken since.

Lack had been making discreet enquiries about Sheila and had been relieved to discover that she didn't have a boyfriend, not so far, at any rate, as anyone could tell.

New Year's Eve was only a couple of nights away. Nearly everyone else in the theatre came from Glasgow and was planning to celebrate it at home with their families. Lack, however, like Sheila, had no family around and couldn't go home as there was a show on New Year's day.

'I was wondering if you'd be interested in going to a dance after the second show on New Year's?' he asked nervously.

She looked at him quizzically. 'What about Trisha?' she asked before she could stop herself.

'What about her?'

'Aren't you and she . . .' wondering if his blank expression was sincere, '. . . friends?'

His laughter was infectious. 'Goodness, no. Well, yes of course we're friends, but . . . you didn't think that . . .'

She felt herself blush scarlet, at a complete loss for words. It was a long time since she'd felt herself attracted to a man.

'So how about Hogmanay then?' he asked eagerly, pretending not to notice her embarrassment.

'I'm afraid I've already promised to go to a small "do" with Pat McLuskey,' she said with undisguised disappointment. 'I'm sorry.'

His handsome face clouded. 'That's rotten luck for me.'

At that moment he seemed so young and vulnerable that her instinct was to sweep him into her arms and cuddle him like a child. But he wasn't a child, she reminded herself. He was a fully grown man who'd coolly stood up to John Kelly's knife. Suddenly she had the suspicion that this young and vulnerable reaction to her refusal was an act. He was an actor, after all. How many unsuspecting females had he twisted around his little finger with this pose, she wondered, but with no trace of anger.

'Can't I persuade you to change your mind?' he cajoled.

'I've given my promise to go, and I never break my promise,' she replied firmly.

'Oh, well. Integrity is a good quality. Some other time, perhaps,' he said, shrugging.

'Perhaps.'

'There's no need to worry about me. I can aye go to the McKillops on my own,' Pat McLuskey said when Sheila told her about Lack's Hogmanay invitation.

'You'll do no such thing,' snapped Sheila. 'Anyway, I've already agreed to go to the McKillops, and I've no intention of letting either you or them down.'

It was late that night. Sheila had just arrived back from work to the room they shared to find Pat in the process of painting her toenails blood red. During the week they both worked days, including Saturdays, and alternate evenings. In the daytime they made and maintained costumes; in the evenings they had to be on hand for emergency repairs.

Sheila found it a fairly exacting job, due to the long hours more than anything else, but one she enjoyed. Her life was now as different to what it had been at Dragonholme as chalk to cheese. She often thought about the village and her family, but tried not to remember her time at the Hall or James Campbell. When she did allow herself to think about him, the warring emotions of loathing and betrayal, disgust and disillusionment brought so much pain and confusion that it nearly tore her apart.

'Has Mr Lack nowhere to go then?' Pat asked, glancing up from her task.

'So it would seem.'

'Ach, we can't leave the poor man all alone on Neer'day, that just wouldn't be right at all! And him a Sassenach, too. What will he think of Scottish hospitality?' Pat had been in the theatrical profession for over twenty years and had spent too many lonely nights on her own not to want to help someone in the same situation.

'He's bound to find some party or other he can go to,' argued Sheila. 'There are always stacks of them on New Year's Eve.'

'Do you like him?'

Sheila tilted her head, apparently absorbed in consideration of Pat's painted toenails. 'I hardly know him,' she answered offhandedly.

'That's not what I asked you, hen. Do you like him?' Pat persisted.

For some reason, Sheila found it hard to meet Pat's eyes. 'Well, I certainly don't dislike him,' she replied.

'Then why don't we have a wee word with the McKillops and see if they'll extend their invitation to include Mr Lack? I'm sure they'll be agreeable.'

'I know he has a car, so that would mean a ride to Maxwell Park and back again,' Sheila said.

Pat bent again to her toenails. Sheila might pretend the car was an important item of consideration, but she wasn't pulling any wool over Pat's eyes. Sheila was keen, which made Mr Lack the first man she'd ever shown any real interest in since coming to work at the Queen's Theatre sixteen months before.

*　　*　　*

Sheila and Pat, the pair of them dressed to the nines, arrived outside Lack's dressing room. 'You knock,' Sheila whispered to Pat, suddenly as nervous as a girl.

The door was opened almost immediately by Lack still in his dressing gown, a towel draped round his neck. 'Come in, come in,' he greeted them. 'I'm sorry I'm running a little behind.'

The dressing room was tiny and rather smelly. Sheila noticed that the ceiling was not only badly cracked, but was actually coming away in bits.

Lack saw her staring round. 'Hardly the Ritz, I'm afraid, but then one doesn't exactly expect luxury in the theatre.'

'This dressing room *is* the Ritz beside some I've seen,' laughed Pat. 'I could tell you stories that would curl your hair.'

'I'm sure you could,' he smiled.

There was an opened bottle of wine on his dressing table and three glasses. With a mock bow, he filled the glasses and handed one to Sheila and one to Pat. 'To get the evening started,' he toasted, raising his own glass.

'Wine!' laughed Pat. 'I don't think I've ever had wine on New Year's Eve before.'

Lack dived under his dressing table, re-emerging with two bottles of Glenfiddich. 'I wouldn't want to break any old Scottish traditions,' he winked. 'So I bought these to bring along.'

Pat's eyes shone. 'With a couple of bottles of that there's not a house in Scotland you wouldn't be welcome in,' she said, winking back.

Sheila sipped her wine. It was excellent. Judging from his taste in drink and clothes, Mr Lack was used to the very best. 'Nice claret,' she said appreciatively. 'It's a long while since I had any.'

Lack stared at her in astonishment. An ordinary person in Glasgow knowing about wine was about as rare as finding gold nuggets down a coalmine. 'You're a connoisseur?' he queried.

'Hardly! But I can tell the difference between a beaujolais and burgundy, or a hock and sauterne.' There were still some things she had to thank James Campbell for, she thought ruefully.

'It's all either red or white to me,' laughed Pat.

'Do you drink Scottish wine yourself?' Sheila asked Lack, a mischievous twinkle in her eye.

'Scottish wine? Surely there's no such thing?'

'Oh, there is indeed. And it's world famous, isn't that so Pat?'

Pat nodded her agreement.

'Scottish wine? But grapes don't grow in this climate.'

'Who mentioned grapes?' teased Sheila.

He knew then that his leg was being pulled, but decided to go along with the gag anyway. 'So where do I try this famous Scottish wine?' he asked.

'Well you certainly won't get it from the same place you get Scottish champagne.'

'Scottish champagne now? I suppose that's world famous as well?'

She pretended to give that much thought. Having difficulty in keeping the laughter that was bubbling inside her out of her voice, she answered, 'It's famous all right, but not quite as famous as the wine. What's your opinion Pat,'

Pat shook her head. 'I agree. Not *quite* as famous.'

'Would you like to try some Scottish champagne?' Sheila asked.

'You mean you have some here?'

'Oh yes!' she grinned.

What on earth was she going to come up with, he wondered, thoroughly enjoying this little game. 'Then I'd love to.'

Sheila laid down her glass and went to the sink in the corner. Filling a teacup that was on the soap ledge, she took the cup to Lack and presented it to him.

'Water!' he exclaimed.

'Also known as Scottish champagne.'

'And Scottish wine?'

Sheila pointed to the bottles of Glenfiddich. 'What the posh sometimes call whisky,' unable to contain her laughter any more.

'A good one,' he acknowledged, and removed his dressing gown to reveal he was fully dressed with the exception of his jacket and tie.

Sheila watched him intently as he knotted his tie. His concentration on what he was doing had produced a deep furrow at the top of his nose, and, for some inexplicable reason, she found it fascinating.

When he was finally ready, he opened an old cake tin standing on one side of his dressing table and took out a single red rose and a box of chocolates. The rose he handed to Sheila, the chocolates to Pat.

'A rose in December! How on earth did you manage that?' Sheila asked in amazement.

He gave her a knowing wink, but didn't reply.

'You appear to be extremely resourceful,' she said.

'Aren't all actors?' he joked, but he was obviously pleased by her appreciation.

'I'll go and get the car,' Lack said as they came on to the street. 'I park it behind the hotel.'

A few minutes later the car purred into view. Sheila gaped in disbelief and Pat's mouth dropped open as she whispered, 'What a stunner!'

It was a Rolls-Royce Silver Ghost. The woodwork was yellow, including the toolbox on the right-hand running board; the running boards, mudguards and general bodywork matt black; the hood and headlights gleaming white.

'Climb aboard!' a grinning Lack said, and opened the passenger door for them.

Pat went into the back expecting Sheila to sit with Lack, but Sheila climbed in with Pat instead. Glancing at Lack she caught the look of disappointment in his expression.

A Silver Ghost, Sheila thought in some awe. How did

a struggling young actor come to own a car like this? 'This is yours?' she asked.

'It is, indeed. It was a present for my twenty-first,' he replied, as though it was the sort of present everyone got for their twenty-first.

'Somebody must like you a great deal,' Pat said, running her hand over the dimpled black leather on which she was sitting.

It was his mother, actually, who'd given it to him, Lack explained, adding, a little shamefacedly, that his mother had always been in the habit of spoiling him. And having been made a gift of a Silver Ghost he certainly wasn't going to refuse to accept it, now was he?

Pat hastily agreed, saying he would have to have been ninepence in the shilling to refuse something as beautiful as this. She'd be happy to accept a Silver Ghost any day of the week, she laughed.

Sheila asked Lack if he knew the way to Maxwell Park, and he replied that he thought he did, but perhaps she should come up front to be on hand to guide him in case he went wrong. Somewhat primly she retorted she could guide him just as well from the back of the car, thank you very much.

Pat turned her face away from the pair of them, and smiled.

Maxwell Park was on the south side, and it took them just over twenty minutes to get there. The tenement where the McKillops lived was at the end of a quiet cul-de-sac tucked away from the main thoroughfares so Lack had no qualms about leaving his car there.

They mounted stairs that were well-kept and had recently been whitewashed at their ends; the landing windows they passed gleamed. As Glasgow tenements went, this was quite clearly one of the better examples.

Jack welcomed them warmly with a kiss each for Sheila and Pat, and shaking Lack's hand vigorously, stated he was delighted Mr Lack could join them for Hogmanay. Lack then passed over his two bottles of Glenfiddich, and Sheila the bottle of blend she and Pat had brought along as their contribution, and away in they went.

Sheila counted fourteen people already in the front room, Maureen McKillop immediately coming over to the newly arrived party to express her delight that they'd come. Maureen then took them round and introduced them to the others who were, without exception, neighbours from up that close or from closes nearby.

There was a friendly atmosphere in the house which made Sheila feel right at home. Turning to comment on this to Lack, she discovered he was already chatting to, or being chatted up by, a good-looking (although, in Sheila's estimation, blowsy) young woman called Christine Templeton.

Dancing was in progress, the music coming from a phonograph that had been installed on top of the sideboard. The carpet in the room had been rolled up and the furniture pulled back, and everyone had the look about them of people out to enjoy themselves.

Sheila watched Lack dance with Christine, miffed that he hadn't got up with her first; but then if Christine had asked him he could hardly have refused her, she told herself, could he?

A man called Rog asked Pat on to the floor, saying that as his wife had gone to the toilet he was free to enjoy himself for five minutes. Clutching Pat to him he went straight into an old Glasgow dancehall favourite called the Palais Glide, or, alternatively, in the rougher establishments Ra Moonie.

'Sorry about that, I was abducted,' Lack grinned at Sheila on his return from the makeshift dance floor. To which she replied, a little more frostily than she'd intended, that as abductions went he'd given the definite impression of suffering no pain.

Sheila puzzled Lack. At times she seemed to like him, quite a bit he thought, while at other time he might have been something decidedly nasty the cat had dragged in and presented to her.

136

'You've got a sharp tongue in your head. Has anyone ever told you that before?' he asked.

Instead of answering his jibe she handed him her empty glass, obviously wanting it refilled. Instead, he set it down on a handy surface and gave her a razored smile.

'Why don't you two show us what you can do?' suggested Pat, dancing past cheek to cheek with Rog, whose wife was glowering from across the other side of the room.

'I don't really feel like dancing just now,' said Sheila.

'That's all right,' said Lack. 'I fully understand if you're not very good at it. Lots of people are unco-ordinated.'

Sheila flushed. Unco-ordinated! What a bally cheek! She retorted hotly that she was not unco-ordinated; in fact she was a damn good dancer, so there Mr High Faluting Englishman!

The slow grin that tugged the corners of his mouth upwards told her she'd fallen for that one hook, line and sinker. Without further comment she followed him to the centre of the floor when he took her hand and led the way.

They danced in silence, each staring over the other's shoulder and wondering what his or her partner was thinking.

The dance finished and they clapped politely. Sheila was about to move off the floor when he grabbed her arm and pulled her back to him. They exchanged a glance, but nothing more.

The next record was a waltz. Snugly they came together and their bodies moved as one. 'Why did you become an actor?' she asked, genuinely curious, for although she was now well used to actors after sixteen months in the theatre it still seemed to her a strange profession for a man to follow.

He explained that when he was at school it had been his intention to go into business, then halfway through his fifth year he'd been approached to take part in a play, which he'd only eventually reluctantly agreed to, thinking he would be bound to hate it. But it hadn't turned out that way at all. On the contrary, he'd found being in front of an audience thrilling and exciting in the extreme. When the play was finally over he'd known, beyond the shadow of a doubt, that being on stage was what he wanted to do with his life.

'But don't you find it boring repeating the same performance over and over?'

He laughed warmly. No two performances were the same, he explained. Each was different, depending upon the mood of the actors and, of course, on the reaction of the audience. Certainly no two audiences were ever identical.

It was during the first performance of that school play that he'd discovered what it was like to be truly alive, for every nerve end in the body to be jumping with excitement, even terror. Once experienced, it became a drug that had to be repeatedly administered till at last one was a hopeless addict.

The thought of ever having to give up the stage was just too awful to contemplate, deprived of the liveliness and exhilaration he felt when treading the boards would be tantamount to being dead.

As Lack spoke his voice assumed a vibrancy that was almost contagious. She had rarely met a man so completely caught up in and committed to his chosen profession.

They were in the middle of their sixth dance when the record was stopped and Jack McKillop told everyone to listen for the bells that would herald midnight and the dawning of the New Year.

While the gathering waited expectantly Maureen McKillop hastily passed round drams. Sheila was holding hers and straining her ears like all present when she became aware that Lack's arm was around her waist.

She looked at him and smiled, and as she did the bells started to ring.

'Wait for it!' whispered Jack McKillop urgently, for it was unlucky to toast the New Year until after the last peel had sounded. 'A happy 1914 to one and all. May it be the best and most prosperous year of our lives!' Jack cried as soon as the bells had died away.

'A happy New Year to you, Mr Lack,' Sheila murmured, mesmerized by his pale blue eyes which appeared to be getting larger and larger the longer she stared into them.

'I think it's time you called me Andrew,' he replied.

'A happy New Year, Andrew'.

'A happy New Year, Sheila,' he said, linking his arm with hers. Arms entwined they toasted the New Year.

Then amid the shouts and laughter welcoming the new year, he kissed her.

'Come in!' Sheila called out when there was a knock on the Wardrobe door. It was Andrew whom she'd been expecting for a fitting.

The play following the pantomime was called William Wallace, and was about the legendary Scottish hero's struggle against the English prior to his execution at the London site of Smithfield, where he'd been hanged, drawn and quartered. Andrew was cast as an English major.

It was six days since Hogmanay, during which time Andrew had thought a great deal about Sheila, and she about him. Yet since the night of the party they'd only said hello to one another in passing.

Sheila had wanted to stop and chat on several occasions, but her pride hadn't let her. He was the man, after all! It was his place to stop her. If he didn't want to go out with her again, that was his misfortune.

Brusquely she told him his costume was the one on top of that hamper over there, indicating the hamper with a nod of her head. 'You'll have to try it on,' she snapped.

Pat suddenly announced she'd make some tea, and left

the room to fill the kettle as there wasn't a tap in Wardrobe.

There was a screen which Andrew went behind. 'I really enjoyed myself at the McKillops,' he called over the top. 'That was a New Year party I won't forget in a hurry.' There was no reply. He thanked Sheila again for taking him along.

'Your coming along was Pat's idea,' she replied tartly, the words no sooner out of her mouth than she regretted them, for as true as they were, they were hardly the full truth.

Andrew winced. Jesus, she had a tongue on her! Despite that, he liked her. The question was, did she like him? For the past six days he had thought of little else; but she blew so hot and cold that it was impossible to tell.

Take the party, for example. She'd been great fun in the dressing room beforehand, then distant in the car during the drive. Once at the party she'd finally thawed, but on the drive back she'd again sat in the back seat like some tailor's dummy, only speaking, and then curtly, when spoken to. What was a man to make of such behaviour? He was damned if he knew.

He struggled into his britches, which were far too tight. He could only do up half his buttons. He emerged from behind the screen just as Pat returned, saying that tea would be up in a jiffy, and did he like Abernethy biscuits? 'I may never be able to eat again,' he winked, holding his britches together.

'Let's have a look at you then,' Sheila said, laying down the costume she'd been working on and coming to stand in front of him.

The coat more of less fitted, she thought. Well enough anyway to get away with. But the britches were another matter entirely.

Andrew squirmed, then made himself stand stock still when he saw Pat's look of amusement. He wasn't a person easily embarrassed, but the sight of Sheila fiddling around with his trousers might just do it.

Sheila told him to take the britches off again, which he did, but not before returning behind the screen first. He obviously had no intention of allowing Sheila to see him in his undershorts. This wasn't lost on Sheila who, having retrieved the britches from where he'd slung them over the top of the screen, grinned at Pat. Pat mouthed back, 'Maybe he's got sparrow legs?', causing Sheila to snicker and Andrew to stick his head round the side of the screen to see what was going on.

After the fitting and after tea and Abernethies, Andre lighted himself a cigarette, chatting happily away.

Sheila paid him scant attention, pretending to be engrossed in her sewing. With Sheila silent, Pat did most of the talking, yammering away like some demented budgie. She didn't fail to notice, however, that although Andrew was listening to her, replying enthusiastically, every so often his eyes strayed towards Sheila.

Finally and reluctantly, Andrew said he had to be going. He stubbed out the remains of his cigarette. 'Will you need me for another fitting, then?' he asked Sheila. Without looking up, she replied that she would, and that she'd leave a message for him on the notice board when he was to come again.

Andrew had presented himself in Wardrobe still undecided whether to ask Sheila out or not, but he now made up his mind he would do, half expecting to be turned down.

Clearing his throat, he said he intended driving out into the country this coming Sunday for a breath of fresh air, so much needed after being cooped up in the theatre day after day, and he was wondering if Sheila would like to go with him. He'd thought they might stop at a hotel for lunch, or at a nice pub if they could find one.

Sheila paused in her sewing, for just a heartbeat. So he *did* want to see her again! Why then had there been six whole days of what amounted to his snubbing her? She would refuse him, she thought, then told herself not to be so stupid, say no now and that could well be the end of it between them. On the other hand, she didn't want to appear too available.

'Pat and I – ' she started to say.

'Pat's to come also, that was what I meant the three of us going for a spin together,' he quickly interjected.

Liar! she thought, and gave Pat a look that told Pat she was to accept the invitation.

'I'd love to go,' Pat smiled.

'Agreed then,' said Andrew, and swiftly arranged a time to call and pick them up.

After he'd gone Sheila glanced over at Pat, and they both burst out giggling.

'You're not making it easy for the poor fellow,' Pat said when their giggling, which had come close on hysterical, had finally subsided.

Sheila's reply was that anything easily got wasn't respected, she had no intentions of being a piece of theatrical fluff to be picked up and laid down whenever he felt like it, and the sooner he learned that the better.

She returned to her sewing, and within seconds was humming happily to herself, planning what she would wear.

Pat listened to the humming, wondering how she could side-step the Sunday spin without it being obvious that that was what she was doing.

He was an excellent driver, Sheila thought, the Silver Ghost responding to his every touch as though it were an extension of himself.

Her thoughts drifted to Pat whom they'd left back at the digs suffering from bad monthly pains. She hoped Pat was all right and felt guilty about leaving her, but Pat had been insistent she and Andrew go ahead without her.

It was a bitter January day, the wind swirling and gusting round the Rolls as they drove through the bleak but attractive countryside. Off to the left were white-tipped hills, while over to the right, just out of sight, was the Firth of Clyde.

'Do you think we could stop for a few minutes?' asked Sheila. 'I'd like to walk over and see the Firth.'

Andrew immediately checked his mirror, then drew the car into the side of the road, thinking he wouldn't mind a stretch of the legs at all.

Getting out of the Rolls, they made for the Firth – together, yet apart. There had been a barrier between them since Andrew had picked her up, and both were painfully aware of it.

He'd made a mistake in asking her out again, he was thinking, she didn't like him, was only tolerating him for reasons of her own.

They topped a rise and Sheila came up short, sucking in her breath at seeing the blue-grey waters of the Firth spread before her.

'I've missed the sea so much since being in Glasgow, but I suppose that's only natural having been born and bred beside it,' she said wistfully.

'So where is it you come from?' he inquired.

'A wee fishing village I'm sure you've never heard of. It's called Dragonholme, and is over on the east coast not far from St Abb's Head,' she replied, her voice filled with love and longing.

'A fishing village. Does that mean your people are fisherfolk?' he asked, intrigued.

In halting tones she told him about the disaster, and how she'd lost her da, three brothers and an uncle and her fiancé in one fell swoop; and how her ma, broken-hearted by what had occurred, had lost the will to live.

Andrew listened, appalled. What a terrible thing to have happened! How awful it must have been for her. 'I'm sorry, truly I am,' he whispered.

She tried to put on a brave smile, but it came over more as a grimace than a smile.

Andrew picked up a stone and threw it at the Firth, but

they were still too far away for the stone to hit the water. It bounced off a small tussock instead.

'Is it because you're still in love with your dead boyfriend that you're so prickly with me?' he asked quietly.

'Prickly?' Sheila echoed.

Not wanting to look into her face right then he picked up another stone and threw that. 'You blow hot and cold with me. I never know what's going on.'

But she countered his question with one of her own. 'Why did you wait six days before asking me out again?'

'I couldn't make up my mind whether or not you liked me, and it seemed up until just now you didn't. But having learned of Eric I can't help but wonder if it's not that you dislike me but can't forget how much you loved him?'

Sheila took a deep breath. What a muddle – and it would seem the blame for that was hers. 'I like you fine,' she said slowly. 'Very much so, in fact; but I'm a bit chary of your motives.'

'What do you mean by that?' Andrew demanded in undisguised amazement. She told him actors came and went and she had no intention, no matter how much she liked him, of being someone's Glasgow conquest. For what else would it be, especially with the difference in class between them. She was working class, there was no hiding that. Just as there was no hiding his real background. Extremely rich middle-class men didn't have serious relationships with working-class girls. Affairs, yes, but not serious relationships. 'Do you think I'm so simple that I don't know that?' she asked at last.

'I see,' Andrew murmured. By God, she'd thought this through far more than he had. It was a huge relief to know she did like him. Perhaps as much as he liked her.

In reply he said that her argument about their difference in class was correct, but only as far as it went. His background might be middle class, but he was no longer that, for as an actor he was officially, by law, classed as a rogue and a vagabond, and as such she was his better.

144

Sheila laughed in spite of herself. 'You're making it up,' she accused.

'Not so!' he protested. Actors *were* officially classed as rogues and vagabonds, alongside beggars, sundry villains and the like, and had been since the Middle Ages. 'Of course, he continued. 'If you look at it another way, in reality we are classless, mingling as we do with the very highest and lowest, the proud and the humble.'

'You've a way with words all right,' she smiled. 'I'll have to give you that.' She then went on to say that he might be a classless rogue and vagabond, but what about his family – they surely weren't?

'I am my own man,' he said, bowing theatrically but with his eyes serious. 'I don't need anyone's approval to take up with someone, or for anything else I might want to do.'

Well, thought Sheila, I guess that's pretty clear. There was no question that he was telling the truth.

She then asked him what his plans were for when he left the Queen's Theatre at the end of the season, and he replied he wasn't sure yet. He could ask to stay on for another season (and he considered the chances high that the management would agree to this), or he could try to get into one of the other two repertories that the grey city boasted.

'But eventually?' Sheila prompted.

Eventually it was the West End for him. That had always been his dream. He needed a few more years' experience, of course, but then it was Shaftesbury Avenue. He wouldn't be satisfied until his name was in lights; top of the bill.

He would make it, too, Sheila thought. He had the talent, he had the looks, and he certainly had the drive. 'By then Glasgow and the people you met there will be only a distant memory,' she teased.

'And who do you mean by that?' he asked, only partially joking.

Sheila looked away.

He went on. Who was to say, he wanted to know, what would be the case? He certainly had no way of seeing into the future. It seemed to him she was trying to run, gallop even, before she could walk. They'd only just established they liked one another, for goodness sake, and already she had him forgetting her. Why not take things a step at a time and see how they developed?

Was she being over cautious, she asked herself, or just over-reacting against the hurt of losing Eric – and that other hurt, her betrayal by Campbell? Or was she merely using her common sense? Perhaps it was a combination of both, she decided. She did have a fear of being hurt again, of having love snatched away – but there was nothing foolish in that. How else was she to protect herself?

She suddenly realized that the barrier which had been between them was gone. Glancing over at his handsome profile, she felt completely at ease in his company. At ease and happy to be with him. It had been a long time since she'd felt so whole and so good.

They sat and watched the ever-moving sea. Sheila could have watched all day without ever being bored. Some seagulls passed overhead and Andrew remarked that it must be a marvellous sensation to fly, to be able to wheel, dive and soar as those gulls were doing. He said, dreamily, that he'd give his eye teeth to be a bird for just ten minutes.

Later Andrew turned to her and asked her how a fishergirl from the untamed coast had come to be working in the Glasgow theatre. She didn't want to tell him about James Campbell, so she told him that her mother's death had been the last straw, she'd just had to get away from Dràgonholme because of the many painful memories the place held for her. 'I just got on a train,' she said softly. 'And when it ended its journey in Glasgow, I stayed.'

As for getting a job in the theatre, the answer to that was simple. Pat McLuskey had already been staying at the house she'd taken digs in, and through her she'd got the job at the Queen's Theatre. The theatre needed a second wardrobe mistress; she'd therefore applied for the position, and landed it. Shortly after this, because they got on so well together, she and Pat had decided to share a room to cut down their expenses.

Andrew said he admired her for taking on and making a success of a job she'd had no previous experience with, to which she replied that wasn't true. She'd been brought up mending, patching, altering and re-making the family clothes. She could turn a shirt collar, put in a buttonhole, or even cut out with or without a pattern if called upon to do so; the position of wardrobe mistress had held no mysteries or terrors for her; what she had to do was only what she'd already been doing all her life, only with fancy costumes rather than ordinary clothes.

They talked at length till finally both were freezing from the cold. He raced her back to the Silver Ghost, and allowed her to win.

They had lunch in a wee pub called The Clansman's Arms and then drove further up the road and parked in a spot overlooking the Firth.

They talked and talked, delighting – even revelling – in one another's company.

When they finally parted late that evening it was with the utmost reluctance, each hating the thought of being away from the other.

It was a click, as the Glasgow expression went.

That Tuesday Andrew asked Sheila if she'd care to come back to his rooms after the second show for a bite to eat. He was a dab hand with the frying pan he assured her, and promised he'd turn out something tasty.

Sheila retorted she wasn't going to have a man cook for her; she'd never be able to take him seriously again. Andrew bowed his head, pretending to be chastised. She could cook, and he would open the wine – but would she come?

'No funny business?'

'No funny business.'

Then she would come.

Crown Crescent had once been very grand; the homes of wealthy tea importers and successful merchants; but now it was tatty at the edges, a geriatric giving way to age and mounting neglect.

Andrew's rented rooms consisted of a bedroom, reception room, kitchen and toilet, and were on the ground floor. 'Well what do you think?' he asked anxiously when they were inside.

Her impression was of genteel shabbiness; like the building, the contents of the rooms had seen better days. The carpet was threadbare in places, the two armchairs had bits of stuffing hanging out, and the pot containing the aspidistra was badly cracked. 'It seems very comfortable,' she proclaimed.

Andrew breathed a sigh of relief that the place had found favour. He showed Sheila where everything was in the kitchen, then returned to the reception room where he lit the fire he'd laid before going to the theatre. When he was certain the fire had taken hold he opened a bottle of claret and took a glassful through to Sheila, who said it was just what the doctor ordered.

She made scrambled eggs, which they decided to eat sitting on the floor in front of the now blazing fire. As he poured more wine she asked him to tell her about his career to date.

He'd started at the Theatre Royal, Brighton, he told her, where he'd spent five seasons in all before moving on to the New at Nottingham. After the New he'd gone to the Grand at Swansea, from there to Canterbury, and then to Glasgow.

Soon the eggs were gone and more wine had to be opened. Andrew talked non-stop as he described the many plays he'd been in, and the parts he'd taken.

Sheila was completely relaxed, her initial nervousness at coming to his rooms having disappeared within a few minutes of actually entering them. She closed her eyes and let the heat from the fire wash over her. This was bliss!

It was past three a.m. when the Silver Ghost pulled up in front of her digs. 'I enjoyed that tremendously,' said Andrew turning to her in the darkness.

'So did I.'

'I feel I've known you all my life instead of only a short while.'

She moved towards him ever so slightly in the dark.

He kissed her, and she experienced the same overpowering sensation she'd felt when he'd kissed her at the McKillops' Hogmanay party.

She whispered good-night. He came round to her side to help her from the car, and kissed her again, standing watching as though entranced as she hurried off into the shadowy, gas-lit close to swiftly disappear up the stairs.

It was hours later before she finally got to sleep because of thinking about him. Andrew had exactly the same problem.

Weeks flew by, turning into months, and Andrew asked the management if he could stay on for another season. The management informed him that the Queen's Theatre would be delighted to have him continue in its employ.

Summer officially arrived to find Andrew playing in *Trelawny of the Wells* by A. W. Pinero, taking the part of the flamboyant Ferdy Gadd (for which he'd received excellent notices) and rehearsing Shakespeare's *Julius Caesar* during the day.

One night during the Trelawny run, 28 June to be exact, Andrew, having given the matter a great deal of thought, brought Sheila home to his rooms after the show with the intention of springing a surprise on her.

Sheila dropped into a chair as soon as she entered the flat. 'Lord, am I whacked,' she sighed. *Julius Caesar*, due to open the following week, was proving a particularly heavy play from the wardrobe point of view because so many costumes were needed, a lot of which Sheila and Pat were having to make themselves.

Andrew poured two hefty whiskies and gave her one. 'You take a drink of that,' he instructed. 'Then close your eyes and hold out your left hand.'

When her eyes were firmly closed he groped in his pocket for the small box he'd acquired at the jeweller's earlier that day during his lunch break, and placed it in the palm of her hand. As he stepped back her eyes immediately snapped open again.

Sheila stared at the box for a few seconds, then placed her drink carefully on the floor. Slowly, with trembling fingers, she opened the box. In the middle of the pale blue satin interior was a diamond ring.

All she could hear was the hammering of her heart. 'What's this?' she whispered.

'A surprise.'

'A surprise? But what does it mean?'

He knelt beside her. 'It means that I'm asking you to marry me.'

She looked up at him, then brought her gaze back to the ring. 'Why?' she demanded softly.

He knew what she wanted him to say, so he said it, and it was the truth. 'I love you,' he whispered. 'I love you more than I ever thought possible.'

Tears came into her eyes which she quickly wiped away.

'It'll mean moving around a bit until we eventually get settled in London. Will you mind that?' he asked.

She shook her head. As long as they were together, that was the main thing; she'd have gone to Timbuctoo if he'd wanted.

'I love *you*, Andrew,' she admitted. It was the first time she'd ever told him.

He took her hands in his and said that he could no more imagine life without her now than he could imagine being anything other than an actor; as far as he was concerned the match was perfect. Sheila's eyes were filled with tears as she whispered that she couldn't imagine life without him either.

He watched eagerly while she tried on the ring which, completely against the odds, was a perfect fit.

It was a gorgeous ring. Sheila held it up to the light, causing its stones to shoot off bluish rays. It must have cost a great deal, but that didn't matter at all. If it had been made of tin she would have been just as proud to wear it.

Throwing her arms round him she pulled him close and kissed him. 'Oh my darling,' she whispered, holding him tightly. 'I have never been so happy in my life. I never dreamed it was possible.'

Andrew looked down, as though studying the carpet. 'As we're now engaged,' he said hesitantly, 'I was wondering if . . . how about you staying the night?'

'Do you take back the ring if I don't?' she teased.

Smiling, he shook his head.

She wanted to stay with him – very much so. But one thing had to aired between them. It was a subject she'd skirted clear of before because it belonged to the past and had nothing to do with him. But now that he'd asked her to be his wife it was only right and proper that he knew. 'I'm not a virgin,' she said bluntly, suddenly, her voice and body tense.

He'd been almost certain that she wasn't, despite her steadfast refusal to sleep with him, and had asked himself if that mattered to him, to which the answer had been an unqualified no. She'd loved Eric and given herself to Eric – how could he hold that against her when he was asking her to do the same? She would have married Eric if he had lived; now she would marry him, which was his good fortune.

'Well I'm not a virgin either, so neither of us can complain,' he replied.

She laughed. It was an honest answer, like the man himself. Then she was in his arms again, kissing him, touching him, being kissed and touched in return.

Breaking away, she disappeared into the bathroom. She took her time, finally slipping into one of his clean shirts. She looked at herself in the mirror, then combed her hair again. She wanted to be just right for him.

He was sitting up in bed reading the paper with a frown on his face when she returned. 'What is it?' she asked.

Immediately he tossed the paper aside. 'Some Austrian Archduke has been assassinated at a place called Sarajevo.'

'Is that important?'

'Only to the Austrians I should think,' he said, and held out his arms for her.

Sheila was trying to get a stain out of a white toga and Pat was hemming a skirt when the door to the Wardrobe banged open and Andrew burst in, standing rigidly in the doorway staring at them.

'We've just declared war on Germany,' he announced in a tight, dazed voice. The date was 4 August.

'Oh my God!' exclaimed Pat, sinking back on to the cutting table.

Sheila was stunned. Like many she'd convinced herself it would never come to this, that sanity would prevail.

'Listen!' said Pat, and crossing to the closest window, opened it wide. The sound of cheering and singing invaded the Wardrobe, a little way off at present but coming closer with every second.

A few minutes later an excited procession passed along the street below, some men waving their caps as they marched, others their fists. A few women were dancing with their skirts pulled up almost to their knees while others were holding poles from which union jacks and lion rampants fluttered. Children of all ages were dashing in and out of the adults. The atmosphere was of a carnival.

'War,' whispered Sheila, the reality sinking home, and glanced at Andrew in sudden fright.

'It'll all be over by Christmas, bound to be,' Pat murmured.

The three of them stood at the window watching the procession till it finally tailed off, then vanished from sight.

'All over by Christmas, bound to be,' Pat repeated, this time with more conviction in her voice.

Sheila stood watching in the wings while Andrew and the rest of the cast formed themselves into a line to take their bows. It was the final performance of the first week of *Julius Caesar*.

The house was only a quarter full, disappointing for a Saturday night, even if it was Shakespeare; but with the country newly at war people were bound to have things on their minds other than entertainment.

The performance had been a splendid one, but nonetheless the applause was thin, starting to die away after only the second bow. The Deputy Stage Manager running the Prompt Corner gave the cue and a stage hand started to run down the curtain.

And then it happened; a solitary female voice, reedy but filled with emotion, began singing 'God Save the King'.

The man on the curtain paused, uncertain whether to carry on or not. He looked over to the bewildered DSM who didn't know what to do either.

A second voice joined the first, then another and another, till the national anthem was ringing throughout the auditorium.

The actors, caught with the rag still above their heads, came to attention and joined in.

Sheila could feel her skin prickling with the sentiment

of the moment, with the unity of everyone there. Here was a reflection of the national will, of defiance and stubbornness, of loyalty to, and support for the Crown. The message was clear and unequivocal; it wasn't only God Save the King; it was also sod the Kaiser.

There are moments in the theatre, often unscripted, which are electrifying, and this was one of them.

The conclusion of the anthem was followed by a few seconds' hiatus, then simultaneously, as though cued, everyone began to clap. And this time the clapping, despite the small numbers involved, threatened to raise the roof.

Sheila noticed that when Andrew and the other men came off stage after the rag had finally been lowered their chins were jutting out and they were walking with more pride than she'd ever previously seen. Already they were like soldiers, soldiers marching into battle.

She felt a wave of fear and nausea come over her.

Later that night, after they had made love and were lying together, his arms still around her, her head against his shoulder, he began talking about what he called the 'grand finale'. Everyone had been full of it backstage, and the management were so impressed they were going to have the national anthem sung after every show, the cast and other employees taking the lead.

And talking about rumours, he went on, unaware of the look of worry that had come into her eyes, had she heard that German soldiers were cutting the breasts off captured Belgian nurses?

But she had a rumour of her own to tell him; a great battle had been fought in the North Sea and the German navy was now at the bottom.

Andrew laughed. The way he'd heard the story it was the British dreadnoughts which had been sunk.

'Norrie Brunton, the man they call Caveman, has joined up. He expects to be going away sometime next week,' said Sheila in a low voice.

Andrew said that men were joining up in tens of

thousands, the response, apparently, to Kitchener's poster 'Your Country Needs You!' That poster with its pointing finger seemed to be everywhere. And every man who saw the poster knew the finger was pointing directly at him.

She reached out just to touch him, to remind herself of his solidity, of his aliveness, of the exquisite beauty of their love. Had it been such a short time ago that she had believed she would never again be happy? Never again know love?

She comforted herself with the thought that the recruiting offices were accepting single men but not married ones yet. Like everyone else, Sheila believed that the conflict would be over sooner rather than later – long before they got round to taking married men. It was up to her, therefore, to save Andrew from his own impetuousness.

'Why don't we get married right away?' she asked, suddenly cuddling against him.

'There's no rush is there?' he asked smoothly, knowing damn well that she believed there was.

'Well,' she said softly, almost shyly, kissing his chest. 'I could get pregnant any day . . . I wouldn't want that without being married.'

Andrew smiled to himself, kissing the top of her head. She thought she was being clever, but she wasn't pulling any wool over his eyes. He knew precisely what was going on in that pretty head of hers, and if it was possible he loved her all the more because of it.

The theatre was going dark for three weeks after *Julius Caesar*, he reminded her. For the first blank week he had to be away from Glasgow on business, unavoidable business, but they'd be married the moment he got back. 'How's that?' he asked, his lips seeking out hers.

'You promise?' moving her mouth just out of reach. 'You won't change your mind?'

'I swear it.'

'And what's this urgent business?'

'Just something I've got to see to in England.'

'But you'll be back in a week?'

His hand moved along her body in a way that was both startling and familiar. 'In a week,' he whispered. 'In just one week.'

Sheila glanced yet again at her watch. It was six minutes to eleven and they were booked to be married on the hour. Where oh where was he?

'Are you sure he knows the address?' asked Pat.

'Of course he does,' snapped Sheila. She'd told him no less than four times when they'd spoken on the telephone the night before last. He couldn't have got it wrong.

Perhaps his train was late? Or perhaps he'd missed the damn thing altogether! She'd strangle him if he had, she promised herself.

She'd wanted to meet him at the station, but he'd been insistent that they meet in front of the Register Office, although for the life of her she couldn't think why.

Martha Street Register Office she'd told him. She could hear the words as she'd said them into the telephone echoing in her mind. A sudden terrible thought struck her. Was there more than one Martha Street? Could he be even now standing in some other part of Glasgow, cursing her the way she was cursing him?

Control yourself, girl, she told herself. If there was another Martha Street the chances of it also having a Register Office must be . . . what? A million to one? Something like that.

'The train might have got stuck at Beattock – that's always happening,' Pat suggested.

He should have come back yesterday, then. He should have given himself some time in hand, Sheila thought.

'How do I look?' she asked Pat for the hundredth time.

'Absolutely smashing,' Pat replied, unable to resist a smile. In fact, Sheila looked exceptionally beautiful today, despite her nerves.

156

Sheila smoothed down the sides of her skirt. She was wearing a grey, two-piece costume she'd bought in Arnott Simpson, considering it elegant and just the thing for a wartime register wedding. Only now she wasn't so sure. 'Is it too severe, do you think?' she wondered out loud.

'It's just perfect,' Pat assured her, trying to hide her own jitters as best she could. Where was the bloody man! Typical actor, thought Pat, a rotten timekeeper.

Perhaps he'd got cold feet and was standing her up? As soon as the thought occurred to Sheila she started to tremble all over. He wouldn't do that to her – not her Andrew, surely! Tears started to stream down her face.

Suddenly Pat clutched Sheila's arm. 'Chalky White,' she said, pointing to a familiar figure hurrying towards them. Chalky was an actor in the company, and a great friend of Andrew's.

Sheila realized then that Chalky wasn't alone; that he was with the figure in uniform striding alongside him. A look into the face above the uniform caused her to give a small cry of anguish, for the face was Andrew's, the uniform that of the Royal Flying Corps.

Andrew, grinning sheepishly, immediately began to apologize for being late. En route from the station, he and Chalky had stopped off for a quick drink and somehow they'd spent longer at the bar than they'd intended. Chalky was to be the Best Man, he explained.

It was plain to Pat that Sheila wanted to be alone with Andrew. 'Come on, Chalky,' she said, grabbing him by the arm. 'Let's go inside to find out what room we're meant to go to.' There was no doubt it was an order. Meekly, he followed her up the steps and in through the glass-panelled doors.

Sheila stared at the uniform and the face smiling at her above it. He was handsome in it, right enough, there was no denying that. Then, the tears still streaming down her face, she laid into him. Why hadn't he told her what he planned to do? Why had he gone sneaking off behind her back to join up?

157

His defence was that he'd known she would have made it as difficult for him as she was able, if she'd known. Could she deny that? Of course she couldn't. And as for being sneaky, what did she think she'd been in trying to get him to the altar as quickly as possible just to save him from entering the Forces?

Sheila dabbed at her eyes, trying to save her make-up from any further destruction. 'What about the theatre?' she nearly whispered.

'It's all taken care of,' he assured her.

'How long before you have to return to England?'

'Three days,' he replied, not looking into her eyes.

'I remember that day we went down to the coast, you said you'd love to be able to fly. It seems you're about to achieve your ambition.'

'That's why I chose the RFC,' he replied quietly.

'I could hit you!' she choked.

'I'd prefer it if you kissed me,' he smiled.

'I would understand if you didn't want to marry me now until all this is over,' he whispered, not disentangling himself from her embrace.

She wished her tears would stop. 'If we've only got three days then we'd better make the most of them,' she said at last.

Hand-in-hand, they climbed the steps and went into the Register Office.

5

It was early November. Sheila was sitting in Wardrobe, staring at the latest death and casualty lists issued from the great and terrible battle being fought at the Ypres salient in Flanders, a battle that was now raging into its fourth week.

Day by day, Sheila had been following the seemingly

endless lists in the newspapers, growing more and more appalled at the carnage being wrought, all the young men dying so far from home.

She thanked God her Andrew was still in England. At least she thought he was. He certainly had been up until a few days ago according to his latest letter which had arrived that morning. It was encouraging to know casualties amongst the RFC and their naval equivalent, the RNAS had so far been light. She could only pray they continued that way.

Sheila gratefully accepted the cup of tea Pat handed her. 'How frustrating it is to be doing such silly work in times like these,' she sighed to Pat. 'I should be doing something for the war effort. Making some contribution.'

Pat mumbled her agreement, peering over Sheila's shoulder at the printed lists. Pat had lost a cousin the previous week at a place called Messines Ridge.

Pat thought about her cousin who'd come from down in the borders where his family had farmed since the days long ago, when the area had been known as The Debatable Lands, debatable between Scotland and England that is.

He'd been a carrot top with a wandering left eye she recalled; small, but wiry, and surprising in strength for his size. He'd been a lot younger than she, by twenty years or more, and the last time she'd seen him he was only a wee lad, mad keen on collecting birds' eggs. Now he was dead at a place called Messines Ridge, and the thought brought a lump to her throat. In her jewellery box back at the digs she still had a blown blackbird's egg he'd given her.

'Ever heard of the VADs?' Pat asked.

Sheila had. There had been several references to them in the newspapers recently. 'Aren't they nurses?'

'Voluntary Aid Detachments,' explained Pat. 'They're women volunteers who assist the nurses,' going on to say that she knew there was a branch of the organization not

far from the theatre. I heard about it in the McKillops'
cafe,' she added.

Helping the sick and wounded appealed to Sheila. Not
only would it be a contribution to the war effort, it would
also be a constructive one.

'I'd be willing to join – what about you?' she asked Pat.

'I'll find out what I can, shall I?' offered Pat. 'And I'll
fix an appointment for the two of us as soon as possible.'

For the first time since Andrew had gone back to
England, Sheila felt bright and cheered within herself.

Commandant McNair of the St Andrew's Ambulance
Association, one of the number of societies affiliated to
the British Red Cross Society, was a fierce-looking
woman who gave the impression she could've dealt
singlehandedly with the entire German Army, and probably the Austro-Hungarian Army as well.

'So you want to be VADs,' she growled, prowling
round Sheila and Pat, eyeing them from head to toe.

'If you'll accept us,' Sheila answered politely.

Commandant McNair stuck her face close to Sheila's
and said it wasn't all forehead bathing and hand holding
you know. Many of the things a VAD was expected to
do were dirty, disgusting, and anything but romantic.
How would she feel about washing a soldier's shitty
backside for example?

Sheila replied coolly that she'd had three brothers, so
having to wash a man's backside, shitty or otherwise,
wasn't going to offend her any.

Commandant McNair grunted; this one was a definite
possible she thought. Transferring her gaze to Pat she
asked Pat what her reaction was to what she'd just
said.

Pat answered she'd spent nearly her entire working life
in the theatre, which was just like that – apparent gloss on
the outside, an awful lot of shit underneath. She'd cope.

'You'll have to study before going on the wards.

You'll need a first-aid certificate and another in home nursing first,' Commandant McNair explained.

'How long will that take?' asked Sheila. McNair replied that that depended on what the person doing the studying had between her ears.

'And how many hours would we be expected to work in a week?' asked Pat, bravely.

The Commandant replied simply, 'As many as you are needed. Some of our women are putting in a hundred hours plus on the wards.' Why did they think more volunteers were so desperately needed?

Pat was taken aback. She'd thought this was a part-time organization. If the women were putting in so many hours, were they being paid? Commandant McNair explained tartly that their ladies did not expect a pecuniary reward for what they did. The society was strictly a voluntary one.

'Well, I'm sorry for taking up your time,' said Pat, blushing. 'But I'm a working woman and I need to earn my living.'

'And what about you, Mrs Lack?' Commandant McNair queried, turning on Sheila.

With Sheila things were different. Prior to leaving, Andrew had told her he had a monthly allowance paid into his bank account, an account he had instructed the bank to make into a joint one. While away he would have his RFC pay to take care of his needs. His allowance was therefore available to Sheila to either save or use as she saw fit. Because of this, unlike Pat, she didn't have to continue to earn her own living.

Going behind her desk, the Commandant wrote Sheila's name and address in a black book. That done, she informed Sheila that she was accepted to start studying. When could she begin attending the daily classes?

'I'll have to give proper notice at the theatre first. As soon as that's served, I'll be free to start the classes.'

Leaving the Commandant's office they made their way back to Wardrobe. 'I'm going to miss you like hell, you know,' said Pat glumly once the door had shut behind them.

'We'll keep in touch,' promised Sheila.

Pat pulled out a bottle of sherry she'd secreted away. 'Sod these poxy costumes – let's get drunk,' she said, trying to sound cheerful.

Sheila put her arms around Pat, hugging her warmly. 'I'll get some glasses,' she half laughed, half cried.

Sheila rubbed her eyes which were sore from staring at the textbook in front of her. Time for a break she decided, and yawning, rose and crossed to the window.

Since their wedding she had been living in what used to be Andrew's rooms, and was now well settled in. She had rearranged things to suit herself, including getting rid of that dreadful aspidistra and replacing it with several attractive potted plants she'd bought from the local florist. She'd been brought up to believe that aspidistras were unlucky; no fisherman would give one house room.

The street outside looked eerie. The streetlamps, dimmed since September, combined with the light fog to make the city streets look both foreign and unreal.

Staring into the soft yellow and grey gloom, Sheila thought of Andrew who'd been over in France for some weeks now. He had gone to join the No. 5 Squadron, flying a plane called a Henry Farman which he described as a sort of box kite with wings.

According to Andrew, his main job was that of reconnaissance; flying over enemy positions and then reporting back what he'd seen. He'd been at pains to tell her that none of the planes on either side were armed, if you discounted pistols and rifles, that is. The greatest danger, apart from the wind carrying you so far behind enemy lines that you couldn't get home again (the wind, he said, always favoured the enemy in this respect) was ground fire. The trick was to stay above that. He, of course, always made sure that he did.

Andrew had become friendly with a man called McCudden, of whom he thought particularly highly, and another named Strange who'd made a reputation for himself by going aloft with a machine gun strapped to the nacelle of his Farman. But the CO, a Major Higgins, had promptly commanded him to dismantle it on his return to the ground.

In Andrew's estimation, the men of the RFC were an odd bunch: nearly all individualists, many of whom had been private flyers before the war; others roped in from various cavalry regiments in the belief that a keen eye and good sense of balance were essential in flying aeroplanes.

They may have been an odd bunch, but they were also a terrific bunch. Andrew thought each and every one of them deserving of respect and affection.

It was the poor bloody infantry he felt sorry for. Dug into their trenches, they were taking a terrible pasting. He was glad he'd joined the RFC. Unwittingly, it had been the wisest of moves on his part.

As for the flying itself, he absolutely adored it, and they all spoke well of his ability, even McCudden, who was far and away the best flyer in the Squadron.

With a wrench, Sheila brought her thoughts back from Andrew and France. It was time to return to her studying. There was a lot for her to get through yet before being able to finally call it a night.

She returned to sit again at the table, and within seconds was once more immersed in her textbook.

Cowcaddens General Hospital was a Gothic edifice of dirty grey stone and towering spires, looking to Sheila like the evil magician's castle of fairy tales.

Once through the doors the smell hit her immediately; a combination of antiseptic, anaesthetic, and . . . And what? It was something she couldn't put a name to. Later she did. The hard-to-define ingredients were very obvious really; they were called fear and pain.

The highly polished floor squeaked beneath her duty shoes as she followed the signs directing her to the administration section.

There were nine girls already assembled in the sparsely furnished room into which she was eventually shown. All of them turned to stare at her as she came in. Automatically she smiled, but not all of them smiled back.

She made a beeline for an empty chair in a corner and sat. A dark-haired girl close by nodded to her, and she nodded in return; but the girl didn't make any attempt to start a conversation, so neither did she.

An eleventh girl arrived, went through the process of being scrutinized, and joined several girls standing together whom she evidently knew.

Sheila was the only one from the St Andrew's Ambulance Association. The rest were from either the Red Cross or the St John Ambulance Association, obvious from the colour of their uniforms: blue for the Red Cross, grey for St John, with the Red Cross or St John emblem on their apron bibs.

'So I told her, she didn't have to worry about that as she'd probably seen more cocks than many a chicken farmer,' a tall girl with sandy-coloured hair and a beaky nose said loudly in a frightfully Kelvinside accent. Her companions burst into laughter, while most of the others in the room smiled, some nervously.

'You *didn't* say that Georgina!' one of the tall girl's companions exclaimed in an equally plummy voice.

'I most certainly did,' Georgina replied, and she and her companions burst out laughing again.

Georgina and company were unmistakably upper-class girls, as were a number of the others, she judged. The remainder, after careful scrutiny, Sheila guessed to be middle class. Which meant that she, the only working-class woman there, was the odd one out.

Sheila stared at the braying Georgina. That's a right bitch, that one, she thought.

A final girl arrived, completing the group, and directly

behind her a nurse who introduced herself as Matron Carswell. There was a brief speech of welcome, then Matron Carswell read out a list of names: the VAD and the ward she was assigned to. Sheila's ward was called McLaggan.

On reaching the end of the list, Matron Carswell snapped her notebook shut and told them to find their own way to their assigned wards; it would be good practice for learning the layout of the hospital, she said, and swept from the room.

Girls assigned to the same ward were teaming up to find their way together, but Sheila had to go on her own as she'd been the only one assigned to McLaggan. She finally found it, on the fifth floor, but as she entered through its green swing doors an agonized scream rang out from within.

'Who are you?' a voice demanded.

The speaker was in the uniform of a Ward Sister and looked desperately tired, the sort of tired that comes from a combination of strain, overwork, and a great deal of lost sleep.

Sheila gave her name, and the information she'd been assigned to McLaggan by Matron Carswell.

'Bed six on the left, assist the nurse there,' Sister snapped, hurrying past Sheila and out of the ward.

Bed six had screens around it. Sheila went quietly behind them, there to discover a rather horsey-faced nurse removing the covering from a dressing trolley. The patient was a young man in his late teens whose left arm was heavily bandaged.

'Excuse me,' Sheila whispered hesitantly. 'Sister sent me to assist.' Barely looking at her, the nurse told her to remove the bandage. The young man watched fearfully as she started to do so.

The bandage came away, and the dressing with it, losing such a terrible stench that Sheila thought she might be ill.

The nurse then handed Sheila a metal bowl and told her

165

to stand a little to the side while she attended to the wound which went clean to the bone and was suppurating badly.

The bowl contained strong antiseptic into which the nurse dipped a wad of cotton wool. She then applied the sodden wad directly to the wound.

Sheila blanched and the young man whimpered. 'Sorry, Tim, but it has to be done,' the nurse said shortly. Disposing of the first wad, she then applied a second.

The nurse re-bandaged Tim's arm herself, doing so briskly and efficiently, yet with care and tenderness. When Tim had been attended to, the nurse instructed Sheila to bring the screens down to bed eleven where another dressing had to be changed, then wheeled away the dressings trolley leaving Sheila to get on with it.

As Sheila manipulated the first of the three screens down the ward, she saw that Sister was standing at the top of the ward watching her. She also counted two nurses other than horsey face moving amongst the beds, and one other VAD.

The man in bed eleven only had one leg, bandaged from mid calf downwards, and was unconscious. When the screens were in place round the bed, the same nurse reappeared with the trolly, from behind another set of screens, and told Sheila to remove the bandage, then disappeared again leaving the trolley behind.

Slowly, Sheila unwrapped the bandage, revealing a foot that was completely black. She stared in horror when one of the toes suddenly fell off.

Trembling all over, she bent down and picked it up. It was dry to the touch, and black inside as well as out. There was no blood.

For a wild moment she had the insane idea that she could somehow stick the toe back on. What with? Glue? she asked herself and gave a short, hysterical laugh.

A hand appeared to take the toe from her grasp. Glancing up she saw it was Sister. 'It wasn't my fault. It just dropped of its own accord,' she stuttered.

'First day on the wards?'

Sheila nodded.

It was best for them to be thrown in at the deep end, that way time was saved on weeding out the ones who were temperamentally unsuitable and time was of the essence, Sister thought.

'Can you continue?' she asked.

Sheila took a deep breath. She was going to see an awful lot worse than a toe falling off, she told herself. 'I'm all right now,' she answered gamely.

Sister personally put a new dressing and bandage on the black foot, telling Sheila in a soft whisper as she worked that it was doubtful the patient would last the day. He was a captain in the Seaforth Highlanders called Haliburton who was being kept heavily sedated with morphine, receiving an injection every two hours.

When Captain Haliburton had been attended to, Sister told Sheila to go away up to her room which was just inside the ward doors and clearly marked. The kettle was kept there, and Sheila was to take it into the sterilizing room opposite and brew up. 'You'll find everything you need in the cupboard underneath the poisons cabinet,' she added cheerfully as Sheila walked away.

By the end of Sheila's first shift, which lasted twelve hours, she had swollen feet and numbed senses.

She had also wheeled Captain Haliburton's body down to the mortuary.

As the days passed Sheila's life became a continual round of cleaning, bed making, blanket baths and temperatures.

More wounded arrived, some by sea, others by rail, a great many still verminous and filthy from weeks in the trenches, the ones who'd come by rail often exhausted by extended weeks of travel.

Each man was supposed to be labelled with his name, number, regiment, type of wound and whether or not an anti-tetanus injection had been given, but sometimes the label read GOK: God Only Knows.

Wounds often went septic and the pus had to be drained out through tubes which it was Sheila's duty to clean. This tube cleaning was constant, as were changing the dressings and the application of hot fomentations.

Ether and chloroform were notoriously difficult to administer and tended to have an adverse reaction on the patients; pain killers were distributed so sparingly that they might have consisted of a hundred per cent gold dust.

Gradually Sheila got used to the stink of suppurating and septic wounds till finally the smell ceased to bother her, even the noxious stench of gangrene.

Then, in March, news started to filter back of a great new battle being fought at a place called Neuve Chapelle, and soon after that the casualties began to arrive in torrents, packing every ward to capacity. When ward saturation was reached, patients spilled out into the corridors which soon became lined with beds.

It was then that the decision was made that the VADs would take up residence in the hospital, only leaving on their days off. This was a decision regrettably arrived at, Sister assured them, but necessary due to the ever mounting pressure on the hospital. She hoped they all understood. The only space available for a dormitory for the VADs was in the bowels of the hospital, directly behind the mortuary.

Two days after the announcement, Sheila, clutching a suitcase containing personal belongings, presented herself at the dormitory where she was assigned a bed.

The first night confusion reigned. 'It's like being back at bloody school!' Georgina Murchison-Stewart announced. She was the same Georgina who'd been part of Sheila's intake, and over the next few days she set herself up as self-appointed leader of the VADs.

'What about you, Lack, where do you come from?' Georgina called out to Sheila one evening, addressing her loudly from across the dormitory.

Sheila was sipping a cup of cocoa. 'The name's either Sheila or Mrs Lack,' she replied levelly, heartily disliking Georgina and the way Georgina had about her.

Georgina's eyes narrowed. Up until now, she had more or less dismissed Sheila as beneath her contempt, but something in Sheila's tone warned her that here was another very strong personality – perhaps even one to rival her own.

Georgina's cronies were all staring curiously at Sheila. From her speech she was plainly working class, yet there was nothing subservient or deferential about her. If she knew she was inferior to them she certainly didn't show it.

Sheila continued sipping her cocoa, knowing Georgina's eyes were riveted on her.

'Where do you come from *Mrs* Lack?' Georgina asked eventually, smirking to her friends over the cleverness of her own mockery.

The dormitory had gone quiet. Georgina and her cronies weren't the only ones curious about Sheila. Though there had been a few other working-class VADs at this hospital, she was currently the only one, and it was obvious that if the others accepted her at all it was only because there was a war on.

'I come from the east coast of Scotland,' she said evenly. 'From a village called Dragonholme.'

'And what do people do in Dragonholme?' asked Georgina archly.

Sheila smiled her sweetest smile, 'They fish.'

'A fishergirl!' Georgina exclaimed in her most patrician tones.

Elspeth Crichton, one of Georgina's pals, sniggered behind her hand.

'Is your husband a fisherman then?' asked Georgina. She might have been interviewing a potential scullery maid.

169

'He's at the Front.'

'Ah, a Tommy!' winking at the audience. It was clear what she thought of Tommies.

'And do you have a man at the Front?' Sheila asked with a smile. She already knew the answer from a conversation she'd overheard in the canteen.

Georgina scowled, but made no reply.

'Do you?' Sheila persisted.

'I have many men, if you must know,' Georgina snapped.

'Of course,' Sheila agreed sweetly, and, turning her back on Georgina, effectively dismissed her.

Georgina's face flushed bright pink with anger. She had no boyfriend, at the Front or anywhere else, a situation that did nothing to improve her disposition. She glanced around edgily. Some of the girls were grinning, others denied their poker faces by the expression of amusement in their eyes.

I'll get you for that you little peasant, she thought, glaring at Sheila.

The following night, after what had been a particularly arduous day (they'd lost four men on the ward and two from the corridor outside the ward), Sheila came down to the dormitory from the canteen where the food had been of its usual low standard.

She sat on her bed to take off her shoes, and right away the niff hit her. When she saw the bump under the bedclothes she thought, Christ! they've stuck an amputated limb in my bed!

But it wasn't a limb, as she discovered on peeling back the bedclothes; it was a dead tunny roughly three feet long.

She stared at the fish, thinking how incongruous it looked in these surroundings. Across the dormitory Georgina and her cronies were giggling, obviously considering this a great jape, to use one of their own words.

A girl in one of the beds next to Sheila, saw the tunny and screamed, which caused the giggling to erupt into full-blown laughter.

Grasping hold of the tunny's tail with both hands Sheila lifted it up so that the entire dormitory could see it. 'Has anyone lost a sardine?' she inquired straight-faced, which produced hoots from all round.

She had a sudden inspiration then of how to turn this to her advantage. Walking down to the one table that served the entire dormitory for letter writing and the like she heaved the tunny up on to it. She'd be back in a tick, she said, and hurried off to the kitchens where she succeeded in borrowing a boning knife.

Returning to the dormitory she flourished the knife aloft, declaring that as a person or persons unknown had been kind enough to donate the fish, the very least she could do was give the dormitory a professional demonstration on how to dress it. All those interested gather round, she instructed, and every single girl did, even Georgina and her chums, albeit bitterly disappointed that this wasn't turning out at all the way they'd hoped.

Sheila hadn't lost the knack of her old skills, gutting and boning the tunny in a few seconds. When she finished with a flourish the watching girls applauded.

'Now, who would like something decent to eat after that rotten food we had in the canteen?'

Sheila took the tunny to the kitchens, where she persuaded the staff to allow her to use one of the ovens. When it was cooked to a recipe of Peg's she took it back to the dormitory where everyone (with the exception of Georgina and her group) had a good tuck in.

'Some bright idea,' muttered a piqued Georgina, glowering at Elspeth whose idea it had been.

'It looks delicious. I wish I had some,' Elspeth murmured wistfully in reply.

Sheila's bed reeked of tunny when she got into it, but that didn't bother her in the least. One up for us fishergirls she thought jubilantly, starting to drift off to sleep.

For the first time in a long time she dreamt about the Dragonholme disaster, seeing again the *Bluebell*, the *Gypsy Queen* and all those other bonny boats disappearing into the sea. Vividly, she saw the *Gypsy Queen* beneath the water and Eric, struggling frantically, floating off to be swallowed in a single gulp by a monstrous tunny the size of a whale.

She awoke just before dawn covered in cold sweat and filled with fright.

Nor did she get back to sleep before it was time to get up and start the long hard day ahead of her.

On 18 April Sheila was called into Sister's office. 'It seems your husband has connections in high places. He's back in Glasgow and you're to be given seven days off. He'll pick you up at the front entrance at four-thirty,' she said shortly.

Sheila stood staring at Sister, trying to make sense of her words. Andrew was home. Andrew was in Glasgow. Giving a cry of delight, she leapt in the air.

'I take it,' said Sister, 'that this is good news.'

'Oh, yes, the very best,' Sheila replied excitedly.

Seven days' holiday to spend with Andrew, just like that, completely out of the blue. It was unbelievable!

'He's timed things well as we're comparatively quiet at the moment,' Sister continued, her mouth unsmiling, but her voice almost humorous.

Sheila glanced at the clock on the wall behind Sister's desk. There were thirty-five minutes before his arrival. She was restless with impatience for those minutes to tick away.

'Well,' said Sister drily, 'I can see I'll get no more work out of you today. Why don't you go off duty now and get yourself ready?'

'Oh, thank you, Sister,' Sheila effused, so excited that she reached out to shake the older woman's hand. 'Thank you so much.'

As the door closed behind her Sister called out, 'Remember, Mrs Lack, no running in the corridors!'

At twenty-five past the hour, Sheila was standing outside the front entrance, smiling expectantly. She had butterflies in her tum and kept hopping from foot to foot, causing more than one person entering the hospital to give her a sideways glance.

Dead on time, the Silver Ghost, retrieved from the garage which had been storing it, came into view. Then the car was parked and Andrew was whirling her round and round, the pair of them laughing joyously, unable to stop themselves from kissing. A passing doctor gave them a wolf whistle, but neither paid any attention.

She had so many questions to ask – thousands it seemed – but for the moment it was enough to have him there beside her, with his arms around her and his lips on hers.

'Oh, Andrew,' she said over and over, her heart so full that she could barely speak. 'Oh, Andrew, I've missed you so.'

'Not half as much as I've missed you, love,' he laughed. 'This is one of the first times in my life that I felt justified in using my connections to get special privileges.'

'So how *did* you manage to pull this off?' she wanted to know, so happy to be sitting beside him, so far away from the nightmare of the war.

Just for an instant the smile left his face. 'I'll explain about that later,' he said, brightening again. 'Later,' giving her meaningful wink.

'Oh, you'll have forgotten by then,' she laughed.

It was only later, while she lay on the bed, watching him across the room as he poured them each a whisky, that she remembered how close they really were to the guns and the deaths.

She noticed then how much older he looked. Of course, all the men who came back from the Front had aged but with Andrew it was something more.

Something about his manner; about the way he moved and did things. The expression in his eyes. It was not just his body which had been changed by the war: it was his heart and mind as well.

'How did you get your leave?' she asked again.

He came to the bed and sat beside her. 'It's a compassionate leave,' he said slowly. 'The old girl's dying. I just got word a few days ago. That's why everything was so rushed.'

'Your mother?' Gently, she took his hand. 'But what happened?'

'The doctors say it's cancer. They don't give her more than a few months to live.'

He would be driving home in the morning to spend some time with his mother before she went, and he'd be taking Sheila with him.

'If you . . . if you'd rather go by yourself– ' she began.

'No,' he said, taking her once more into his arms. 'I wouldn't.'

They set off early the next morning, and arrived in Manchester late that afternoon. It was Sheila's first trip south of the border. Her excitement delighted him.

The Lack house was situated in the suburb of Withington, just off the Wilbraham Road. Set in its own grounds it was the largest house she'd ever been in, with the exception of Dragonholme Hall. It was constructed of what had once been red bricks, which were now black with soot and grime. 'That house is a hundred and twenty-seven years old,' Andrew informed her as he parked the Silver Ghost in the driveway. 'And was probably only its original colour for twenty-seven of them.'

Of course, she had known all along that Andrew's family was rich – his father had been a successful industrialist – but she had not quite realized just how rich. Not even the Rolls had prepared her for this.

174

'Don't be nervous. Mother will adore you, I know she will,' he assured her as he helped her from the car.

But Sheila was nervous, and even Andrew couldn't calm her. She prayed that Mrs Lack wasn't going to be some grand lady who despised her on sight. She didn't want Andrew to be caught between them, his mother and his wife.

Ollerenshaw, the butler, answered their ring. 'Mr Andrew,' the old man cried in delight. 'It is absolutely marvellous to have you home.' And then added, the perfect English butler again, 'I am very sorry about your mother.'

Andrew introduced Ollerenshaw to Sheila. 'It is an honour and pleasure to meet the young master's wife,' he said solemnly. 'All of us are looking forward to having you here.'

Taking them inside the house, Ollerenshaw showed them the room that had been specially prepared for their coming. Andrew left Sheila there to get washed and changed while he went to see his mother.

On the writing bureau near the window was a picture which caught her attention. It was old and sepia tinted, the photograph of an earnest young man and a bonny young woman, clearly his wife. Sheila recognized them immediately as Andrew's parents – the resemblance was unmistakable.

In the past, Andrew had often spoken to her about his father, for whom he'd had great admiration. Oliver Lack had inherited a small ball-bearing factory which he'd soon turned into a large ball-bearing factory. One by one, he'd bought other small factories after that, and done the same to them. At the time of his death he'd owned seven booming factories in all.

Oliver Lack had always planned that Andrew, his only child, would succeed him in business. He'd been bitterly disappointed when Andrew had announced his intention to become an actor.

Oliver and Sarah Lack had done their utmost to

persuade Andrew to change his mind, but to no avail. Finally, though reluctantly, they'd accepted that Andrew would follow his chosen profession, the theatre.

It was to their eternal credit that once they'd accepted this there had been no recriminations, and the pair of them had come to see Andrew the first time he'd gone on stage, even though the part had been a dismally small one.

When Oliver Lack died, his factories had been sold, and the realized capital invested. When Sarah Lack followed her husband, everything would go to Andrew.

She was just finishing making herself presentable when Andrew reappeared. 'My mother would like to meet you now,' he said, looking at her with pride.

'How do I look?' Sheila asked. She'd chosen to wear a simple but attractive dress that she'd run up for herself when working at the Queen's Theatre.

'Absolutely fine,' Andrew answered, giving her a kiss.

'You're certain it's all right?'

'Couldn't be more so.'

'How is she?' she asked at last, as casually as she could.

Andrew's eyes clouded over. 'Skin and bone. I nearly cried at the sight of her.' He was silent for a moment, staring out through the window behind her. 'But she can't wait to meet you.'

Andrew led her along the corridor, and up a flight of carpeted stairs. Pausing before an oak door he gave Sheila's arm a reassuring squeeze. Then, taking an audible breath he rapped on the door.

A reedy voice called 'Come in.'

Inside the bedroom, the curtains had been drawn, the one source of illumination a bright bedside lamp. Mrs Lack, white-haired and terribly frail-looking, sat propped up against a bolster and pillows. She wore a shawl round her painfully thin shoulders.

Death was already in the room. Sheila could smell it. It was a smell she'd become well acquainted with at the hospital.

'It's good to meet you at last, my dear,' Mrs Lack smiled, her voice little more than a whisper.

Sheila came forward and took the dry, skeletal hand in her own. 'It's good to meet you, also,' she said sincerely, and, on a sudden impulse, bent down and kissed the old woman on the cheek.

Her eyes shone as they moved up and down her daughter-in-law. 'Bring Sheila a chair over so she can sit beside me. She and I must get acquainted,' she ordered Andrew with unexpected vigour. He immediately brought the chair and placed it where his mother instructed.

Sheila's nervousness evaporated completely as she and Mrs Lack, who insisted she call her Sarah, began to chat.

They spoke about Sheila's job as a VAD and her previous employment at the Queen's Theatre where she'd met Andrew. Then she talked about Dragonholme as she hadn't talked about it in years.

Minutes ticked past to become half an hour, then an hour. Finally Sarah announced that she was tired, and had to sleep. But would Sheila and Andrew come to her again after their supper? Sheila spoke for both of them. 'Of course we will,' she said. 'You just rest.'

Sarah glanced up at her son. A soft, knowing smile twisted the corners of her mouth. 'You picked a good woman, Andrew. I heartily approve and so would your father.'

'I knew you'd like her,' beamed Andrew.

'If only this war hadn't . . .' Sarah trailed off in despair. She'd have given every penny she possessed for the war not to have happened, and Andrew not to have gone into uniform.

But it had, and he had, and there was nothing she could do about it.

As Andrew closed the door behind himself and Sheila, they could hear his mother weeping.

*　　*　　*

Two nights later Sarah Lack died in her sleep, not making it to the end of the month after all.

He'd got home just in time, Andrew said to Sheila, then broke down into floods of tears. He'd loved his mother dearly, and they'd been very close, despite the disappointments he might have caused her.

Sheila took her distraught husband into her arms and rocked him back and forth as though he were a child.

6

It was 15 July 1916, and the Battle of the Somme had been raging for a fortnight. Already the casualties were enormous, stretching even further the already thinly stretched medical facilities and personnel. Several days after the start of the battle, word had arrived back in Britain that more doctors, nurses and VADs were desperately needed. Sheila, who'd volunteered some time previously, was one of those now told they were going to France.

The night before, she'd left Portsmouth in a destroyer. Only halfway across the Channel she'd become aware of the far off sound of the guns. Since then it was a sound to which she had become accustomed, getting steadily louder the nearer they got to the Front.

She was tired, irritable, hungry and extremely thirsty. There was no food on the train, or water, except what individuals had brought along with them, and no one seemed to have any idea of when they were likely to arrive at their destination.

Rising, she made her way to the toilet, only to discover, as she had the previous seven times she'd tried, that it was engaged. 'Damn!' she muttered, and fought her way through the crowded corridor and back to her seat.

She thought of Andrew safe in Egypt, where he'd been posted directly after his leave. At least that was one less fear to contend with. The intense heat and boredom were his principle complaints, with bedbugs and flies coming a close second. According to him the most popular form of entertainment was a game they all played of seeing who could get most bugs skewered on a pin.

She smiled to herself. As far as she was concerned he could stay in Egypt till the war ended. Far better bored and sticking bugs than hazarding his life at the Front.

The others from Cowcaddens General with whom she'd come over had left her at Boulogne. From there they were proceeding to St Omer. Her own orders were to report to a Casualty Clearing Station, a CCS at Maricourt, which was apparently just to the rear of what, until the first of the month when the Somme offensive had started, had been the most forward British positions.

Tired of thinking and worrying and wondering, she finally closed her eyes and fell into a restless sleep.

It was in the early hours of the next morning that the train shuddered to yet another of the many halts that had taken place during the journey. This halt, however, was different. Word spread rapidly from carriage to carriage that all medical personnel were wanted outside on the platform.

After the heat and fug of the train the outside air was cold and sharp. Sheila stamped her feet, rubbed her hands briskly together, and wondered what this was all about. She soon found out.

A hospital train emerged from the dark to stop at the other side of the platform. Less than a minute later the first fleet of ambulances started drawing up outside the station, ambulances packed to overflowing with wounded.

The hospital train had been carrying its own special complement who'd begun unloading equipment the moment the train stopped. Many of these now broke away to make for the queuing ambulances.

Lights were strung overhead and fires lit to boil water. A stretcher was dumped in front of Sheila, and a doctor in attendance brusquely told her to do what she could for the patient. Somebody called out a name and the doctor hurried off.

Sheila bent to her patient instantly. He'd been shot in the side of the head and through the chest. A grip as strong as a vice grabbed her and pulled her down.

'Trones Wood. We all went in and only I came out again,' the man choked, blood running down the side of his chin.

She stared into the man's eyes, unable, somehow to turn away. The eyes flickered, then closed for the last time.

Gently, Sheila disengaged the hand still gripping hers.

Seven hours later the hospital train finally pulled out leaving the dead behind for burial and a platform stained bright with blood.

Welcome to France, she thought as she climbed back aboard her own train and returned to her seat. Welcome to bloody France.

It took Sheila three days to get to Maricourt. She finally managed the final stage of her journey by hitching a lift with an ammunition lorry going up to the Front.

The CCS consisted of a group of large tents clumped together, surrounded by an assortment of smaller ones.

The first thing Sheila did was seek out and report to Matron Fenwick whose name was on the orders, who said she was pleased to have Sheila with them. As Sheila was Scots she'd billet her in with the only other Scots VAD they had.

Fifteen minutes later the other Scots VAD finally showed up at the spot where Sheila had been told to wait. Sheila was astounded to see who it was. Just my luck, she thought with a sigh.

Georgina Murchison-Stewart stared at Sheila out of a

face haggard from strain and fatigue. She'd come to France just a little over eight months earlier.

Without uttering a word of greeting or even acknowledgement, Georgina instructed Sheila to follow her, taking her to the Quartermaster's Store where Sheila was issued with three army blankets and a large canvas bag in which, she was assured, she would find everything needed for comfort.

She was rather sceptical about that claim – *everything* she would need for comfort in one canvas bag – but later found this to be absolutely correct.

On opening this Pandora's box, she discovered a folding cot, a cork mattress, a washstand, a small table, a canvas pail in which to carry water, a lantern, an enamelled plate, a drinking cup, knife, fork and teaspoon. The claim hadn't been exaggerated after all.

On leaving the Quartermaster's Store, they went to a two-man tent, which, Georgina informed her, would be their temporary home.

Oh, Lord, thought Sheila, who'd been hoping against hope that it would be a larger tent, housing a number of women.

And then, like dawn rising out of a bleak night a smile came on to Georgina's face. 'I can't even begin to tell you how marvellous it is to have someone here from Glasgow, particularly someone I know!' she said, and fell upon Sheila to hug her tightly.

'Do you remember that tunny?' Georgina laughed, when at last she'd released Sheila.

Sheila nodded. 'How could I ever forget that blessed thing?' laughing as well. It was going to be all right between them; Georgina had changed since coming to France.

The days that followed were a nightmare as the Battle of the Somme continued and thousands of wounded passed through the Maricourt CCS.

Trones Wood, which she'd first heard of from the lips of a dying soldier in an unknown railway station, became engraved on her heart as a place of terrible human suffering and destruction. So also did Bernafax Wood, Caterpillar Wood, Bazentin-Le-Petit Wood and Contalmaison.

In yet another wood called Delville, the South Africans went in and were annihilated, fighting gallantly and gloriously to the bitter end. As the South Africans were making what would turn out to be their supreme sacrifice of the war, their British comrades of the 3rd, 7th, 9th and 21st Divisions, fighting on either flank, were also suffering horrendous losses.

Then the Anzac Corps came into that part of the Line, only to be mown down along the narrow front from Guillemont to Bazentin-Le-Petit.

Sheila overheard an Australian Lieutenant describe, bitterly and with awe, where he and his men had fought as 'a place so terrible a raving lunatic could never imagine the horror of it'.

After the Anzacs came the tanks, few in number, but, when working, effective in the extreme, striking terror into the German infantry as they crawled along the tops of the German trenches enfilading them with continuous machine-gun fire, closely followed by small parties of Tommies throwing hand grenades on the survivors.

Sheila woke with a start, wondering what had wakened her. Then she heard a rustle in the darkness and knew Georgina was also awake.

'Would it disturb you if I put my lantern on?' she asked softly.

'Not at all,' Georgina answered immediately. 'The only reason I haven't put on mine is because I didn't want to wake you.'

Sheila's lantern filled the tent with a soft, yellow, glow. Sitting on the ground in front of her cot with a drinking cup in one hand and a half empty bottle of gin in the other, was Georgina. Swallowing the contents of her cup, she grimaced as though taking medicine. 'Want some?' she asked, holding up the bottle.

Sheila hesitated for a second. It was against station rules to drink, even off duty, but something in Georgina's expression caused her to pass her own cup across with a sleepy smile. 'What are we celebrating?' she asked, as Georgina poured her out a large measure.

'Nothing,' Georgina said, lifting her own cup in the air in a mock toast. 'This is called medicine to help you get to sleep.' With that, she tossed back her drink and immediately poured herself another.

'Do you often have trouble sleeping?' Sheila asked, trying to sound as causal as possible as she watched the other woman take another greedy swallow of gin.

'Oh, no,' Georgina laughed without any humour. 'Not often. Sometimes I'm so exhausted I could sleep standing up.' She stared down into the clear liquid in her cup. 'Sometimes. But other times I close my eyes and all I see is an endless line of dead and dying soldiers.' She lifted her eyes to Sheila's, almost defiantly. 'Just like the line I see when my eyes are open.'

It took no imagination for Sheila to see it too. Scots lads, English boys, Welsh and Irish, Canadians and Indians, South Africans, Frenchmen and even Germans, all marching by, waving, cheering, grinning like kids on an outing, and disappearing down a long road at the end of which they would be blown away like so many leaves in a high wind.

Outside, it began to rain, the drops hitting against the canvas making a disconsolate sound which seemed to echo the mood within the tent.

'How long have you been seeing this procession?' Sheila asked quietly, her eyes not moving from the other woman's pale, strained face.

'Since the middle of my fifth month,' Georgina answered, her voice flat. 'It was right after this boy I used to know, this boy from Kelvinside, died in my arms of gas gangrene.' A tremor ran through her that was noticeable even in the poor light. 'He'd always been such a lovely lad. When we were young, I'd been pretty sweet on him, I suppose. You know, the way kids are.' Tears filled her voice and her eyes. 'He was one of the funniest people I've ever known. He made everybody laugh.' Silent sobs shook her body.

At that moment, an 'Archie', as the German flak was called, cracked directly above the tent. Both women jumped. A few seconds later, another cracked not far away in the direction of Mametz.

Georgina, a wry smile on her lips, poured them both more gin. 'I buy this from one of the ambulance drivers. You can bet he does a brisk trade.' Against the background of the rain, Georgina's voice sounded like a cry for help. 'Lots of people have trouble sleeping.'

Thinking of what had to be faced daily at Maricourt, Sheila wondered how long it would be before she, too, was doing business with the ambulance driver.

Sheila stared up at the place in the sky where a hapless, dark FE was desperately twisting and turning, trying to evade a German Albatross D1 which was hot on its tail.

Because of Andrew, she had taken an interest in the air war, and had learned to identify most of the machines by sight.

Of late the tide had turned against the RFC and RNAS, both of which were taking an exceptionally hard hammering.

Thanks to the technical advance of aeroplanes and related equipment the air war had changed dramatically since Andrew had been at the Front. It was a long time now since pilots had been limited to taking pot shots at one another with pistols and rifles. Now the war in the sky was just as deadly as on the ground, perhaps even more so.

Of the German aces Oswald Boelcke was the most feared, replacing the now dead Max Immelman, killed in June, as the German Number One: while on the British side the violin-playing Albert Ball was without question the highest rated.

Sheila had no way of knowing it, but the pilot of the Albatross she was watching, just returned from the Russian Front where he'd been flying bombers, was a young Prussian aristocrat who would shortly become the greatest ace of them all, Baron Manfred Von Richthofen.

As she continued to watch, the FE began wheeling all over. Obviously the plane was being flown by an experienced pilot who knew he mustn't let the Albatross get in the blind spot behind him.

Then more planes appeared, and suddenly the sky was full of them.

The original FE flattened out, having apparently lost sight of the Albatross for the moment. The much faster Albatross surged up beneath the FE so close that Sheila held her breath for a collision seemed imminent, and at that point-blank range Richthofen fired.

The FE's propeller slowed, jerked, then stopped; and the British machine went down, swinging and jerking with the observer's head no longer visible in the front cockpit.

The FE turned over and next moment two bodies fell from it, one still as it plummeted to the ground below, the other futilely grabbing at empty air as though in the hope the air might somehow suddenly turn into something solid on to which he could grasp.

Sickened Sheila averted her head as the living airman smashed into the earth a little beyond the station. Then she ran towards him, knowing the impact must have been fatal, but going to him anyway. Just in case.

High overhead, the Red Baron saluted his fallen foes.

★   ★   ★

It was a Friday afternoon and the Battle of the Somme was now into its third month. The weather had been atrocious all day, which had stopped planes going aloft. It didn't, however, stop the infantry, who were now not only fighting the Germans but also the infamous Somme mud, many of them not certain which they hated most.

Sheila had become so used to fatigue that she couldn't remember what it was like not to be dropping from exhaustion. That afternoon marked thirty-six hours since she'd last been to bed.

She hardly noticed when it began to rain again, rain that beat against her face and made her already wet clothes even wetter.

She plunged a hypodermic into the arm of a Tommy who, as part of Gough's Army, had helped take Thiepvel, and smiling told the man he was one of the lucky ones; it was Blighty for him.

The soldier, with three fingers and a foot missing, agreed that yes, he was lucky; then the injection started to take effect and he began to drift off to sleep.

Sheila gazed about her, wondering which section to go to next.

'Hello, Sheila,' said a sudden voice behind her.

She turned and blinked. 'Yes?' She had a vague sense that she knew this airman who was staring at her so intently, but so great was her tiredness that she couldn't understand why he seemed so familiar.

He could see how worn out she was by the dark rings under her eyes and the gauntness of her cheeks. 'Oh, my darling!' Andrew cried and swept her into his arms for a kiss.

'Andrew!' she gasped when the kiss was finally over. She held him at arm's length and gazed at him in total wonder. How grand he looked. The tan and moustache suited him, no wonder she hadn't recognized him right off. 'Oh, Andrew! Is it really you?'

He lifted her off the ground in an ecstatic hug. 'Of course it's me, you silly,' he laughed. 'Of course it's me.'

When at last he released her, he asked, hopefully. 'I've got three days; can you get away?'

But Sheila shook her head. That was impossible, with the battle still in progress. 'But how did you get here?' she wanted to know, suddenly afraid that his presence must mean that he'd been posted to the Front.

'No fear, my love,' he said, unable to stop touching her. 'I've been posted to England.' He shook his head, 'Surely there's some place we can talk that's out of the rain?'

'There's the mess.'

Georgina, who'd come over to see what was going on and had been listening to the conversation suddenly intervened. 'Bugger the Mess,' she shouted. 'There's the tent with a bottle of gin in it. You two go there, I'll cover for Sheila for a couple of hours.'

'Are you mad, Georgina?' asked Sheila her hand held tightly in Andrew's. 'I can't take that amount of time off. Besides, we'll be for it if we're caught with a man in our tent.'

'There are occasions,' said Georgina in her old voice, 'when rules should be broken. And this is most certainly one of them.'

'It would appear to be our only chance of being alone together,' Andrew said quietly but with insistence.

'Well . . .' Sheila looked from one to the other. 'Well, what the hell.'

Once inside the tent, she rooted out Georgina's gin, pouring Andrew a fair-sized measure and herself a smaller one.

He took a sip of his drink, but almost immediately laid it aside. 'Come here to me,' he commanded softly. 'Come here.'

She had thought about this moment for so long – through all these nights and days of hell. To touch him again; to lie in his arms. She'd planned to look beautiful for him. Instead she looked like something the cat hadn't even bothered to drag in, but had turned up its nose at disdainfully.

'I don't give a damn how dirty you are, or how louse ridden,' he whispered, removing her clothes. 'You're my Sheila, the woman I love. That's all that matters.'

Later, when it was over, they began to catch up on one another.

'I've been trying to get posted back to France for ages,' he said, ignoring the flicker of fear in her eyes. 'But I got nowhere. Then six weeks ago, new orders came through for me out of the blue.'

She was suddenly cold all over, her happiness already dissolving in reality. Sheila shivered. 'Not to the Front?' she whispered.

He turned to give her a level, serious gaze, but couldn't hold it, for he could see how desperately anxious she was. A smile twitched at his lips.

'Not to the Front, worse luck. I've been posted as an instructor at London Colney.'

Relief rushed through her. 'How long do you expect to be there?' she asked as calmly as she could.

He shrugged. 'Your guess is as good as mine. What I can say is I would be very surprised if it was for less than six months. I've never heard of anyone being posted as an instructor for less than that.'

Six months – possibly longer. With a bit of luck, he might even ride out the rest of the war in that posting. She thought of Kaiser Bill, and raged inwardly at him for starting this terrible business. If he was made to roast in Hell for all eternity for what he'd done, it wouldn't be punishment enough.

She glanced sideways at Andrew, and prayed for the umpteenth time since he'd gone into uniform that he'd come out of the war in one piece. Please, God, she said silently. Please.

And when it was all over, as some day it must be, it would be back on the boards for him, and with her to help him he'd carve out a name for himself, a name that would blaze out in lights on Shaftesbury Avenue.

Her rage gave way to a warm tingling of pleasure, for

in her mind she could see those lights, and Andrew the world-famous actor.

There was only one thing more to make her dream complete; his child, his children.

She ran a hand down his arm, on to his chest, then across the tightness of his belly to hold him again. Six months more of safety. It was more than most people got – but not nearly as much as she wanted.

'Oh, Sheila,' he sighed. 'I do love you.'

After Andrew had gone, promising to come back next day, she returned to her duties. About twenty minutes later a nurse stopped by where Sheila was changing a soldier's bandages to inform her that Matron wanted her right away.

Matron Fenwick glanced up at Sheila's approach, her mouth forming into a thin, disapproving line. She was terribly disappointed, she said, having hitherto thought very highly of Sheila who, it now seemed, had let her down. In curt tones she informed Sheila that a man had been seen leaving her tent. 'What do you have to say for yourself?'

Jesus, Sheila thought, and they'd been so careful, too. It just went to show you, there were unseen eyes everywhere in a place like this. Wearily she nodded, and said it was true, but it wasn't the way it looked.

'How was it then?' Matron Fenwick snapped.

'The man wasn't just any man. He was my husband, Lieutenant Andrew Lack of the RFC. He's just come over from England to try and spend a few days of his leave with me. Of course, I had to tell him that was impossible.'

The hard lines of Matron Fenwick's face immediately softened. 'And how long has it been since you last saw him?'

'Over a year. He's been in Egypt.'

Matron Fenwick picked up a pencil and fiddled with it. The matter had been officially reported, so an official reason, in other words an acceptable excuse, would have to be recorded. 'You wished to discuss certain important domestic matters in private, and there was no private space available?' Matron Fenwick suggested.

Stunned it took Sheila a few seconds before nodding her head in agreement. It was certainly as near the truth as dammit. Bless you, Matron, she thought. You're a real smasher!

'How long's his leave?' Matron asked quietly.

'He can stay round here for three days, then he's got to return to England. He's to be a flying instructor at London Colney.'

Suddenly overwhelmed by everything, Sheila swayed grabbing hold of Matron's table to stop from tumbling over. Hastily she apologized.

'When did you last sleep?' demanded Matron.

'Over forty hours ago now,' Sheila replied, giving a small grin.

Matron Fenwick went back to fiddling with her pencil. She was completely whacked herself, having been on the go just as long as Sheila, but she hadn't had the shock of suddenly being reunited with her husband. Nor would she ever be reunited with Charlie; he'd died of gas poisoning at Ypres.

In a gruff voice Matron Fenwick told Sheila to go and get her head down. In her present state she'd probably kill off more Tommies than she'd help. 'And has your husband arranged to see you again?'

'Yes, Ma'am. He's returning to Maricourt tomorrow. But I'll send him packing straight away.'

'You'll do no such thing!' Matron Fenwick rapped out in reply. There might be a war on, but that didn't mean it had to be all pain and suffering; there was room for a little joy and happiness as well. 'Where is he staying?'

'With No. 11 Squadron. Andrew has friends in the squadron.'

Matron Fenwick's features lit up with interest. No. 11 Squadron was Albert Ball's wasn't it?

Albert Ball was a great hero, held in highest esteem by the British Forces and public alike. During this Battle of the Somme his reputation had become one of almost Godlike proportions.

'I want you to take twenty-four hours' leave, starting from the moment your husband gets here tomorrow,' said Matron Fenwick.

Sheila was astonished. 'But I can't possibly!' she protested, though only half-heartedly. 'Not while the battle is still in progress.'

Matron Fenwick told Sheila to let her worry about such things. Besides there were five new VADs due in later that day, so Sheila's absence wouldn't be that noticeable. 'I only wish I could send everyone off for twenty-four hours. Heaven knows they need and deserve it. But, of course, that's quite out of the question,' Matron Fenwick sighed.

Returning to her tent Sheila discovered that Andrew's personal smell had remained behind him. Closing her eyes she savoured it, then with a smile began to undress.

When Georgina found her later she was still smiling, only half undressed, and curled in her cot sound asleep.

He'd said he'd come at the same time as yesterday, and almost exactly to the minute, he arrived. Sheila was ready and waiting for him when he showed up in a staff car driven by a Sergeant Roper, a blunt Yorkshireman from the Dales.

Andrew let out a whoop on hearing that Sheila had twenty-four hours' leave, immediately bundling her into the back of the car and instructing Roper to get them out of there before the good Matron Fenwick had a change of heart.

As the car roared off, he kissed her. She wriggled out from under him, 'We'll be seen,' she laughed.

'I don't give a fig who sees us,' holding her tightly. 'Right now I'd snap my fingers at old "Boom"

Trenchard himself.' Trenchard was the head of the RFC in France.

Just beyond Maricourt, they came upon an infantry battalion waiting to go into the line. The men were sitting quietly, many with cigarettes dangling from their lips, all with packs hanging heavily from their shoulders. None were talking; every one of them resigned to his fate.

As the staff car passed the battalion their colonel glanced at his watch, and they all rose to their feet and adjusted their equipment. Then they went marching down the road to meet whatever lay in store for them.

A grim-faced Sheila watched them go, wondering how many would end up in Maricourt before the day was over, and how many would die out there in the terrible grey mud.

Andrew tried to break the sudden gloom that had sprung up between them by saying cheerfully that with only twenty-four hours at their disposal he didn't think it worth their while trying to get out of the battle zone, and he was certain there wouldn't be an inn or hotel in the area that hadn't long since been taken over by the various Services and Armies; which left Château Roisselle, 11 Squadron's current, and temporary HQ. How would she feel about them spending her leave there?

'I'd be happy to spend the entire twenty-four hours in a trench, as long as you're with me,' she smiled.

The Château Roisselle had seen better days. Two of its four spires had been blown off, and there was a boarded-up hole in a side wall where it had taken a direct hit from a British gun when in German hands.

There were several large, fairly level fields on the right of the château which were used as an airfield. Repair and overhaul facilities had been set up, and mechanics could be seen busily working on aircraft as they drew up. The squadron itself was in the air, away on a mission.

Andrew took Sheila into the château where arrangements were quickly made. Sergeant Dummit, a fierce-looking fellow with the black patch of a pirate over one eye, said a bath would immediately be drawn for Mrs Lack, and in the meanwhile refreshments would be sent up to Andrew's room. It seemed that there were no inflexible rules any more in this terrible war. Life would only concede so much to death.

The château had at one time been opulently furnished, but that had been before the war. The rich colours that had been everywhere were now faded, the rugs and carpets in ruin. There were pinpricks of light in the roof where it had only recently been strafed by a German aeroplane.

On entering their bedroom, Andrew closed the door behind him, then pulled Sheila into his arms. They were still kissing five minutes later when there was a discreet knock which turned out to be Dummit with an ice-cold bottle of champagne and the news that Sheila's bath was ready.

Once Dummit had left them, Andrew opened the bottle with a bang, and poured champagne straight from the bottle into Sheila's mouth, then into his own. He swallowed some, put his hand behind her head, brought her lips to his and kissed her again then forced what remained of the champagne in his mouth into her's.

Sheila shrieked and jerked away, champagne running down her chin. 'What sort of trick was that?' she laughed.

'A most deliciously insanitary one,' he replied.

The last thing she did before leaving the bedroom to meet the returned squadron was to put a dab of precious perfume (the only bottle she possessed had only a few drops left in it) behind both ears, and wished again that she had a civilian dress to wear instead of her VAD uniform.

The chatter of conversation ceased the moment she appeared. 'Oh, I say. Isn't she an absolute corker!' a voice exclaimed, followed by another angrily telling the first to mind his manners.

Sheila smiled as she descended the stairway. Andrew, eyes shining with pride, hurried forward to greet her with a soft hello.

Andrew started his introductions with James McCudden, a handsome man with an aquiline nose. 'My oldest friend in the RFC!' Andrew declared as McCudden shook her hand and welcomed her to the 11th.

Round the gathering they proceeded, Sheila's hand pumped again and again, and even kissed by a chap called Rodders who proclaimed loudly that the Frenchies weren't the only ones who could be gallant.

'And this is Albert Ball,' Andrew said.

Albert Ball was young, slim, and clearly of a highly strung, nervous disposition. His eyes had a brooding, intense quality and were strangely unblinking, which she found unsettling, yet attractive at the same time. There had been a Siamese cat in Dragonholme once. Albert Ball reminded her of that cat.

Ball shyly shook hands with Sheila, muttering that Andrew was indeed a lucky fellow, and he would be honoured if the pair of them sat next to him at dinner.

'The honour would be ours,' she replied.

More champagne appeared, and Rodders confided to Sheila that the cellar was full of the stuff. 'The Hun made such a quick exit that the champagne got left behind,' he laughed. 'For which 11 Squadron is extremely grateful.'

They had no sooner sat down to dinner, Sheila on one side of Ball, Andrew on the other, than a glass was rapped with a fork and Lieutenant Walters asked them to drink a toast to their new comrade, Lieutenant Arthur Pyle, who'd joined the squadron two days previously and made his first kill that afternoon by shooting down a Roland.

'Lieutenant Pyle!' rang round the room.

'Speech! Speech!' someone cried out, followed by the table being thumped repeatedly by a battery of fists.

Blushing furiously Pyle came to his feet. He cleared his throat, drank some . champagne, then cleared his throat again. 'This is even worse than facing the Hun,' he admitted, which earned him clapping, cheers and a piercing whistle from Rodders.

'Tell us the story of what happened,' Lieutenant Lewis prompted. It was a tradition in the squadron for pilots to recount their first hit.

He'd got the Roland more by luck than skill, Pyle told them in an embarrassed voice. He and Sam Moxby had been flying at seven thousand feet above Baupaume when they spotted a Roland and LVG, but not the balloons which they'd been expecting.

He and Moxby had attacked simultaneously with their Le Prieur rockets, he the Roland, Moxby the LVG. Streaming flames the LVG fell away, but although his rockets streaked round the Roland they didn't hit it.

The Roland then dived, he went after it firing his Lewis, and the Roland, silly sod of a pilot, instead of pulling away from the bullets, turned straight into them. Raked from front to tail the Roland went into a spin from which it never recovered.

'And that was how it was,' Pyle said in conclusion.

Albert Ball led the applause which consisted of thumping the table with both hands and singing, 'For He's A Jolly Good Fellow'.

Pyle, relieved that was over, sat down and beamed around him. Someone then presented him with a large tankard of champagne that he was obliged to see off in one go.

When Pyle had accomplished this the applause became even more thunderous. Lieutenant Morgan-Jones jumped up on to the table, where he thumped his feet instead of his hands.

Just as well it's an extremely strong table, thought Sheila, as knives, forks, glassware and dishes went flying.

The meal itself turned out to be superb, by far the best she'd had since coming to France. The pudding was a lemon sorbet that literally melted in the mouth.

Unfortunately not many of the pilots ate theirs, pelting one another with it instead.

The champagne continued to flow in a never-ending river. Bottles of whisky, brandy and port were brought in as alternatives. Sheila noticed that Albert Ball was one of the few who drank sparingly.

During an ebb in the hilarity, Rodders asked Andrew what machine Andrew would be teaching the new boys to fly on at London Colney. 'The BEs,' he replied.

Hearing him, Ball looked up suddenly and, in an angry voice, declared that the BE was a bloody awful plane. 'It's too stable by half,' he continued. 'Flying one in France is tantamount to suicide, if you ask me.'

Silence fell around the table. Every eye was trained on Ball. 'The BE can't climb to the height required in the time required to outmanoeuvre the German machines,' he went on. 'They're no match at all for the German planes, if you want the simple truth.'

Suicide! 'Do you mean they're unsafe?' asked Sheila, thoroughly alarmed.

Ball chuckled dryly. 'Quite the contrary,' he said. 'They're safe as houses. They're ideal for training, but they're lethal in action.' Ball's expression became sour and morose. 'No 11 Squadron's fortunate because we're equipped with French Nieuports,' he explained to Sheila. 'But many of the other British squadrons are still flying the BE and FEs and even antiquated Farmans against Fokkers and Albatrosses that can dance rings round them.'

As for the newer planes the Royal Aicraft Factory were coming up with most of them were worse than useless.

The trouble was that the scientists and engineers at the Factory refused to accept the facts. According to them, and their slide rule calculations, the new British machines were unbeatable, a theory the Germans disproved daily by shooting them wholesale out of the sky.

Ball's eyes flashed with fury. If the situation was bad before, it was even worse now that the Germans had taken to flying in formations they called Jagdstaffels, or hunting squadrons, equipped with fast intercept fighters flown by pilots of picked and proven quality.

'Jagdstaffels,' Sheila repeated. The very word tasted of terror and death.

'Staffels for short,' Lieutenant Walters said quietly.

Ball opened his fist, then closed it again. The RFC had to have a plane of comparable standard to the German fighters, he said, swinging round on Andrew, and they had to have it in *quantity*. If they didn't, and he shrugged, then there wouldn't be an RFC left before long. And without the Flying Corps, Haig and the Army might just as well pack their kitbags and go home, for the war would be lost.

Ball fixed Andrew with his gaze and said that as an instructor at London Colney Andrew would undoubtedly have occasion to speak with the scientists and engineers working at the Factory. Somehow Andrew must impress on them the dire necessity for a new fighter that performed *in the air* as well as it did on their damn silly pieces of paper. Such a new fighter must come soon, or it would be too late.

Sheila stared in awe at Albert Ball. The power and the passion coming from him at that moment was so strong it was almost tangible. Ball, she realized, wasn't merely a derring-do fighter, but a man of intellect and imagination as well.

Albert Ball uncurled his fist like a flower greeting the morning Sheila thought, and held it out to Andrew. 'Will you do your best on behalf of all pilots and observers in the Corps to talk some sense into those thick heads over there?' he asked quietly.

Andrew accepted the hand, shaking it with strength and resolution. 'I'll make it a personal crusade, you have my word on that,' he replied.

Ball nodded, then suddenly smiled. The spell was broken.

Shortly after that, Albert Ball excused himself, saying he was off to bed.

Sheila watched Andrew watch Ball go, Andrew's expression one of candid admiration.

All these bonny men are heroes, Sheila thought. Every last one of them.

Sheila woke to the sound of throbbing engines. Beside her, Andrew stirred, then also awoke.

Her mouth was dry and she felt washed out. Too much of that champagne last night, she told herself, thinking that it might have been too much, but it had been lovely.

She listened to a plane take off, followed by a second and a third.

'The dawn patrol, they go out every morning at this time to try and catch the German bombers,' Andrew said, giving her a kiss.

After the squadron had gone they lay in each other's arms in silence; he wishing he was flying with No 11, she thankful he wasn't.

Outside the window the many lamps and torches that had been used to illuminate the take-off area were now extinguished, and gradually the room darkened.

Suddenly, Sheila felt frightened. She snuggled up closer to Andrew, putting both arms around him and holding him tightly.

Somewhere a bird started to sing. She remembered a wounded Tommy at Maricourt telling her that he'd heard one singing in the middle of No Man's Land, only seconds after the guns stopped.

Soon she would have to return to the horrors of Maricourt, to the stream of wounded that arrived daily from the Front, to blood and pain and that awful despair.

But not yet, not quite yet. For the moment she had the song of a bird, and she had Andrew. She couldn't have asked for anything more.

'Make love to me darling,' she whispered.

Slowly and tenderly he obeyed her, as though trying to make it last forever.

Later, when the squadron returned, they went down to breakfast. Sheila was halfway through her egg when she remembered there was something she wanted to ask Rodders.

She looked around for him, but he wasn't at the table. There was another empty chair which she realized should have seated Lieutenant Pyle.

She turned to McCudden whose grim expression told her what she wanted to know. Rodders and Pyle hadn't come back from the dawn patrol.

It was the afternoon of 6 April 1917, and the newspaper Sheila was reading cried the news that America had, at long last, declared war on Germany.

Like the rest of the country, Sheila was filled with elation – and profound relief. This *had* to be the beginning of the end for the Germans.

Laying the paper aside, she ran a hand across her brow. It had been a long, wearying journey from Maricourt.

Her leave was for a month, but she wouldn't be returning to Maricourt at the end of it. When she'd left Maricourt was in the process of being dismantled and moved to a more forward position.

What had been the Maricourt CCS was to be set up again at Rancourt where fresh personnel would be taking over. All the Maricourt personnel had been given long overdue leave, and would be going to new postings on their return to France.

Sheila had said good-bye to Georgina several hours before at Euston station. Georgina was taking the train from there to Glasgow, while Sheila'd travelled across town to catch a train for London Colney just south of St Albans.

She'd considered telegramming Andrew from London that she was coming, but had decided against it. The distance was so short, she'd probably arrive before the telegram.

Nor had she written to him from France to tell him she was coming. They'd only been notified three days before their departure so there'd been no time for anything but packing up. It was going to be quite a surprise for Andrew when she turned up out of the blue. She could hardly wait to see his face, or have him in her arms again.

How marvellous it is to be home again, she thought as the train puffed on. Even if home for the moment was England rather than Scotland. If Andrew could get some leave of his own, perhaps they could go up to Glasgow. She'd missed the grey city far more than she'd ever imagined she would.

They would stay in their rooms in Crown Crescent, which had been kept on all this while, and she would see darling Pat again. She'd had a number of letters from Pat in France. She was still working at the Queen's Theatre, where the programme was now, according to Pat, a constant diet of patriotic plays and shows.

Thinking of the theatre filled her with warmth – that daft world whose inmates took it all so seriously, where magic really did exist, and where happiness of unbelievable intensity could be caused by a full house and good review.

Strangely, she hadn't missed Dragonholme at all. It was as if that part of her life had receded so far back in time that she'd only dreamt it.

She dozed for a little while, dreaming that she was back working with Pat, and that Andrew was again playing the pirate chief in Sinbad the Sailor. She smiled in her sleep to see Andrew being whacked on the bottom by Sinbad, and he, clutching himself, leaping up and down shouting 'ooh! ooh! ooh!'

Finally arriving at London Colney, she got a taxi to take her to an inn close to the aerodrome.

As soon as she'd registered, she explained the situation to the landlord's wife, who gave her permission to ring the aerodrome on the pub telephone. On getting through she asked for Andrew, but was told that he wasn't available. She left a message telling him of her arrival, and where she was to be found.

There was still no sign of Andrew when dinner time came around, so she asked for a tray in her room.

She was in the middle of her meal when the door suddenly burst open, and there was Andrew, dishevelled and out of breath. 'I only got your message ten minutes ago,' he gasped. Then they were hugging and kissing as though neither had believed they would even meet again.

'How on earth did you get here?' he demanded at last.

Quickly she told him about the CCS at Maricourt being closed down, and moved to Rancourt, and how she, and everyone else there, had got leave as a result.

'Just think, we've got an entire month together now. Isn't that wonderful!' she exclaimed, nearly breathless herself with excitement. But then she noticed a worried look in his eyes. 'What's wrong?' she asked quickly.

'Nothing,' he assured her, the look gone. 'You just look very thin.'

'Oh,' she said lightly. 'I had a bout of dysentery a little while ago. But I'm all right now.' She couldn't look at him without smiling. 'I've never felt better in my life.'

'You should have written and told me you were ill,' he admonished.

She laid a palm against his cheek. 'You're so gorgeous,' she said softly, staring at him as though she would never see enough.

'Oh, no,' he whispered, beginning to undo her blouse. 'You're the one who's gorgeous.' The blouse slipped to the floor. 'Even thin as a rail, you're the most beautiful woman I've ever known.'

'You'll never leave me, will you Andrew?' she breathed, wanting to hold him so close that they could never be parted.

'Nothing could make me leave you,' his lips on her face, her neck, her breasts. 'Nothing in the world.'

And so lost was she in the passion of their lovemaking

201

that she forgot about the fear which shadowed her every moment, forgot about the world in which they lived, where happiness was a moment with no past and no future.

'Nothing at all,' he repeated.

And so joyous was she at his touch, that she believed that what he said was true.

But even as he entered her, a voice in the back of Andrew's mind was saying, tomorrow, tell her tomorrow.

The next morning, he insisted on taking her first thing to the aerodrome.

'But why?' she asked, laughing as he pulled her from the bed. 'At least give me time to get dressed.'

'I told you, woman,' he said, scooping her into his arms. 'I've got something I want to show you. Now, either you get dressed right now, or I'll carry you there just as you are.'

There were several aircraft dotted about, but Andrew led Sheila to a model she had never seen before. 'Well, what do you think?' he asked, running a hand lovingly over the plane's fuselage.

'I can tell she's a fighter and a beauty,' agreed Sheila. 'Is it new?'

Did she recall the mission Albert Ball had charged him with at Chateau Roisselle?

'Oh,' said Sheila. 'Now I understand.' She should have realized from the excitement in his eyes.

'Well, this is the machine Ball says we need. It's called the SE5. Isn't she something?'

'You've flown it then?'

His smile grew even broader. 'I've done a lot more than that,' he grinned. 'I'm her test pilot. Many of the modifications we've made on her have been the result of my flights.'

Test pilot! Angrily, she turned on him, close to tears.

202

'You never told me you were doing anything so dangerous!'

'For God's sake, Sheila. There's nothing in this war that isn't dangerous.'

'No,' she sighed at last. 'I suppose there isn't.'

'There's something else,' he said slowly.

'Something else?'

And then he told her that a new squadron, No. 56, was being formed at London Colney. 'It'll be the first to fly the SE5s in combat,' he announced, unable to contain his excitement. As though in a trance, she listened while he talked about the new squadron's mission in France, where it would be commanded by Ball, and would, as Andrew put it, give Baron Von Richthofen hell.

'When does the squadron leave?' Sheila asked, when finally he was through.

'We leave tomorrow at dawn,' Andrew answered quietly.

For several moments she just looked at him, unable to accept what he was saying – what she had known for a long time he was going to say. 'What do you mean, *we*?'

'James McCudden's taking over from me as instructor,' he said flatly. 'I've requested to join the 56th and I've been accepted.'

If she had found him with another woman she couldn't have felt more betrayed. 'You requested to go?'

'We're to be based at Vert Galland.'

Vert Galland? There were two CCSs near there. She would somehow have to manipulate it so that she was posted to one of them. If she and Andrew were both going to be in France then she was going to do everything in her power to ensure they were close to each other. Tears sprang to her eyes, sobs shaking her body. To hell with her month's leave, she thought. She didn't want that now. All she wanted was to get back over there, as soon as possible.

'Things could have been worse, you know,' he said,

taking her into his arms. 'We could have passed one another en route.'

Crying even harder, she clung to him as though nothing would ever pull her from him.

'You have to understand, love,' he said gently. 'I can't train these young lads, then send them over to fight a battle I'm protected from. I couldn't live like that.'

She didn't sleep a wink all night, although, for his sake, she pretended to.

They'd agreed not to say good-bye. 'Well,' she'd said, as jauntily as possible, 'it's hardly worth the breath. I'll be seeing you at Vert Galland before you're even settled in.'

She lay still, her eyes closed while he rose from their bed to dress. Barely breathing, she listened to him grope about in the dark.

When he was dressed he came around to her side of the bed where he stood staring down at her for several minutes. Reaching down he lightly touched her hair, then tip-toed from the room.

After he'd gone she sat up, leaning against the head-board, and wept. Once she was composed again she got dressed and went downstairs. Letting herself out into the pub's rear courtyard, she stood shivering in the morning chill, her gaze focused on the distance.

Dawn was breaking when the first flight of 56 Squadron took off, five brown birds winging their way heavenward, the front bird flown by Andrew.

'Good luck my darling, see you soon,' she whispered, blowing a kiss in the direction of the vanishing plane. From the aerodrome, a second flight took to the air.

She waited till the last plane of the third, and final, flight had vanished from view, then hurried back indoors to pack her things.

Her key to returning prematurely to France lay in Glasgow with the St Andrew's Ambulance Association and/or the Cowcaddens General Hospital.

The sooner she was in Glasgow the sooner she'd have the new orders and the posting she had to have.

Sheila stumbled through to the toilet, her hand clasped over her mouth. This was the third morning in a row that she'd been nauseous. She put it down to the upset stomach that had been bothering her off and on for the past week.

It was a few days over a fortnight now since she'd arrived back in Glasgow. Despite all her efforts, she still hadn't succeeded in cutting short her leave. The powers that be had decreed she was to have a month off, and the powers that be seemed determined that a month off was what she was going to have, whether she wanted it or not.

Pat McLuskey arrived just after midday with a bottle of milk and six fresh eggs, intending to make an omelette for their lunch.

When she suggested this, and that perhaps they could put some onions in the omelette if Sheila had some, Sheila went a pale shade of green and sank into a chair.

'What in the name of the Wee Man's the matter with you?' asked Pat, her face serious with concern.

Sheila ran a hand across her face. 'I'm feeling hot and cold at the same time,' she explained. 'And I ache all over. I've been sick three times this morning, as well.' She smiled wanly. 'It's been like this for days and days. Do you think I'm coming down with the flu.'

'And it's only in the morning you're being sick?' asked Pat.

When Pat had established that Sheila had also been off her food it seemed to Pat she might have the answer. It certainly wasn't flu. 'You could be pregnant, you know,' suggested Pat.

Pregnant! Sheila made a rapid calculation, then shook

her head. 'Sixteen days is far too soon for me to be showing any signs,' she said firmly.

'That's just where you're wrong,' countered Pat. 'The body is quite capable of showing signs this early on.'

Could she be pregnant? Sheila wondered.

'You'll be delaying your departure now,' Pat said.

But Sheila looked shocked. 'I'll be doing no such thing!'

'But if you are pregnant, you owe it to yourself and the baby not to go back to France,' argued Pat.

'What if I'm not, though? What if it's only a bug I've picked up?'

Pat knew only too well how headstrong and stubborn Sheila could be, whether wrong or right. She would have argued further if she'd thought it would have done any good, but knew it wouldn't. On the contrary, it would only make Sheila more determined.

It was 8 May, the day Sheila had anxiously been awaiting, for it was the day she was to start back to France – and Andrew.

Commandant McNair, of the St Andrew's Ambulance Association, had finally arranged for her to be posted to Larache, the closest of the two CCSs near to Vert Galland.

Pat had come around to see Sheila and Georgina off. Georgina, at this moment fetching a taxi, would be travelling to France with Sheila, though her destination was a general hospital in Hazebrouck.

'Look out the window to see if there is any sign of Georgina,' Sheila said impatiently.

Pat leaned out into the street. 'There's a taxi turning into the far side of the Crescent,' she called back.

'That'll be her,' Sheila shouted excitedly, and hurried through to the bedroom to put on her cloak.

In the bedroom, she paused to glance around her. Three or four months and I'll be back here, she thought.

She was now certain that she was carrying a child; his child, their child – hers and Andrew's.

She had decided to keep her secret for as long as she was able so she could spend as much time near Andrew as possible.

Her reverie was interrupted by voices in the reception room. Georgina was here, the taxi was waiting, it was time to go. As excited as a child herself, she gathered up her things and charged into the other room. But the moment she saw Georgina's face she knew something was wrong. 'What is it?' she whispered, her eyes darting from one friend to the other.

In reply, Georgina handed her the copy of the Glasgow Herald she was holding, but Sheila wouldn't touch it, recoiling from the newspaper as though it were alive.

Georgina knew then she was going to have to break the news verbally, to have to actually speak the awful words. 'Albert Ball and five other members of his squadron were shot down and killed yesterday,' she recited as though the paper's words had been burned into her brain. 'I'm afraid . . . I'm afraid that Andrew was one of them.'

A voice, which Sheila recognized as her own, spoke from what seemed a long way off. 'They're quite certain Andrew's dead? There couldn't be some sort of mistake, a mix-up perhaps?' asked the voice.

'There's no mistake,' Georgina said softly.

In her mind's eye, Sheila saw again the FE she'd watched shot down over Maricourt, and the still alive pilot falling . . . falling . . . falling. . . .

Pat sprung forward to catch her just before she hit the floor.

PART THREE

The Steering Star
1923–24

'I must go down to the seas again, to the lonely sea and
the sky,
And all I ask is a tall ship and a star to steer her by. . .'

From *Sea-Fever*, by John Masefield

Sheila laid down the Fair Isle she was knitting for wee David with a sigh. How boring life had become since her son started school when he turned five in January, she thought. Before that she was always busy just taking care of him, even though the money she had come into on Andrew's death had made it unnecessary for her to ever work again. Ever work or ever worry. Though she had known the Lacks were well-off, she hadn't quite realized just how well-off. She now had money beyond her wildest dreams. Money enough to send her son to the finest school in Glasgow, money enough to have anything she desired, money enough to never have to worry again about anything in the future.

Directly after Andrew's death – while the war dragged on and the estate had yet to be settled – she moved back to Crown Crescent with Pat. Without Pat's support and companionship, she doubted that she would have made it through those awful months, her heart and spirit broken, Andrew's child growing within her despite her terrible grief. If there had been no Pat to buck her up and keep her going, no Pat to help her to the hospital that bitter winter's morning, the snow feet deep on the road and a razor-sharp wind blowing off the Clyde on the day that David was born, Sheila doubted that she would be here at all, snug in her posh house in Kelvinside with her best friend and darling son.

Sheila's reverie was interrupted by Pat's return from shopping. Pat no longer worked in the theatre, but as Sheila's companion and housekeeper, an arrangement with which they were both extremely happy. Sheila enjoyed having a friend around the house to chat to, and Pat, who lost her job when the Queen's Theatre closed late in 1919, was relieved to have a secure position as well as a long-term friend.

Pat could have found a position elsewhere as a wardrobe mistress, but she preferred working for Sheila, or, to be more precise, she preferred helping Sheila with David, whom she loved as her own.

Pat was talking about her trip into the town. While Sheila listened, she noticed for the first time how peaked Pat was looking. It had been a long, grey winter for them all. Perhaps she should take Pat and David for a drive in the country now that spring was here.

'How about a cup of tea now?' asked Sheila once Pat's tale was over of the wifey in the tram who'd been so fat she'd got stuck in her seat. 'You look like you could use a pick-me-up.'

'I'll make it,' said Pat, already on her way to the kitchen.

That evening, as she was tucking David up in bed, he suddenly asked Sheila to tell him about Dragonholme. 'What's brought this on?' she laughed. Although she'd often told him about the village, he'd never before expressed any special interest in it.

It was then that she had the idea. 'I'll do better than that,' she promised, kissing him soundly. 'What if you and Pat and I all take a drive to Dragonholme next weekend?'

Immediately David sat up. 'Will I be able to go out on a fishing boat?' he asked excitedly.

'I couldn't promise you that,' she laughed. 'But if there's a boat in the harbour I'll see what I can do about getting you taken aboard and shown around. How's that?'

'Oh,' cooed the little boy. 'That would be marvellous. I can hardly wait. You won't go and change your mind, will you?'

'Of course not,' she assured him. 'I want to go as much as you do. We'll leave directly after breakfast on Saturday and stop for a picnic lunch on the way. How's that?'

212

Sheila's heart was pounding as she left David's bedroom. She hadn't had any contact with Dragonholme since running away from James Campbell all those long years ago.

After Andrew's death she hadn't been able to bear the thought of returning to Dragonholme, the scene of the other great losses in her life. It had taken all her strength to cope with Andrew's death without having to face those other ghosts as well.

Now it seemed enough healing had taken place within her for her to be able to return. And with that decision all the love she'd always had for her home returned as well. For the first time in a long while she felt really excited about something – excited and, yes, thrilled.

Sheila stopped the Silver Ghost at the top of the descent into Dragonholme, staring down at the place where she'd been born and raised.

She gazed over the cluster of houses, remembering each individual one, and the families who lived in them, as though she'd been away only a day or two.

Finally, she turned her eyes out to sea, out to the spot where the disaster had occurred, where her childhood had vanished into the depths of the sea.

Tears glistened in the corners of her eyes as she saw again that violet glow and angry black clouds; heard again the crashing thunder and remorseless wind.

'Are you all right Mummy?' asked David, his hand reaching out to take hold of hers on the steering wheel.

'I'm fine, darling,' she replied in a voice trembling with emotion. 'There's nothing for you to worry about. I'm just very happy to be home in Dragonholme after all this time.'

Pat stared worriedly at Sheila guessing the real reason for her tears.

From there they drove to the family house. Sheila

remained sitting in the car, staring at the house for several minutes, before going in.

'It's awfully small,' said David, impatient to get out of the car. 'I want to see inside.'

Some of the furniture and bits and pieces had gone, otherwise it was exactly as she remembered. Glancing round she visualized the family as it had been: Davey with his battered old clay dangling upside down from his mouth; Peg kneading dough on the table; Bob in his chair day-dreaming about Thomasina McLean; Dougal and Jack, having just popped in, sitting by the range arguing about something or other while Davey looked on.

Sheila went ben to the room she used to share with Bob, crying out with delight to find her kist still where she'd left it.

Eagerly she opened it, staring down at the once-treasured items she'd gathered together for her marriage to Eric. She explained to Pat about the contents of the kist as she rifled through them; the four pillows and two bolsters, the four fluffy white blankets and two baby blue ones, the half-dozen sheets made of Egyptian cotton, the twelve Turkish towels.

She would take the kist with her when they returned to Glasgow, she told herself. It would occupy a place of honour in the Kelvinside house.

'Oh, but it's grand to be back!' she exclaimed, closing the lid of the kist again.

She took David and Pat to the smokehouse, showing them round it, pointing out things she thought might be of interest. This was another place laden with memories for her, and filled with ghosts.

Then she led the way to the house loft where, in bad weather, the nets had been hung up to dry, and the spare ones stored; the tarry smell of them lingering though the nets were so long gone.

'Can we go to the harbour now?' David asked, having been as patient as a small boy could be while his mother rooted around what he saw as a musty old cottage.

'Right,' she cried, grabbing his hand. 'We'll start for the harbour this instant. Come on Pat, we'll leave the car here.'

Tom Taggart's chandler shop had closed down, that was her first surprise. The second came as they neared The Haven, her da's favourite pub, which stood dark and cheerless in the afternoon sun. 'I don't understand it,' she said turning to Pat with a bewildered expression. 'Everything seems to be shut down.'

And so many houses were empty, just as her own home was. Some were boarded up, but most were simply empty, their doors snicked shut, their occupants vanished.

This wasn't the Dragonholme Sheila knew; the one whose memory had comforted her when she felt most frightened and alone.

What had happened to the busy little village filled with life and laughter that had once been her whole world. Now it was little more than a ghost town; little more than a shell.

There were four boats tied up in the harbour. 'Look, David,' Sheila cried excitedly, her heart fairly leaping at the sight of them. Coming closer, she saw they were the *Foamcrest*, the *Nonsuch*, the *Silvery Dart* and the *Rising Sun*, three Zulus and a Scaffie, all survivors of the disaster that now seemed to her to have happened a lifetime ago.

The closest was the *Foamcrest*. They strolled along the quayside to it, Sheila enthusing as they walked. 'It was aye a bonny boat,' she smiled. 'I can remember when old man Olafson bought it to replace the *Jean*. He was right proud of it. You would have thought it was the finest boat in the land.'

A man came on deck and bent to pick up some gash tackle. He was heavier than when she'd last seen him, and the beard was new, but she recognized him instantly.

'Hello, Duncy!' she called out, smiling.

He paused to glance over at her, frowning in puzzlement for a few moments. Then a smile of recognition lit his face. 'Sheila Beattie!' he shouted, and jumping down beside her, vigorously pumped her hand.

'How's Marika and the family?' she asked.

'Marika's fatter than ever. And there are three weans now; another boy and girl to add to the first girl we had,' Duncy replied with a grin.

Sheila introduced Pat, then David. Solemnly Duncy shook hands with David, saying that it was a great pleasure to meet a son of Sheila Beattie's. 'You ma's an old friend of ours. Why, I can remember when she was no bigger than you are now.'

'Here, less of the old,' chided Sheila gaily. 'And it's Sheila Lack, not Beattie.'

Sheila explained that David was desperate to have a look over a boat. 'Are you now?' he asked, turning to David. 'Then you've come to the right place.'

Duncy helped David clamber on board the *Foamcrest*. Leaning over the side, David called to Sheila, 'Aren't you and Pat coming too?'

'Women aren't allowed on the boats. It's bad luck. Pat and I will wait for you here. By the way, Duncy,' she asked, as they were about to go below. 'When did you start crewing for the Olafsons?'

Duncy, suddenly sombre, turned back to the side. 'Ronnie Olafson was washed overboard during the war,' he said quietly. 'Since then I've taken his place.'

'Sheila! Sheila!' shouted a voice behind her as David and Duncy disappeared into the *Foamcrest*.

Sheila turned on hearing her name shouted, and there was Rhona flying towards her with outstretched arms.

They embraced, kissed, and embraced again. 'Mrs Johnstone cried the news to me that you'd been spied coming down here. I came running right away,' said Rhona breathlessly.

Trust Mrs Johnstone, Sheila thought. At least some things hadn't changed.

'What happened to you? Why did you disappear like

you did?' demanded Rhona, oblivious to Pat's curious stare.

'My ma's death rather threw me – after everything else that happened,' she said quickly. If no gossip had been spread after her flight she wasn't going to start it now.

'Aye,' said Rhona, suddenly subdued. 'I thought that was what it was.'

'My son's on board the *Foamcrest*. Duncy's showing him round,' Sheila went on, changing the subject.

Rhona's mouth opened wide in surprise. 'A son! When did you get married? Where's your man?'

'It was a long war,' Sheila smiled ruefully. 'I'll tell you about it later.'

'Oh, lass,' whispered Rhona.

'And this,' said Sheila, pulling her forward, 'is Pat McLuskey. My dearest friend.'

Rhona immediately asked them to come up to tea. 'That would be lovely,' agreed Sheila. 'We'll be along just as soon as David is finished aboard the *Foamcrest*.'

'Wonderful,' beamed Rhona. 'I'll get away back and put the kettle on. We'll have a proper chat, just like the old days.'

David was full of the *Foamcrest* when he eventually, and reluctantly, rejoined his mother. Did she know what a warp was? He did, Duncy had explained that to him along with so many other things that he could barely get all the words out of his mouth fast enough.

'Marika will never forgive me if you leave without calling in,' said Duncy.

'I'll pop in some time this evening. I couldn't go without seeing Marika.'

'Right, then,' said Duncy. 'We'll be expecting you. And what about your husband? Is he with you too?'

Sheila took hold of David's hand. 'My husband died in France,' she said shortly.

Duncy muttered that he was sorry, and ruffled the lad's hair. 'My father was a famous pilot who flew with Albert Ball!' announced David. Duncy gave a wan smile. Suddenly Sheila asked the question that had been troubling her since coming in sight of the harbour. Where were the other boats?

Duncy turned his face out to the sea. 'This is all that's left,' he said, as though from far away. 'The other five boats that survived the disaster were sunk in the war with all their crews. Three of them on the Dover Patrol, two in the Adriatic.'

'That's all?' she whispered, her voice like an echo. Only four boats left from the Dragonholme fleet. Four boats and a handful of men. If the disaster had crippled the village, the war had substantially destroyed it entirely.

'Are we going to have tea now?' David interrupted her reverie, disturbed by the look on his mother's face.

'Aye, love,' she smiled. 'We're going to have tea.'

Rhona welcomed them at her door, Ian standing beside her. Ian had grown into a fine young man with a serious air about him.

To begin with, David was shy of his much older cousin, but Ian put him at his ease with his quiet, gentle way. Before long they were playing together in a corner of the kitchen. At least, David played while Ian looked on.

'I'm sorry I never got in touch,' Sheila apologized, once they were settled down over their tea. 'I always meant to, but somehow I just never did. I hope I didn't cause you any worry.'

'Oh, no,' smiled Rhona. 'I know that bad news travels the fastest.'

As the afternoon dwindled, Sheila told Rhona about France – and about Andrew. Once it had seemed that it was happiness that bound people together; but now, she thought, noticing the sympathy in Rhona's eyes, that it was loss.

'With the village in such decline, how on earth are you managing to get by?' she asked at last.

Rhona gave a wry grin. 'I gather shells from the

218

seashore and make them into ornaments which I sell, in Edinburgh,' she explained. She went to a cupboard and came back with a box of tiny figures made of shells.

'What a clever idea!' exclaimed Pat.

'How did you ever think of it?' asked Sheila.

Rhona confessed that she hadn't. Ian had brought home a book from school about Iceland. Leafing through it, she'd come across a large picture of seashell ornaments.

'I thought they were very appealing, so I decided to have a go at making my own. After all, what did I have to lose except a little effort and a pot of glue?'

It had taken her a while to get the hang of it. Then she'd made a round hundred and, using up her tiny savings, had taken them to Edinburgh in the hope of selling them to one of the big Princes Street shops.

'And it worked!' she laughed. 'That shop took a thousand a year, while another in the old part of the city had a standing order for seven hundred and fifty. I'm still in my parents' house, but it's been mine since they died, so it's not the lap of luxury we're living in,' she went on. 'But it keeps the roof over our heads and the wolf from the door.'

'Well I certainly have to hand it to you,' said Sheila. 'You've got more spirit than most people. By the way, what happened to Maggie?'

'Oh, Maggie and Ian flitted through to Portnessie soon after you left. But what about yourself?' asked Rhona. 'What are you doing now?'

Rhona was delighted to hear that despite all the tragedies she'd withstood, Sheila at least had no worries about money. As she said to herself, if your husband was destined to die young far better he left you wealthy than poor.

But what of Ian, for whom she'd aye had a soft spot – how was he getting on?

'Well,' said Rhona proudly. 'Miss Dalziel, his teacher, says he's very brainy and could go far, given the chance.'

She did not have to add that it was unlikely that chance would be given. 'One thing's certain, though,' she said sharply. 'He'll not be going to sea.'

It was clear to both Sheila and Pat that Rhona was more worried about her boy than she would admit. He was due to leave school fairly soon, but then what? There were only two choices: either he helped Rhona with her small business, hardly a job for a lad with his brains; or they upped sticks and flitted through to Edinburgh in the hope that he'd find a suitable position there.

'And what about all the folk who've left Dragonholme?' asked Pat. 'Where have they gone?'

Rhona sighed. 'Dragonholme was largely a village of widows and weans after the disaster,' she said slowly. 'After the war there were more widows and little chance for any more weans.'

Some of the old folk, like Handy Dandy and Tom Taggart, had passed on and were buried in the village cemetery. A number of the wives, the younger ones that is, had eventually moved away to bide with relatives elsewhere, or to look for new husbands, or both.

As for those who'd been children at the time of the disaster, most of those were grown up now, the lads leaving first to try and find a berth somewhere, inevitably putting down roots in the port that adopted them, and the lassies following. For them there was no point in staying on in a village with no young men.

Rhona sighed again. With no work and no men and no babies being born, or precious few anyway, it was only a matter of time, and a short one at that, before Dragonholme ceased to exist altogether.

'But why hasn't the laird done something to help?' asked Sheila. After all, he was supposed to be the protector of the people.

Rhona rolled her eyes. 'It's years since James Campbell even set foot in Dragonholme,' she informed them. 'Of course he knew the state the village was in. How could he possibly not when he lived in Dragonholme Hall? But it's as though he's lost all interest in the village,' she went on. 'It's almost as though he's turned against us.'

'That doesn't sound like the James Campbell I remember,' said Sheila.

'Aye, well he's had his share of misfortune, too,' said Rhona, not unsympathetically. 'First Robert was killed in the war, then Drew. When Mrs Campbell got the second telegram it was too much for her. She had a heart attack and died herself there and then.'

'Oh, the poor man,' said Pat, momentarily forgetting the things the poor man himself had done.

'Poor Mrs Campbell,' whispered Sheila. Her money certainly hadn't brought her happiness.

It wasn't until later that she wondered if James's abandoning of Dragonholme had been because of her; because it was her village, forever associated with her in his mind.

'We won't get out of touch again,' she assured Rhona as they parted. 'You can be sure of that.'

Sheila paused to listen to the fair-sized sea that was running, whitecaps rolling off it to pound against the shoreline. She'd just come from Marika and Duncy's where she'd spent a good hour talking over old times and renewing her friendship with them.

Before Marika and Duncy she'd been to see Miss Dalziel, the schoolmistress, who'd given her much to think about concerning Ian.

As there was a cold bite to the air she didn't stand listening to the sea for long, but hurried on her way, her feet clattering on the cobbles as she walked.

Coming up to The Halibut's Tail, Sheila saw it was still open and, on the spur of the moment, decided to take herself in for a dram.

The pub was empty except for Mr Meekie the landlord who insisted on buying her the drink, although it was obvious trade was so poor he could ill afford the gesture.

The paint was flaking from the walls, and all joy had gone out of the place. She sat on a chair by the miserable peat fire and stared into her whisky, thinking about what Miss Dalziel had told her.

Ian was a brilliant scholar, quite gifted, according to the schoolmistress, and most certainly had what it took to go to university. The big stumbling-block were the entrance exams. Quite simply Ian needed better tuition than it was Miss Dalziel's ability to provide. Without that tuition there was little chance he'd pass the exams.

It seemed to Sheila, as she sipped her drink, that the answer to the problem was Kelvinside Academy. Of course that would necessitate Ian moving through to Glasgow, or even he and Rhona together, should Rhona not want to be parted from him.

Money would be no problem of course. She could set them up in a wee house of their own if that was what they wanted. Then again, they could stay in her house in Kelvinside: it was certainly big enough, God knew.

If Rhona elected to go with Ian, though, that would be one more family gone: another nail in the coffin.

Finally Sheila decided to talk the matter over with Mr Lumsden, the Academy's headmaster, before mentioning it to Rhona and Ian.

She glanced up as a second customer entered the pub, a young man whose face was vaguely familiar.

The young man ordered two half pints at the bar, and stood talking for a few minutes with Mr Meekie. Then he ordered two more drams of whisky, picked them up and strolled over to where Sheila was sitting.

'Will you allow me to buy you a dram? A sort of thank you for the bit of help you once gave me,' he asked, smiling.

By his speech and manner he was clearly from the village, but she couldn't put a name to the face.

Noticing her puzzlement, he gave an amused laugh. 'I know I've changed but surely you recognize me?' he said.

'Give me a clue. Remind me about this bit of help I once gave you.'

He sat down and placed the fresh dram in front of her. He had warm brown eyes that were twinkling mischievously, and enormous broad shoulders, muscular even by fishermen's standards.

The young man gestured about him. 'Do you remember a night just before the disaster, when you and Eric Gifford, on your way home from here, rescued a lad who was having a rather nasty brothering?' he smiled.

It all came flooding back then: Tarry Dunbar and the crew off the *Locarno*, the boy with the trousers round his ankles while Tarry painted his crotch and backside with tar.

'You're wee George Jorgesson!' she exclaimed.

George nodded, joining in her laughter. 'That's who I am, right enough.'

'Not so wee anymore,' Sheila murmured, indicating his massive shoulders, and they both laughed more.

'I owe my life to that brothering, and Tarry's cruelty,' he reminded Sheila, for as a result of the brothering he'd been in bed for a month, and consequently he'd missed sailing aboard the *Locarno* when the fleet went out after the big shoal.

They reminisced for a while, then Sheila asked George if he was crewing one of the four remaining boats left to Dragonholme.

'No I'm not,' he said. 'I left Dragonholme before the war, and settled in Eyemouth. I've been crewing there for a real nice man named McFadyen. Or I was anyway. Unfortunately McFadyen's decided to retire because of his age. He's got the arthritis bad.'

'So what will you do now?' asked Sheila.

George sipped his dram, becoming almost morose. 'It's on account of his decision to retire that I'm here in Dragonholme.'

McFadyen's sons all had boats of their own, so the old man's would be up for sale. 'He's given me first refusal, because he knows I'm mad keen for a boat of my own.'

223

George had some money of his own put aside, but not nearly enough for the boat's asking price. He'd gone to Edinburgh in the hope of raising capital there, but to no avail. The Edinburgh bankers had turned him down flat because he didn't have any collateral, as had the Glasgow bankers when he'd tried them.

As a last resort he'd returned to Dragonholme to ask James Campbell to lend him what he needed, but Campbell's reaction had been the same as the bankers: no collateral, no loan.

'You took a risk in going to Campbell,' commented Sheila. 'It would be just like him to buy McFadyen's boat for himself, to add to his Portnessie fleet.'

George shook his head. 'I knew I was safe on that score. McFadyen bought his boat, the *Sheila B.*, from the laird in the first place. It's the only boat James Campbell's ever been known to sell. He wouldn't want it back.'

The *Sheila B*! Sheila dropped her gaze so George wouldn't see her smile. So James had got rid of the boat he'd named after her. My God, she thought, he must have been angrier than I thought.

It was clear that George was unaware that the boat had been called for her; he wouldn't have mentioned its name quite so casually if he had.

Sheila could picture the trawler as she'd last seen it, a sweet craft right enough. And for the first time in all these years felt a pang of almost affection for the man who had named it.

'What do you intend doing now?' she asked.

'There's nothing I can do. It's lost to me. I'll stay the night with my ma, then go back to Eyemouth in the morning and tell McFadyen to put the *Sheila B*. up for sale.'

As though it was only a matter of curiosity, she asked him about the state of the industry since the war. George brightened. 'It's never been better. The great shoals are now greater than they've been within living memory.'

George's eyes sparkled. 'If only I could get hold of a boat I could easily pay its costs off within a few years.'

'And what price is McFadyen asking?' The amount he named was reasonable enough.

It was on the tip of her tongue to tell George she would lend him the money, but it was always her policy to sleep on any important decision if she could, and that was what she would do now.

Going up to the bar she ordered two more drams.

Sheila woke with a start having been restlessly tossing and turning since going to bed several hours before. She and David were in what had been her ma and da's bed, Pat through in the other room in her old one.

She turned to look at the snoring David. How she loved that wee boy. He had become her whole world.

The *Sheila B*, that's what was running around and around in her head. That's what had woken her.

Something was bothering her about lending George the money to buy the boat, but what? It certainly wasn't the amount involved. Even if she lost the lot, which she'd ensure couldn't happen, it was money she would never miss. So what was niggling her?

And then the answer came to her. How blind could she be? Rather than helping George buy the boat she should be buying it for herself. It was named for her after all – and it would be a damn fine investment. And, she thought with a tingle of excitement that she hadn't felt for years, it would really anger James Campbell.

Her own boat, a thrill ran through her just to think about it. And she could . . . oh, the things she could do.

She sat up, her mind racing as she made plans. Without her realizing a part of her that had been empty for a long time had begun to be filled again.

At breakfast next morning Sheila announced to Pat and David, somewhat mysteriously, that she was going off for a few hours on a matter of business, and she thought it best they remain behind.

'Oh, fine,' Pat replied, 'I'll take David down to the shore to play.'

Shortly afterwards, George was astonished when Sheila knocked on his mother's door to say she'd give him a run down the coast to Eyemouth, if he wanted, an offer he readily accepted.

He stared in wonder at the Silver Ghost, giving Sheila a strange sideways glance before getting inside.

It didn't take long for them to reach Eyemouth where the Eyemouth fleet lay in the harbour. It would be another couple of months yet before it set off for the Shetlands and the northern fishing grounds.

The fleet was a bonny sight, she thought. One which stirred memories long forgotten and brought her heart into her mouth. And there was the *Sheila B*. tied alongside the other eight steam trawlers of the fleet.

Sheila stopped the Rolls by the quayside, then got out and strolled over to look at the boat.

The *Sheila B*. had been so well-cared for that it might have been newly launched instead of thirteen years old. Nor was she worried about the state of its engine; an owner who cared for the outside of the boat cared for the inside as well.

So that was it. Her mind was made up – if indeed it wasn't before. 'Will you introduce me to your Captain McFadyen?' she asked George, standing by her side.

George nodded, wondering what the hell she was up to. They climbed back into the Rolls and he gave her directions to the McFadyen house.

Lang Jake McFadyen was as tall as his tee name suggested, and well into his seventies. Because of arthritis his back was permanently bent, his hands hooked into claws, and when he walked it was with a shuffle. She couldn't understand why he hadn't decided to retire earlier.

Mrs McFadyen showed Sheila into the best chair,

then hurried off to put the kettle on. Lang Jake and George sat over the table facing Sheila.

Sheila came straight to the point. She told Lang Jake she was interested in buying his boat and as George hadn't had any luck in coming up with the money would he consider selling to her instead.

'Is that right? You can't raise the asking price?' George nodded reluctantly.

Jesus, but she was quick off the mark, George thought. And not a word about what she intended all the way down here. She might have said! Rising, his face flushed, he stalked from the room.

Sheila stared after him, thinking what a fool she was not to have said something to him. Of course he'd think she'd been using him. With difficulty she brought her attention back to Lang Jake who was regarding her with an amused and patronizing expression.

'Ach, you can't possibly be serious, Mrs Lack. It's unheard of for a woman to own a working boat,' Lang Jake chuckled.

'It may be unheard of, but there's no law against it,' she replied sweetly.

Lang Jake knocked dottle from his clay, then began cleaning out the bowl with a stained pipe cleaner. He could hardly wait to get out and tell his mates about this.

'I want that boat,' Sheila stated quietly, steel in her voice.

Lang Jake laughed. 'You're havering, woman. What can you possibly know about herring boats and the like?'

Sheila fixed him with a cold stare. 'My father was Davey Beattie, the last admiral of the Dragonholme fleet. If you'll recall, he went down with my three brothers in the disaster.'

That wiped the smile off Lang Jake's face. 'I myself worked for James Campbell as his personal assistant. He taught me a great deal about the fishing industry.'

It was now plain to Lang Jake that this was no ordinary lassie, this one knew how to stand up for herself in a

227

man's world, and probably win gey often as not. He'd be wrong to dismiss her lightly.

'So your maiden name would've been Sheila Beattie,' he mused.

She knew what he was getting at. 'If you're asking is the boat named for me, it is.'

'Well, well,' murmured Lang Jake, tamping down his new fill.

Mrs McFadyen bustled back in carrying several plates stacked high with potato scones, crumpets and tea cakes which she laid on a pouffe beside Sheila.

Lang Jake was remembering Davey Beattie whom he'd met on a number of occasions, the last time in Southwold when they'd had a good bucket together. He'd liked and respected the man.

Sheila was now absolutely determined to have the boat. Not conscious of the gesture, she stuck her jaw out defiantly.

'You've no mad notions about actually sailing aboard the boat yourself have you?' he asked at last. 'There's not a crew in Scotland or England would entertain such a thing.'

'I have no intention of going to sea myself,' she said shortly. 'I'm only too well aware of what fishermen think about women aboard boats. No, I just want to be the owner.'

Sheila mentioned the price that George had been asked. 'Aye,' said Jake. 'That's a special price for George, whom I'm very fond of. The price to anyone else would be higher than that.'

Sheila pretended to consider this. 'And what do you think about George as a potential skipper?' she asked.

'George is a natural seaman,' a new look coming into his eyes. 'Young as he is, he'd make a fine skipper.'

That was what she had wanted to hear. 'I'll tell you what,' she now said. 'If you sell it to me at the price you'd expect from anyone else, I'll make George skipper.'

This was a big chance for George, and well Lang Jake

228

knew it. Sure, George would get another berth easily enough, but being made skipper! Without a boat of his own he could wait a dozen years or more for that to come about.

Lang Jake grinned inwardly. He liked this woman's style. She certainly had a shrewd head on her shoulders. How could he possibly turn down his price *and* such an opportunity for George? He couldn't – as she'd been counting on. He named a fair market sum and, with no dickering, she agreed.

'You'll be making history,' Lang Jake said, extending his hand.

History. She hadn't thought of it like that, but it was true enough. She spat in her hand before slapping it into his.

Lang Jake roared with laughter.

George was standing outside staring glumly down at the harbour and the boat that was meant to be his.

He looked up at her approach. He didn't have to inquire what the outcome of her meeting with Lang Jake had been, the answer was written on her face.

'Congratulations,' he muttered, averting his eyes.

She thanked him for that, then gently reminded him that the *Sheila B.* had already been lost to him. If she hadn't got it someone else would have.

'There used to be a small repair yard in Eyemouth,' she went on. 'Is it still in operation? Do you have any idea how busy it might be right now?'

'Oh, aye,' he said slowly. 'It's still going strong. Last I heard it wasn't turning down any new orders, if that's what you mean.'

That was lucky, Sheila thought. It saved her contacting Tom McIndoe up in Aberdeen to find out if he could fit in what she wanted done.

'How would you like to skipper the *Sheila B.* for me?' she asked suddenly.

George turned to her in amazement. This was the last thing he'd expected.

Sheila went on. 'There are two conditions, though. First is that the *Sheila B.* is converted into a drifter, for I'll not run a trawler. Second is that its home port becomes Dragonholme. Now what do you say?'

'Can I choose my own crew?'

'Skipper's privilege,' she smiled

He looked down at the *Sheila B.* which he'd thought had gone out of his life forever, then back at the woman beside him. 'Done.'

If Glasgow had a Bohemian quarter then this small enclave of mean grey streets just off the Byres Road was it. In these ramshackle tenements students from the Art School congregated along with theatrical people and down-at-heel intellectuals. It was an area frowned on by the good folk of Glasgow who are inclined to view any artistic aspiration or endeavour as the pursuit of the shirker.

The close Sheila turned into had grey slate underfoot and was lined halfway up its walls with cracked and chipped tiles, the rest covered with ancient whitewash.

She found the name she was seeking on the third flight up; G. Hurley the name plate proclaimed. She knocked and waited.

She'd written to Graeme Hurley the previous week suggesting she call round at this time and speak with him, but had received no reply. Despite this, partly because she was the persistent type, but more because Graeme Hurley had come so heavily recommended, she'd decided to call anyway.

After a minute, with no response from within, she knocked again. Mr Lumsden, the headmaster at Kelvinside Academy, had warned her Hurley could be strange in his ways, and had explained why.

She knocked a third time, and was rewarded by hearing the faint tread of a footstep.

The door slowly opened and a pale face poked round. 'Yes, what is it?' the face asked.

Sheila stated, in her most officious voice, who she was, and that she'd written him for an appointment.

Graeme Hurley coughed, a barking cough that quickly splintered into a series of hacking smaller ones. Disappearing behind the door he spluttered into the handkerchief he was never without.

When the coughing attack was finally finished he told her she'd better come in, then led the way along a dark and dingy hallway.

The parlour he ushered her into was light and airy, which were about the only good things that could be said for it. The ceiling, particularly its fancy plasterwork, was encrusted with dirt, the wallpaper might have been up a hundred years or more.

Seeing Sheila glancing around, Hurley muttered apologetically that he was a bachelor and housework wasn't exactly his strong suit. When he asked if she'd care for a cup of tea she hastily declined.

Sheila began to wonder if she'd made a mistake, then reminded herself it was as a tutor she was interested in Hurley, not for his housekeeping abilities.

He was somewhere in his mid-thirties she judged, and not such a bad-looking chap either, now that she had a chance to study him properly. His skin was striking, being extremely sallow, almost translucent in places, while his eyes were the saddest she'd ever seen. The eyes of a poet she thought, a description that fitted them perfectly.

Hurley ran a hand through his deep auburn hair, then coughed again, turning away quickly when he did. Sheila sat on a none too clean armchair and waited for the coughing to subside.

'Sorry about that,' he mumbled when it was over.

'That's all right. I understand.'

There were many he would have challenged for making such a statement, but he didn't Sheila. Reaching into his inside jacket pocket he pulled out her letter and waved it at her as though it was a flag. He said he was surprised old Lummie had recommended him after giving him the sack. 'You did know I had the sack didn't you?' he asked aggressively.

Sheila cleared her throat. 'Mr Lumsden told me he'd regrettably had to let you go because of your health.' A teacher who had to take as much time off as Hurley did, Lumsden had explained, was unfortunately no use to him, no matter how excellent that teacher was.

Hurley tossed the letter aside and said perhaps Sheila could explain the situation to him herself.

Sheila started at the beginning, with her idea to send her nephew Ian to university, should he be capable. She then related the conversation she'd had with Miss Dalziel.

Her next step had been to see Mr Lumsden, to ask if Ian could be taken on at Kelvinside Academy. Very politely, Mr Lumsden had turned Ian down.

If Ian had been younger, Mr Lumsden said, he would have been delighted to accept the lad, but not now when Ian was deficient in so many pertinent studies for the university entrance exams, and would need so much personal attention.

'Mr Lumsden didn't think it would be fair to Ian to take him on at this late stage,' she went on. 'Psychologically. If he was as bright as Miss Dalziel said he was, it could damage him to be so behind the other boys.' She smiled wanly. 'He seemed to think that Ian would completely upset the balance of the class.'

Graeme Hurley broke in to say that he totally agreed with Mr Lumsden. No good school would take Ian on at this late stage. 'Some of the not so good ones might,' he added. 'But the chances they could get him through the exams at this stage are slim.

'Tell me more about Ian's background,' he prompted.

She told him of Dragonholme, of the disaster in which Ian's father, Jack, had been drowned, and of how Rhona now earned a living making ornaments out of sea shells. When she was done, she asked if Hurley had any tutoring engagements at the moment. Hurley shook his head. He told Sheila he had a small private income which took care of his needs; he didn't have to work. He didn't have to add that since leaving the Academy, he hadn't.

'Mr Lumsden said you were one of the best all-round teachers he'd ever come across. That if anyone could help Ian you were the person.'

Hurley opened his mouth to reply, but before he could do so a fresh bout of coughing hit him, far more severe than the other two.

Sheila watched in pity as the coughing wracked his body. Finally she rose and went through to the kitchen where she ran a glass of water and brought this back to him. He grabbed the glass and greedily drank its contents.

'Where were you gassed?' she asked when he had recovered enough to answer.

He gave her a baleful look. 'The Somme.'

There had been a number of mustard gas attacks by the enemy during the battle, all of them towards the end. 'You were lucky to survive the gas,' she said kindly. 'Not many did.'

This time his look was one of irritation. 'What would you know about it?' he snapped.

'I know because I was there,' she replied evenly.

He blinked in astonishment. 'You were?'

'I was a VAD with the Casualty Clearing Station at Maricourt. I was there for nine months.'

His breathing was a lot easier now, the searing agony that had seized his lungs had subsided. But he knew it wouldn't last for long. He had at least a dozen major attacks every day, and innumerable minor ones.

He excused himself and left the room to fetch a clean hanky. When he returned, he told her he'd come through

Maricourt in mid-October, having been gassed at Le Transloy. 'I can recall the action,' she said, 'but not you.'

He gave her a wry smile. 'I'd be surprised if you did. The CCS was bursting at the seams with casualties when I was there. Even if you'd tended me yourself, why should you remember me?' The look in his eyes was almost a challenge. 'Or I you, come to that?'

A very bitter man, Sheila thought, watching him closely.

Returning to the subject of Ian, Hurley said he'd like to help, he genuinely would, but unfortunately he was going to have to decline. 'To put it bluntly,' he said defensively, 'I don't think I have the strength for a task like this.' It was clear she was being dismissed.

With a flash of insight, Sheila realized that Hurley's health was only part of his problem. He'd also lost confidence in himself. What a waste, she thought, what a terrible terrible waste.

Rising, she said she was sorry to have bothered him. He replied that he'd enjoyed the company as he didn't have all that much.

He led the way back down that dark and dingy hallway to the door which he opened for her. There she paused, reluctant to be defeated.

She was going down to Dragonholme in a couple of weeks, she told Hurley. Why didn't he come with her and meet Ian? There could be no harm in that. She'd be interested to hear what he had to say about the lad. When Hurley didn't answer right away she added, 'Some sea air would be good for your lungs.'

Hurley glanced away. 'I'm sorry,' he mumbled.

Sheila moved towards the stairs, then suddenly wheeled around again. In a voice ringing with scorn she said, 'I'm sure there were many who fell at Le Transloy who, if it was possible to ask them now, would gladly trade places with you. Rotten lungs and all. And becoming you they wouldn't funk the rest of your life, they'd make the best of it, thanking God they were alive to do

234

so.' And with that she marched off down the stairs. When she got home she thought what an awful thing that had been to say to the man. Nonetheless, it was what she'd felt and, harsh as her words had been, she couldn't regret them.

Two days later the telephone rang in the Kelvinside house. It was Graeme Hurley to ask Sheila if the invitation was still open for him to accompany her to Dragonholme.

She told him to bring pyjamas, they'd be staying overnight.

It had been a quiet drive down, David in the back with Pat and asleep for most of the time, Hurley up front beside Sheila. He only spoke when spoken to, and spent most of the ride staring out at the passing scenery with those sad and suffering eyes of his. She didn't know what he was seeing, but it certainly wasn't the view.

Between Hurley's agreement to come to Dragon-holme and the visit itself, Sheila had corresponded with Rhona, asking Rhona's permission to bring Hurley to see Ian, and explaining what she hoped it might lead to. She also asked Rhona to help her by making temporary accommodation arrangements for the crew of the *Sheila B*. They would make their own permanent ones in due course.

Rhona had been enthusiastic about Hurley – she and Ian were looking forward to meeting him.

Immediately after the introductions, Rhona put out the lunch, a large fish pie that gave off clouds of steam when she cut into it.

David tucked into his plateful, declaring it scrumptious. Pat said it was so delicious she was certain to have some more. But Hurley only picked at what he had in front of him, finally leaving most of it with the excuse to Rhona that he never had much of an appetite.

Rhona was dishing up the rhubarb tart and custard

when Hurley got a major attack, jumping up from the table so quickly he knocked over his chair he fled the house.

Rhona, her face filled with concern, watched his blundering exit, then turned to Sheila who explained to her and Ian about Hurley having been gassed in the war.

'Poor man,' said Rhona, shaking her head in sympathy.

After about five minutes Hurley returned and tried to apologize, but Rhona shushed him, saying apologies were completely unnecessary.

'Does it hurt when you cough like that?' Ian asked.

'Like the Dickens,' Hurley replied, almost smiling.

It had been a simple enough exchange, but Sheila, watching the look that passed between them, felt some sort of bond had been established between the pair of them. A good sign, she thought.

After lunch Sheila suggested that Hurley and Ian be left together for a while. Before departing for Glasgow, Hurley had told her he intended giving Ian a series of short tests.

Sheila went outside, glancing at her watch. It was nearing time for the arrival she was so eagerly looking forward to. 'Come on, David,' she called. 'I'm taking you down to the harbour. There's a surprise there for you.'

David was instantly excited. A surprise! What sort of surprise? Laughing, Sheila replied that if she told him it would cease to be a surprise, so he'd just have to wait his horses.

On reaching the quayside, Sheila glanced back the way they'd come to see the villagers coming down to join them. Within a few minutes almost the entire village of Dragonholme had gathered.

'There it is!' cried Lena Murray a little later, pointing.

Sheila's heart swelled within her when she picked out the *Sheila B.* in the distance. She'd spoken by telephone to George the previous day and he'd assured her the

236

conversion was a first-class job; the Eyemouth yard had done the boat proud.

'I can't see,' complained David. She picked him up and pointed to the boat. 'That's ours, David. Yours and mine. We own it,' she said proudly, her eyes shining.

David squealed with delight, giving his mother a big wet kiss on her cheek. He wanted to know if he could go out on their boat, and was disappointed when she replied not yet. 'When you're a little older I'll ask George to take you out for an hour or two,' she promised.

David wasn't pleased. 'I want to go today,' he insisted but Sheila was adamant. Not until he was older. He would have to settle for that.

As the *Sheila B.* sailed into the harbour, George sounded its horn again and again. The onlookers clapped and cheered.

She had instructed that the name *Dragonholme* be emblazoned on the boat's stern, denoting Dragonholme to be its home port. More than one of those present had tears in their eyes.

George skilfully manoeuvred the *Sheila B.* into the old *Bluebell* spot, then a member of the crew jumped ashore and demanded to know which of the ladies was Mrs Lack. When Sheila said she was Mrs Lack he handed her the for'rard line and said George had thought she'd like to tie off the *Sheila B.* for its first time in its new home port.

It was a gesture she appreciated. Calling David to her side she told him they'd do it together. There was a rousing cheer from the crowd.

When the boat was secure, George came on to the quay-side and introduced his crew to Sheila and the villagers.

There were five crew, plus George, three of them married, the other three bachelors. She shook each of the five by the hand and welcomed them to Dragonholme.

'When will your families be arriving?' she asked.

'They'll be getting into Dragonholme in two days time,' a crewman named Shet Perlie informed her.

Sheila replied that that was excellent, and that

237

appropriate accommodation had been arranged for all concerned, but before they were shown that accommodation would they care for a drink?

The crew of the *Sheila B.* greeted that with broad grins and a nodding of heads. She then said to the other fishermen present that she hoped they'd join them at The Halibut's Tail so the men could all get acquainted. 'The drinks are all on me,' she laughed.

'This is the happiest day Dragonholme has known in a long time lass,' gossipy Mrs Johnstone said to Sheila as the men made their way to the pub. In that instant the germ of an idea was born in Sheila's mind.

At The Halibut's Tail Mr Meekie welcomed them with open arms.

That night, after David was asleep Sheila, Hurley, Rhona and Pat sat down with a bottle of whisky. Hurley said he agreed with Miss Dalziel, Ian was university material, no doubt about it. But Ian did need considerable coaching, both in new subjects and in those he was already studying, if he was to pass the entrance exams.

'So will you take him on?' Sheila asked bluntly.

Hurley rubbed his jaw, his eyes all the while studying her. 'It would be an honour,' he said at last. 'I'd enjoy teaching a boy with so much intelligence and potential.'

Rhona was smiling, but it was a strained smile. 'Well,' she said, 'I'll wind up the ornament business and we'll move through to Glasgow as soon as possible.'

'That's that then,' said Sheila, topping up their drams.

Hurley announced he wanted to make a toast. Raising his glass he said: 'To Ian getting into Glasgow University! And may he turn out to be an even better novelist than Sir Walter Scott.'

Rhona's glass stopped halfway to her mouth. 'What do you mean "novelist"?'

'Hasn't Ian told you? That's what he wants to be,' Hurley grinned.

Rhona gave a tiny laugh. 'This is the first I've heard of it.'

'He can certainly tell a marvellous story when he wants to,' said Pat. During her previous visit, Ian had regaled her with several tales he'd made up.

Fairy-touched, Sheila thought. That was how Ian had always been described since a wee boy. Aye, he'd make a fine novelist. What more ideal calling for a person the fairies had touched than that of a writer?

She woke next morning to the clamour of gulls screeching on the roof. Beside her was David, and beyond him Pat. The three of them had had to share the front bed while Graeme Hurley took the back room.

David would sleep for a while yet, Sheila thought, and Pat was still well out for the count. She decided to get dressed and go outside to have a look down at the *Sheila B.* for the sheer pleasure it would give her to see it there.

Slipping out the front door, she was surprised to find Hurley standing gazing out to sea. 'You're up early,' she said.

He gave her a smile. 'I've already been for a long walk along the seashore,' he said enthusiastically. 'Now I'm absolutely ravenous. I can't wait for breakfast.'

Sheila stared at him in amazement. 'That's certainly a change of tune from yesterday when you told Rhona you never had much of an appetite,' she remarked.

Hurley grinned. 'It's years since I've felt this hungry. Maybe you were right about the sea air. In fact, I actually got a decent night's sleep for the first time in years.'

'That's marvellous!' she said, looking at him more closely. He did look better: there was even a hint of colour in those sallow cheeks of his.

Hurley ran a hand through his hair, then gazed back out to sea, in the same way he had in the car during the drive down; staring at one thing, but seeing quite another.

Beside him, Sheila followed his gaze and sighed, thinking about the idea Mrs Johnstone had given her yesterday afternoon. My God, what an achievement that would be. That would be something to be really proud of! Could she pull it off, though? She watched the colour of the water change beneath the sunlight. Why not? At least she could give it a damn good try.

She glanced at Hurley's face, and was shocked to see it had become contorted in agony, twin rivers of tears streaming from his eyes.

'What is it?' she asked hesitantly.

He'd forgotten she was there. He groped for his hanky, embarrassed that she'd seen him crying.

He'd never spoken about this to another soul, but felt he could with her. She'd been there, after all; she'd know what he was talking about.

In a voice that seemed to come from far away, he talked of the Somme and the horrors he had seen there.

He told Sheila of his friend Brian Robertson, drowned before his very eyes in a huge shell crater filled with mud that Brian had stumbled into.

They'd done their best to get Brian out, but the mud had defeated them, dragging the screaming and pleading Brian down to his death with a final obscene plop.

'That terrible mud,' he said quietly. 'We all had nightmares about it. That vast ocean of mud, rippling when the wind blew, filled with traps for the unwary, traps that claimed victims with horrible regularity.

'I'm haunted by Brian's screams,' he said. 'His and the screams of the others.'

Sheila shivered in the warm morning air. She had heard other accounts of the mud related to her while at Maricourt, often by men she'd later learned had gone back to the mud, to be claimed by it in turn.

Hurley talked on, describing the action at Le Transloy when he'd been gassed, saying how he'd fumbled for his mask, while all around him men were writhing as their lungs burned out. 'It felt like my lungs were on fire,' he

240

said. Holding his breath, he'd slipped the mask on, then beat as hasty a retreat as he could.

He'd passed Sarge Copland running round in circles like a chicken with its head cut off, and John Mitchell whose eyes had been bulging so much they'd made him giggle hysterically inside his mask, and Lance Corporal Timms, quite dead, kneeling as though praying, and all the while the gas swirled around, not that much deeper in colour than many yellow fogs he'd experienced in the depths of a Glasgow winter when every fireplace in the city was going full blast.

Sheila suddenly realized she had a pain in her right hand. Glancing down, she found blood between her clenched fingers. She'd made so tight a fist she'd broken her flesh with one of her nails.

When Hurley was finally finished, he hung his head for a few moments, then turned his gaze back to the sea.

They stood for a little while in silence, the world waking up around them, each remembering.

Eventually, Sheila broke the silence.

'If you'd like that breakfast now I'll cook it for you.'

He faced her with a smile. 'That would be lovely.'

After breakfast they discussed the return to Glasgow. It was agreed that they'd start directly after lunch.

Sheila wanted some time on her own to think, so she arranged for Pat to take David off to play. When they'd gone, she went down to the quayside where she sat on a coiled rope staring at the *Sheila B.*, in her mind going over and over the idea she'd had the previous afternoon. It could work; she was certain it could.

When Sheila spied George she waved him over and they sat together for a good hour while she fired questions at him. If he thought she was behaving peculiarly, he didn't show it.

When lunchtime came Sheila went to Rhona's. Hurley was sitting in front of the fire with his shoes off and a cup of tea in his hand. 'I've come to a decision,' he said when Sheila came in. 'I've been waiting for you to announce it.'

Immediately, she was alarmed. Had he decided against tutoring Ian, after all? Was he going to give up already?

Clearing his throat, Hurley said he couldn't remember when he'd last felt so well. 'Since this morning, I've been like a man reborn,' he beamed. 'I would never have thought it possible. It seems to me,' he went on, 'that I could stay that way if I remain in Dragonholme. It's the air,' he laughed. 'You told me the air would do me good.'

Hurley glanced over at Rhona, then back to Sheila. 'It also seems a great shame to me that Rhona would lose her small business by coming through to Glasgow. She needn't do that if I stay here.'

This was something Sheila hadn't even dare hope for. She looked over at Rhona. It was clear how relieved she was at the thought of not having to leave her home.

Hurley went on to say there was little left for him in that dirty city anyway. Here he not only had some of his health back, but had found the beginnings of a sense of peace as well.

Hurley stared at Sheila. She knew he was now talking again of the Somme. What had passed between them that morning had been some sort of exorcism for him, or at least the start of one. Dragonholme wasn't only good for his physical health.

Hurley said he would return to Glasgow with them that day as planned, for he had to put his affairs there in order. Then he'd come back to Dragonholme with all speed, and begin the task of getting Ian ready for his exams.

Sheila told him he could use her house here as long as he liked, for which he thanked her. He would take her up on that offer until he could make other arrangements.

With a sniff Rhona turned again to her cooking. She'd been dreading going to Glasgow. Her stay there would have been purgatory – she who was used to village life and the fresh smell of the sea forever in her nostrils. She would have suffocated in the city, stifled by its claustrophobia. Aye, that would have been the way of it, sure as eggs were eggs, and herring herring. She offered up a silent prayer to God, thanking him for her reprieve.

When she dished out the lunch, Graeme Hurley got twice the plateful anyone else did, and he ate every last morsel of it.

The great day arrived for the boats – they could hardly be called a fleet anymore, although Sheila intended altering that – to sail north. She motored down to see them off.

George, starting his first season as skipper, was the proverbial cat with two tails, and one who'd fallen into a bucket of cream at that.

Sheila met the wives and weans who'd moved through from Eyemouth, already knowing from Rhona that they were well settled into their new homes.

Houses had been easy to find for these families, thanks to so many in the village lying empty. George, of course, had been staying with his ma, the other two members of the crew having gone into digs which they'd return to when the *Sheila B.* fished the home waters and again at the end of the season.

As was traditional, everyone in the village came down to the quayside to wish the boats and the men who sailed them good luck.

Graeme Hurley stood with Rhona and Ian. Only the week before he'd moved out of Sheila's house and into a small cottage he was renting from the Dragonholme Estate.

Sheila looked from the *Sheila B.* to the other boats. The age of sail was definitely past, she thought; steam was the thing now, and the thing into which she'd be putting her money. But you had to hand it to the sailing craft, they had style and romance.

She grinned to herself. She could just hear Davey, her da, telling her not to be so soft; there was nothing in the least romantic about fishing boats, sail or otherwise. But he'd have been wrong; there was.

The Rising Sun, the smallest of the boats, was first away, then the *Foamcrest*, *Silvery Dart* and *Nonsuch* in that order. Last of all, and as far as she was concerned best of all, was the *Sheila B.*, George blowing its horn as the villagers cheered and waved, no-one cheering louder or waving harder than Sheila herself.

They waited on the quayside until the last boat had vanished over the horizon, then reluctantly turned for home.

Sheila had only taken a few steps when she happened to glance up at the cliffs towering over Dragonholme. Automatically, she held her breath.

There, looking down on her, a figure on horseback was silhouetted against the bright sky: a figure she recognized instantly.

James Campbell had also come to see the boats away.

8

Sheila thought the *Friend's Good Will*, squat and truncated in appearance, an ugly vessel. It certainly had nothing like the graceful lines of the *Sheila B*. But the *Friend's Good Will* was up for sale. It was the first steam drifter to come on to the market that season, and Sheila was determined to buy it.

She'd driven up to Buckie two days before, in order to have a comprehensive report made on the boat. The report had been favourable. Despite being sixteen years old, the *Friend's Good Will* was still structurally and mechanically sound and had a long working life yet remaining to it.

The reason the boat was on the market was that its owner and skipper had suffered a serious accident off

Lerwick. His hip had been severely crushed, and as a result of that he'd never walk again, far less go to sea.

The sale of the *Friend's Good Will* was to be by public auction on the quayside beside the boat. When Sheila arrived there was already a small knot of people there.

She was well aware of the curious glances cast in her direction. A good-looking and expensively dressed woman all on her own wasn't exactly a common occurrence at such an occasion.

After a while a man came over, raised his cap, and asked her if she wasn't the Miss Beattie who'd worked at one time for Mr Campbell? She nodded that she was.

The man introduced himself, and Sheila recalled doing business with him years ago. They shook hands, then chatted for a few moments, after which he melted back into what had become a sizeable throng.

She wasn't worried about the ever-growing numbers, though. Most of those present would be spectators come to watch the bidding.

Dead on noon, the advertised time, the auctioneer jumped on to a small platform, banged his gavel, and announced the start of the sale.

A number of people looked at Sheila in surprise when she made her first bid. None of them had ever known a woman to bid before. The auctioneer paused, momentarily thrown. 'Are *you* actually bidding?' he asked Sheila in a pedantic schoolmasterish tone.

Biting off a blistering reply, she said in a loud, clear voice, 'Yes, that's correct.'

The auctioneer looked around, presumably for advice. When none was forthcoming, he shrugged and continued with the business in hand.

One by one the bidders dropped out, until the only ones left where Sheila and someone on the far side of the assembly, hidden from her view.

Sheila raised her bid again and again, and still the other bidder continued to top her. She chewed her lip when what she'd set herself as a maximum price was reached, then bid once more.

There was no hesitation from the other bidder in topping her yet again. Telling herself that this was absolutely her last bid, she went up a double amount.

The auctioneer had hardly recognized this last bid of hers when she was topped a final time. The auctioneer looked at her inquiringly, and waited.

Having set her heart on owning that boat it took all her self-control to shake her head, knowing the price the *Friend's Good Will* was already fetching to be well in excess of its actual value.

The auctioneer offered the *Friend's Good Will* one last time, then banged his gavel. 'Sold to Mr James Campbell!' he announced with finality.

Sheila flushed with rage. James Campbell! She should have known! Who else could be so determined?

As the crowd began to disperse she noticed that several of the men were smirking at her, obviously pleased to see her lose out after having had the audacity to intrude on what they considered a male province. Silly sods, she thought. They hadn't heard the last of her yet.

She was about to move off when suddenly James Campbell was there in front of her, his face so hard and expressionless it might have been carved from granite.

'Hello, Sheila,' he said.

He'd aged considerably since the last time they'd met. His hair was grey, his body now so thin that his clothes just seemed to hang on him.

'You did that for spite didn't you?' she snapped back instantly. 'You've no need for a drifter. You know damn well you only have trawlers in your fleet.'

The very sight of her was driving him wild. Though his face showed no emotion, he wanted to sweep her into his arms, to kiss her, to hold her to him, and never let her go.

But all he could say was, 'Is that any way to greet an old friend?'

'You mean that stealing my boat from me *is*?' she countered.

If she could convert a trawler into a drifter, then why shouldn't he do the reverse? he teased, smiling thinly. He'd known she'd be stumped for an answer to that one.

James Campbell's penetrating gaze made her want to squirm. He seemed to be staring into the very depths of her being. She had forgotton how powerful a man he was.

Disarmingly he then confessed that the reason he'd attended the auction in person was so that he could speak to her.

It surprised and disturbed her to realize that her heart was pounding.

As for his buying the *Friend's Good Will*, he genuinely had intended converting the boat and adding it to his fleet (which was a lie, his intention all along having been to do as he was about to do). But as Sheila had accused him of spite, and because she obviously wanted it so much, then she would have it, a present from him to her. And with that he handed her the boat's purchase papers and other documents.

She stared in astonishment at the papers in her hand.

'Now, can we go somewhere where we can talk?' He knew a pub that was rather nice where they could have a drink together.

'Talk about what?' she demanded, finally finding her voice.

'About something very much to your advantage,' he replied mysteriously, all his old charm still with him.

Perplexed, she just stared. The last thing she wanted was a drink and a chat with James Campbell. But still she could not find it in her to say no.

'Let's go then,' she replied stiffly, avoiding his eyes.

She flinched when he took her arm, but didn't object or remove it from his grasp.

In the pub he settled them into a quiet corner. When he returned with their drinks he asked her why she'd been after the *Friend's Good Will*. 'I can understand why you bought the *Sheila B.*,' he smiled. 'She was named for you, after all. But why the *Friend's Good Will*?' He'd obviously been puzzling over that.

There was no reason why she shouldn't tell him, she thought. He'd find out soon enough.

She couldn't help the anger that crept into her voice. 'I'm only doing what you, as laird of Dragonholme, should have done,' she said. 'And that's to breathe life back into the devastated village.'

She explained that it was her plan to buy as many boats as she was able, boats that would be based at Dragonholme, and whose crews and families would live there.

Men and work, those were the keys to revitalizing Dragonholme. By bringing in both she'd restore the village to the thriving community it had once been.

All the while she spoke, he said nothing. He could feel his own blood moving as though it had been sleeping for years.

She was right about the village, of course. He had not so much neglected it, as abandoned it. As though by watching it shrivel he was getting back at her. Oh, the fire of her, he thought, as she went on excitedly about her plans. Had he ever known anyone else with so much spirit?

At one point he'd considered selling the Hall, taking himself away from the places forever associated with her in his mind. But in the end he hadn't been able to sell. No matter how much it hurt, he couldn't bring himself to sever the tie with the place where he'd spent the happiest days of his life.

'So the rumour's true that you've come into a fortune?' he asked at last.

She nodded.

'Your husband was killed in the war I heard?'

'Aye.'

'I lost my two lads then. And Fiona of the shock.' He

stared at his hands against the top of the table, then raised his face to hers with something of a smile. 'But I expect the gossips have told you all about that.'

'I'm sorry,' she whispered, almost speaking his name.

'Fiona opened that second telegram, read its contents, screamed, and fell down dead. Just like that. I'll never forget that sound till my own dying day.'

She took a sip of her drink. Since the disaster it just seemed to have been death, death and death again.

'You said you wanted to talk about something that was very much to my advantage?' she prompted.

'I really did think I'd got over you,' he began slowly, his voice barely audible. 'That I'd pushed you into the background once and for all. Then you returned to Dragonholme, and all the old feeling erupted. And I realized that I'm still as much in love with you as I always was.'

'I don't love you,' she said, her voice as hard as rock. 'I will never forgive you for what you did to my family. For what you did to me.'

Breath hissed from him. 'So that was the reason you ran away. You found out.'

'I overheard you and Dunwoodie talking that night you were both drunk.'

His hand grabbed hers across the table. 'I know I was wrong, but that doesn't make my love wrong.'

She jerked her hand free. 'I don't want to hear any more.'

'You've more than yourself to think about, you know. You've a son, you must consider what's best for him. It's not good for a boy to be brought up without a father.' He leaned towards her so that she could almost feel his breath. 'Marry me and I'll be that father to him,' he pleaded.

She couldn't believe what she was hearing. 'Are you mad? Marry you? After what you did?'

'You're not thinking my proposal through,' he argued.

My God, she thought, he is mad! 'What is there to think through? My mother would have lived longer, and certainly in far easier circumstances, if it hadn't been for

249

what you and that pig Dunwoodie did. And what about
the hardship you caused my sisters-in-law and their
children?'

'But I loved you. I only did what I did because I loved
you.'

She didn't know whether to laugh or to cry. 'Love? Is
that what you call love? Do you know, I think you must
be the most selfish bastard I've ever known.'

'I don't know what else I can say to convince you.'

She moved as though to stand up. 'There's nothing
you can say.'

His face had lost all its colour. She had to accept his
proposal, she had to. In all the fantasies he'd had since
learning of her return – in all the fantasies he'd had when
it seemed he would never see her again – she always
forgave him in the end.

'I don't want you to ever speak of this again. It's a
ridiculous suggestion,' Sheila said, suddenly on her feet
and pushing in her chair.

There was no trace of his usual composure as he staggered to his feet. 'There's nothing ridiculous about it,' he
said in a choked voice.

She stared at him levelly, all the old anger burning once
more. 'You disgust me,' she said. 'You fill me with
disgust.'

But, in his mind's eye, he could see her as he'd often
dreamed of her, her body naked and her arms reaching
out for him, her smile warming him, his own self dissolving in the ecstasies of love.

With a sudden movement he grabbed her wrist,
squeezing it so hard she gasped with pain. 'You don't
mean that,' he whispered.

She tried to pull herself free, but he wouldn't let go.
She had no wish to make a scene.

'If you won't be my wife at least consent to be my
mistress again. It can't have meant nothing to you. You
loved me once. You'll love me again. Just give me a
chance.'

'You've had your chance, James Campbell,' she said with all the dignity she had.

Then the volcano of his emotions erupted, so that he lost all control over himself.

Regardless of where they were, he threw himself on her, pressing his lips against her unwilling ones in a kiss.

Sheila struggled against his assault. With her free hand she struck at his face, raking her nails the length of his cheek.

With a cry of pain, he pulled away from her. The side of his face was marked with four thin lines of blood.

'Try to force yourself on me ever again and so help me God I'll kill you,' she spat out in fury.

His passion spent, he felt only humiliation and shame. He'd made a complete fool of himself, and how that hurt – far more than a damaged cheek.

'Get away from me,' she ordered.

Another customer walked the length of the bar for the water jug, turned and glimpsed James's face, looked startled, then scuttled back the way he'd come.

James groped for his handkerchief, holding it to his bleeding cheek. He wanted to lash out, hit someone, and the someone he wanted to hit most of all was himself.

As he rose to go his gaze lit on the purchase paper and other documents for the *Friend's Good Will*, lying beside Sheila's drink. His hand swooped down to snatch them. In a voice that shook he told her he was damned if she was going to have that boat after all.

It was such a pathetic gesture, that all she could do was laugh.

To James Campbell, that laugh was as sharp as a knife, and far more lethal. He strode from the pub, banging the door behind him. Outside, he would have sworn that he could still hear her laughing.

'Campbell was right about one thing,' Pat was saying. 'David does need a father. It's not good for a boy to be brought up with only women.' Sheila had just related to her what had happened in the Buckie pub.

Sheila was tired after the drive down from the north, but, despite the lateness of the hour, it would be a good while yet before she'd be able to sleep. There were too many things running around inside her head for that.

'Are you saying I'm spoiling David, or mummying him?' she asked slowly.

Pat shook her head. 'No, of course not. All I'm saying is that any child lacking one of its parents will grow up sort of lopsided, if you know what I mean.'

Sheila had never thought of it like that. She pictured David upstairs in his bed, and her heart went out to him. But she had herself to consider also, or was that selfishness on her part?

'It's been six years since your Andrew died, and you're still a very attractive woman.' Pat paused. 'How old are you?'

Sheila had to think for a moment. 'Twenty-eight. Twenty-eight, my God.' Until recently she'd felt more like fifty.

Pat shrugged. 'You've a whole life still ahead of you. I'm sure Andrew wouldn't have wanted you to go on playing the widow forever. He'd want you to find someone else, just as you found him after you lost Eric.'

Pat was right, of course. And Andrew would have agreed with her. But not yet, she wasn't ready for another man yet. She needed more time to heal the wound of grief still open within her. Only since she'd repaired her ties with Dragonholme had the ache begun to diminish.

She changed the subject, then after a while went up to her bedroom, taking a large whisky with her.

Damn James Campbell for buying the *Friend's Good Will* out from under her, she thought angrily. If it hadn't been for his interference the *Friend's Good Will* would now be hers. How long till another stream drifter was put up for sale? God alone knew, it could be weeks, or months, and in the meantime she was seething with impatience. How long could she wait?

Well, she decided at last, exhausted by her own busy brain, she would continue going after boats as they came on the market, but she could also help matters along herself. It was so simple a solution that she wondered that she hadn't thought of it before: she would have more boats built for her.

And she knew exactly who she wanted to build them.

Tom McIndoe was a right old man now, his hair snow white, his shoulders stooped, his face tramlined with age. But he still owned McIndoe's Shipyard, and still ran it with a rod of iron. He also still built some of the bonniest boats to be seen in any herring fleet. When Sheila had been James Campbell's assistant she'd often dealt with Tom, and the pair of them had been great pals.

He greeted Sheila warmly, ushering her to a hard-backed chair.

Sheila liked Tom McIndoe's office. It was a real man's place, smelling strongly of tobacco smoke and male bodies. There were plans and drawings everywhere; on top of his desk and strewn all round it.

She came straight to the point. She wanted him to build four drifters, similar in line to the *Sheila B.*, but completely up-to-date.

Tom nodded. 'Aye,' he said in a deep, rough voice, 'I can do that, no bother. Mind you, they'd cost a fair bit.' He judged her with his open blue eyes. 'I presume the person on whose behalf you are acting is aware of that?' He knew she hadn't worked for James Campbell in years, but she had explained very little in her letter.

'I'm not acting for anyone. I want those boats for myself.'

Tom sat back in his chair with an astounded expression on his aged face. A woman owning fishing boats! He'd never heard the like.

'I take it you've no objection about building for a woman?' Sheila asked drily.

Tom stared up at the ceiling while he considered whether he did or not. Just because he hadn't done it before didn't mean to say he shouldn't, but it was novel, oh, aye, it was certainly that!

'As far as I'm concerned a woman's money is the same colour as a man's,' he replied at last, with a broad smile.

'There speaks a true Aberdonian,' Sheila grinned back. 'Now what about delivery, when can I have them?'

Tom rose from behind his desk and told her to come with him to the window. There he pointed to the yard below which was bustling with activity, and where a number of new hulls could be seen in various stages of construction.

With proud satisfaction in his voice, he informed her that the yard was working flat out, with orders stacked up waiting their turn. It would be two years before he could deliver the four drifters.

Sheila's dismay and disappointment were evident. Two years was an absolute eternity.

'I can't deliver before then,' Tom assured her.

She stared down at the yard, her gaze moving from hull to hull, the majority of which were going to be trawlers. She watched a gang of riveters, admiring the dexterity and expertise with which they drove home each individual rivet.

Two years? That wasn't satisfactory at all. Turning to Tom she said so, and added, sadly, she'd have to take her business elsewhere.

'But we're the best,' he said reasonably.

'*One* of the best,' she corrected him.

He repeated it would have to be a two-year delivery date. She repeated that that was unacceptable and she'd have to take her business elsewhere. Her mind was already considering the alternatives.

It went totally against the grain for Tom to let an order slip away like this. There had been too many lean times in the past when the yard had been empty and he'd have given an arm and leg for one drifter, far less four. Frantically he began mentally rejigging schedules, trying to find some way in which to accommodate this determined young woman.

A silence hung heavily between them for a full minute, then, with a sigh, Sheila thanked him for seeing her and said she'd be getting along.

Her hand was actually grasping the door knob when Tom said softly that with an awful lot of switching about he could deliver two of her boats in six months, the other two a year after that.

Sheila knew once an initial compromise had been made the way was open for others to follow. Without turning round she said two in six months, the remaining two six months after that.

Tom stuck a finger in a hairy ear and waggled it up and down. He replied somewhat grudgingly, that if she recalled he always sealed a new order over a dram. She answered she took water with hers.

They had three whiskies each, by the end of which Sheila had bargained the price down considerably.

She was happy, jubilant, and slightly drunk when she finally returned to her hotel.

Six weeks later, Sheila was back in Aberdeen to attend the sale by public auction of the pipe stalkie, the *Rowland*. Steam drifters were often called pipe stalkies by Scottish crews because of the tall, thin, funnel sprouting behind the wheelhouse.

The weather, despite it being July, was wet and blustery as she strolled on to the fish wharf where the auction was to take place. Some minutes later the auctioneer climbed on to the makeshift platform that had been erected for him and announced the start of the sale. As he spoke Sheila became aware of an all too familiar figure staring at her coldly, and her heart sank.

James Campbell, graven-faced, thought to himself that he was going to enjoy this. He was newly determined that if he was to be denied, then so also would she be. He'd made up his mind to destroy her dream of revitalizing Dragonholme, and in the process be revenged for the rejection and humiliation he'd suffered that day in Buckie – that he'd been suffering since the day she left him.

Her worst fears became justified as the bidding progressed. Eventually, she too dropped out knowing that even if she'd bid every last penny she possessed James Campbell would still have topped her.

She felt sick when the *Rowland* fell to him. You bastard, she thought, but refused to let her frustration and anger show.

James Campbell shot a smile of triumph in her direction, then, in a gesture of dismissal, turned his back on her.

'It would've looked grand tied off in Dragonholme harbour,' a voice said beside Sheila.

The speaker was a woman Sheila recognized, but couldn't quite put a name to. Realizing this the woman smiled and said, 'Aye, it's been a long time, right enough. I'm Mrs Burnside now, but you knew me when I was cried Rosie McCullough.'

Rosie was one of the many lassies who'd finally been forced to leave Dragonholme because of the shortage of men. She now told Sheila she'd come to Aberdeen where she'd married a fine, handsome man by the name of Hector Burnside. Prior to the sale, Burnside had been skipper of the *Rowland*.

Rosie went on to say she and her husband had heard how Sheila had bought the *Sheila B.*, and when they'd seen her there that day they'd rightly assumed she was after the *Rowland*, 'We'd been sore hoping you'd get it,' she finished.

Sheila was puzzled, and asked why Rosie and her husband should want that. Rosie replied wistfully that she had a great hankering to go back and live in Dragonholme. If Sheila had got the *Rowland* her Hector had been going to ask if he could keep his job as skipper. If Sheila had agreed, that would have meant they could have set up home in Dragonholme rather than Aberdeen.

Sheila asked where Hector was now. 'He's gone to ask James Campbell about staying on as skipper. But we don't hold out much hope of success. Campbell has a habit of promoting skippers from within the Portnessie fleet.'

Rosie was exactly the sort of person Sheila wished to bring back to Dragonholme. She would gladly have reinstated Hector as skipper, providing his previous employer gave him a good reference that was.

They talked about the past for a few minutes, and as they chatted it came to Sheila that perhaps she could bring Rosie back to Dragonholme after all, for wouldn't she be looking for a couple of skippers in three-and-a-half months' time?

She knew Hector Burnside would almost certainly still be unemployed then, for with the season under way skippering jobs wouldn't exactly be thick on the ground.

Sheila told Rosie that. 'If your Hector doesn't get the job with Campbell,' she said, 'then I'd like a word with him. I'll be in my hotel room all evening if you care to call for a drink. If you don't I'll know he's got the job.'

Rosie's eyes lit up, and she was effusive in her thanks.

Sheila left the wharf feeling a little better and in a fighting mood.

At the back of seven, Sheila had just finished putting a telephone call through to David and Pat when there was a knock on her door. Rosie and Hector, she thought, crossing to it; but she was wrong, for when she opened the door Tom McIndoe, clutching his bowler, stood revealed.

Tom, looking quite wretched, apologized for disturbing her, and asked if he could come in.

She took his hat and light coat, which she put to one side, then offered him a dram. 'You'd better pour yourself a glass as well, lassie,' he advised. 'For I'm the bearer of bad news.'

Sheila glanced at him sharply. This must be some sort of ploy on his part to postpone the delivery dates he'd agreed to. Aye, he's had second thoughts, and is now trying to pull a crafty one on me, she told herself, handing him his whisky. But she was wrong.

Tom swallowed his hefty dram in a single gulp, shuddering as it went down. He glanced hopefully across to where the bottle stood, and Sheila told him if he wanted another to help himself.

Tom was hating every moment of this. It ranked high amongst the worst things he'd had to do in his entire life. 'I was going to write,' he said to Sheila. 'But I heard you were in town for the auction of the *Rowland*, so I thought I'd come by and see you instead.'

He shifted uncomfortably where he stood, his ears a bright pink from embarrassment.

Alarm suddenly locked her body. There was something wrong here, something far worse than she'd at first imagined. 'What is it Tom?' she asked quietly.

Tom drank more whisky, after which he asked her if she had a family. 'Yes,' she said in surprise. 'I have a wee boy called David. He's just over five years old.'

Tom nodded. With a lad of her own she might understand. 'I have three sons,' he said. 'They're all grown up now, of course. They're working in the yard. They're good sons. Grant, the eldest, he'll become head of the firm when I die.'

Tom rubbed his forehead, finished what remained of his dram, and poured himself a third without even bothering to ask. Rounding on Sheila, eyes wide and vulnerable, he told her he was hellishly sorry but he had to cancel her order; he couldn't build the four drifters for her after all.

She stared at him as though he'd suddenly started speaking in a foreign language. 'What?'

Tom took a deep breath, then began to explain. James

Campbell had been to the yard several days previously. Campbell had come to ask if it was true he was building boats for her, and he'd told him the truth.

Campbell had then threatened him. If he went ahead with the order, Campbell would ensure no further orders were ever placed with the yard. And furthermore, the existing ones, with exception of hers, would all be cancelled.

Tom said he was in no doubt whatever that Campbell was capable of carrying out such a threat, for in recent years he had become undisputed leader amongst the fleet owners. King Campbell the man was even cried by some. If Campbell put the word out that his yard was to be banned, then banned it would be.

Tom went on to say he had his three sons to think about. If it had only been him he'd have told Campbell to take a running jump and damn the consequences, but the yard was bread, butter and the future for his lads. Matter of principle or not, it wasn't in him to take that away from them.

Having got that off his chest Tom sat and slumped over his again empty glass.

She couldn't blame Tom. The poor old man had been put in an impossible position. And Tom was right in considering James's threat not to be an idle one; James Campbell didn't make threats he wasn't prepared to carry out.

Crossing to Tom, she knelt by his chair and put her arm round him, telling him not to worry, she'd get her boats somehow, and she was only sorry he'd had to go through what he had.

She added she could well appreciate what it had been like for him to have to come and tell her this.

'What on earth did you do to him lassie?' Tom asked thickly.

'It's not what I've done to him that counts,' she smiled. 'It's what I'm going to do.'

* * *

It was four days since the Dragonholme boats had arrived back to fish the home grounds, and marvellous hauls they were having; a continuation of the superb catches they'd been taking in the northern waters. As seasons went, this was proving to be a bumper one for them.

Sheila was extremely pleased with George Jorgesson, who'd turned out a first-class skipper, just as Lang Jake McFadyen had said he would, with a nose that could sniff out herring the way a dog can aniseed.

George and the *Sheila B.* were out at sea that morning, while Sheila herself was in Portnessie to attend yet another auction of a pipe stalkie. She had high hopes of getting the boat in question, having indulged in what Pat McLuskey described as 'a wee bit of stage management'.

The auctioneer was the one who'd been at Buckie. A dozen or so feet to Sheila's left stood James Campbell, over on her right Hector Burnside.

She and Burnside hadn't even looked at each other, far less acknowledged one another. Nor would they.

The *Lorella* had been built in Berwick in 1910, and was a good, solid, reliable boat. It had been recently painted; black, French blue, and grey, which enhanced its appearance.

The bidding got off to a brisk start, nearly all eyes coming to rest on James Campbell when he made his first offer. It was now well known that he'd bought the last two drifters to come on the market and had converted them to trawlers in his own Portnessie repair yard.

Hector Burnside, appearing anxious and concerned, joined in the bidding, giving the man who'd topped him a glowering, sideways, glance.

One by one the bidders dropped away till at last there was only Sheila, James Campbell and Hector Burnside left. Finally Sheila shook her head when the auctioneer looked to her for fresh bid, and turning, swept through the crowd and off the quayside.

The next ten minutes were agonizing ones. Then Hector Burnside came bursting into the hotel lounge where she'd arranged to meet him, his face wreathed in smiles.

Sheila wanted to let out a whoop, but managed to restrain herself.

'He fell for it, just as you thought he would. He made no more bids after you'd gone,' Hector told Sheila, handing her the *Lorella*'s purchase paper and other documents, which she accepted with a trembling hand.

Two boats she now owned. Two out of the twenty she meant to have. Putting the purchase paper and other documents to her lips she kissed them.

'Pick a crew, but don't be hasty. Take your time. I want the best of those still looking for berths. And when they and the *Lorella* are ready, join up with George Jorgesson and the other Dragonholme boats,' Sheila ordered.

'I will Mrs Lack,' Hector replied respectfully.

'You've taken quite a chance in what you've done, you know. It won't take James Campbell long to find out we've put a fly one over on him, and he isn't a forgiving man.'

'I have what I want in being a skipper again, and Rosie has what she wants by being able to go back and live in Dragonholme. Sure, I've stuck my neck out, but as far as I'm concerned it's worth it. Anyway, I've every faith that you'll see I never get into the situation where Mr Campbell is able to carry out a reprisal against me,' Hector replied honestly.

She was touched by his declaration: and it served to remind her she was now responsible for people other than David and Pat.

'I'll do my best never to let you down, Hector. You have my oath on that.'

Sheila laughed with delight as she completed the second box of herrings she'd gutted since the boats had come in a short while before.

261

She'd come down to the shoreline to 'watch their arrival, and a braw sight it had been, too, with the *Sheila B.* leading them in.

It was Shet Perlie's wife who'd asked if she'd like to lend a hand, and she'd immediately answered that she'd be only too happy to.

When the last box had been filled and loaded she went down to the water's edge where she washed the knife she'd been loaned by Agnes Perlie.

As she did this she thought of how much she was enjoying living again in Dragonholme where she, David and Pat were settled into the family house for the summer. If it weren't for David's schooling, she'd sell the house in Glasgow and move back on a permanent basis.

She spied Rhona further down the shore, and waved. Rhona was holding a bag, which told Sheila that Rhona was out collecting seashells.

Sheila made a gesture that indicated drinking tea, and Rhona shook her head and pointed to the bag. The message was clear: Rhona had a lot more shells to collect before the tide, already well turned, came in.

Marika strolled over. 'Just like old times, eh Sheila?' she said happily.

'Almost,' Sheila replied, thinking it would be like old times indeed when there was a full Dragonholme fleet again, and the men living in the village to crew such a fleet.

'Mrs Johnstone isn't feeling too well and has taken to her bed. I dropped by earlier for a wee chaff,' said Marika.

'Is she bad?'

'Nothing that a few days in bed won't cure. That and a dram or two.'

Sheila smiled. Mrs Johnstone was well known to like her dram, although that was something the biddy could little afford nowadays.

'I'll drop by later with a half bottle,' Sheila said.

Sheila returned the knife to Agnes Perlie, saying she'd

fair enjoyed that. Then she went back to the house where she found Pat knitting and David playing with some tin soldiers behind a chair.

'There's a letter come for you – I put it over there beside the bread bin,' Pat said.

Sheila read the letter through, swearing under her breath. 'It's from the Renvoize Yard in Cornwall. They've turned me down as well,' she said angrily.

Pat's mouth tightened with concern. 'They were the last were they not?'

'The last in a long list from Lerwick to Falmouth. Every British yard that builds fishing boats has now turned down my order.'

She screwed the letter into a ball, and threw it from her. King Campbell was what Tom McIndoe had said James was cried, and by Christ that was right enough.

'Is there nowhere else you can try?' asked Pat.

'Perhaps Holland or Brittany, but I would have imagined he would have thought of that. He has strong connections over there as well. I've no doubt he can cut me off there just as he can here,' Sheila answered, her voice leaden with despair.

David glanced round from behind the chair where he was playing, saw his mummy's expression, and burst out crying.

Sheila immediately went to him and scooped him into her arms. She rocked him back and forth in an effort to console him.

'You look so unhappy,' he wailed, and hugged her tight.

Tears sprang into her own eyes then. He was such a dear wee lad, and aye concerned for her, just as his father had always been.

She took him over to where there was a bottle of lemonade – lemmy loo he called it – and poured him a glass. That stopped his crying, and brought a smile of pleasure to his face.

'Didn't you once tell me that Georgina pal of yours

from the war belonged to a family that owned a big Glasgow shipbuilding yard, a yard that's built several of the P&O and Cunard ships?' Pat said suddenly.

It was something that had come to Pat just as she was going off to sleep the night before, and which she'd forgotten about again until the last few moments.

'Yes I did,' Sheila answered, recalling the conversation. The yard in question was the MS Yard in Yoker, a large concern and the fount of the Murchison-Stewart money.

'Well maybe they can help somehow. If nothing else it's at least worth a try,' Pat suggested.

'But they build ocean liners!' Sheila protested.

Pat shrugged. 'It seems to me it wouldn't do any harm to have a word with them. They can only say no like everyone else after all.'

Pat was quite right; they could only say no, Sheila thought. She had everything to gain, and nothing to lose.

The big problem was that she hadn't been in touch with Georgina for ages. They had seen one another, and frequently corresponded, after the war. Then Georgina had married a stockbroker chap called Donald Galloway, and their relationship had petered out.

'Well?'

Sheila refilled David's glass, and gave him a quick kiss on the tip of his nose.

'I'll write this evening,' she replied.

Georgina lived in the Newlands Manor House, a splendid example of the very best of Scottish architecture. Newlands was an area in Glasgow's south side where the toffiest of the toffs lived, and the Galloways were the toffiest of the lot.

Sheila exclaimed on seeing that Georgina was pregnant, with only seven weeks to go.

Georgina, the picture of blooming motherhood, told Sheila this would be her third: there being Katie, whom

Sheila had met, and Kirsty, whom Sheila hadn't yet met.

Sheila handed over the mindings she'd brought, and said she'd have to send something for Kirsty. Georgina told her the girls were upstairs; they'd be down shortly.

Georgina commented on how well Sheila was looking, and expressed disappointment that she hadn't brought David with her. Sheila explained there'd been a long-standing arrangement for Pat to take him to Calderpark Zoo that day. He was mad keen on snakes, and this was to be a special treat before he returned to school at the conclusion of the summer holidays.

'Oh but it's grand to see you again!' Georgina breathed, and coming to Sheila swept her into her arms, hugging her hard.

They talked of Maricourt. Sheila told Georgina about Graeme Hurley who'd passed through there near the end of the Somme, and how Graeme was tutoring her nephew in Dragonholme, and doing a grand job of it too.

'And how about you, have you found anyone else yet?' Georgina asked.

Sheila gave a small smile, and shook her head.

Georgina returned Sheila's smile, but her eyes showed her concern. It was a long time since Andrew's death, and if Sheila hadn't been counting the years, she had.

Over coffee, Sheila got down to the real reason for her visit. 'This isn't purely a social visit, Georgina. What I wanted to know was if your family still owned the MS Yard.'

Georgina gazed at her over her cup, one eyebrow raised in surprise. 'Yes, we do. My brother Johnnie's in charge since father retired and took mother off to live in the south of France.' Georgina sat her cup down on its saucer, waiting for some explanation. 'Well?' she said at last. 'Are you going to tell me what is going on?'

Sheila slowly stirred her coffee. 'I'd like to meet your brother. I'm looking for a man who knows about boats.' And with that, she launched into her story.

*   *   *

265

Georgina brought Johnnie down to Dragonholme the following Sunday. She'd persuaded him that he'd been working too hard and needed a break; and that a day trip to her friend Sheila's on the coast was just what the doctor ordered.

Georgina and Sheila had already decided that Georgina wouldn't tell Johnnie that Sheila particularly wanted to speak to him. That fact would emerge in Dragonholme.

Johnnie Murchison-Stewart was short and stocky with a broad, flat face. Physically, he and Georgina were as different as chalk and cheese. All they had in common was their sandy-coloured hair, and the fact that neither of them would have won a prize in any beauty competition.

Georgina and Johnnie arrived in Dragonholme at lunchtime to find the cold buffet that Sheila and Pat had prepared already on the table.

Sheila took to Johnnie right off. There was a bluff, no nonsense quality about him that reminded her of Davey, her da.

'I hope the drive here wasn't too much for you,' Sheila said to Georgina as they sat down to eat. 'It's a pretty long ride.'

'Not at all,' Georgina assured her happily, helping herself to the ham. 'If anything, I feel elated by it.'

'Georgina's been telling me about the little tent you had to share at Maricourt,' Johnnie said conversationally. 'It's just as well you got on together.'

'We didn't always. Not when we were at Cowcaddens General Hospital,' Sheila admitted with a smile.

Georgina blushed.

'Oh?' prompted Johnnie, looking from his sister to her friend.

'When I first met her she considered me a right little peasant,' Sheila grinned.

'I wish I could deny it,' said Georgina ruefully. 'But, unfortunately, it's true. I was a proper stuck up prig in those days.'

Johnnie helped himself to bread. 'If the war did

nothing else it helped change a lot of out-of-date attitudes, and a damn good thing too.'

There followed a conversation about how the class structures had begun to change during the war, and were continuing to change. The old barriers between the classes were now not nearly as rigid as they once had been.

'I'm glad something decent came out of all that awfulness,' Sheila said quietly but not without bitterness.

Pat and Georgina exchanged an anxious look. Neither of them had any doubt as to what – or whom – she referred.

An awkward silence settled on the company for a few seconds, finally broken by Sheila herself when she asked, 'What did you do during the war, Johnnie?'

Normally he glossed over his years in service, but now he felt it necessary to go into some of the details. 'I was a junior officer in the Navy, for most of the conflict. Aboard the *Galatea*, a light cruiser.'

'I know that name,' Sheila said thoughtfully.

'The *Galatea* had the dubious honour of being the first British ship to make contact with the German fleet at the Battle of Jutland. She was talked about in the newspapers a lot for a while.' Even in the homely warmth of Sheila's cottage, he could vividly recall that long ago afternoon of 31 May, 1916. He gave a wry smile. 'I was very lucky. Just before Jutland I was nearly transferred to the battle cruiser *Queen Mary*, which was blown up and sunk with her entire crew.'

Again, a heavy silence settled over the table while everyone thought about the twists of fate by which men lived and died.

Johnnie's talking about the sinking of the *Queen Mary* gave Sheila the opening she needed. 'As someone who's been close to being sunk yourself, you'd be interested in the Dragonholme disaster,' she said.

Johnnie raised one sandy eyebrow. 'What disaster was that?'

'Why don't you and I walk down to the beach after lunch and I'll tell you all about it,' she smiled.

Across the table, Georgina gave her a small nod of approval.

As Sheila and Johnnie strolled through the village after lunch, she chatted on about Dragonholme, and her childhood there. She spoke of Davey, her ma, her brothers, and Eric. She could speak of them now without pain, but not without sadness. Then she spoke about the Dragonholme fleet.

'They were such bonny boats, she sighed, her eyes far away. 'All twenty-eight of them. And I tell you this, Johnnie, when they came sailing into harbour laden down with fish, and the wives and the sweethearts and the friends were all there waving and calling to them, and the seagulls were circling and shrieking above, and . . .' She trailed off, tears falling down her cheeks. 'There wasn't a better or more inspiring sight this side of Heaven,' she finished. in a whisper.

Her words touched Johnnie deeply. His eyes rarely left her as they continued down to the beach.

They stopped a few feet up from the furthest reaches of the water, and there Sheila told Johnnie how the disaster had happened, and how it was now her dream to rebuild the lost Dragonholme fleet and save the village from extinction. He listened to her entire story without saying a word.

Sheila laid Johnnie's letter down, feeling sick with disappointment. When Pat and David arrived back at the house almost twenty minutes later they found her sitting staring blankly into space.

'What's wrong with you?' Pat demanded.

Sheila took a deep breath, and brought herself out of her dream. 'I've finally heard from Johnnie Murchison-Stewart at MS,' she said.

'He received Mr McIndoe's plans safely then?' Pat asked excitedly.

'Yes, he did.'

Walking back from the beach the day he and Georgina had visited Dragonholme, Johnnie had quizzed her about drifters, the building of which he'd admitted he knew nothing about.

He'd wondered if Tom McIndoe up in Aberdeen would let him have the plans for the boats that Tom had intended building. She had said she would write to Tom and ask him to send Johnnie the plans, pretty certain that Tom would comply for friendship's sake.

'Well, when do you get your boats?' Pat prompted.

Sheila smiled hollowly. 'I don't.'

'What? But I thought he'd committed himself.'

'I was taking a lot for granted, apparently. He said he would like to build them for me, and I suppose in my enthusiasm I took that to mean he would.'

Pat took the letter Sheila handed her. 'So why won't he?'

'Not won't, *can't*. He'd hoped to be able to manipulate the orders his yard has on its books so that he could fit in my tiddlers. Apparently he's tried, and it's impossible. Every square inch of the yard is booked solid for years to come. So far in advance he can't even give me a date when he could start work on my order.'

'Oh, lass!' Pat whispered. This was a cruel blow indeed.

'It seems James Campbell has beaten me after all,' Sheila said. But her tone was more angry than resigned.

Sheila's eyes opened suddenly, and she wondered what had wakened her. It wasn't David, who was sleeping peacefully by her side.

She was about to turn over again, when she heard a scraping sound right outside the front door, followed seconds later by a muffled cough.

Sheila froze. As was the custom in Dragonholme, the door wasn't locked. Whoever was out there only had to turn the handle to walk right in.

There it was again, more scraping; as if the person was running something over the door. What could be going on?

Moonlight shone through the window. With that to guide her, she slid noiselessly from the bed, tip-toed over to the range, and picked up the old brass-handled poker standing there.

Her heart was racing, the blood pounding in her ears, as she stealthily crossed over to the door, stopping, breath held to listen. All she heard was the rustle of a breeze, nothing else.

Lifting the poker high, she grasped the door handle and jerked the door open suddenly. But whoever had been there was gone.

Something flashed down the road, black on white. Putting a hand on the door she started to lean forward to try and get a better view, then pulled her hand away with a cry. The door was covered with something which from the smell and texture could only be one thing.

In the still moonlight her eyes scanned the sleeping houses and shadowy landscapes, but there was nothing to be seen. What sort of person, she wondered, would do such a filthy thing? And why to her? With one last look around, she went back inside, this time bolting the door behind her.

After washing her fouled hand, she sat herself down on one of the kitchen chairs. She was too awake now to go back to sleep, her mind spinning with turbulent thoughts. In all of Dragonholme, there was no one she could think of capable of such a disgusting act. There was no one who wasn't her friend. Was it some sort of joke she wasn't seeing because it was in such bad taste? No, that couldn't be it. If it wasn't some crazy outsider, it must be someone with a grudge against her.

And then she thought of James. As crazy as it sounded, there was no one else it could be. He was the only person in Dragonholme with any reason to hate her or to wish to frighten her.

Well, she was damned if she was going to let him get away with it. She'd confront him, face to face, and tell him what she thought of this sort of childish, revolting behaviour.

Her first impulse was to get dressed right then and march into the Hall, waking them all up if necessary, especially his lordship.

On second thoughts, though, she decided to wait till morning, when she would be in total control of herself when she saw him. She knew James Campbell well enough to know that he regarded female emotion as weakness. If she went to him now she would only end up in tears of rage and hurt.

She would shed no more tears for James Campbell, she decided grimly. Not one.

The next morning, having got up early to clean off the door before David could see it and upset himself, she told Pat what had happened during the night. Directly after breakfast she climbed into the Silver Ghost and pointed it in the direction of the Hall.

It was her first visit there since she'd run away to Glasgow. Seeing it up close again brought a sudden rush of memories and feelings that made her heart skip a beat.

Annie Tripp had left James's employ shortly after Fiona's death, as had Agnes and Pat Dyer. Annie, she'd been told, was living in London, working for a family in Bloomsbury. She had no knowledge of where either Agnes or Pat might be.

She'd heard that a lot of the Hall had been closed down, and even from the outside she could see that this was true. It didn't take an expert eye to see that exterior

271

maintenance had been badly neglected. The roof and large areas of the walls needed attending to.

She remembered the roof of another grand house, then. One which when she'd seen it had been recently strafed by the guns of a German aeroplane. In the peaceful morning she shuddered at the memory. All those dear dead boys, including her own Andrew, blown away like so much chaff in the wind.

She thought of Lieutenant Lewis who'd been among those sitting down to dinner that night in the chateau. It had been a relief to discover he'd survived; she'd read recently he was making something of a name for himself as a writer.

James McCudden, Andrew's friend had been among those killed, though in his case, ironically, as the result of a simple flying accident towards the end of the war when he'd stalled on take-off and crashed into a wood.

She wondered if Château Roisselle had been restored to its former glory after hostilities ended, hoping it had. As for Dragonholme Hall, she considered it criminal that James Campbell was allowing it to rot around him. In its own austere way, it was every bit as imposing as that French château.

The butler who answered her knock was new to her. 'Good morning,' she said in her most formal manner. 'I would like to see Mr Campbell. Tell him Mrs Lack is here.'

The butler eyed her coldly, making no move to show her into the house. 'I'm afraid the master is not up yet,' he informed her archly. It was obvious he didn't consider Sheila a good enough reason for disturbing the laird.

'Oh no?' said Sheila, her temper boiling again. 'Well it's about time he bloody well got up,' and with that she brushed past the astonished man and into the small reception room. It had a musty smell about it, and was crying out for a good airing. She ran her hand along the top of a picture, and the rim of a vase, wiping the dirt from her fingers with a grimace.

Some minutes later James appeared in the doorway, a dressing gown hastily thrown over his pyjamas. His hair was dishevelled, his eyes puffy, and his cheeks flushed. It took no special talent to guess that he'd been drinking heavily the night before.

'Why have you come bursting into my home like this?' he demanded, though it was clear he was more astonished than angry to see her.

'Shit.'

James blinked, visibly taken aback.

'Shit, or if you prefer, shite,' she repeated, her colour high with anger and her eyes ablaze.

He had the uneasy thought that were she a man she would hit him.

'I've no idea what you're raving about,' he snapped back. 'It's a little early in the morning for visiting.'

'Did you do the smearing yourself, or did one of your toadies go sneaking down to my cottage last night and do it for you?' she yelled, stepping towards him with a hand raised.

James cleared his throat, suddenly realizing that she was serious. 'I think you'd better sit down and explain to me what this is all about,' he said calmly. 'Just what are you accusing me of?'

God he was good, she thought. She'd expected some show of guilt or embarrassment, but there was no hint of either. In a voice rigid with frost, she described the events of the previous night, and how her reasoning had inevitably brought her to him. 'After all,' she concluded, 'you're the only person around who has ever tried to hurt me or mine.'

When she was done, he turned on her angrily. 'What sort of man do you think I am?' he shouted. 'Do you think I run around in the middle of the night, playing practical jokes?'

'I know exactly what kind of man you are, James Campbell,' she replied, looking at him as though she could see right through him. 'That's why I'm here.'

He offered her a seat, but she refused to sit down. 'Well, this time, Mrs Lack,' he said smoothly, 'you are very wrong. You might ask yourself what you think I have to gain by such a trick.'

She drew herself up to her full height, eyeing him coldly. 'A man who wouldn't stop at depriving a poor widow of her rightful monies, wouldn't stop at smearing a little shit on a door. A man who would destroy an entire village just because of his own stubborn pride is capable of anything. I don't think that what you do or do not have to gain has anything to do with it.'

Speechless, he stared at her for some seconds. For the first time since she ran out on him he understood not only that she didn't love him, but that she felt nothing but contempt for him. All these years he had kept within him the secret thought that she loved him still, that the joy with which she had filled his life and his dreams had touched her too. Even now, even after his humiliation in the pub, he had refused to believe that there was nothing left, that he had destroyed her feelings for him so completely that nothing could redeem them.

'I didn't do it,' he said softly, incapable of fighting. 'I swear it.'

Her expression didn't change, but a sudden look of uncertainty flashed through her eyes. 'If you didn't do it, or arrange to have it done, then who did?' she asked challengingly.

But it was there, just a shadow of fear, just enough to make his heart ache. If only he didn't still love her. If only he weren't even now prepared to do anything she asked, to make any sacrifice, anything at all, if only she would be his. 'I'm afraid,' he said, his tone one of dismissal, 'that I can't help you there. Perhaps you have more enemies in Dragonholme than you thought.'

'But you still maintain it's not you?'

'Not this time,' he smiled. If she would give him a sign, if she would ask for his help, then he would give it.

She picked up her purse from the table on which she'd

laid it. 'You're not only contemptible,' she said hotly, her colour rising with her voice. 'You're despicable as well.'

'You don't need the butler to see you out, do you? You know the way well enough, I'm sure.'

The outside door banged behind her. Sheila stood on the steps for a minute, collecting her wits, wondering what to believe. From behind the heavy door of Dragonholme Hall, she thought she could hear the faint sound of James Campbell's laughter.

Sheila was chaffing with Betsy Thomson, wife of one of the *Lorella*'s crew, when she saw a familiar car appear in Brae Street. It was the car in which Johnnie Murchison-Stewart had brought his sister Georgina to Dragonholme the Sunday they'd come down together.

Hastily, Sheila took her leave of Betsy and hurried after the car which was now headed in the direction of her house.

'Johnnie!' she cried in greeting as he climbed out of the driver's seat. She could see now that he was alone.

Glancing round he caught sight of her, and gave her an acknowledging wave.

'Well this is a pleasant surprise,' she said to him on reaching his side.

'I was going to write, then decided to come down instead,' he smiled.

A tightness in his voice told her something was wrong. 'Come away in and we'll have a cup of coffee, or a dram if you prefer?'

'I'll have both if you don't mind,' he laughed as they went inside.

Pat was there with David and Ian. Sheila poured Johnnie a stiff whisky, then made coffee for the three adults. When Johnnie kept to polite conversation, she realized he wanted to talk to her privately, and suggested they go back outside, which he readily agreed to.

'Now what's this all about, Johnnie?' she asked, perching herself on a front mudguard of the Silver Ghost.

Johnnie's eyes clouded with the shadow of anger. 'I had a visit at the yard from your Mr James Campbell,' he said heavily.

'Oh, aye?'

'I've no idea how he found out, but he knew that you'd approached me to build four drifters for you.'

'And?'

'What he didn't know was that I'd already turned you down. He thought I'd be going ahead with the order.'

Sheila stared at Johnnie attentively. 'So what happened?' she prompted.

'He threatened me!' he exploded, his expression still showing his astonishment. 'The man had the gall, the bare-faced cheek, to threaten me!' It was obvious that no one had ever threatened him before.

Sheila had to restrain a tiny smile. 'Then you explained to him you'd turned me down and that was that?'

Johnnie's chin rose aggressively, proudly. 'I did nothing of the sort. I told him my affairs were none of his business, and for him to get the hell out of my office!'

Now she did smile, her laughter easy and warm. 'Good for you. And did he?'

'He did indeed. But not before saying I would never get another order from the Yellow Funnel Line, in which, apparently, he has a great many shares – and a great deal of influence. And that their current order with us would be cancelled.'

'What size of ship is that to be?'

'An eighteen-thousand-ton cargo vessel for the Far East run.'

Sheila blanched. 'You mustn't lose an order that size on account of me, Johnnie. If you won't tell him, then I'll see he finds out that you're not building my drifters.'

'Oh, but I am!' Johnnie winked. 'I couldn't very well not do them now.'

276

Sheila's heart leapt. 'But you've no space at the yard. You said so in your letter.'

'I have space now that I won't be building for Yellow Funnel. I intend building your four drifters in the space their ship would have needed.'

'But it'll cost you financially. My four drifters will come nowhere near compensating you for what you'll lose on the other order.'

A hard, determined expression came into Johnnie's eyes. 'I will not be blackmailed, Sheila. Not by Campbell or anyone else. All his interference will achieve is to allow me to do what I would have preferred all along. To build your boats. The loss of a little income is neither here nor there.'

'He has so much influence . . .'

'Not in my world he doesn't. About all he can do is cancel the Yellow Funnel order and that's it. Frankly, Sheila,' winked Johnnie, 'if I'd understood from the beginning what a pompous tyrant the man was I would have said yes if it meant building them in the road.'

'Oh James Campbell, you had me beaten and didn't know it. Now you've inadvertently given me, and Dragonholme, a reprieve! Sheila could contain her excitement no more. On sudden impulse she jumped to her feet and threw her arms around Johnnie.

'You won't be sorry,' she laughed.

It was the week before Christmas, 1923. Sheila, David and Pat were at the MS Yard for the handing-over ceremony. The four drifters had been launched a fortnight previously; since then the finishing touches had been made, and they'd been fitted out.

Sheila was ecstatic about the boats; even Tom McIndoe with his vast experience of building fishing craft couldn't have come up with better. Johnnie, and the MS Yard, had done her proud.

David clutched Sheila's hand and stared at the drifters

riding in a line. The foremost was called the *Andrew*, after his father, the one behind the *Davey B.*, after his grandpa, the third the *Peg B.*, after his granny, and the fourth the *Dougal B.*, after the oldest of his uncles who'd been killed in the Dragonholme disaster. He liked the *Andrew* best, although it was no different from the others.

He looked round for George Jorgesson, who was somewhere about. He wanted George to take him on board the *Andrew* so he could go behind the wheel and pretend to steer. George was good at games and pretending with him. George was fun.

Johnnie was standing beside Sheila ticking items off a list. He was triple checking to ensure everything was just as it should be. He intended the handover to be as smooth as silk.

The crews of the four drifters were present, all men hand-picked by George and Sheila. They would be sailing the boats down the Clyde, round the top of Scotland, then southwards to Dragonholme where the boats would remain till the start of the season.

Of the twenty-four men who'd be working the boats, twenty-three were new to Dragonholme, sixteen of them bringing families with them when they'd arrived to take up residence. The population of the village had now doubled since Sheila bought the *Sheila B*.

David spied George and waved to him, wriggling his hand free from his mother's when George beckoned him over. Sheila let David go, then turned to Duncy Laidlaw with a smile as he came up to her. She'd made Duncy skipper of the *Peg B*.

'I thought this the appropriate moment to thank you for the chance you've given me, Sheila. Neither Marika nor I will ever forget it,' Duncy said shyly.

'I know you could have been a skipper before now if you'd chosen to leave Dragonholme, so it's no favour I'm doing you: only giving you what's long past your due,' Sheila said lightly.

'No one will work harder for you, I promise you that.'

'I know,' she answered softly, giving his hand a squeeze.

She watched Duncy walk away, lurching from side to side in a typical fisherman's gait. The boat cried for her Ma would be well safe in his hands. Peg would have been pleased he was to be the skipper – she'd always had a soft spot for Duncy Laidlaw.

Johnnie made his final tick. All was now ready; the handing-over could take place. He signalled to the two apprentices waiting close by, who immediately ran off to his office. Then, in a loud voice, he called everyone to gather round, raising his hands for quiet. When he had it he made a short speech about the drifters and how pleased the yard had been to build them. With that, he presented the papers of ownership to Sheila. It was now her turn to make a speech.

There were tears in her eyes which she couldn't hide. 'I just want you all to know how proud I am – for myself and for my son – to be the owner of these very special boats. I wish all who sail in them well, and that every trip will be a successful and prosperous one.' She smiled through her tears as the crews raised a cheer. Her voice trembling, she went on to thank the yard workers who'd built the boats, saying what a grand and expert job they'd done. Putting her hands together she applauded their effort and the fishermen joined in.

At the conclusion of her speech the two apprentices pushed their way through the crowd, each carrying a crate of whisky and a box of glasses.

Drinks were quickly poured and the new drifters toasted by name.

When that was over, George started getting the fishermen aboard. He himself was sailing on the *Dougal B.* as an extra crew member. Sheila had wanted him to be with the boats on their passage round the top of Scotland, for he was now admiral of her six boats, if not yet admiral of the other Dragonholme four as well.

'Without you this day would never have been possible. I'm forever in your debt,' Sheila said to Johnnie.

Johnnie blushed, glancing down at his shoes.

'Johnnie?'

He looked up again.

Taking hold of his lapels she kissed him squarely on the lips. 'Thank you,' she whispered.

George, standing to one side waiting for a word with Sheila before he too got on board, watched the gentleness of the kiss she gave to Johnnie. Of course, he should have known there was more between those two than a contract. For the first time, he really looked at Johnnie Murchison-Stewart – at his appealing face and expensive clothes; at his obvious poise and self-assurance.

Ach it was a daft notion anyway, he told himself, to think a man like he had a chance with a woman like Sheila. Daft beyond belief to even think that she would ever let his rough hands touch her, would ever touch his lips with hers.

As the four drifters steamed off down the Clyde Sheila gave a special wave to George, who was staring straight at her, and wondered why he didn't wave in return.

9

Sheila swallowed some beer, glad to wet her throat. It was absolutely boiling in the Community Hall where Rhona and Graeme Hurley's wedding reception was being held. She took another swig, and sighed with happy weariness. She'd just come off the dance floor and was feeling exhausted but merry.

Sheila stared across to where Rhona was chatting with Mrs Jorgesson, George's mother. How radiant Rhona looked; how radiant and how happy. Aye, ecstatically happy. It was a long time now since those nightmare days after Jack's death – those lonely, empty years.

It was just over a month ago that Rhona had come to

the house one night in a fit of giggles, to tell Sheila she was getting wed to Graeme. She was carrying his child.

As for Graeme himself, the man was hardly recognizable as the whey-faced cougher Sheila had brought to Dragonholme only one year before. The good sea air and Rhona's cooking (for, though he had his own wee house he'd eaten most of his meals with Rhona and Ian) had worked wonders. There was now permanent colour in his cheeks, sparkle in his eyes, and a new excitement in his heart – though that was more down to love than diet, Sheila thought.

The reception had been deliberately timed for the night before the Dragonholme boats sailed to the northern fishing grounds. That way, there were two celebrations instead of just one. For days before, Sheila had been driving everyone mad with her plans for the party, and indeed, the whole village seemed to have been involved in them. And now the whole village was here laughing and dancing, talking and smiling – almost as though the past had never happened.

She glanced over to where Rhona's Ian was shyly talking to a lass belonging to one of the new families, a bonny lass who was hanging on his every word.

They were all pleased with Ian's progress. Graeme Hurley was doing as marvellous a job with the boy as with himself.

Sheila gazed contentedly around the hall. It had been a long time since she'd felt so excited and so alive – so full of purpose. Could it have been only a year ago that the thought of David's going to school had filled her with such dread and a sense of futility? Only a year ago that she had felt so tired and so old? Then the only joy in her life had been her son – now it was her life itself that offered joy.

Sheila was just wondering if she was up to another whirl around the dance floor, when she spied her other sister-in-law, Maggie, and her husband, Ian McPherson. She had seen them once or twice during the past year, but had never had the opportunity or the desire for a serious conversation. Seeing them both across the room, obviously enjoying themselves, she decided that the time might be right for the word she'd been wanting to have with McPherson. By all accounts, he was prospering in Portnessie and had a finger in a number of lucrative pies.

Even as she approached them, a smile on her lips, Sheila was thinking to herself that the years hadn't changed Maggie at all. She was still the same bitch she used to be, a little older and leaner now, a little less hungry and less frightened, but still petty and obsessed with her own interests.

'Well, Sheila,' exclaimed Maggie as she came up to them. 'How nice to see you. And what a smashing party this is. It must have cost a fortune.'

Sheila gave the other woman an unenthusiastic hug and shook Ian's large, rough hand. 'You're looking well, the two of you,' she said sweetly. 'I hope you've had enough to drink and all.'

They stood chatting for a while, Maggie seeming to confine her comments to how the other women looked or danced or how drunk their men were, until finally Sheila could take no more and turned to McPherson with a different look in her eye and a different tone in her voice. 'I think,' she said, 'that I might have an idea you'd be interested in.' Instantly, he was all ears. Sheila Beattie's reputation as a shrewd and astute businesswoman had not escaped his notice.

Sheila told him about her plans for revitalizing the village. 'My original aim was to own twenty boats by the end of five years,' she explained. 'But lately I've been thinking of increasing that figure. If the six boats we're sending out this year make the same sort of profit as the two we had last season, nothing, in fact, will stand in my way.'

The problem, she continued, was that with the village beginning to get back on its feet there was a new need for the shops and businesses that had previously closed down to open again. The chandler's was a prime example of what she was talking about. Already it was so desperately needed that it couldn't fail to start to show a handsome return within a couple of years for whoever had re-opened it.

Then again there was Ian's father, who was somewhere in the hall. He wasn't getting any younger. How would the Dragonholme fish get to Portnessie when the old man died. Wouldn't it be worth Ian's while to consider going into partnership with his da? Once the partnership was formed they could modernize, get rid of the old horses and carts and replace them with lorries which were far more efficient, and less expensive to run.

Ian's initial response was no less than she'd expected. 'Why don't you invest in all this yourself?' he asked.

'I might be well off,' laughed Sheila, 'but I'm not Carnegie. The bulk of my capital is tied up in my boats. I don't have anything extra.'

Maggie chipped in then. 'If these shops and all are such excellent investments why hasn't the laird been tempted? Isn't James Campbell known as a man always out to further line his pockets whenever possible?'

Sheila had to laugh. 'James Campbell has lost all interest in Dragonholme,' she explained. 'He never comes near the village any more. He'd be the last person to invest, profit or no.'

Ian stroked his chin. 'Well,' he said at last. 'You've certainly given me a lot to think about. It'll all need looking into, of course. But, aye, I'm interested, right enough.'

They left it at that. After a few minutes, Sheila excused herself to go and check on David, who was careering about the hall with several of the other children present.

He had a dirty face from crawling underneath chairs, and a skinned knee, but he was obviously thoroughly enjoying himself, so Sheila left him to get on with it.

Hector and Rosie Burnside danced by, Rosie

wheeching and kicking the air as they went past. Sheila looked for George, thinking she'd like to have a dance with him, but he was nowhere in sight.

She was a wee bit concerned about George. It was nothing she could quite put her finger on, but over the past months it seemed to her that he'd been more and more formal with her rather than less. Even though they had had to work so closely and she had come to rely not only on his skill and expertise but on his quiet support and understanding, she sensed that they were less friends now than on the day she re-met him in the pub.

She had a birl with Shet Perlie instead, then was collared by Miss Dalziel who asked if she might have a word.

Miss Dalziel said she wanted to speak to Sheila about Graeme Hurley because Hurley was employed by Sheila. Now the thing was this; she'd been soldiering on as schoolteacher past normal retirement age because, with the state the village had been in, she'd known no one would replace her, and what would have happened to the small amount of children left to Dragonholme then?

But it wasn't a small amount anymore, thanks to the new families Sheila was bringing in; and the truth of the matter was that with the increased numbers she just couldn't cope. She wanted to stand down and spend the days left to her at home and in her garden.

The obvious choice to replace her was Hurley, a far, far, superior teacher to what she'd ever been. With him at the school it wouldn't only be Ian Beattie who could pass university entrance exams.

But as Sheila was Hurley's employer she felt it only right and proper to get Sheila's permission before talking to Hurley himself. If he agreed to apply for the job there would be no question about him being appointed, she could vouch for that.

Sheila said of course Miss Dalziel had her permission to speak to Hurley. She didn't see why he couldn't be schoolteacher and also tutor Ian.

The newlyweds weren't going away on honeymoon, so Miss Dalziel said she'd have a chat with Hurley sometime during the next week.

This was excellent news, Sheila thought after Miss Dalziel had left her, and felt as pleased as if she'd arranged it herself. A teacher of Graeme Hurley's ability would do no end of good for the youth of Dragonholme, and give Hurley a fine secure post into the bargain.

She glanced round to see Ian McPherson staring at her thoughtfully. Waving, he then turned his attention back to Maggie who was deep in conversation with Lena Murray.

She had lied to Ian. It was well within her financial ability to open up some of the shops and other businesses she'd spoken to him about, but she didn't want to. She felt that it was important that Dragonholme belonged to all its people, not to one person alone.

About an hour-and-a-half later, she found David fast asleep behind the casks of beer that made up a large section of the bar, and decided it was time to go home. She told Pat to stay, but Pat insisted on going home as well. They agreed to take it in turns to carry the sleeping boy back.

Having made their good-byes they went out into the cool, starry night. 'He's becoming a ton weight,' sighed Sheila as they made their way along the time-worn path. 'Soon he'll be too heavy for the two of us combined.'

They were just passing the graveyard, walking slowly and companionably beneath the familar sky, when a figure suddenly leapt out from behind a headstone and struck Pat a blow on the temple which knocked her senseless to the ground.

It all happened so quickly that Sheila could only stand and gape, her arms automatically tightening around her sleeping child. Then the short, stocky figure whirled on her.

Sheila broke into a run, but had only got a few yards when the assailant caught up with her. An arm encircled

285

her throat, and at the same time she was punched in the back so hard that she dropped David.

She tried to scream, but couldn't find the air. She heard David start to cry, then she was propelled into the graveyard itself where she was flung to the grass between two stones.

Her only thought was of David. It didn't matter what happened to her as long as he was all right. 'Run, son! Run!' she gasped as hands frantically tore at her dress. All she could see was a hideously distorted face looming over her.

She tried to scream as he tugged and tore at her underdrawers but had barely the strength to whimper. With one last effort she started to sit up, only to be hit savagely in the mouth and knocked prostrate again.

Her underdrawers ripped and fell apart. She moaned in revulsion as a hand grabbed and squeezed her viciously. Then she heard him fumbling with his own clothes.

'Mummy!' David called out from close by. He hadn't run as she'd told him to.

The man laughed, a sound with no humanity in it, and threw himself on top of her.

But he never entered her. Just as he was about to, he suddenly flew sideways, rolling over and over in the sloping grass.

Quickly George bent to Sheila. As he did, the attacker leapt to his feet and went racing off through the graveyard.

When Sheila saw George's anxious features peering down at her she let out a cry of relief. Then David, tears streaming from his eyes, was in her embrace, she instantly calming, and soothing him, telling him it was all over now, George had come to their rescue and frightened away the nasty man.

George hurried over to Pat who was groaning as she started to come round. The temple where she'd been hit had already swollen into a sizeable lump.

He decided to leave Pat for the moment, and ran in the

direction the would-be rapist had taken, Sheila shouting after him to be careful.

Still consoling the extremely distraught David, Sheila tugged her dress down to cover the lower half of her body which had been completely exposed. Her now useless underdrawers lay to one side, having been ripped right down the middle. She shuddered to think what had so nearly happened to her.

Sheila and David made their way to Pat who was sitting up and nursing her head. 'It feels as if it has been used as a football,' she moaned.

They were all standing holding on to one another when George returned. 'I'm afraid the bastard's got clean away,' he said angrily. 'Did you recognize him by any chance?' he asked Sheila.

'No,' she sighed. 'He must have been wearing a mask – his face was all distorted.'

George stared out across the silent stones. 'All I saw was what he was doing to you,' he said thickly.

'About to do,' she whispered gently. 'You stopped him before he did.'

'Thank God for that,' he said, thinking that wouldn't make any difference if he could yet get hold of the man; he'd still beat the bastard to a bloody pulp.

He'd escorted them to their house before returning to the reception to warn those there of what had happened. His intention was to roust out a number of the men still sober enough to be of any use and make a search of the village and seafront. 'It was lucky I decided to go home right after you,' he said to Sheila as they walked, 'or there's no knowing how things might have turned out.'

On reaching the house, he ushered them inside, then waited till Sheila had locked the door. They watched him run as fast as he was able back to the Community Hall.

Sheila got David stripped and into bed where he lay noisily sucking his thumb. She then attended to Pat's bump, putting a hot bread poultice on it to bring down the swelling. Sheila didn't have to tell Pat how lucky she'd been; a blow such as she'd had could quite easily have been fatal.

When the hot poultice had been bandaged into position, Sheila took off her clothes and went to the sink where she gave herself a good all-over wash. In the middle of this she started to shake, her body convulsed with sobs. Pat came over to her and the pair of them clung to one another. 'I could murder a drink,' Sheila said at last. While she put on her dressing gown, Pat poured them both large drams.

Sheila sat with David until he finally drifted off in a troubled sleep. Then she joined Pat sitting by the range where they talked in low tones, speculating about how George and the others were getting on in their search.

A little under an hour later George returned to tell them their attacker hadn't been found. The men had scoured the village from top to bottom, but to no avail.

With no hesitation, he accepted a dram from Sheila. 'Every man in Dragonholme's been accounted for,' he told her. 'So your attacker was most definitely an outsider.' He took a grateful drink, 'Everyone's pretty relieved about that, I can tell you.'

George added that Ian McPherson, who'd aided in the search, would be reporting the matter to the police in Portnessie.

George finished his whisky, and Sheila promptly poured him another. He watched her as she set the bottle back down. She was pale, her features drawn; he thought she looked absolutely marvellous.

He asked her if, in the light of what had happened, she wanted her boats to delay sailing northwards for several days, but she said she didn't see any advantage in that – in her opinion it was best things went ahead as planned.

'You're no doubt right' he agreed. 'The boats will have to go sooner or later. I just hate the idea of the women being left alone when there's a maniac on the loose.' But did not add that it was she who particularly concerned him.

288

'Aye,' laughed Sheila. 'We fisherwomen are a tough breed, God help us. Besides, we won't be completely alone. Graeme Hurley, Mr Meekie from The Halibut's Tail, and a few others will still be here.'

George sat with them a few minutes longer, then left, and Sheila set about changing Pat's bread poultice which had gone cold.

'A helluva nice man that,' Pat said.

Sheila agreed; George was a helluva nice man. It was on the tip of her tongue to tell Pat the story of George's brothering when she and Eric had rescued him from Tarry Dunbar and the crew of the *Locarno*, but decided against it. For some reason, she didn't want anyone laughing at George, not even in Pat's good-humoured fashion.

Later, when Pat was asleep, Sheila sat in front of the grate with a dram in her hand, her face serious with thought. James Campbell, had he been behind that night's attack? If he had been then this was a frightening dimension to his vendetta against her. Fouling her door was one thing; tonight's incident quite another. Though she could believe him capable of anything – some part of her refused to accept this.

She was certain of one thing: the man himself hadn't been James. He'd been the wrong shape, and even if he'd somehow disguised his shape, she'd still have known if it had been him. A dozen different things would have given that away.

On the other hand, of course, it was entirely possible that her attacker was completely unconnected to James, a violent lunatic simply passing through the district.

Sheila sipped her whisky, then worried a nail. So what should she tell the Portnessie police when they arrived to take a statement from her? Did she tell them about the trouble she'd been having with James? Or not? Did she explain the reason for their rivalry? Make the private past public knowledge and cause for gossip and speculation? Would that help either of them?

But then if he was involved, might not even scandal be preferable to a successful repeat of tonight's attempt? Who was to say it would have stopped at rape? Might not murder have been the end result?

Sheila wiped clammy sweat from her forehead, and drank more whisky.

Only after hours of agonizing, did she decide to give James the benefit of the doubt. She would not mention her suspicions to the police when they came. Sheila sighed as she prepared for bed. In her heart of hearts she just couldn't believe that James Campbell was responsible for the night's events.

Pray God that she wasn't wrong.

Sheila stared up at the partially completed hulls of the three new drifters Johnnie was building for her. They were going to be real beauties, just like the other four from the MS Yard. These were to be called the *Jack B.*, *Bob B.*, and *Albert B*. The first two after her brothers, the last after Albert Ball.

She was in Glasgow to finalize the sale of her house in Kelvinside. She, David and Pat had moved, lock stock and barrel back to Dragonholme three weeks before.

The only thing that had stopped her moving earlier was David's education, but with Graeme Hurley now ensconced as Dragonholme's teacher she had been able to take David away from Kelvinside Academy secure in the knowledge that he would continue to be taught to the same high standard.

And oh how marvellous it was to be back living permanently in Dragonholme! All three of them were loving it.

She glanced over to where Johnnie was deep in conversation with one of his gaffers. Dear sweet Johnnie; he'd become a good friend to her. And she hoped she'd become the same to him.

No, friendship wasn't the right word, she told herself.

It was more than that. He was something of a cross between a father and a brother to her.

'Mrs Lack! Mrs Lack!'

Sheila looked round to see Sandra Urquhart, Johnnie's personal secretary, running towards her.

'You're wanted urgently on the telephone by Miss McLuskey,' Sandra gasped, her face flushed and her eyes worried.

Fear gripped Sheila. Something must have happened to David! Pat would be ringing from the village's one telephone box, the only telephone in Dragonholme. It could only be an emergency.

Side-by-side Sheila and Sandra hared for Johnnie's office. Sheila snatched up the telephone as soon as they were in the room. 'What is it Pat?' she demanded, trying to prepare herself for the worst.

Something had happened all right. George Jorgesson was in hospital in Peterhead. All Pat could tell Sheila was the name of the hospital and that George was in a bad way. She had no other details.

'I'll have to go to him,' Sheila shouted into the receiver, not waiting for Pat's reply. 'I'll leave immediately.'

She drove away so quickly her tyres actually smoked. She barely said good-bye to Johnnie.

What in God's name had happened?

The all-pervading smell of the Royal Victoria Hospital, Peterhead, brought back a host of memories – buried memories of Cowcaddens General and Maricourt.

She found out which ward George was in, made her way there and asked to see Sister. Sister McKechnie couldn't have been anything other than a nurse. Everything about her from the tone of her voice to her air of efficiency epitomized the species.

Sheila introduced herself, explained she was George's employer, then asked the extent of his injuries and present condition.

291

George hadn't been in an accident at sea, as she'd decided must have been the case, but a fight ashore. Until a few hours ago the doctors had thought him to have internal injuries, but it had now been established that he didn't.

What he did have was severe bruising. So severely beaten was he, in fact, that he would be off work for the next several weeks. The doctors were adamant about that; he was to have as much rest as possible until the bruising had disappeared, otherwise there could be long-term damaging effects.

'Of course,' replied Sheila. 'That's only reasonable.'

'To you, maybe, but not to Mr Jorgesson,' said Sister McKechnie. He seemed intent on getting back aboard his boat as soon as possible. Sister was obviously determined that this wouldn't happen. 'I'll keep him where he is now until I think he's recovered sufficiently to be discharged,' she concluded.

Sheila said that sounded just like George, who must be fretting in the extreme of being laid up. She appreciated it wasn't visiting hours but could she still see George? 'I've driven all the way from Glasgow to see him,' she pleaded.

Sister McKechnie pursed her mouth. 'That would be highly irregular,' she said shortly.

Sheila replied that she was only too well aware of how big a favour she was asking; rules were rules after all, that's what had been drummed into her when she'd been trained.

'You were a nurse?' Sister McKechnie asked, her look softening fractionally.

'VAD. I served in France.'

'I also served in France.'

Within a few minutes they discovered several people they knew in common.

'Wait here,' Sister told Sheila at the end of their conversation, and disappeared out of her office to order screens put round George's bed.

'Follow me,' she instructed when she returned, and led Sheila down the ward to George's bed where the screens were already in place.

Sheila whispered a thank-you to Sister McKechnie, then turned to the heavily bandaged George. 'I should have thought to bring you some grapes,' she smiled.

'I'm glad you didn't. I hate grapes,' George said, trying to match her smile, but ending in a wince of pain. 'I feel as though I've been run over by a road roller.'

'You look it,' Sheila winked.

George started to chuckle, and winced again.

Sheila ignored the chair provided, and sat on the edge of the bed. 'Tell me about it.'

'I finally met up with the skipper of the *Zodiac*, a huge brute of a Highlandman called Red McGregor,' George explained.

Sheila sighed. All the way here she'd been wondering if this might be to do with the *Zodiac*, one of the Portnessie fleet that had been giving her boats a lot of trouble recently, and costing her a considerable amount of money.

The *Zodiac* had been using its propeller to slice through the warps which held and controlled each individual net, as well as smashing the buoys keeping the net afloat so that the net sank to the bottom and was lost.

Five of Sheila's nets had been lost this way during the past two-and-a-half weeks, and now her admiral had been hospitalized.

George went on to say that the morning before, the *Sheila B*. had been peacefully fishing when the *Zodiac* was spied bearing down on it; and it was obvious what the Portnessie boat's intentions were.

He had already briefed the crew what to do in such an event. They immediately winched the warps aboard and brought lengths of heavy chain on deck. These chains were then attached to the warps at the points where the warps were normally just under the water, and the warps let out again, the chains disappearing into the sea; and the

Sheila B. had pretended to go on fishing. It had been George's ruse, and a good one.

As he'd expected, the *Zodiac* had borne down on the *Sheila B.*'s warps, and just as its propeller was about to make contact with them he had winched the warps in several feet.

His plan had worked as he'd hoped. The warps had been sliced through all right, but at the same time the lengths of chain had wound themselves round the *Zodiac*'s propeller, causing one of the blades to shear away.

The *Zodiac* had wallowed helplessly while the *Sheila B.* retrieved its net, then the *Sheila B.* had steamed away leaving the *Zodiac* to its own devices.

'It was a damn ingenious plan,' Sheila said. 'What happened next?'

After unloading their catch last evening, they'd all gone to Mother Mary's Bar for a celebration on having got their own back on the *Zodiac*. Unknown to them, the *Zodiac* had been taken in tow by another Portnessie trawler and later that evening was brought into Peterhead where it would be laid up until its propeller had been replaced.

At this point of the story George stopped, embarrassed. Continuing, he said it had been about half past eight when the lads had moved on elsewhere, leaving him at Mother Mary's on his own.

Misunderstanding his embarrassment, she asked where the others had gone.

He told her didn't know where they'd gone on to.

'George Jorgesson, you're fibbing,' she teased. 'Tell me where they went.'

There was no getting away from telling Sheila, it was clear she wouldn't give up. 'You promise you won't tell anyone? Some of the men are married,' he stammered.

Sheila grinned. She was pretty certain she knew now what was coming next. 'I promise.'

In a small voice George said his crew had gone to a

brothel much frequented by fishermen, a place where the prices were reasonable and the lassies clean.

'But not you?' Sheila teased.

George blushed, and glanced away. He hadn't gone with the lads because there was only one woman who interested him nowadays; the one sitting on his bed.

But Sheila didn't notice his discomfort. 'Go on George,' she urged.

He told her it had been shortly after the lads had left him that Red McGregor and the crew of the *Zodiac* had appeared in Mother Mary's, having been scouring Peterhead for him and the crew of the *Sheila B*.

McGregor had introduced himself, then said he intended revenging what the *Sheila B*. had done earlier to the *Zodiac*.

He had replied it was McGregor's fault. It was the *Zodiac* which had started it all by cutting warps. But the fiery McGregor wouldn't accept his action had been justified. Like all natural bullies McGregor loved dishing it out, but couldn't take it in return.

'Did you find out if McGregor's warp cutting was on James Campbell's instructions?' Sheila asked.

'Aye,' said George. 'That much came out in my brief conversation with McGregor.'

McGregor had gone for him and, although he'd done his best, it had been no contest. The last thing he remembered prior to waking in Accident and Emergency was Red McGregor lifting him high into the air, then throwing him through an opened trap in the bar floor into the cellar beneath.

Having explained to Sheila what had happened, George then said he just had to get out of the hospital and back aboard the *Sheila B*. Tied up in Peterhead harbour the boat was losing money, and the men not earning.

'Don't you worry about the boat,' she assured him. 'I'll sort everything out.' She then asked him to recommend a member of the crew to take over as skipper, and while he was ashore she'd have Hector Burnside act as admiral.

She assured George he wouldn't lose financially because of this. He would still get his full share. She would also come to a personal arrangement with the man taking over as skipper.

George insisted he was well enough to return to sea that very day. Sure he'd be stiff and sore for some time, but he'd manage.

Sheila could see how stubborn George was going to be, and knew him quite capable of running away from the hospital the moment he was mobile. 'You'll stay ashore until I say otherwise,' she ordered, 'or I'll sack you.'

George was in no doubt Sheila would carry out her threat. She wasn't the type of person to make one unless she meant it. Reluctantly he agreed to stay where he was: he'd have agreed to anything rather than lose captaincy of the *Sheila B*.

It was then that Sheila had an idea. Excusing herself from George she found Sister McKechnie in the linen cupboard, and there explained what she had in mind. Sister was uncertain till Sheila gave her word as an ex-VAD that George would be properly cared for.

'Well,' said Sister slowly. 'I could certainly use the bed.'

Sheila shook her hand before she could change her mind.

Rejoining George, Sheila told him he'd be leaving the hospital next morning after breakfast. 'I'll drive you to Dragonholme to do your recuperating there,' she explained. 'When you're fully fit I'll drive you to wherever the *Sheila B*. is offloading. How's that?'

'Thanks,' George said, briefly but gratefully.

'I'll be telling your ma exactly what you can and can't do, and you'll obey her to the letter, or suffer the consequences,' Sheila warned.

'I understand.'

'Good,' said Sheila. 'Then we've got a deal.'

A few minutes later Sheila was heading for the harbour. As she walked, she was thinking about James Campbell and Red McGregor.

When Sheila arrived back at the hospital next morning she found George ready and waiting for her in Accident and Emergency. He was still on the trolley used to wheel him down from the ward.

Two porters took the trolley out to where the Silver Ghost was parked, then manhandled George into the front passenger seat.

'Tell me all you know about this Red McGregor?' Sheila asked George once they'd left Peterhead behind.

'As I said to you yesterday, he's a Highlandman. Comes from a fishing village called Findochty over in Banffshire. He's got a well-deserved reputation for being vicious and cruel. Because of that he's had trouble in the past keeping steady employment. I heard he left the fishing boats for a while and joined the Merchant Navy, then suddenly a month ago, he reappeared as skipper of the *Zodiac*.'

'Does he still live in Findochty?'

'I've no idea. I would have thought myself he'd be based in Portnessie now he's with the Portnessie fleet. What I can tell you is his crew must be the dregs. No decent fisherman would sail under the likes of that scum.'

Sheila pressed for further information, but that was all George knew about Red McGregor. She lapsed into silence, sunk in thought.

A dozen or so miles down the road George broke into her reverie by asking what had happened about the man who'd attacked her the night before the boats had sailed north. She'd never said another word about it since.

'The police investigated the matter, but no arrest was ever made. There didn't seem to be any clues.'

'Yon bastard will never know just how lucky he was I didn't get hold of him,' George said quietly.

There was a depth and intensity in George's tone that startled Sheila so much that she glanced sideways at him. What she saw was written clearly on his face caused her to catch her breath. It was if a door had suddenly been opened through which she could see for the first time what lay beyond. Now she knew why he'd been acting so strangely of late. It was nothing whatever to do with his position of admiral as she'd thought, but because he was in love with her.

They hardly spoke for the rest of the way.

'So how is he?' Pat asked, handing Sheila a glass of wine. It was night and Sheila had just arrived in; David was upstairs fast asleep.

Plonking herself into a chair, she told Pat about George's fight with Red McGregor, and why it had occurred.

'It's a bad business, right enough. We can only be thankful he wasn't injured worse than he was,' Pat agreed grimly.

'James Campbell ordered the *Zodiac* to cut my warps. McGregor admitted that to George,' Sheila continued.

'So what are you going to do about it?'

Sheila ran a hand across her face. She was so tired she could hardly think straight.

'Why don't you have a word with Johnnie? There must be some awful hard men working in that yard of his. Perhaps one of them could sort out this Red McGregor,' Pat suggested.

'No, I won't meet violence with violence. Knowing James Campbell, that's a game I'd end up losing in the long run.'

'What will you do then?'

'I haven't the foggiest yet. But I'm going to have to think of something.'

Sheila drained her glass, and Pat said she'd pour her a refill.

298

When Pat returned to Sheila's chair with the wine it was to find Sheila fast asleep, and gently snoring.

As she seemed comfortable enough Pat covered her with a travelling rug, and left her there.

Sheila carefully unwrapped the bandages round George's torso, and was encouraged by what she saw. He was healing fast.

'I think you can have the bandages off for good next weekend,' she said, starting to bind new ones on in place of those she'd just removed.

'I can hardly wait. He does nothing but moan about the itching,' Mrs Jorgesson sniffed.

'Well they do, like mad!' George complained.

'He's just a big wean,' Mrs Jorgesson said to Sheila, knowing that would infuriate George, which it did.

'Don't make them so tight this time, you constrict my breathing,' George said to Sheila.

Her response to that was to pull the bandages even tighter. He yelped, and glared at her.

'The tighter the better,' she smiled sadistically.

'Will I get the lad's present you made for him?' Mrs Jorgesson asked George.

David was instantly all ears and attention. 'What present? What is it?' he demanded eagerly.

'Just a wee something,' George replied.

Mrs Jorgesson left the room. David literally vibrated with impatience till she returned with a fishing line which she handed to him. The line was wound on a beautifully carved wooden frame that had been varnished a dark oak colour. It wasn't just a fishing device, it was a work of art.

Somewhat embarrassed, George shrugged and said it was only a minding he'd knocked together from some old bits and pieces that had been lying around. The line itself, complete with hook and lead weight, had been cut from a long line used to catch white fish out of the herring season.

It was clear to Sheila how much love and care George had put into the gift, and she was touched by it.

'Thank you, George, it's really smashing,' David breathed, clutching the gift to his chest.

George gave a soft laugh. It pleased him greatly that David was so thrilled. Reaching out, he ruffled the boy's hair. 'When your Ma says it's all right for me to leave the house I'll take you down to the harbour and show you how to use it properly,' he promised.

'How about tomorrow, Mummy? Can George take me to the harbour then?' David pleaded.

'Well,' said Sheila thoughtfully. 'I don't suppose a little light activity would do George any harm. All right. Tomorrow it is.'

David gave a whoop of delight. Good old Mum!

'Thank God. It'll be like being let out of prison after a spell inside,' sighed George.

Sheila finished her bandaging and stood up.

'Have you time for a cup of tea?' asked Mrs Jorgesson.

'No thanks. I'm due to call in at the chandler's shop for a chat with Ian McPherson. I'll have tea there. Have you heard that the shop is doing so well Ian is going to open a new general store soon?'

Mrs Jorgesson's eyes gleamed. 'Aye, I did hear. It's right good news so it is. It makes you feel the village is well and truly coming alive again.'

'It's rare news indeed,' agreed George.

It was all beginning to come together – just as she'd hoped and planned – Sheila thought. Then she remembered the *Zodiac* and Red McGregor.

'I received a letter from Hector Burnside this morning to say the *Zodiac* cut the *Peg B.*'s warps day before yesterday, and its net was lost,' she told George.

George's face clouded with anger, and frustration. 'The *Zodiac* has got to be stopped, or you might not only end up losing money, but become a laughing stock into the bargain.'

It was later, when she got Brodie's report, that Sheila

300

remembered what George had said about being made a laughing stock; and decided, in light of the information Brodie had given her, that that was the weapon to employ against McGregor.

Mr Brodie was a small, rotund man who wore rimless spectacles perched on the end of his nose. He reminded Sheila of a mole.

It was Johnnie who'd helped Sheila find Mr Brodie, whose offices were above a pawnshop in Glasgow's Trongate. The faded gold lettering on Mr Brodie's door proclaimed him to be a Private Investigator.

Mr Brodie came well recommended. A man to be trusted, and a most diligent worker, Sheila and Johnnie had been told.

Mr Brodie had shown Sheila to a chair, then had sat facing her. 'Now what can I do for you, Mrs Lack?' he had asked.

He'd listened intently, occasionally making a note on the pad in front of him, as Sheila spoke.

'Being the sort of person McGregor is he must have something to hide – something the police might be interested in, for example,' Sheila had concluded.

Brodie nodded; his brief was explicit. 'And for how long do you wish me to go on digging?'

'As long as it takes,' Sheila had replied, convinced there had to be a 'something' in McGregor's background.

After Sheila had gone Brodie had got out his map of Scotland and looked up Findochty. He'd never heard of the place.

That's where he would start.

James Campbell had been knighted to become Sir James Campbell of Dragonholme. To celebrate the event he was throwing a hoolie for the men of his fleet who were now fishing the home waters.

301

Sheila sat in the Silver Ghost outside the hotel where the hoolie was being held, the palms of her hands damp with sweat, telling herself to get on with it. She turned to the pretty lassie sitting beside her. 'Will you be embarrassed?' she asked.

'For what you're paying me, I'll walk in there starkers,' Chrissie McGowan replied in her distinctive working-class Glasgow accent.

Sheila grinned. 'That won't be necessary.'

'I just hope this doesn't backfire on you,' Chrissie said.

'So do I,' Sheila said drily, and got out of the car where she waited for Chrissie to come round and join her.

It was the beginning of September, and so far that season Sheila's boats had lost nearly two dozen nets, thanks to Red McGregor, the *Zodiac* and James Campbell. Tonight, she hoped, was going to be the end of it.

As they entered the Buccleugh Hotel, Sheila recalled staying there all those years ago when she'd worked for James. It seemed like more than a lifetime ago. Where had that girl gone, she wondered, as they passed through the lobby.

The hoolie was at the rear of the hotel where Sir James had taken over the grandly styled ballroom. A sit-down meal had been served earlier, after which the tables and chairs had been removed, and the musicians brought on. An adjoining cloakroom had been turned into a bar where drinks were being dispensed in a never-ending flow.

Sheila stopped dead centre of the main ballroom entrance and stared around. By sheer willpower she demanded her presence be noticed, and was gratified to see that it was. Shock waves began to ripple through the room as she made straight for a face she recognized from the past.

She had chosen her outfit carefully. In a simple black dress with matching shoes, she looked stunning as she scythed through the crowd to Tod McAlpine, who used to be a friend of her brothers. A plumpish female, clearly

302

Mrs McAlpine, stood at Tod's shoulder, and beside Mrs McAlpine a man Sheila was certain had been at her da's funeral.

As she walked, voices whispered all around her. Out of the corner of her eye she saw a woman nudge the husband in the ribs.

On reaching Tod she said hello. Then, without waiting for an introduction to Mrs McAlpine, she asked Tod which of those present was Red McGregor, skipper of the *Zodiac*.

The atmosphere was electric. Many of the dancers had stopped to stare in her direction – as more and more people in the room were doing.

Tod glanced about, then pointed to where a group of men stood drinking. 'McGregor's among that lot, he's the chap with the red beard,' Tod said quietly to Sheila.

Sir James, deep in conversation, was almost the last to become aware that something untoward was happening. Frowning he looked around to see what was going on. It was then that he saw Sheila, making for McGregor, and momentarily lost his composure.

Long before Sheila reached McGregor's group she was the focus of everyone's attention. Even the musicians had stopped playing, several of them climbing on to their chairs to get a better view.

Sheila heard her name whispered over and over, Mrs Lack who owns the new Dragonholme pipe stalkies, aye, her that was Davey Beattie's lass.

She stopped about three feet away from the man with the red beard. McGregor had small mean eyes in a fleshy face; he also had the most massive chest she had ever seen. His arms were thick with muscles. Poor George never had a chance, she thought.

She froze inside for a moment, not at all sure she could pull it off after all. Then she saw amusement in those dark, vicious eyes and something else – contempt? Yes, that was it. He was contemptuous of her.

Her resolve instantly hardened again. She would go through with what she'd come to do. As she could gut a herring with a knife, so she'd now gut this bastard with words.

'I wanted to see the scum who's been cutting my warps,' she said in a loud, ringing voice.

Sir James started to force his way through the crowd, then halted, not at all sure how to handle the situation.

McGregor looked Sheila up and down, the way a farmer might a cow at an auction. If he'd been hoping to phase her by this action he was disappointed. 'How's that boy you call your admiral?' he asked, sneering.

McGregor's question gave Sheila the perfect opening, and saved her having to use the one she'd already worked out in advance.

'The boy, as you call him, is twice the man you are McGregor,' she replied.

McGregor gave a roar of laugher. 'How can Jorgesson be twice the man when I beat the shite out of him!'

Sheila smiled. 'I was talking about being a man where it counts,' she said. Around her, the room was so quiet you could have heard a feather fall.

The dangerous eyes became hard as flint. 'What are you talking about?'

A laughing stock was the phrase George had used to her, and that was what she intended making of McGregor. Individual pride and prowess; fishermen held these virtues above all else, and consequently were particularly vulnerable on either count.

'Maybe George Jorgesson can't beat you in a fight, but there's other things he can get up besides his fists.'

McGregor went white, throwing the myriad freckles dotting his face into sharp relief.

Sheila stared at McGregor, waiting for the denial she knew would come.

'You're a fucking liar!' McGregor snarled, knotting his hands into fists, wishing she were a man and could be beaten into silence there and then.

'Why did you never marry, McGregor?' she asked sweetly despite the trembling in her legs.

'That's none of your business!' he blustered in reply.

Close by a young woman sniggered which enraged McGregor even further.

'I don't talk to fools or women,' he shouted, making to push her aside.

Sheila held her arm out straight in front of her, the hand flopping. 'I've got a new Tee name for you McGregor. Forget being called Red, from now on you're Droopy McGregor.'

McGregor seemed to shrink where he stood, his face contorted as though her laughter was causing him physical pain.

'I say it's a lie, and it's your word against mine,' he countered when her laughter finished.

Sheila crooked a finger, and instantly Chrissie McGowan was by her side. She could see the panic in McGregor's eyes and guessed correctly he was desperately trying to remember if Chrissie had been some woman he'd failed with in the past, in the days before he'd finally given up trying.

Sheila stared at McGregor, knowing his impotence had been the result of a fight he'd been involved in many years previously. Mr Brodie's report had been most thorough.

'Do you still maintain I'm lying?'

'Yes,' he hissed in reply.

'Then I'd like you to meet Chrissie McGowan, the best looking prostitute in Glasgow's Blythswood Square. All you have to do to prove me a liar, and that you are the man you claim, is take Chrissie upstairs to a room I'll pay for, after which Chrissie can come back and give us the verdict.'

One of McGregor's group guffawed, a bad mistake on his part. McGregor's fist lashed out and the man fell to the floor with a bloodied mouth.

'That's enough. This has gone far enough,' Sir James said, having finally decided to intervene.

305

Sheila swivelled to confront her main adversary. 'McGregor didn't cut my warps of his own accord, but on your strict instructions. Well no matter how many of my warps are cut, or nets sunk, my boats will continue to fish and try to restore life to a village that has suffered the greatest disaster the east coast has ever known.

'I can only say this; if the positions had been reversed my da and the men of Dragonholme would have done everything in their power to help Portnessie revive, not try to hinder it by despicable means.

'By doing what you are doing you demean the men who work for you, and the good name of fisherfolk in general,' Sheila said.

A growl of approval filled the room. They all knew about the warp cutting, but few had agreed with it. The Dragonholme boats posed no threat to their living, so why should this action be taken against such close neighbours? It was a question nearly all the Portnessie fishermen had asked themselves, and not one had come up with an acceptable answer.

Sir James could feel the mood had swung against him. Sheila had won this particular battle, no doubt about it. To continue warp cutting after what she'd just said would be to lose the men's goodwill; and that he wasn't prepared to do.

Sheila read her victory in James's face. Now was the time to go, she told herself, and turned on McGregor.

'Goodnight Droopy,' she smiled, winking.

Laughter errupted throughout the room.

Sheila and Chrissie McGowan swept from the ballroom, the laughter buoying them on their way.

'Oh but that was rare!' said Chrissie, wiping tears from her eyes once they were outside.

Sheila ran behind the Rolls to be sick.

10

It was early Saturday evening and, as had become her custom since taking up permanent residence again in Dragonholme, Sheila had gone to the Fairy Dell to gather wild flowers for the next day's church services.

She did the gathering, and delivered them to the church. Later Mrs Mitchell would come along and do the arranging. Mrs Mitchell had been arranging the church flowers for over twenty years.

Mr Mitchell was dead. He'd been one of those to survive the disaster, only to lose his life on the Dover Patrol during the war.

The Mitchells had two sons. The oldest had come back to the village with his family when George had offered him a berth aboard the *Albert B*. The other son was currently working on a boat of the Dunbar fleet, but also would return to the village when a place could be found for him aboard one of Sheila's boats.

David always accompanied Sheila on her trips to the Fairy Dell, carrying her basket there and back again. He thoroughly enjoyed the church flower picking, as Sheila called it.

The Fairy Dell was sheltered on three sides by the tall firs of Loki's Wood, and all manner of wild flowers and herbs grew there in profusion. It was by far and away the best spot for flowers and herbs for miles around.

Sheila hummed to herself as she picked the best out of a clump of bluebells. She'd just had a letter from Johnnie that morning confirming her order for two new drifters. In his reply Johnnie had said he hoped to have them built and ready for the start of the next herring season.

She had nine pipe stalkies at sea now; two more would bring her total to eleven, and the Dragonholme contingent to fifteen in all. Just a little over half of what the original fleet had been before the disaster.

She paused in her musings when a shadow fell across her's, a shadow that had a long protrusion in front of it.

She straightened and turned, putting a smile on her face as she did. The protrusion was a shotgun.

The man was short, stocky and white-haired. He had a thick beard, and full moustaches, and was a stranger to her.

Or was he? There did seem to be something oddly familiar about him. Something about his hard, empty eyes. Involuntarily she shivered.

David didn't like those eyes either. Coming to his mother he took hold of her skirt and pressed himself against her.

'Can I help you?' Sheila asked.

The twin barrels of the shotgun slowly rose till they were level with her midriff. The finger curled round the right-hand side trigger tightened.

'Oh have I dreamt of this moment, bitch,' the man whispered in a voice that made Sheila's flesh creep, and David press himself even harder against her.

And then she knew. She realized just who the stranger was. No stranger at all, but Wally Simpson, who'd once been James Campbell's ghillie, and who'd so mistreated her.

'You!' she gasped.

Simpson laughed evilly. 'I've been watching you a long time now bitch, waiting to pay you and his High and Mightiness back for what you did to me all those years ago; and this is it.'

'Don't be so ridiculous,' she said bravely, and grabbing David's arm made to move off.

She heard the shot as though it had happened somewhere else. With a cry of pain she tumbled to the ground. The hand she put to her cheek came away again bright red with blood.

'You leave my Mummy alone!' David yelled, and launched himself at Simpson.

'David!' Sheila shrieked, quickly crawling after him.

Simpson whirled the boy around, and put his free arm under David's chin, exerting just enough pressure not to choke the lad, but hold him still.

Sheila froze, and stared up into those cruel eyes that she now recalled so well.

'Let the boy go' she ordered.

Simpson brought the shotgun up, and rested its barrels on David's right shoulder. He then slid the barrels backwards till their ends were pointed directly at David's ear and about an inch away from it.

She couldn't believe this was happening. One minute she and David had been having such a lovely time together, the next . . . this nightmare brought on by a monster out of the past.

'Bang!' laughed Simpson.

Sheila gasped.

'I'll do anything, anything at all. Just let the boy run home,' she pleaded.

'It was a grave situation when I last had you on the ground,' Simpson said, and chuckled.

Grave situation? What was he babbling about? 'I don't understand.'

'Thinking about it afterwards I was pleased that your friend intervened, for now I've come up with something far far better. A plan that's going to kill my two birds with the one stone.'

David began to cry.

'I still don't understand.'

'I was wearing a mask. Does that help?'

Sheila gazed at him in horror. 'That night after the Hurleys' wedding! It was you!'

'In the dead centre of Dragonholme. Get it? *Dead centre*. A joke,' Simpson explained and chuckled again.

So the attempt hadn't been engineered by James. Her instincts had been right after all.

She remembered other things. 'And the fouling on my door. Was that you as well?'

'An indication of what I think of you,' Simpson leered.

'Mu . . . mmeee,' whispered David.

'Don't worry, darling. Everything's going to be all right,' she soothed, trying to put assurance and conviction into her voice.

Part of her mind was numb; another part was whirling madly around and around.

Madly. *Mad*. The world leapt out of her. Mad. Of course, the man was out of his mind.

She looked again into those eyes – and saw something there she hadn't seen before. Something that caused her stomach to contract into a tight knot of fear and the blood turn to ice in her veins. 'Let the boy go, please. He never hurt you,' she pleaded.

Simpson released David, who immediately ran to Sheila to be enveloped in her arms.

'Get up bitch,' Simpson commanded, gesturing with the gun.

'We're going for a walk now, down to the shore,' Simpson said.

She put her hand to her damaged cheek. At least the bleeding had stopped.

David clutched on to her as she stumbled in the direction Simpson indicated. Perhaps somewhere along the way they could make a break for it, she thought.

'Try anything funny and the lad gets it first, understand?' Simpson said, as though reading her thoughts.

Soon the Fairy Dell was lost to view behind them, while ahead the blue glint of the sea could now be seen.

'What did you mean, kill two birds with one stone?' Sheila asked as they trudged along.

'*My* two birds I said. You being one, his High and Mightiness the other.'

There it was, he planned to kill her. But it wasn't herself she was concerned for, it was David. It was inconceivable to her that her son would also die at the hands of this maniac.

'You'll hang, you know. You can't get away with it.'

'Oh, but I can. I only plan to attend to you. The lovely part is that Campbell will get the blame and he'll be the one to swing for your murder.'

'Why should the police think he killed me?'

'Because when your corpse is found this shotgun I'm holding will be lying alongside it, and the gun belongs to Campbell.'

'Campbell will deny it,' she said, her heart filled with despair.

'That won't do him any good. It's common knowledge he's been your enemy this long while. The law will put two and two together, and come up with five.'

Sheila thought of George Jorgesson. If only he'd been there to intervene as he'd done that night in the graveyard. But George was hundreds of miles away in the southern fishing grounds.

'It wasn't easy getting into the Hall for this gun. It's taken me ages to work out my plan so I wasn't caught or spotted. And it had to be a Saturday, the day you'd be going to the Fairy Dell. I didn't want his High and Mightiness finding out about the theft and reporting it, did I?' Simpson laughed.

They struggled down a slope, and along a path that brought them to the entrance of Kettil's Cave.

'In you go,' Simpson instructed.

Sheila recalled that day long ago when she'd brought a picnic down to James Campbell who'd been with his Coble in the Cut beyond.

As if reading her thoughts Simpson said, 'It's also common knowledge that this is a favourite haunt of Campbell's and that he brings that wee boat of his in here a lot. The fact you're discovered here will damn him even more.'

David sobbed, a sound that threatened to tear Sheila's heart apart. There had to be a way out of this for him, there just had to be!

They emerged from the rear of the cave into Kettil's Cut. As she'd known it would be, the tide was going out.

The water was choppy and full of swirls and eddies.

There was only one thing she could do to give David even the semblance of a chance: she must jump Simpson and keep him occupied as long as she could while David ran for his life.

But that wasn't going to be easy. So far Simpson had maintained a distance between them which made that impossible. The answer was to keep him talking, caught up in what he was saying, while she inched towards him.

'What I must ask you is why? So the laird fired you, and thrashed you into the bargain for what you'd done to me, but that's no reason for murder. Not after so many years.'

Simpson's eyes narrowed, and his mouth thinned to a slash. 'I had everything when I worked for Campbell: power, position, security. Then you came along and tried to undermine my authority. You, a chit of a lassie, putting yourself up against *me*!'

'Your so-called authority wasn't based on respect but fear and bullying. You hated me because I was the only one with the guts to stand up against you,' she snapped back, slowly moving herself and David closer to Simpson.

'Do you know what I was reduced to after the laird threw me off the Dragonholme Estate? Seasonal work, picking potatoes and the like. And when that wasn't available I starved, and had to sleep rough without even a roof over my head.'

'Why didn't you get another job as a ghillie?'

'Why don't you ask James Campbell. He saw to it that no one would give me a decent job again.'

'In other words, what you threatened Hay with happened to you. I'd call that justice,' she declared.

She'd succeeded in making him so furious that he didn't notice her getting closer and closer. Another foot should do it, she judged.

And, please God, when I shout to David to run, make sure that he does. Like the wind.

'I walked the streets of Edinburgh for a while, begging for a crust. Can you imagine the humiliation of that?'

'I wouldn't say it was nearly as humiliating as being nearly raped,' she mumbled.

'You deserved what happened to you!' he roared.

'And so did you, Simpson. Every humiliating second of it.'

She let David go, and tensed her body in preparation. One more step, that's all she needed, one more step.

Then the unexpected happened. There was a creak of wood, and snap of sail, and James Campbell's Coble shot into the Cut with James just about to lower canvas.

James saw Sheila, and paused in what he was doing to frown.

Simpson stared out over the Cut at the Coble and James in astonishment. This was the last thing he'd expected.

Sheila took her chance and threw herself on to the shotgun. 'Run, David! Run!' she screamed.

But despite the tears David was his father's son. He had no intention of running away and leaving his mother fighting with this nasty, scary man. He began pummelling Simpson with his tiny fists.

James stared at them in stunned bewilderment. What was going on?

Sheila knew she couldn't keep it up for long. Physically, she was no match for the powerfully built Simpson who still retained a great deal of the strength he'd had when younger.

A barrel of the shotgun went off, the blast deafening to Sheila whose head was less than a handspan away from the stock. Shot ricocheted off the rockface beneath them, all of it whistling harmlessly away, most of it peppering the sea like suddenly falling hail.

Uttering an oath, Simpson swiped David aside, sending him rolling to the edge of the rockface where it fell almost perpendicularly into the water below.

Sheila, her head still ringing from the blast, twisted

313

round to see what had become of David, momentarily relaxing her grip on the shotgun. It was enough for Simpson, who tore the gun from her grasp, then hit her with it, thwacking both barrels hard against her belly.

Sheila went down, gasping for air. Why oh why hadn't David run as she'd told him to?

James snatched up a barbed steel gaffe and drew it back to throw it as a spear. He was about to launch the gaffe at Simpson when Simpson fired the second barrel.

James dropped the gaffe as he was lifted right off his feet, and thrown backwards. The next thing he knew he was in the sea, and sinking fast.

Simpson was enraged. This ruined everything, the lovely beautiful plan he'd hatched to kill the Beattie bitch and send his High and Mightiness to the gallows. Those hard, cruel eyes came to rest on David at the edge of the rockface.

Sheila read Simpson's intention in his face. 'Nooo!' she shrieked.

Simpson's right boot lashed out to thump into David's chest. Uttering a thin, keening cry David vanished over the rock edge to be swallowed by the broil beneath.

Simpson snapped the shotgun open, and fumbled for cartridges. But before he could reload Sheila was upon him. Wailing, she clawed ribbons of flesh from his cheeks with her nails.

The water round James was streamered in pink as he fought his way back to the surface. He wondered where the colour was coming from, then realized that it had to be from him. He glanced down to see that blood was covering his chest.

David had been lucky. He'd gone under, and come up again. His flailing hands had banged against a spur of rock a little above the waterline, and this he was now grimly hanging on to.

The undertow tugged at his small body, seeking to drag him out of the Cut into the open sea. His teeth chattered with fright as he doggedly clung to the rockspur. Directly above him he could hear his Mum and the crazy man fighting.

James gratefully gulped in air when he finally broke surface. He was facing out of the Cut, so the first thing he saw was his Coble drifting back the way it had just come in.

Sheila fought like one possessed. Knowing David could barely swim, and what the water was like in the Cut, she believed him dead or drowning.

James's only thought was to get to Sheila. His strokes were feeble and when he coughed blood flooded from his mouth. But he made himself go on. He must save her: nothing else mattered.

Sheila managed to knee Simpson with all her strength.

Screeching in agony, Simpson whirled around, away from Sheila, and by doing so went right over the edge of the rockface. He was still screaming when he hit the water.

'The boy! The boy's underneath you!' James shouted, having spied David himself.

'Mummee, I'm here,' David cried plaintively.

The mists of rage that had taken possession of Sheila vanished, throwing herself flat she looked over the edge of the rockface. Sure enough there was David clinging on for dear life.

She pulled herself over the edge as far as she dared, and stretched down her right arm, the stronger one. 'Grab hold and I'll pull you up,' she commanded.

Simpson's hands shot out of the water behind David, followed instantly by Simpson's head and shoulders.

Simpson glared malevolently up at Sheila, then brought his gaze on to David struggling to catch hold of his mother's straining fingers.

Simpson reached out and caught hold of the same rockspur that David was hanging on to. Then he put a palm on David's head, and forced it underwater.

Sheila scrambled to her feet again and was about to jump on top of Simpson, but James reached the ex-ghillie

315

first. James's arm went round Simpson's throat and squeezed.

Simpson let go of David as he fought for air and freedom, but James would allow him neither.

James took a large breath and forced himself back down into the depths, taking the struggling Simpson with him.

David was again clinging to the rockspur, coughing, spluttering and crying.

Sheila was about to try and reach him a second time with an outstretched arm when suddenly she had the idea of using the shotgun to give her extra reach. She snapped the gun shut before poking it and herself over the rock edge.

'Grab on to it David,' she yelled.

David grasped the end of the barrels with one hand, then the other.

Slowly he climbed upwards slipping once, but swiftly recovering.

When David had a secure grip of her arm Sheila let the shotgun go, its usefulness over. She hauled David up the rest of the way till at last he tumbled over the edge to collapse in a sodden heap beside her.

'Oh!' she choked, and began crying tears of relief.

'Mummeee!' David wailed, and buried his face in her bosom.

'It's all right, it's all over now,' she told him, stroking his dripping hair. Then she remembered James, who'd just saved her boy's life.

Crawling back to the rockface edge, she gazed over. There was no sign of either James or Simpson.

Part of the water had darkened in colour. Moments later, Simpson bobbed to the surface floating face down. He was obviously dead.

When James resurfaced Sheila thought he too was gone, but after a couple of seconds his eyes blinked open. He was dreadfully weak.

'Over here,' Sheila called out. It was plain that he was disorientated.

He didn't have it in him to swim properly, so he paddled towards her as best he could.

Sheila glanced over to where she'd last seen the Coble, but it was gone. Simpson's corpse, floating spreadeagled downwards, was rapidly following suit. Soon it too would be out on the open sea.

James was lightheaded, his senses reeling. He eventually reached the spur of rock and crooked an arm over it, gasping for breath. Each breath was a sheet of searing flame.

Sheila reached down and he was able to grab hold of her extended hand.

'Wait a minute yet,' he said, staring at the stained water around him. He could only just see her, staring down at him with a look of tenderness and compassion that he'd never thought he'd see again. 'Is the boy all right?' he whispered.

'Yes, he's fine. But we must get you out of that water.'

James grimaced as the swell banged him against the rock wall. The pain was building quickly now, he was ablaze inside with it. 'All right,' he said, nodding.

Sheila strained, and he made what effort he could.

It wasn't all that far, the length of her arm, he thought. It might have been a million miles.

He made a second attempt, and this time didn't even manage the few inches upwards he had before. Releasing her hand he grasped hold again of the rockspur.

Sheila stared at him. She'd been able to haul David all the way up. But David was a wee boy. A full-grown man, and one as badly wounded as James, was a different proposition entirely.

'Try once more,' she urged. Miracles had been known to happen after all.

'It's no use, Sheila, it can't be done. You know that as well as I do,' he gasped.

She read in his expression that he was resigned to his fate. 'I'm sorry,' she whispered, fresh tears streaming down her face.

317

'So am I, Sheila, but not for this. For all the horrible and misguided things I've done to you.' His voice faltered. 'Everything I did was prompted by love, Sheila. You must believe that.'

'I know,' she sobbed. 'Oh, James I do believe you.'

'Can you possibly forgive me?'

'Yes,' she choked out. 'Yes, I can.'

Neither of them thought to suggest she run for help. They both knew there wasn't time for that.

'One last touch?' he pleaded, and held up a straining hand.

Their fingers pressed together, then his moved away. She saw that he'd let go of the rockspur and was being taken by the tide.

'Away home now,' he said evenly.

At the spot where the rear of Kettil's Cave opened out on to the Cut she paused. A wind sighed in off the open sea, and somewhere a herring gull screeched raucously.

She turned to give James a farewell wave. But there was no-one there to wave to.

Postscript

Sheila and David were on the cliffs overlooking Dragonholme. They'd just come from Dragonholme Hall where they'd left Johnnie Murchison-Stewart and Helen Drummond, the woman Johnnie would shortly be marrying.

Johnnie's and Helen's had been a whirlwind romance, and in Sheila's opinion they were a couple ideally suited to one another. She couldn't have been more happy for Johnnie, and had already promised to be godmother to the first wean when it arrived.

After James's death, Dragonholme Hall and the attendant estate had been put up for sale, and Sheila had seriously considered buying them. In the end it had come down to a straight choice, the Hall and estate, or Dragonholme fleet restored to what it had been before the disaster. Her capital wouldn't stretch to both. Her decision had been to continue rebuilding the fleet.

All this had coincided with Johnnie's romance, and when she'd confided to him that she'd have to give up the idea of owning the Hall, he'd surprised her by asking if she'd mind if he went ahead and tried to purchase it, confessing he was another who'd fallen under the spell of the village and its environs.

Mind? She'd been delighted. And that was how the new laird of Dragonholme Hall had come to be Johnnie Murchison-Stewart.

Johnnie and Helen intended honeymooning abroad, then returning to the Hall. As Johnnie still had to run the MS Yard in Yoker he'd be keeping on his Glasgow residence, but he and Helen would be down at the Hall at every possible opportunity.

'Look!' shouted David excitedly, and pointed southwards, out to sea.

Sheila raised her eyes. There were tiny black dots on the southern horizon. Hastily she began counting them.

'Is it George, Mummy? Is it the boats coming home for the winter?' David demanded.

She remembered a far off day when she'd stood almost on this exact spot and watched the old fleet come in from the north. The day she'd first met James Campbell.

So much had happened since then; so very much. In a way, well . . . it was as if the wheel had come full circle.

'It must be, the number's right,' she replied with a laugh.

David let out a whoop. George was coming back to Dragonholme. George who was a man, and his pal, and so much more fun to be with than women.

'You've missed him, haven't you?' she smiled.

David nodded.

She'd missed him too, and had thought about him a

great deal. Thoughts that had nothing to do with him being a good sailor.

'Let's go down and meet him,' she said.

Hand in hand Sheila and David made for the road that would take them down into Dragonholme, and George.